A New
Life in the
Château

Sarah Long is a London-based author of four previously published commercial fiction novels and one hilarious memoir about her ten years living in Paris. She is a married mother of three.

Also by Sarah Long

And What Do You Do?
The Next Best Thing
Le Dossier
Invisible Women
A Year in the Château

A New
Life in the
Château

Sarah Long

ZAFFRE

First published in the UK in 2025 by
Zaffre
An imprint of Bonnier Books UK
5th Floor, HYLO, 103–105 Bunhill Row,
London, EC1Y 8LZ
Owned by Bonnier Books
Sveavägen 56, Stockholm, Sweden

A CIP catalogue record for this book is
available from the British Library.

Paperback ISBN: 978-1-80418-121-8

Also available as an ebook and an audiobook

1 3 5 7 9 10 8 6 4 2

Typeset by IDSUK (Data Connection) Ltd

Printed and bound in Great Britain by Clays Ltd, Elcograf S.p.A.

Zaffre is an imprint of Bonnier Books UK
www.bonnierbooks.co.uk

For Julia

PROLOGUE

The room was bathed in a golden pink glow as Simon reached up to hang the final piece of wallpaper. He smoothed down the edges against the neighbouring strip, then descended the ladder to complete the task.

He stood back to admire the effect – the flock paper had a velvety richness to it, the rosy highlights offsetting the auburn hair of Apolline who was posing now in front of the wall, the picture of DIY chic in her faded dungarees, the famous tresses tied up in a green scarf.

'Messieurs, mesdames, I present to you, the Jean-Honoré Fragonard suite,' she said, taking a bow for her audience of one.

It was the latest guest room to be decorated, as the chateau gradually opened its arms to a wider world, inviting paying guests to experience the life of a seigneur. Apolline was one of the first and Simon thanked his lucky stars that she had arrived in their midst. What were the chances? Charming and helpful, she was also stunningly beautiful, and Simon was hopelessly in love with her. He hadn't told her. There were complications, not least the fact that he was married to Beth.

He clapped his hands and looked at her in adoration. She was so French, and so perfect.

'Bravo, *mon assistante*, we have done a magnificent job, and now I must reward you with an aperitif. Shall we take a glass of crémant up to your studio, I want to choose one of your new vases for my daughter.'

Apolline was a talented potter, on top of everything else. She had set up her wheel in an attic room, turning out beautiful objects that were often sold to departing guests eager to take home a memento of their holiday.

'Yes, let's go,' said Apolline, 'I have one in mind for you. But also, I want you to show me the book you are writing. I am intrigued by the concept, and I know it will be brilliant because I have seen how your mind works, during our interactions.'

Our interactions, here's to more of them, thought Simon.

'That's very flattering,' he said, 'but it's still in its early stages, I'm not sure you'd find it interesting.'

'Please, I want to see it.'

Her insistence was gratifying, he couldn't wait to settle in beside her and watch her read his words.

'All right then, let's clear up quickly and get down to it.'

They put away the tools and Simon took the brushes to clean in the bathroom basin. She inadvertently brushed against him as she manoeuvred the ladder out of the room and he wondered if she felt the same electric shock that he did.

His phone pinged.

Shit, it was Beth. He'd forgotten he was supposed to pick her up from the Paris train. Talk about a mood spoiler.

'Sorry, Apolline, I've got to collect Beth and Leo from the station, they're back from the city.'

'No problem, we can do the vases and your book another time.'

'We must. I want you to read my stuff, I really value your opinion, you know.'

What an amazing artistic collaboration it would be, him admiring her pots while she was moved to tears by his writing, how infuriating that they couldn't do it right away.

'Why don't I go and fetch them?' said Apolline. 'I know you want to condition those brushes with the special product you were telling me about.'

She was teasing him now, but he knew she shared his enthusiasm for all their joint ventures. Even hanging wallpaper was an exciting adventure when they did it together.

'Would you mind? That would be amazing, the train's due in twenty-five minutes.'

'See you later.'

She touched him lightly on the shoulder on her way out. He massaged softener into the bristles of the brush and wondered what on earth he was going to do.

Part One

Autumn

CHAPTER 1

'As happy as God in France'. It was a German expression that perfectly expressed Nicola's feelings on this warm September afternoon, as she soaked up the sun on the terrace.

She was sitting on a stone bench next to her friend Beth. Behind them, the chateau rose up in all its glory, turrets reaching for the sky. Before them lay the walled gardens spilling over with Michaelmas daisies, the orchards heavy with fruit, the lake reflecting the late sun, the lush beauty of the domain they were privileged to call home.

She turned to Beth, wanting to share the joy.

'Do you know, I love every season here at the chateau, but autumn is my absolute favourite. What's yours?'

Beth gave her a sour look.

'What are we, six years old? Or maybe this is a BFF quiz, how well do you know your best friend, is she an autumn or a summer person?'

'Don't be prickly. Anyway, you're not my best friend. I don't have one, since we are well beyond playground age. But if I was forced to choose, I suppose it might be you.'

Beth nodded her assent.

'All right then, on that basis, I'll play your silly game. I'm going to say winter. Sharp frosts, warm stews, footprints in the snow, logs crackling in our many magnificent fireplaces.'

'Fair enough, that fits, for you are indeed a hard and frosty person. Come on, let's walk down to pick up some windfalls. Leo needs some *reine de reinettes* for dinner tonight.'

She picked up her plum-stained wicker basket and led Beth down the wide stone steps that had accommodated so many dainty French silk-stockinged feet through the centuries and which now, miraculously, belonged to them and a handful of friends. British risk-takers who, on a whim, had turned their backs on the prospect of a conventional retirement and pooled their resources to buy up the vast Renaissance beauty, the merciless money pit, that was Chateau Lafarge.

It was five years since they'd taken the plunge, a roller coaster of highs and lows, as you might expect when nine people trade in their familiar, nuclear households for a sprawling, palatial commune in the French countryside, an ambitious renovation project that was now – finally – reaching completion. Planning meetings over generous aperitifs, noisy dinners in the chandeliered dining room, squabbling over the budget, exploding lavatories, leaking roofs, long days up ladders, learning to love French workmen – there was never a dull moment. There was also one heartbreaking tragedy they could never have anticipated. Now, they all agreed, Chateau Lafarge was their forever home, it was impossible to imagine living anywhere else.

The orchard floor was littered with apples and they soon filled the basket. The windfalls kept them going throughout September, before the proper harvest took place, when they stripped the trees of fruit for sale at the local market.

'It's autumn in the palm of your hand,' said Nicola, feeling the warmth of the fruit and holding it up for inspection. 'Look at that maggot, they always target the sweetest ones.'

'The windfalls are the tastiest,' said Beth, 'which is lucky as they're the only ones we get to eat. I know you can't sell them, but you can't beat them for flavour. Maybe you're right, I'll forego winter and nominate autumn as my favourite. Or spring. All that hope, new life, sap rising, daffodils, first warm day of the year. Can you imagine living in a land without seasons? No need for a winter coat, same weather all year round, absolute hell.'

'Singapore, Dubai, the Amazon basin,' said Nicola, 'wearing the same tropical shirts day in, day out.'

They shuddered at the thought.

'Shall we go back and deal with these?' said Nicola. 'Orchard-fresh butter-fried apple garnish for our iconic autumn dish, *poulet vallée d'auge*.'

It was a treasured local recipe, chicken steeped in Calvados, cider and crème fraîche, the very essence of Normandy.

The two women held the basket between them, one handle each to share the weight, and made their way slowly back to the chateau, through the side entrance into the scullery, or *arrière-cuisine*, where Leo was dabbing at a bowl of dark mushrooms, exotic as lilies with their folds of delicate flesh.

'Leo, are you *sure* they're edible?' asked Beth, staring doubt-fully into the sink. 'I know you double-checked, but the name *trompettes de mort* doesn't exactly inspire confidence. Horns of death, it's kind of asking for it.'

'A hundred per cent, just watch me.'

Leo dramatically lifted one to his lips and nibbled off the top.

'I'm the royal food taster. If I'm still alive by dinner time, you'll know it's OK. Delicious in fact and will be even better fried in garlic butter and parsley. There's always a frisson, isn't there, eating self-foraged mushrooms. The faint, thrilling risk that you might just get a poisonous one and turn green and die like the old king in *Babar the Elephant*. We need that, at our age – the danger of the unknown. It's our version of living on the edge.'

'Not the most glamorous of deaths,' said Nicola.

'Let's not talk of death. What do you think of my outfit?'

Leo peeled off his pinny and struck a model pose, one leg forward, his elegant frame and black hair perfectly set off by a pair of teal velvet trousers and a cropped turquoise jacket.

'I hate you, you're such a clothes horse,' said Beth. 'You're literally the same shape as when I first clapped eyes on you a century ago.'

She and Nicola had met Leo at university, and it was fair to say the years had been kind to him. He acknowledged the compliment by running his hands up over his face, as if to forbid it from collapsing

'Thanks, you must admit I work at it. And, of course, I haven't been ravaged by childbirth and the cares of raising a family, unlike you heroic ladies.'

'Ravaged, thanks very much!' said Beth. 'I'll take that remark as directed at me, given that Nicola could still pass as a schoolgirl. From behind and from a vast distance, obviously.'

She kissed Nicola on the cheek, then sat down at the table to deal with the apples.

'You know I don't mean it,' said Leo. 'You are superb, the pair of you. I was merely paying tribute to your incredible contribution to peopling the planet, while all I had to worry about was keeping my looks. Nicola, darling, come and help me finish the table. Tonight is an historic occasion, it deserves a very special decor.'

Nicola followed him through the *arrière-cuisine* into the main kitchen, then into the dining room – the first of the vast reception rooms that interconnected across the breadth of the chateau in a miraculous procession of grandeur that still took their breath away. Nicola had counted the paces once, walking from one end to the other. If you included every floor, up and down the staircases, you could easily achieve your daily step count by marching once around this palace, not something that was feasible in the terraced house in London she'd previously called home, where naturally she didn't have the run of thirty-seven rooms. Fifty-three, if you included the attic, not to mention the various outbuildings that made up their demesne – barns, a cider press, a dovecote, most of them now pressed into residential service for their expanded community.

When the nine friends signed up for this new life, it was an exciting adventure that flew in the face of what was expected. Not for them the life of nuclear couplehood promised by brochures for retirement flats and Saga cruises. Oh no. This was to be a non-stop house party, with a carefully curated set of like-minded friends. It was also, whisper it, a blessed escape from family responsibilities. Of course they would miss their adult children, but how marvellous, actually, to take a bit of distance from them, and not be so available to hear about their career and relationship crises, the gritty details of them making their way in the world. The merry pensioners would live in a sexagenarian bubble, their cares behind them, as they devoted their remaining years to the French pleasures of friendship, love, wine, food and *la culture*.

But it was not to be. Nature has a way of laughing at your plans, and a child-free universe would not be tolerated. The band of nine chatelains had expanded with the arrival of a baby boy – the dauphin Louis – born to Fizz, Will's second wife and the only female resident of reproductive age. As if that wasn't enough, Nicola's daughter Maddie was so entranced by the chateau after spending her maternity leave there that she'd upped sticks and moved in permanently with her husband and daughter. It took a little adjustment, but the new arrivals were warmly received into what Simon termed the hippy commune for non-hippies. Which was just as well, since both mothers were expecting another child in the spring. The world must be peopled, as Leo liked to remind them all, and it's not as if they didn't have the space.

Tonight's dinner was a special occasion because it marked the end of an era. Chateaux don't run on thin air, as self-appointed accountant and unapologetic tightwad, Dougie liked to remind them. Every winter, he stood guard by the thermo-stat in the entrance hall, ensuring that nobody tried to turn it up a notch. He put in a bulk order for thermal underwear and encouraged vigorous exercise and the wearing of multiple lay-ers. On the bleakest days, when the wind howled over treacher-ous frosts, and he could almost see the heat escaping through the rattling windows, he would think back to his cosy home in Cambridge, where he and Mary could sit in their shirtsleeves through the cruellest conditions, such was the quality of their home insulation.

This year, it all came to a head with the arrival of the January fuel bill, when it was agreed that something must be done. The residents had various income streams between them, but until now the only money generated by their gas-guzzling chateau came from the fruit and vegetables they grew in the fields and sold at the farmers' market, alongside pots of home-made jam with frilly lids which Beth pronounced very Women's Institute. It became clear there was one crop they could no longer afford to ignore, and that was what Dougie referred to as Paying Guests.

Paying Guests, what a terrible term! The overtones of post-war households eking out a living by taking in lodgers was *not* what they were looking for. But luxury accommodation in guest suites in a distant wing of the chateau, that was a different matter. Leo had been charged with the decoration, taking his inspiration from Baudelaire. 'Do you know that poem, "*L'invitation au Voyage*"?' he'd asked the others. '*Luxe, calme, volupté,* I'm thinking gleaming furniture, polished by the years, rich ceilings, deep mirrors, oriental splendour . . . above all, no cushions on the bed, that's common, and no chocolates on the pillow, though I may allow a mini fridge and tea- and coffee-making facilities to encourage them to keep to their rooms and leave us in peace.'

The rooms were completed over the summer, the wall colour refreshed three times by Will under Leo's direction, and their first guests were arriving tomorrow, seduced by the promise of the *chambres d'hôte d'exception*. So tonight, for the last time, the residents would be having a private dinner *en famille*. The term used loosely of course, but the chateau family was as tightly intertwined as any biological version.

Upstairs, in what was arguably the best bedroom in the chateau, Simon was lying on the quilt, glass in hand, watching with a critical eye as Beth changed for dinner.

'I'm not sure that dress plays to your strengths.'

Beth shot him a look of hatred.

'And what would those be, in your opinion? My strengths?'

'Don't be like that! I'm only being constructive. It's just a bit . . . tight across the haunches. Maybe you should go for something more loose-fitting.'

'And maybe you should take a long hard look in the mirror before you start hurling insults my way. You and your strap-on belly, the worst kind of dangerous fat for a man of your age. Not helped by whatever it is you're drinking. Can't you wait to have your aperitif downstairs with everybody else?'

'Touché!'

He raised his glass and blew her a kiss.

'I'm a creative person, you know I need my stimulus.'

Since renouncing his career in advertising, or, to be more accurate, since it had given up on him, Simon had turned his hand to creative writing. He'd completed one novel, yet to find a publisher, and was currently working on a personal memoir of the pandemic, *Après Moi, Le Déluge*. The title was, in Beth's opinion, misleading, quite apart from being ridiculously grandiose. Firstly, he'd only had a very mild dose of it, and secondly, there was no deluge.

'As for my substantial girth, you must agree it lends me a certain gravitas, emphasised by my statement shirts.'

He patted his stomach, clothed in a flamboyant silk shirt depicting orange birds of paradise on a blue background. He took great pleasure in selecting fabrics, which his tailor in England made up for him, in ever increasing sizes. There was always excitement at the chateau when the latest parcel arrived, and Simon gave a fashion parade in the ballroom.

Beth zipped herself into her dress then stretched out on the bed beside him.

'It's going to feel weird, isn't it, having guests in the chateau? Paying ones, I mean, as opposed to our own visitors.'

'Flinging open the doors to the great unwashed,' said Simon.

'Hardly unwashed. They'll be discerning types who want an upmarket chateau experience. I hope they don't find *us* on the unwashed side.'

'Washed-up old hippies, which is what we are, really. Yuppies turned hippies.'

'We weren't all yuppies! Certainly not our darling aesthete Leo. And Dougie and Mary never cared about money, they were learned scholars!'

'All right, yuppies and blue stockings turned hippies. I'll count Dougie as a blue stocking, as we're all gender fluid these days.'

'Change is good, though, isn't it?' said Beth. 'We weren't sure how it would feel having Maddie and John and their baby moving in, and then Fizz having one, but in fact it's been great.'

'The place is turning into a nursery. Sinister breeding ground for expat Brits planning to take back control of Normandy, it's the Hundred Years' War all over again. But yes, I concede the babies are a worthy addition, the circle of life and all that.'

'Very *Lion King*. You'd make a great Mufasa, but I'm not holding my breath for our very own prince Simba.'

Beth and Simon's daughter Eva lived in London with her long-term boyfriend James, who had failed to endear himself to her parents, on account of his extreme self-absorption. Their relationship didn't appear to bring much in the way of sunny uplands, rather it was a rich source of problems, a bone they endlessly chewed over. Eva blamed pressure of work – she was a medic and James did something unfathomable in finance, which was supposed to explain his surliness. Even so, Beth would be prepared to overlook his shortcomings if ever he were to provide them with a grandchild. In her close but competitive friendship with Nicola, it was galling to find herself down one–nil on that front, two–nil if you counted the baby Maddie was expecting next year.

'Never mind, big baby, her time will come, you *will* be that doting grandmother.'

'Don't call me "big baby"! It's a horrible name.'

'It's affectionate, you should be grateful! Here, join me in a glass of this, it's like sherry, but nicer.'

He reached down into his bedside cabinet and brought out an extra glass and the bottle of Pineau des Charentes he'd placed there earlier.

'Look at us, furtively sipping sherry in our room,' said Beth, accepting the glass and walking to the window. The sky was soft with pink and mauve light, throwing the trees into dark relief. 'I hope we get a sunset like this tomorrow, for the guests. First impressions are so important, aren't they? Especially here where you literally live in the weather.'

They had often commented how they rarely noticed the weather when they lived in a city where it was the unremarkable backdrop to the day's business. Here at the chateau, your mood was determined by the sky. It was impossible to feel downbeat when the sun was sparkling on the blossom, or the mist was suspended like a magic cloak over the fields, or a carpet of snow covered the grounds like a heavenly cloud. But when the rain fell relentlessly against a sullen grey outlook and you needed the lights on all day long, it was tempting just to stay in bed, hibernating until a chink of light crept between the dark velvet curtains to lift your spirits and call you up again.

Simon checked his phone.

'Set fair for the week, according to Meteo France. And they are usually gloomier than BBC Weather whose forecasts I prefer, as a glass-full kind of chap. I take it back about your dress, by the way. It emphasises your curves. In fact you look rather stunning, silhouetted in the window. And the green goes perfectly with the *toile de jouy* wallpaper. You look as if you've just stepped out of it, like a happy eighteenth-century countrywoman.'

They had opted for traditional decor in their bedroom. The walls were lined with the same fabric as the curtains, featuring bucolic scenes of men in stockings holding hands with bonneted women in wooded landscapes.

'Anyway, it's now officially aperitif o'clock, shall we go down?'

He stood up and performed a formal bow, then offered her his arm.

'Will you do me the pleasure, big baby?'

CHAPTER 2

Will never expected to become a father again, after leaving his wife for the pretty young temp at the office. One of the many attractive features of Fizz had been her insistence that she didn't want to burden the world – or him – with another drain on finite resources. When she changed her mind and presented her pregnancy as a fait accompli, he'd sulked for a week. But when Louis was born, he experienced a rush of love exceeding anything he'd felt for the sons that Marjorie had presented him with. Possibly because this time round, he was nudging frail old man territory, as opposed to being a thrusting young lawyer out to conquer the world.

The only disadvantage to his born-again fatherhood was the downgrade in their accommodation, now they had sacrificed their chateau room and been exiled to a cowshed. It made sense for them to settle into one of the many outbuildings on the estate. Will could see the practical advantages – no long hike to the kitchen every time the baby needed a bottle – but he sometimes felt that by not living in the actual chateau, his status was diminished. Maybe not exactly to that of a serf, but possibly akin to a tenant farmer, or a gardener, or a stockman, sleeping with his animals in a stone barn with mean little windows offering a view of the chateau to remind you of what you were missing out on.

The barn – Fizz refused to call it the cowshed – was of *colombage* construction, half-timbered with wattle and daub, typical of the region's rustic dwellings, which were increasingly sought after by townies in search of the good life, Parisians fleeing the city for weekends of wholesome fresh air, so highly valued after recent confinements. As far as Will was concerned, it was a bit too cottagey. Small windows made it dark and mean, compared to the spectacular light-flooded rooms of the chateau.

The barn was only a stone's throw away from the chateau, assuming you had a strong arm, but Will still regretted the loss of their original bedroom on the first floor. Every morning when they'd lived in the chateau, he would throw open the shutters and marvel at the commanding views over the lake and the horizon. He would then sweep down the palatial staircase, passing through the grandeur of the interconnecting reception rooms and on to the kitchen, where he would prepare a tea tray for his young wife, and take it back up to her in bed, like a courtly knight.

Now, in the cowshed barn, he lifted the freshly bathed Louis into his cot.

'There you are, little prince, plenty of subjects to entertain you.'

Louis snuggled into his nest of soft toys. He was allowed them now he was safely beyond the age of cot death risk. None of them were paid for, thanks to Fizz's status as an influencer, which brought a regular supply of everything you might need – and much that you didn't – delivered to the chateau door in a yellow post van, driven by a rather cross woman – the *postiers* in France were all female, unlike in London where you rarely had a delivery driver who wasn't a man.

'Look, here comes Mummy.'

He turned to admire his young wife, dressed for dinner in a slinky black number that clung to the undulations of her pregnancy.

'Madame Bovary, your son is ready to receive your good-night kiss.'

Fizz's vlog was originally called Mademoiselle Bovary, featuring winsome photographs of her posing in the Norman countryside, echoing the background of Flaubert's novel. As the youngest member of the chateau group, she could identify with Emma's yearning and alienation. She too had an older husband, though you could hardly compare Will with that poor old plodding doctor Charles Bovary. It had been love at first sight when she was temping at the law firm where Will was a partner, so cool and powerful in his designer suits. Less cool and powerful these days, obviously.

Once she'd given birth, she changed the vlog's name to Madame Bovary, reflecting her new mature status as *mère de famille*, building on her success to achieve an even greater following. But she still had a nostalgia for the early days, before the chateau's renovation and often looked back at those first posts. The one of her in dungarees, hair swept up, straddling a ladder with a paint pot. The tragic one of her standing outside the chateau in the debris of the roof tiles blown off during a storm. The one of her at the seaside in the passenger seat of Will's sports car, with Isadora Duncan-style scarf and sunglasses. Always the young and glamorous member of the party, she had sacrificed her London life for the love of her husband and accepted to bury herself away in the depths of the French countryside.

She approached the cot with her phone.

'There you are, *mon petit dauphin*, just a little piccy now with your darling elephant, that's lovely. I know that will go down so well with your fans.'

Louis offered an obliging smile. He had inherited his mother's willingness to perform for the camera. Fizz scrutinised the photo, admiring as usual the blissful smoothness of her son's skin. High-definition cameras offered no advantages to adults – how she longed for those smudgy images from the golden age of Hollywood when there was no need to apply a flattering filter – but baby skin was so enchanting, like silk.

'That poor child,' said Will. 'More photographed than anyone ever in the history of the world, he'll probably hate you for it when he grows up.'

'We'll cross that bridge when we get to it,' said Fizz, giving him a dazzling smile. 'He's free to delete his virtual footprint whenever he chooses.'

'Change his identity you mean. Go into the witness protection scheme?'

'Now you're being silly. Is the baby alarm on?'

'Yes.'

Will waved the receiver at her.

'Also, the most surveilled baby ever. No action or snuffle unmonitored.'

'Essential, especially now we're relegated to the cowshed. Can't check up on him without putting on coat and wellies and trekking over from the big house. It's nearly time, you can just wash up those tea things, and we'll go across.'

Will meekly headed off to what he liked to call the kitchenette and washed the lentil soup out of the food mixer, setting it to drain alongside the spouted beakers and baby spoons – the paraphernalia he thought he'd seen the back of thirty years ago, when his older sons reached the age of relative reason. Another age, another wife. It was less onerous in those days, as far as he was concerned. He went out to earn the money and Marjorie did everything else. By comparison, Fizz was brutal in the way she divvied up the tasks relating to little Louis. Fifty–fifty, fair to a fault, she even set a timer to mark the point where her shift ended and his began. Which was progress, he supposed, in our egalitarian society, but he wished she could be a little more freewheeling.

She came up beside him, nodded her satisfaction.

'Good work, Daddy. Shall we go?'

He put his arm round her waist, felt the firm tummy where Louis' sister was limbering up, and buried his face in her neck, breathing in the incredible smell of her.

'I'm not your daddy. Remember that.'

Leo was lighting the candles, the final touch in his table preparations, walking the length of the room with a box of long-stemmed matches, admiring the resulting glow. He then set about the tea lights that were laid out in groups on the side tables. It was one of the first things he'd learned about interior decoration – you could never have too many light sources, especially candles. Seven places on each side, plus one at the head of table for tonight's guest of honour, Madame de Courcy, the previous owner of the chateau, who ended her family's centuries-old connection with the site when she sold it to *les rosbifs* five years ago.

'That looks amazing, Leo,' said Nicola, reappearing in a soft pink silk dress that shimmered in the candlelight. 'Do you want to come through now, we're all ready for drinks.'

'You look gorgeous,' said Leo. 'Has Jean-Louis arrived?'

Jean-Louis was Nicola's love interest. Boyfriend. Part-time live-in lover. Significant Other. It was hard to find an appropriate term when you were over sixty, she found. Jean-Louis was not over sixty, as she was reminded every time he took off his clothes to reveal the toned physique of a youngish farmer in his prime. Lucky her.

'Not yet,' she said. 'He's picking up Madame de Courcy, to save her driving in the dark.'

'*Quel* gentleman! She shouldn't be driving at all at her age, in my opinion. She must be a hundred at least.'

'We'll never find out, that's for sure. She was thrilled to be invited.'

When they first took possession of the chateau, Madame de Courcy would regularly let herself in, using the spare key she'd held on to. She would wander round her former home, commenting on the renovation, helping herself to various pieces of furniture which she hadn't meant to include in the sale. In the end, they had to have a word with her, and she tearfully handed back the key. She lived in a small modern house in the village, and though she walked past the chateau most days, she now only came in when she was invited. *Faites comme chez vous*, the new chatelains urged her, make yourself at home. But not all the time, by crashing in whenever you feel like it and helping yourself to our property.

Simon was pouring champagne in the drawing room next door, where everyone was gathered. Dougie leaned forward to read the label as he received his glass.

'Real champagne!' he said, glaring disapprovingly at the contents of his glass. 'That's very rash, I thought we'd agreed it was straightforward sparkling wine from now on, with our cost-of-living crisis. There are so many to choose from – Crémant de Loire, Crémant de Jura, Crémant de Bourgogne . . .'

Simon put a reassuring hand on Dougie's arm.

'Relax, Dougie,' he said, 'I bought this in the *foire aux vins*, an absolute steal.'

The supermarkets all ran wine fairs, regular as clockwork, spring and autumn, when shelves by the entrance were loaded with boxes of wine, raided by customers who had studied the offers, consulted the opinions of *Guide Hachette* and other experts, and arrived at opening time on day one, determined to snap up the best bargains. It was the French version of the Harrods sale, on a national scale.

'Anyway, our fortunes change tomorrow,' he continued, 'with the massive ker-ching of the chateau cash till!'

Dougie shook his head nervously.

'It's only two rooms, not enough for us to behave like wanton spendthrifts.'

'Fat chance of that, Dougie, with you in charge of the books,' said Beth. 'Hurry up with that magnum, Simon, the young parents are parched over there, aren't you, my dears?'

The room was so huge, she had to raise her voice to be heard by Maddie and Fizz who were sitting on the other side, deep in discussion about their children's respective speech development. Fizz liked to point out how Louis tended to achieve his milestones at the same time as Maddie's daughter Lily, even though he was six months younger. Will and John, the less competitive fathers, were nerdily comparing baby alarms, pointing out the technical features on each other's devices.

'Not for me,' said Fizz, as Simon handed her a glass. 'You forget that I am great with child. I think I just heard Madame de Courcy arriving, I'm going to stand over there to get a shot of her coming through the door. That will make a great post, chatelaines past and present. My followers love all that heritage stuff.'

She jumped up and moved to the back of the room by the dining room doors. Will admired her grace, the lightness of her. When his first wife Marjorie was pregnant, she had adopted a lumbering gait, sighing deeply whenever she stood up, as though the transition to motherhood demanded a shift to martyred heaviness.

Madame de Courcy enjoyed making an entrance, and all eyes were on her as she came into the salon, her white hair in an elegant chignon, her walking stick a stylish accessory to her fitted tweed suit as she leaned on the arm of handsome Jean-Louis. He had obviously just had a shower, thought Nicola, his blond hair was still damp and flyaway.

'Smile please, everyone,' said Fizz.

'*Ouistiti*,' said Madame de Courcy, obligingly.

Fizz thought it the funniest thing ever when she first heard a group of French people repeating that word. She'd looked it up and found it defined a type of monkey. Will had explained it was their version of 'say cheese,' and far more effective for producing a wide smile. When you say 'cheese', it actually makes your mouth go into a sort of snarl, but '*ouistiti*' turned even the most morose Frenchie into a grinning ape.

'*Et nous voilà*, here we are!' Madame de Courcy announced, using the royal we, as if giving permission for the party to start. She kissed Simon on both cheeks – she'd always had a soft spot for him – then took the glass of champagne and cast her eyes round the room, settling on the wall lights that had been restored and rewired with impressive results.

'Ah, those sconces,' she said, 'it was such a silly mistake to include them in the sale. I said to the *notaire* afterwards, I made it very clear that they were *not* to be included. I very much meant to take them with me . . .'

'Is she hoping we're going to unscrew them from the walls and hand them back?' Leo whispered to Nicola.

Jean-Louis approached them with an amused expression and shook hands with Leo.

'I think they would look very inappropriate in her bungalow,' Jean-Louis said. 'Such a grandiose style in her small home, it would be *ridicule!*'

He drew Nicola to him and kissed her.

'*Salut, cherie.* You are looking very *ravissante* in that dress.'

She reached up to stroke his hair.

'Still wet,' she said.

'Ah, I remember now, the word you teach me!'

He ran his fingers through his wild blond curls – surely a legacy from his Viking roots, they were early invaders of this part of France.

'Finger-dried!' he said, in his sexy French accent.

'Very good,' said Nicola. 'No hairdryer for you.'

'You're so lucky, Jean-Louis,' said Leo, gazing at him with complete adoration. 'I'd give anything to have your hair, mine takes *hours* to get right. Now, I must leave you and attend to those birds.'

It was a good thing the champagne had been on special offer as they managed to work their way through several bottles before Leo eventually reappeared in the doorway, flushed with the exertion of it all, and announced with a deep curtsey that '*Mesdames, messieurs, le dîner est servi!*'

'Leo, *j'adore* how you speak French,' said Madame de Courcy, rising to her feet, 'and so *courageux* of you all to present these extraordinary feasts with no domestic staff. It was unthinkable during my tenure, that I should do such a thing.'

She had employed a live-in couple for decades, as much a part of the chateau as she was, until they finally retired, which made her realise it was time for her, too, to downsize. Marie-France was a reasonable cook, but not a patch on these English enthusiasts, whose mastery of French cuisine astounded her. She thought it must be because they were from a different class. She had been brought up to leave *la cuisine* to the servants, whereas these less nobly born foreigners seemed to find it a source of enormous fulfilment.

Fulfilment for her, too, as a frequent guest at their table. This evening was no exception. The mushrooms, the *poulet*, the *plateau de fromages* where every cheese was *au lait cru* – these funny British people had an aversion to anything pasteurised – it was all superb, finished with a chocolate souffle of great refinement, created by that charming daughter of Nicola's, who was the very essence of an English rose, a translucent blonde beauty, so like her mother and her baby daughter too, who was a perfect Boucher cherub.

But the highlight for Madame de Courcy was the end of the evening, when Simon had accompanied her on the piano, insisting they were all *begging* her to sing her favourite party song – 'Tout Va Très Bien Madáme La Marquise'. An undeniable classic, she remembered every word without prompting, the hilarious account of denial when Madame la Marquise returns to her chateau to be told by her valet that all is well, apart from her grey mare dying – oh, and the stables burning down – and the chateau too, burned to a ruin following the suicide of her husband . . . *Un vrai regale*! It was an absolute treat, no wonder the *rosbifs* demanded it on every occasion, declaring no evening complete until she agreed to perform it.

*

'Madame la Marquise was in excellent voice as usual.'

Jean-Louis threw his trousers on top of his shirt on the bedroom chair and slid into bed beside Nicola.

'You are sweet to drive her home,' Nicola murmured, half asleep.

'I could hardly allow her to go swaying down the road unaccompanied! Anyway, no chance of *les flics* jumping out to breathalyse me on that short journey. *Bonne nuit, mon amour.*'

Nicola felt the warmth of him against her back as his breathing settled into sleep. Lying in the dark, she allowed her memory to wander back to the first night she had ever spent in this bedroom. It wasn't with Jean-Louis. It was with her husband, Dominic, on the day they all moved in.

Tired and excited from the journey, they had waved off the removal vans and left the boxes piled up in the crystal ballroom while they celebrated their new life with a welcome dinner of chicken tikka masala. Not at all French, but Nicola had brought it over on purpose in the cool box, a nostalgic tribute to the national dish of the Britain the nine of them had left behind.

Just like this evening, they had all drunk rather a lot. Start as we mean to go on, they'd said, the party begins here. Then Dominic had carried her, giggling, up the stairs. He'd always been one for the big romantic gesture. *I'm going to carry you over the threshold*, he'd said as they arrived at the end of the corridor, then he pushed open the door and threw her onto the bed, this bed, the one they'd brought over from their London home.

Dominic. The hot summer day a few short months later when they'd given a lunch party and needed more bread for the evening. Casually hopping on his bicycle, it was only a ten-minute round trip to the boulangerie the way he cycled, he'd be back in no time. The waiting, the growing anxiety. Then the slam of a car door, the arrival of Jean-Louis, walking towards her in his sky-blue shirt, his face so serious as he approached with his terrible news. He'd found him on the side of the road, it must have been a pothole.

What would Dom think of her now, lying in their bed with this man who had brought her the worst news in the world? What did she think of herself? You never knew how things would pan out, could never anticipate what lay around the next corner. Thank goodness. She tucked Jean-Louis' arm around her and drifted into sleep.

CHAPTER 3

The following morning found a muted party assembled for breakfast on the terrace. Hangovers were not what they used to be, as Dougie was regretfully discussing with Mary while they wiped down the surfaces. Gone were the days of sleeping it off, when you pulled a pillow over your head and didn't get up till noon. These days, their ageing body clocks forced them up at seven as usual, which meant the clear-up was complete, the dishwasher emptied, and an impressive cache of empty bottles already removed for recycling.

'It's poor form, I know, to slag off absent members of the household,' said Leo, 'but how come it is always us five who get lumbered with the clearing up?'

He topped up his coffee from the pot and took a bite of fresh buttery croissant, which immediately lifted his mood. Dougie had driven down to the boulangerie first thing to buy a heartening bag of *viennoiseries* – pains au chocolat, brioche, pains aux raisins in addition to croissants, guaranteed to revive jaded spirits.

'Cinderellas of the chateau, that's us,' said Beth, spreading blackberry jam on a yellow slice of brioche, 'while the ugly sisters all sleep it off.'

'Simon would make a great ugly sister,' said Nicola, 'he was born for pantomime. To be fair, he worked hard at the piano last night, so we'll let him off. And Jean-Louis was up early as usual, for the farm.'

'Which leaves those other ugly sisters, Will and Fizz, using their child as a get out of jail free card,' said Beth. 'Now they're over in the barn, we can't even knock on their door to get them up. Same with Maddie and John, at a safe remove in the old cider press.'

Mary peeled off her rubber gloves and helped herself to a pain au chocolat.

'I saw Maddie earlier, taking Lily to school,' she said, 'so we'll excuse her. Anyway, you know me, I can never relax until everything is clean.'

'Which is why you're such a treasured member of our community,' said Beth. 'Advice to any group of friends thinking of buying a house together: make sure you include a clean freak in the mix.'

'But Mary is so much more than a clean freak,' said Nicola. 'She's our resident professor, for a start.'

'*One* of your resident professors,' Dougie reminded them. He, too, was an expert in his field, as competitive as any other retired academic.

'Sorry, Dougie,' said Nicola, 'I forget how frail a scholar's ego is. It's a bitchy old world in the groves of academe, I don't know how you both survived.'

'Former professors, to be precise, ' said Mary, 'although as a committed medievalist, my work goes on in retirement. But never mind my intellectual credentials, you will all find me irresistible when we buy the Paris flat, and you have the use of it. What with my cleaning skills and my Paris bolt-hole, I'll miraculously become Most Popular Person in the chateau, but I won't judge you for being shallow.'

She had received a surprisingly large sum when her mother finally died, after ten years lost in a nursing home. There was a definite upside to being an only child, as Dougie pointed out, especially when it came to the inheritance. They'd decided to spend it on a flat on the Left Bank, to be used for cultural trips to the capital. They would hang around Café Les Deux Magots like Jean-Paul Sartre and Simone de Beauvoir, only slightly less glamorous.

'I can't wait for use of your pied-à-terre,' said Leo, 'so much more relaxing than a hotel.'

He stayed in Paris occasionally, after meeting clients – his reputation as an interior designer was growing – but always felt like a tourist when checking into a mid-priced hotel alongside other budget-conscious foreigners. Having a key to an apartment would make him feel like a real Parisian. He'd checked out the address on his last visit – Rue Jacob, the heart of the Latin quarter. You could feel the poetry and history as you walked through the narrow streets, so different to the Haussmannian grandeur of much of the city which he sometimes found grey and austere in its conformity.

'I'm going to take a final look at the rooms, before our guests arrive,' he said, 'make sure everything is as it should be.'

He walked down from the terrace, following the path that led to the west wing, which mercifully had its own entrance. It kept a notion of family privacy that the guests could access their rooms without traipsing through the chateau, pulling their bags on wheels and chipping away at the paintwork. He knew all about the pitfalls of opening your home to strangers. Up the circular staircase, and there was the corridor leading to what would eventually become a suite of eight guest rooms. He opened the door marked 'Louis XIV' and was satisfied by what he saw.

The curvaceous bed, the armoire, the drapery, the mirrors, everything to suggest the gilded luxury of Versailles. It was a shame they didn't have celebrity guests to christen it, Catherine Deneuve maybe, or Brigitte and Emmanuel Macron. He could just see Brigitte as an eighteenth-century courtier. The bathroom door was discreetly covered with the same patterned paper as the walls, so you had to hunt for the handle, then you opened it to reveal the trio of basin, toilet and bidet, bought for a song at the local *brocante*. Leo was glad they'd agreed to include the bidet, almost a museum piece now, when so few homes installed them. It would no doubt provoke a few sniggers, the British were childish like that, but Leo was a great believer in the efficiency of washing only the important little places, and hoped it would lead to reduced use of the shower built into the corner of the room. He adjusted the towels on the rack to achieve perfect symmetry and admired the line of toiletries supplied in glass bottles solid enough to deter thievery. Miniatures were fair game, but only a very unsuitable guest would dare to stash away a large crystal container as a going-home present. Though he had heard about people travelling with screw-top containers in order to steal shampoo, there was nothing you could do against that level of meanness.

Back in the bedroom, he checked the mini fridge – cunningly concealed within a bedside cabinet – and noted the fresh milk, mini bottles of wine and water. A tray of what lesser establishments would describe as 'tea- and coffee-making facilities' was placed atop a bow-legged table. It was important for the guests to feel they had everything they needed. Anyone staying in this room would have to agree it deserved its moniker. Louis XIV, the sun king, heart of the court, monarch for seventy-two years, famously identified himself with the land he ruled – '*l'état, c'est moi'* a sentiment shared by recent would-be leaders of France. Although Leo couldn't be doing with politics. The great thing about living abroad was that you felt removed from the worries of the world, detached from your home country's concerns, and excluded from those of your host country. Snug in your chateau-sized bubble, with only your guests to worry about.

The village school looked like something from a children's storybook, a pretty stone building with blue-painted shutters, surrounded by trees. Outside the gates, Maddie was waiting for the midday bell, wearing a long floaty dress that rather set her apart from the other mothers, who were chatting in the autumn sun. They were practical countrywomen, sensibly dressed, hardly the epitome of French chic. Maddie supposed you'd have to go to Paris to find those effortlessly stylish women you see in magazine articles about how to wear a scarf like a Frenchwoman. Here, it was anoraks and flat shoes. She'd exchanged words with some of them but felt shy in their presence. The language barrier, for sure, but also the sense of otherness, that her life was so different from theirs. She was one of those British weirdos who'd abandoned their own country to shack up in a run-down old chateau. The chateau was no longer run-down – it was positively luxurious – but she could tell they still thought it was a crazy idea. She'd overheard two of them speculating about how on earth you heat a place that size, whispering that surely *les excentriques* were forced to congregate in one salon while the other forty-nine rooms remained cold and empty.

The gates opened and a stream of tiny children came running out of the *école maternelle*. Such a cute term, motherly school, no thought of teaching them to read or write until they were six, this was a time for holding hands and painting pictures. Some of them stayed for lunch, which involved a compulsory siesta. Maddie had a glimpse of it once, little tots lying solemnly on mattresses, clutching their teddy bears, pretending to sleep. She couldn't imagine it happening in Britain, surely there would be a riot. Next year Lily would be a full-timer, when she entered *moyenne section*, but for now it was half-days only, quite enough to break her into the system. The main aim of *petite section*, apparently, was to get children to like going to school, and Lily loved it.

Here she came now, waving at her mother, face beaming with excitement as if they were reuniting after four months rather than four hours.

'We did a *dessin*,' she said, thrusting a drawing of a deranged-looking animal in Maddie's direction.

'Lovely, darling!' said Maddie, in her default mode of unconditional approval. 'We'll put it on the wall with all your others.'

Driving back to the chateau, Maddie thought how different her life would be now had they not made the move from London. She'd be rushing between the office, the nursery, the childminder, battling traffic and crowded Tubes, anxiously engaging with school waiting lists and catchment areas, huddled together with other city parents, worrying how to do the best for their child.

Instead of which, she was sweeping through the gates of a Renaissance chateau her parents had rashly bought on a whim, along with a bunch of other old people who now made up her immediate social circle. Apart from Fizz – who was weird anyway – she and John saw nobody of their own age, apart from a nodding acquaintance with parents at the school since Lily started there two weeks ago. They agreed they really didn't miss it, they had become so used to socialising via a computer screen, they barely noticed the absence of real-life encounters.

She parked up in their normal spot – under a beech tree at a distance from the chateau – and followed Lily who was skipping through the field towards the cider press barn they had lovingly renovated during her maternity leave, thinking they would use it for visits, until it dawned on them that a far better idea would be to live there all the time.

John looked up from his computer as his daughter bounded in and hurled herself on to his lap.

'Daddy!!'

That was the end of his morning's work. How wonderful to have your day punctuated by the rhythm of your child. He lifted her on to his shoulders and pretended to be a horse clip-clopping round the kitchen, while Lily screamed with delight.

'Goat's cheese salad for lunch?' asked Maddie, opening the fridge. John usually worked at the kitchen table, while Maddie preferred to stretch out with her laptop on the sofa in the sitting room where she could put her feet up. She couldn't imagine ever going back to the workplace after the luxury of working from home. Sitting up at a desk, surrounded by other office slaves, no thank you. Fortunately, their employers took a relaxed view of where their staff spent their working days. Every couple of months, she and John drove *en famille* to London to stay with his parents, who looked after Lily while they put in guest appearances at their respective offices. It made a refreshing change and on the journey home to France they would congratulate themselves – smug alert! – on how they had achieved the perfect work–life balance.

'I thought we were going up to the chateau for lunch,' said John, swinging Lily back onto the ground. 'Aren't we supposed to be gathering for a group viewing of the first guests? Hapless guinea pigs that they are.'

'They're not due until teatime,' said Maddie. 'Let's chill here, shall we? Can you cut us some herbs?'

'Herbs!' said Lily, heading for the door. It was one of her favourite tasks. John followed her out with a pair of scissors to edit her selection. Left to her own devices, she'd uproot the lot. Old iron troughs installed beneath the windows were planted with sage and thyme, basil and dill, while rosemary and bay bushes shared a bed with an old climbing rose which they'd preserved during the renovation of the cider press. John guided Lily to some frothy dill fronds which she cut with serious precision, breathing heavily as she administered the scissors. It was a feature of French supermarkets that you couldn't buy fresh herbs as readily as in Britain, apart from bunches of curly parsley. Maddie used to wonder if every French household grew them in pots on their windowsills to make up for this shortfall. Certainly they grew them in abundance at the chateau.

Maddie served up the grilled goat's cheese slices, melted over toasted baguette, the edges deliciously brown and crunchy, on a bed of lettuce she'd picked from the garden earlier. Lily took fat pinches of dill and sprinkled them over the three plates.

'This is the life,' she said cheerfully, currying favour with her parents by using one of the phrases she often heard them use.

'This is the life indeed,' said John. 'How was school today, Lily?'

'We did a *dessin*.'

She pointed at it, already pinned up on the wall.

'Beautiful,' said John. 'So, we're going to meet our first guests today, Lily. What do you think of that?'

Lily ignored him, focusing on her plate, so John directed his conversation to Maddie.

'Where are they from, do we know?' John asked.

'One couple from Guildford, I believe. Another from Yorkshire.'

'Outsiders! We've become so insular, the shock might see us off.'

Most afternoons you wouldn't expect to find all the chateau residents gathered in the crystal ballroom, but nobody wanted to miss the arrival of the paying guests. Mary was bent over a large board, working on a jigsaw of a David Hockney painting of his Normandy garden which was situated just up the road. She and Dougie had set out to look for his house once, driving slowly through the country lanes like a couple of stalkers, hoping to identify it from the photos in a magazine article. A fruitless task in the end, so she'd ordered the jigsaw instead. Not his finest work – he'd dashed it off on an iPad – but there was pleasure in recognising the familiar skies and trees.

Lily and Louis were playing with a Brio train set, joining the pieces to form a track under the armchairs, beneath the half-attentive gaze of their parents who were more interested in studying their phones.

'I'm not sure those wooden railway lines add anything to the ambience of the decor,' said Leo. 'Far too chunky and modern, I'd be happier with a vintage Hornby set.'

'Don't worry, Leo,' said Fizz, leaning down to stroke Louis' hair as he crawled beneath her chair, clutching a miniature railway bridge, 'we'll be taking them back to our barracks soon, but I didn't want to miss the big arrival.'

Simon was pacing in front of the windows, watching Nicola attending to the plant pots on the front terrace, last minute dead-heading to make sure the garden was at its absolute best.

She looked so young in her jeans, it took him back in a flash to when he was her boyfriend. They were barely out of their teens, a university romance which still bubbled under, if he was honest. For him at least. It got out of hand when they first moved to the chateau, and he became obsessed with Nicola all over again. Embarrassing now to remember it. Beth had been furious with him, but he couldn't help it. He was a passionate man, it wasn't his fault if he was prone to falling in love with people, or re-falling in love in Nicola's case. Anyway, that was all in the past, he and Beth had patched it up. And Nicola was all loved up now with that French farmer – with unseemly haste, some might say – after Dom's tragic demise. He clicked himself back to the present.

'In another age, it would have been the king and his retinue we'd be receiving, or at least other members of the French aristocracy,' he said. 'Instead of which we've got who, exactly? Remind me, Dougie.'

Dougie was sitting in front of his computer, spreadsheets open, a man in charge of his project. He peered at the screen.

'Today we're expecting Nigel Green, from Guildford, and Brenda White, from Wakefield.'

'Ooh, just like Cluedo,' said Beth. 'Reverend Green in the library with the candlestick or Brenda White in the Louis XIV suite with the lead piping?'

'The bookings are going pretty well actually,' said Dougie. 'A steady stream of overnighters and short stays, then one very welcome reservation from an Apolline Granger for two full weeks in October.'

'Two weeks! That's a bit keen,' said Beth, 'surely you'd book for a couple of days and check us out before committing to that.'

SARAH LONG | 41

'She might fear we're fully booked,' said Simon, 'that's why it's best not to show a drop-down calendar. "Contact us to check availability" maintains an illusion of hard to get.'

'Anyway, why wouldn't she long to stay for two weeks?' said Leo. 'She'll have studied the refined detail of my rooms and realised she could ask for nothing better.'

'She's reserved for one person,' said Dougie. 'I explained we didn't offer a single person discount, apart from on the breakfast. She wasn't fussed.'

'Apolline, sounds French,' said Simon. 'Where does she live?'

Dougie scrolled through the email chain.

'Henley-on-Thames. Not French at all.'

'Mysterious,' said Simon.

'Oh, I missed this part,' said Dougie. 'After the single person rate discussion, she says she is "looking for a new environment, somewhere to escape from my circumstances, where I can breathe and feel free". And she instinctively feels that Chateau Lafarge will be perfect for that.'

Will looked up from the floor where he was helping little Louis to slot in the bridge. He loved Brio, he loved it first time round when he snatched moments to play with his now-grown sons, and loved it even more now he had all the time in the world to construct elaborate routes. Next would be the Scalextric toy racing car tracks, still intact from his own childhood. He couldn't wait to unpack all that again when Louis was a bit older.

'That sounds a bit worrying,' he said, 'all that new environment stuff. Sounds like she's looking for a self-help farm, not a centre of luxurious excellence, which is what we're offering.'

'Think of the money,' said Dougie. 'It sounds to me like she could be a well-heeled retired civil servant, maybe. Sensitive and

educated, clearly, a good candidate for my history tours.' His
side hustle was leading scholarly tours of Rouen and the Landing
Beaches, which had proved very successful. It was encouraging
to see how many tourists were eager to acquire some learning
during their holidays.

'Forget Apolline – whoever she turns out to be – I can see
a car at the gates!' said Simon. 'What do we think, will it be
Brenda or Nigel?'

Beth joined him at the window.

'Neither, you blind old fool, that is Madame de Courcy's
Citroën. There's no way she was going to miss out on this
momentous afternoon.'

They watched her drive towards them and park, as usual,
slap-bang outside the front door. Beth went out to greet her,
escorting her in to join the others.

Madame de Courcy stood regally over her walking stick and
nodded graciously to the assembled friends.

'I hope you will excuse me showing up again today. I just
wanted to express my gratitude for the *belle soirée* yesterday, it
was *magnifique*. And now I want you to know that in spite of
my hesitancy over your commercialisation of my family seat,
I understand that you have your reasons. And so, although it
pains me to think of my home being thrown open to all-comers,
in exchange for financial gain, I don't want you to feel guilty on
my behalf. I forgive you.'

'Thanks for that, Madame de Courcy,' said Beth, 'but to clear
up a couple of points, it's not your home, it's ours, and we're free
to use it as we see fit, without any need for your approval.'

With perfect timing, Nicola came in from the garden.

'Hello, Madame de Courcy. I was just thinking of you earlier,' she said, 'and the first time I met you out on the terrace, do you remember? You arrived with a gift of lily of the valley on the day we moved in, it was such a charming gesture. As you know, my granddaughter's name is Lily. I love the continuity there, as though it was somehow meant to be.'

'Grandma!'

Lily abandoned the train set and ran across the room to hurl herself at Nicola.

'Of course, I remember it well,' said Madame de Courcy, mollified, 'but in French we call this flower *le muguet*, always offered on the first of May, so the link to your granddaughter's name only works in English . . .'

'Oh look, someone's just arriving!' said Dougie. 'Who's going to meet and greet? We can't overwhelm them with all of us!'

'Nicola, I think,' said Beth. 'Act casual, everyone, let's pretend we usually spend our afternoons hanging out together in the crystal ballroom. I'm going to take a closer look, but you all stay where you are. Off you go, Nicola.'

Nicola obediently went out to greet the guests, while Beth provided a running commentary from her ringside seat by the window.

'Ooh, she's got red hair! Not ginger, I mean proper tomato red hair . . . and a flowing gown that looks like it's made from curtains. I like her style! Husband quite hefty, wearing shorts – and sandals with socks, of course!'

'Pity we haven't got net curtains for you to twitch,' said Dougie, 'you'd better come away from the window before Nicola brings them in.'

Beth moved to an armchair and an unnatural silence fell upon the room while they waited.

Nicola pushed open the door.

'This is the crystal ballroom,' she said, 'and these are my fellow chateau-dwellers. Say hello to Brenda and Mark, everyone.'

The new arrivals looked around to assess their surroundings. Leo silently judged the heavily built man in shorts and sandals who would shortly be testing the springs of the Louis XIV bed. He hoped they were up to the task.

'Too bad you don't have a moat,' said Mark, shaking his head mournfully. 'I said to Brenda as we drove in, what a shame they don't have a moat. But then I thought, maybe that's a blessing, it would just be another thing to clear up and maintain.'

'Don't listen to that miserable beggar,' said Brenda, 'it's a grand old chateau, exactly as I hoped, just like on the telly! Look at that chandelier, and all those windows! Lot of work went into this, I bet, makes me tired just looking at it.'

Leo liked the look of her. Red scarf to match her hair, bright yellow shoes peeking out beneath her damask coat.

'On the telly?' he said, coming up to shake Brenda's hand. 'Are you telling me we've been on the telly and we didn't even know?'

'You must know the TV show,' said Brenda, 'surely that's what gave you the idea. We all dream of buying a ruined chateau and escaping the rat race, thanks to that programme.'

'We don't watch television,' said Leo, 'we don't have time.'

Fizz came over to put the record straight, she wasn't going to miss the chance of adding a couple of new followers.

'Pleased to meet you both,' she said, 'I know the programme you mean, you must excuse Leo, he's a bit out of touch! I'm very aware of all the media interest in chateau renovation, in fact I have my own YouTube channel, do you know it? I used to call myself Mademoiselle Bovary, but now I'm a mother, it's Madame Bovary. I'll send you the link. In fact, you might like to feature in it, as you're our very first guests, did you know that?'

'Are we really, what an honour! We'd love that, wouldn't we, Mark?' said Brenda.

Mark nodded, it would make up for the disappointment of having no moat if they were actually filmed at the chateau. Shame it wasn't on the TV though, he never watched things on the computer.

Madame de Courcy felt it was time to make her presence felt. She advanced with her walking stick to greet this peculiar couple. So eccentric, the British, this enormous man with his scarecrow hair and terrible short trousers, and his wife, dressed like a perfect fright and with that peculiar hair dye – they really made the others look normal by comparison.

'Allow me to introduce myself. I am Madame de Courcy. My family have owned this chateau for centuries, you could say we are part of the very fabric of this edifice, our roots have run deeper and deeper into this plot over many generations.'

'Oh yes, you really look the part,' said Mark, nodding his approval. He could imagine her featured in an oil painting hanging over the fireplace.

Beth quickly intervened.

'And we bought the chateau from Madame de Courcy five years ago, as a group of friends. You could say we're a kind of collective.'

'I didn't think there'd be so many of you,' said Brenda, gazing round the crowded room. 'On that programme it's just the two of

them living in their great big chateau, along with their two kid-
dies. I see you've made a start there with those two little ones.'

She waved at Louis and Lilly, who stared at her frostily.

'They are recent additions,' said Simon. 'We started off as a
child-free band of nine consenting adults, but you know how
these things happen.'

'Don't we just! Ours are grown now, but they all live near us
in Wakefield, so there's no escape.'

'Ah yes, that is the perfect introduction to my joke,' said
Simon. 'How can you tell if someone's from Yorkshire?'

Brenda shook her head.

'Ignore him, Brenda,' said Beth, 'he has a terrible range of
jokes, believe me. I've heard them all, multiple times.'

'Tell me then,' said Brenda, 'how do you know if someone's
from Yorkshire?'

'Because they tell you within thirty seconds of meeting you.'

'Oh aye,' said Mark, 'I've heard that before, it's a good 'un.'

He looked at Simon with respect.

'Shall I show you to your room?' said Nicola. 'Leo has done a
marvellous job on it. You're in the west wing which has its own
access so you can come and go as you please without having
to come through this way – though of course you are welcome
anywhere in the chateau. And let us know if you'd like to join
us for dinner tomorrow – I know you have other plans for this
evening.'

She took them away, leaving the others to hold the post-mortem.

'Well, well, Simon, mine host,' said Beth, 'are you going to
be greeting all our guests with offensive jokes about where they
come from?'

'He loved it,' said Simon. 'You've got to break the ice, otherwise it feels too weird having strangers in the house.'

'It's such an intrusion,' said Leo. He was stretched out on the chaise longue, hands covering his face. 'I thought I was ready for it, but it's one thing to imagine people you don't know coming to stay, you only have a vague picture of what it might be like. Then you confront the reality. Strangers invading our personal space.'

'That is entirely my point,' said Madame de Courcy. 'Do you not say that an Englishman's home is his castle? In your case, a real castle. And it is a shock to have that invaded.'

'Yet you invade us quite frequently, Madame de Courcy,' Beth teased.

The old lady tapped Beth's arm playfully.

'*Méchante!* Naughty girl.'

'Hold your horses, here come the others!' said Simon, from his vantage point at the window.

'A nice old Porsche, Will, right up your street.'

Will hurried up from the floor to take a look. He still pined for the open-topped sports car he'd driven over when they arrived at the chateau five years ago. His young wife beside him, the wind in their hair, it felt so free. With the arrival of baby Louis, he had traded it in for a functional family car, equipped with infant seat paraphernalia he didn't remember from last time round. He was pretty sure he and Marjorie used to simply chuck the carrycot on the back seat. Things were simpler then.

'Very nice indeed,' he said wistfully, watching a tall man unfold himself stiffly from the driver's seat. It was true that as you got older, it was increasingly difficult to get up from a low-slung seat, maybe he was better off after all with his boring SUV on its big wheels.

'He's wearing a cravat!' said Simon. 'I haven't seen one of those for years. Does he think he's James Bond or something? They're both out of the car now, who's going to greet them?'

'I shall welcome them in,' said Madame de Courcy, who had been inspecting the new arrivals through the window and found them very satisfactory. She swept out to perform her noblesse oblige routine.

'That woman's got a nerve,' said Beth, as she watched the old lady with her head on one side, flirting with cravat-man, gesticulating at the chateau as she gave an animated account of its history. 'Anyone would think she was still the owner. I don't know why we bothered signing that bit of paper.'

'Think of her as added value,' said Simon. 'She entertains the guests so we don't have to, plus she's the real deal – authentically French – that's what people want when they come to stay here.'

He had a point, Beth conceded, as she watched their guests nodding at the old lady's every word, drinking in her stories, then following her into the chateau to meet the real owners.

'You must be Nigel,' said Simon, taking the initiative and shaking his hand. 'Do you know that there were no new Nigels born last year? It's funny how that name has gone out of fashion, you're a dying breed!'

'I know, I'm something of a rarity!' said Nigel.

Thank goodness he'd taken that remark in good part, thought Beth, you could never rely on Simon not to say the wrong thing.

'And I'm Camilla,' said his wife.

Leo looked up from the chaise to see an immaculately dressed woman with the lean physique of a racehorse and elegant grey

SARAH LONG | 49

hair. Sensing a kindred spirit, he volunteered to show them to their room. By the time they reached the chambre Madame de Pompadour, he had established that he and Camilla were distantly related, through the convoluted threads of lineage that only posh people know about. Camilla and Nigel raved about the room, appreciating every aesthetic detail, which gave Leo a warm glow inside. It really was a perfectly marvellous idea to open the chateau to guests. His reservations melted away at the thought of all the lovely people they would meet through this exciting new venture.

CHAPTER 4

On a perfect October morning, dawn was breaking over the misty fields and Jean-Louis was driving Nicola to market in his van loaded up with apples and pears, chard and cauliflowers – products of the fertile Norman soil shared by his farm and the walled garden of her chateau.

He wound the window down and inhaled the crisp air.

'*Ah, ça sent l'automne.* The smell of autumn!'

He produced a roll-up from the crumpled packet in his breast pocket and pulled out the dashboard lighter, applying the hot orange rings to the tip to achieve a satisfying inhalation.

'It's lucky your van is so old,' said Nicola, 'the new vehicles don't come with cigarette lighters.'

Jean-Louis shrugged.

'Then I would use a *briquet*.'

He rattled the collection of lighters in his pocket and turned to her.

'Do you remember the very first time we drove together to the market? I was already in love with you, I felt like a nervous boy with you sitting beside me.'

'Of course I remember.'

It was during the aftermath of Dom's death, she had focused her attention on the market garden operation, growing vegetables, keeping busy to ward off the pain.

'You were not in love with me, I knew that. But I also knew it was only a matter of time until we were together.'

'You prophet! And here we are.'

Over the following months, their relationship had blossomed. The regular trips to market became more than a friendly business arrangement, they became courtship rituals, with Nicola pulling back from Jean-Louis's gentle advances. He was too young, it was too soon. Until she realised it was all right for her to find happiness again.

'My mother adores you,' said Jean-Louis, 'she said again last night how glad she was to have you in her life.'

'That's only because I've finally learned how to cook a *côte de boeuf* the way she taught me.'

This involved flashing the meat under a hot grill for an indecently short time, then flipping it over with a fork for a quick burst on the other side. The combination of scorched surface and almost raw interieur was, admittedly, unbeatable. They had it last night, served up with bearnaise sauce and *frites* deep-fried by Jean-Louis's mother in an old-school chip pan, the type you used to see in lurid public health broadcasts to illustrate how recklessness around boiling fat could set fire to your home.

'She likes it very much when we invite her to dinner.'

'And I like her coming round. I also like it when she goes back to her mother-in-law annexe and we have the house to ourselves. Intimate solitude, we don't get much of that at the chateau.'

Jean-Louis frowned.

'Mother-in-law, it is an ugly word, *belle-mere* is much more beautiful.'

'That's true, but of course neither word is relevant here. As we are not married, just happily semi-cohabiting. I love the way we live.'

She reached across the gearbox to squeeze his hand.

When Jean-Louis' father died, his mother Anne had moved into the farmhouse annexe, leaving her son to occupy the main residence. She had hoped that he might marry and fill it with the next generation of farmers, so was not overjoyed when he took up with someone so much older. But she had made her peace with Nicola, and whilst their arrangement was unconventional, with Nicola dividing her time between the farmhouse and the chateau, Anne appreciated the extended family nature of the set-up. She loved it when Nicola's granddaughter came over to play with the old-fashioned weighing scales in the *laiterie*. Anne could teach Lily to make cheese when she was a little older, it didn't matter that they weren't biologically related, it was family after all, just in a different form.

The sun was fully out when they arrived at the market square, and with practised ease they set up their stall alongside the others, to the background noise of the church clock chimes. Nicola went off to check out the fish stall – they had their new guest arriving this evening who had booked for dinner and Will had asked Nicola to let him know what was on offer, so he could plan his menu accordingly.

She called him to talk through the options.

'Hey, Will. So there's some beautiful red mullet, there's also loads of shellfish – do we know if she likes it? We don't want to find out she's allergic.'

Will was still in bed, Louis playing on the floor beside him, while Fizz was warming up on her yoga mat in readiness for her morning run.

'Shellfish is good!' he said. 'Dougie emailed her yesterday to ask about diet requests, she actually said she adores all seafood.'

'Great, so I'm thinking seafood platter to start – oysters, whelks, those sexy little grey prawns . . .'

'Then maybe a fishy pasta,' said Will, sitting up in enthusiasm at the thought of escaping childcare to get creative in the kitchen. 'I'm thinking, let's cast off the tyranny of French cuisine and go Italian. Linguine with crab, maybe . . .'

'They have some beauties here, claws tied up to stop them snapping your fingers! He also has *palourdes* – clams.'

'Yes, let's go with the clams – *spaghetti alle vongole*! Forget the crab, I remember the last time I cooked it, it was a bit traumatic. Stunning the poor bastards in the freezer, because it's too cruel to drop them into boiling water – it almost turned me vegan. Plus the work! I spent all afternoon scooping out the meat. I don't know why they don't sell it already gouged out in pots, like you find in British supermarkets.'

Nicola made her purchases and returned to join Jean-Louis at their own stall.

'Delicious seafood for our supper with the new guest,' she said, swinging the bags. 'I bought some extra for you and Anne, I'm assuming you won't join us this evening?'

'Ah, a 'fish supper',' said Jean-Louis, proud of his mastery of English idiom.

'No, that would be fish and chips, quite different.'

She opened the bag to reveal its delights.

'*Fruits de mer*, it's a shame we don't translate that as fruits of the sea.'

'Oysters!' said Jean-Louis. 'You are making an extravagant effort for your new guest, I hope she is worth it.'

'Come over later and see for yourself.'

'Thank you, but I will enjoy my oysters quietly at home.

Within the walled garden of the chateau, Will had constructed a beautiful double swing, using the timber from an oak tree that had blown down during one of the dramatic storms that were a feature of country life. It was quite common to find the roads blocked by trees, which would be removed and recycled into building projects or firewood – the pleasing circle of life where nothing was wasted.

Fizz and Maddie had taken their children outside to work off some energy before teatime, culminating, as usual, with Louis and Lily enthroned on the swings, screaming with excitement and urging their mothers to push them higher and higher.

'It's just the most boring thing ever, don't you think?' said Fizz. 'Standing here like lemons, pushing the wretched swings over and over again. They'd go on forever, the little tyrants, if we allowed them.'

'That's not how it looks on your vlog!' said Maddie. 'Rapturous mother and child bonding over the shared experience, is how I'd describe the mood of your last post. I know, because I was the one who filmed it, if you remember.'

'Yes, you did a good job. I swear, though, if I didn't have the motivation to make it all look so wonderful for the record, I'd be on my knees with the relentless monotony.'

She pushed Louis, in sync with Lily now as they stretched their little arms out to each other at the highest point.

'Don't worry, we've got plenty more of this to come,' said Maddie. 'Next spring when we have our new babies, we'll look back on these as the halcyon days. We'll remember how easy it was when you only had one. Anyway, I don't mind a bit of monotony. Especially in this setting, it's not as if we're crammed into the local playground with loads of other families, like we would be in London.'

'At least then there would be people to look at. And people to look at us.'

'Are you suffering from lack of attention?' Maddie teased. 'You've got Dougie over there, tending the veg, what more do you want?'

She called out to him, and he came hurrying towards them, carrying a trug of freshly pulled leeks, slim white stems with leafy green tops.

'Aren't they a picture?' he said. 'The quintessence of the French *potager*, in my opinion. I'm going to make a soup. Delicious and nourishing, and so *cheap*.'

'Fizz has a touch of the rural isolation blues,' said Maddie. 'She's feeling unnoticed, you must assure her that is not the case.'

'Unnoticed, good Lord, no!' said Dougie. 'You are an exceptional young woman, Fizz, it was brave of you to take on this chateau project with all us fogeys – admittedly one of them was your husband, but even so it was admirably unconventional. And now you are noticed by thousands of strangers, I believe, on the internet, thanks to your extravagant photography of our palatial estate.'

'Thank you, Dougie, I appreciate it,' said Fizz, mollified.

'And may I also say how much I admire the disciplined way you are bringing up your son. Mary and I were a little nervous about having another child in our midst, but we are both impressed at your rigour in establishing a routine for him.'

'Oh, it's essential,' said Fizz. 'Will thinks I'm too strict with my timetable, but for me it's exactly the same as with yoga and nutrition. You must establish the rules and the framework and stick with it.'

She really is quite terrifying, thought Maddie. She remembered her mother joking about Fizz, how she and Beth used to refer to her as Templewoman because her body was her temple, balanced in meditation on a mat and filled only with foods approved by the gods of wellbeing. It was odd how she and Fizz had been thrown together here through circumstance. They were chalk and cheese when it came to their attitudes to child-rearing. Benign neglect was Maddie's default mode, let them get on with it as long as they're not being annoying.

'What about me, Dougie?' she asked. 'Don't you admire the way I'm bringing up Lily?'

'Oh, Maddie, that goes without saying,' said Dougie, looking slightly embarrassed. 'You have a more relaxed approach, it's true, but Lily is a delightful little girl. Anyway, I must go off to the kitchen now and make this soup.'

Dougie made his way up to the chateau, admiring the way the stone facade glowed in the warmth of the late sun which offered dazzling reflections from the high windows. For him, October was the best month when the weather was kind, as it was today.

In the kitchen, he found Will chopping chilli at the table, while Simon was opening oysters over the sink.

'Dougie, welcome to the gentlemen's club!' said Simon. 'Care to join us in a snifter? We're getting ahead for dinner.'

He waved a bottle at him.

'We're on the Pommeau. A winning blend of apple juice and Calvados, ideal for this time of day as a pick-me-up, a sort of liquid afternoon tea really. Also, one of your five a day.'

'No thank you, it's a little early for me,' said Dougie. 'Oysters! That's rather extravagant. Is this in honour of our new arrival? We don't want to set the bar too high on the first night. I checked Apolline's email again and she says she'd like to book in for dinner every day.'

'Hardly surprising,' said Simon. 'If she's travelling alone, she's not going to drive off to sit in some quiet French restaurant by herself, is she? It's not like going to a casual British pub, where nobody takes any notice.'

'Oh, I don't know, solo dining can be very rewarding, I find. As long as you take a book to read.'

'We both know that's not true. It's an excruciating exercise in self-consciousness. If you're eating alone, you should be completely alone. Not watching everyone else enjoying lively conversation while you're being Norman no-mates. That's the beauty of our life here, every night is party night, we reject lone-liness and all other annoying aspects of growing older. Ready for a top-up, Will?'

He placed the final oyster on the platter and admired the results, then refreshed Will's glass before topping up his own.

'Look at you couple of dipsos,' said Beth, who had come into the kitchen to make a cup of tea. 'I was wondering why you men were suddenly so keen to take on cooking duties.'

'Prerogative of the chef,' said Simon. 'I'm in a long and vener-ated line. The Galloping Gourmet, Keith Floyd, Anthony Bour-dain, Fanny Cradock's husband . . .'

'What about you, Will?' said Beth. 'Fizz won't be pleased to hear you're having a sneaky afternoon tipple.'

'She won't know, will she?' said Will petulantly. 'Unless you tell her, of course. I'm allowed the odd secret indulgence when I'm off childcare duties.'

'God, I don't envy you,' said Simon. 'Once was enough for me, and that was when I was in my prime. And here you are going round again, poor bastard, with another one on the way. I always say to Beth, you know I'd never leave you for a younger woman because she'd want kids, so you're quite safe there.'

Beth scowled.

'Thank you for that reassurance. And don't be so down on Will, he's delighted he's going to be a dad again, aren't you, Will?'

Will took a swig of his drink.

'The world must be peopled, as Leo likes to remind us. And we all know that Fizz is an unstoppable force. Once she made her mind up, that was it. And, as Simon says, our community life at the chateau is a game changer. I'd find it harder being an ancient new dad if I was in a more conventional set-up. You know, if Fizz was going out to work while I was the nanny, that would be tough.'

'That would be the pits,' Simon agreed. 'If you're going to be an old dad, you've got to have rock star money, or live in a vibrant extended commune. Luckily you fit into one of those categories at least.'

'Seafood heaven!' said Leo, bursting into the kitchen, and catching sight of the platter of oysters. 'I'm glad they're nestling on a bed of ice, we don't want to poison the new girl. Mary and I have just been freshening up her room. What a relief that she's staying for two weeks, I'm through with this endless cycle of changing beds every couple of days.'

'We need to find a cleaner,' said Beth. 'What's the point of living in a bloody chateau if you've got to swab down your own floors? I'm quite a slob as you know, but now we've got the paying guests . . .'

'Stop, don't use that term!'

Leo was still conflicted about opening up the chateau for money.

'All right then, let's just call them guests. Anyway, the point is, it's very obliging of you and Mary to bear the brunt of the cleaning, but the bookings are coming in thick and fast, and once we open the other rooms, there'll be even more to do.'

'That's true,' said Leo. 'I wonder if we could find someone who could be persuaded to dress up in a frilly cap and pinny, that would be marvellous. A French maid straight out of central casting. I could put an advertisement up in the boulangerie.'

Nicola came into the room, still wearing her market-day overalls.

'There you all are!' she said. 'I was wondering where everyone was. We live in this huge house and you're all huddled together in the kitchen.'

'I love you in those dungarees,' said Leo, 'they scream "woman of the soil". How was the market today?'

'The market was great, but more importantly I've just met our delightful new arrival! Apolline *est arrivée*! Not what we expected. Hippy chic, she's driving an old VW campervan. She's parking up now.'

'A hippy!' said Leo. 'That sounds worrying.'

'Not a real hippy,' said Nicola. 'Arty. Bohemian. You'll love her.'

'I'm on my way,' said Leo, whooshing his hair up and giving her a smouldering pout. 'How do I look?'

'Fabulous, as always,' said Nicola.

'Come on, Simon, let's go and say hello,' said Beth. 'Nicola's piqued my interest.'

They followed Leo out through the servants' side entrance and made their way round on to the front drive where a brightly coloured van was parked at an erratic angle near the front door.

'Look at those curtains!' said Leo. 'Ideal for peeking through. And I love the swirly patterns on the orange bodywork, takes me right back to the seventies. And those tiny wheels, not like the great ugly things they stick on modern cars.'

Simon was staring, entranced, at the campervan, taking in the simplicity of the design, the way the body nearly touched the ground, the dainty windows, the big friendly headlights.

'That's freedom, pure and simple,' he said.

'Didn't you used to have a campervan?' asked Beth. 'Back in the dark ages, before we were together?'

'I did. It was even before Nicola.'

'Even before Nicola! That really was the dark ages.'

'It was in my gap year,' Simon reminisced. 'Everyone takes one now, but I was a bit of a trailblazer back then. Well, not exactly – the only people who went on gap years were those who stayed on at school for an extra term after A levels to take the Oxbridge entrance exam. I failed, as you know, which made me even more determined to make the most of those extra months off.'

'I'm glad you failed, otherwise we would never have met,' said Beth.

'True. Anyway, I worked cleaning cars for a local garage, then bought a knackered old VW campervan and drove it all over Europe with my mate Kev. It was magic, we had no money, we'd park up on a cliff for the night, open the roof and heat up a can of baked beans . . .'

He stopped talking as the van door opened and a tall woman stepped out. She was wearing a green velvet dress which offset the wild auburn hair that cascaded over her shoulders.

'Very pre-Raphaelite,' whispered Leo, 'I can just imagine her lifeless corpse floating down the river, decked in flowers.'

'Sshh,' said Beth, 'what a thing to say about our guest!'

She stepped forward to greet the new arrival.

'You must be Apolline, welcome to Chateau Lafarge. I am Beth, one of your hosts. Well done for finding us.'

'Thank you, Beth, it is just as I hoped.'

Apolline spun around to admire the impressive view, taking in the towers and the gardens spilling down to the lake. Beth clocked her small waist, in the way that women do who have lost theirs.

'I think it was a lot of work for you, no?' she said to Beth, her face radiating sympathy and admiration. 'The results are enchanting, I think even more beautiful than in the photos.'

That sexy little French accent, thought Beth, you really couldn't fault it.

Apolline turned to Leo.

'And I recognise you from the website, you are *tellement beau*! I know you are the designer of the bedroom where I shall be sleeping! The suite Louis XIV, so carefully created with a combination of antiques and bold colour use, I can't wait to see it in reality, this is a big excitement for me!'

'You are perfect for the room,' said Leo, flattered by her attention, 'I could have designed it with you in mind.'

So much more appropriate than that couple he'd ushered in when they first opened. He'd worried about them breaking the bed. This graceful apparition was much more on point, she could even be his muse, Lizzie Siddal to his Dante Gabriel Rossetti.

Simon was standing, transfixed, watching Apolline as she chatted with Leo. His open-mouthed expression hadn't gone unnoticed by Beth.

'This is my husband, Simon,' she said briskly.

Simon leaped into action, unleashing what Beth often sharply referred to as the 'oil slick' of his charm offensive.

'Pleased to meet you, we've been so looking forward to your arrival,' he said, shaking her hand and leaning in to admire her green-flecked eyes that were accentuated by the emerald-coloured hairband that pushed her hair off her face. 'Can I help you with your bags?'

'If you like, thank you.'

She reached into the van and pulled out a carrier bag, spilling over with clothes and toiletries and a half-eaten baguette sandwich.

'No suitcases, then?' said Simon, taking it from her.

'No point, they take up too much space. I carry only what will fit into this bag, the rest is superfluous.'

She gave him a dazzling smile.

'That is a wonderful attitude,' said Simon, who couldn't believe how perfect this woman was. 'So much of our lives is superfluous, we should concentrate on the essential. I couldn't agree more.'

He noticed the remains of the sandwich lying on top of the bag.

'Is this the superfluous part of your lunch?'

'I was too excited! I couldn't eat it all. And it is difficult to eat a baguette sandwich while you are driving, I have become used to the British versions, flat triangles, made for lunch on the go. For baguette sandwiches you must stop and concentrate. And there is so little choice here in France. I had forgotten how for your filling, it is ham, or cheese, or ham and cheese! Nothing changes, ever.'

'That's what we love about living here,' said Simon. 'Nothing changes – the French worked out years ago what tastes best, so they stick to it. We find it very charming. We find them very charming. And we love the way they speak – *ton accent est très séduisant.*'

Oh please, thought Beth. *Pass the sick bucket.*

Apolline acknowledged the compliment with a gracious smile.

'Perhaps my years in England have made me more adventurous,' she said. 'Now, will you show me to my room? Or should that perhaps be Leo as he is the creative force behind it? I am so looking forward to getting to know you all. I hope that everyone will be there for dinner this evening?'

'Oh yes,' said Beth, 'we'll all be there, don't you worry.'

CHAPTER 5

'She's a bit of a bombshell, wouldn't you say?' said Mary to Dougie.

It was the morning after Apolline's arrival and they were discussing her in the relative privacy of a first-class carriage on the train to Paris. It wasn't like them to show such extravagance but Dougie felt the occasion merited it. They were finally going to pick up the keys to their flat at the *notaire*'s office, where they had signed the *compromis de vente* a few weeks ago.

Dougie raised his eyebrows.

'A bombshell! I haven't heard that term in a few years. Rather unreconstructed of you, I'd say.'

'That's the freedom of living here, isn't it? We can say outrageous things without anyone jumping down our throats.'

'You don't know that,' Dougie whispered. 'That woman in the seat opposite could be a spy from a French university who's recording you and about to have you cancelled.'

'I'm only speaking my truth. As a plain-ish woman in her sixties, I would describe Apolline Granger as a bombshell.'

'Never plain, my dear. You're always alluring to me. If I'm allowed to say that.'

'You are allowed. Anyway, in addition to being a bombshell, I thought she was also an interesting and engaging woman, didn't you?'

'She certainly knew a lot about Fragonard. We might go into the Louvre later to take a look at that painting of the lovers in the locked room that she recommended. Isn't this wonderful! Our bucolic communal life now balanced by our Paris love nest, it couldn't be better.'

Three hours later, they emerged from St Germain des Près metro station, holding the keys to their new home. Mary had wrapped a scarf around her face whilst on the metro, in a bid to keep out the prevailing smell of bad eggs, a phenomenon she had noticed before on this otherwise excellent public service network. Stepping on to the pavement, she whipped off the scarf and breathed in the crisp air, admiring the perfect way the round lamp topped the elaborate wrought-iron sign, the dark green metal contrasting with the red of the metro sign. Effortless, timeless Paris style. They made their way down Rue Bonaparte, taking in the antique shop windows, then turned into their street, arriving at the ancient-looking double doors of their building. Dougie entered the code and the door obligingly clicked open, admitting them to a quiet, seventeenth-century courtyard. Beside a stone urn, another door opened on to a rickety staircase. They heaved their suitcases up the stairs – luckily only one flight – and were finally turning the key into their very own pied-à-terre.

The sale had included all furnishings, so they were stepping into a ready-made home. Three tall windows gave on to the street, the view that had sold them the apartment. Mary knew she could spend all day reading on the tapestry-covered chaise longue, looking up occasionally to check out what was going on outside. In warm weather, she would open that long window and step out onto the narrow balcony to take a more detailed look at the street life below. It was the best type of privacy. Secluded in this sanctuary, they could nevertheless walk out into the heart of Paris whenever they wanted, mingling with their fellow citizens, or not, according to their mood.

'Perfect, isn't it?' said Dougie. 'I'm going out to buy something to christen it.'

She heard the door close, and the sound of his receding footsteps. For the first time in ages, she realised she was completely alone. At the chateau, you always knew there was somebody somewhere, there was bound to be with so many occupants. She pulled her suitcase into the bedroom, which had the same beamed ceiling as the salon, with a window looking onto the courtyard. The bed pretty much filled the room, and was even made up with sheets. The vendor had been renting the flat as an Airbnb and had left it ready for guests, complete with toiletries in the bathroom. Mary unpacked her few clothes and checked the bathroom, pleased to find it reached her hygiene standards. She then went into the kitchen, delightfully and minimally equipped with only what you need for two people: a few pans hanging from the wall, open shelves displaying clean white crockery, a compact Nespresso machine. What a contrast to the chateau kitchen, loaded with pots and pans to feed an army.

'*Chérie*, I'm home!'

Dougie came in carrying a box of macarons and a chilled half-bottle of champagne, setting them down on the coffee table by the chaise longue. Mary brought through two flutes and two plates and watched him open the box. Inside were twelve exquisite almond meringues, in subtle pastel shades.

'So fortunate having Ladurée just round the corner, I can't tell you how much I enjoyed choosing the flavours. Raspberry, pistachio, lemon, orange water, rose cardamon, coffee, vanilla, and the irresistibly named Marie-Antoinette – look at that light blue colour! Criminally expensive, of course, but needs must.'

He poured two glasses of champagne.

'Here's to our quiet days in Paris.'

They clinked glasses, then jumped at the unfamiliar sound of a ring at the doorbell. Dougie went into the hall to inspect the intercom, pressing what he hoped was the appropriate button.

'*Allo, c'est qui?*' he said, in his best gruff Parisian manner. Maybe Paris, too, was home to those annoying door-to-door sellers of dusters. At least the intercom afforded some screening, unlike in Cambridge when you opened the front door and it was already too late to ignore the young man with his basket of overpriced dusters and gadgets to clean behind radiators.

But it was a familiar voice that spoke to him now.

'Hello, Dougie, surprise!! I had a last-minute meeting in Paris, so thought I might just pop by to inspect the premises, can you let me in?'

'Leo! It's been so long.' Dougie rolled his eyes at Mary who had come out to see who it was. 'Do come up and join us.'

Apolline was not a morning person, the generous breakfast table laid out in the dining room was of no interest to her, though the other guests – a greedy couple from Brighton – had hoovered their way through the croissants and polished off the hand-strained *faisselle* which Leo had prepared the night before. Instead, she had made herself a coffee in her room – which was entirely to her satisfaction – before taking a tour of the grounds, then wandering into the grand salon to see who was around.

Simon was doing *The Times* crossword on his tablet. He'd been watching her through the window, hoping she was heading this way.

'We missed you at breakfast,' he said, 'hope you slept all right?'

'I slept like a dormouse! Or, as you say in English, like a log! Felled by that magnificent dinner. I've heard from my friends that the best cooks in France are English, and that point was proved last night. I always feel in England that the tendency is to smother mediocre ingredients with confusing different flavours, but in France, the ingredients speak for themselves, they require only simple treatment, which you and your friends seem to understand perfectly.'

She was wearing a long crimson skirt, with a soft purple oversized jumper that made her look poetic and fragile in Simon's eyes.

'Ah yes, we're all competitive cooks here,' he said, 'just wait until it's my turn. I'm thinking about a *tarte des demoiselles tatin*, a gorgeous upside-down tart, to use up some of those endless apples that dominate our autumn.'

'I look forward to it. I'm here for a good long stay, so I can judge you all. Like *The Great British Bake Off*, or MasterChef. I know all the cookery shows. That is how I perfected my English, I watched them on my own and assimilated the language by osmosis.'

Simon wanted to ask why she watched them on her own, but thought it was too soon to pry.

'You live in Henley-on-Thames, I believe?' he asked. That was neutral enough.

'Yes. It's very pretty. Houses with lovely gardens running down to the river which is full of people rowing boats at great speed.'

'It's a British thing,' said Simon. 'We excel in all sports that involve sitting down – rowing, cycling, sailing, sliding down mountains on a dustbin lid. What took you to Henley in the first place? Was it your work?'

'I went to live in London as a *jeune fille au pair* for a few months during my studies. And then I stayed on, you know how these things go . . .'

Simon loved how she said the words '*jeune fille au pair*', it sounded so much more attractive than the clunky English 'au pair girl'. He wondered how long ago that was. It was hard to guess her age, probably late forties. He and Beth had a French au pair living with them for a while when Eva was a child, but Bénédicte turned out to be a stern young woman and a devout Catholic. Simon had been rather hoping for a *Bonjour Tristesse* situation, the novel by Françoise Sagan was still one of his favourites, but alas it was no-go. Apolline would have been a much better proposition.

'I won't press you for your life story,' he said, 'it's only day one after all.'

'I'm surprised to find you here,' said Apolline, 'you told me last night that the mornings are your prime writing time. I thought you'd be at your desk engaged in the next chapter of *Après moi, Le Déluge*.'

'Well done for remembering the title! I'm on my way, just warming up with the crossword. It's my morning ritual: sit in this chair, study the clues, breathe in the atmosphere of these old walls and thank my lucky stars for that view out over the lake. Enhanced this morning, of course, by the sight of you taking the air.'

'You old smoothie, I heard that!'

Will came into the room with Louis trotting beside him.

'Good morning, Apolline,' he said, 'I hope you're not being harassed by this man, I'm afraid he's a dinosaur from an earlier age.'

Apolline shook her head.

'Not at all, I am never afraid to accept a compliment. You will find Frenchwomen are less aggressive on that front. And I must compliment you in turn, Will, on your *spaghetti alle vongole*. It was sublime. This must be your son; I didn't meet him yesterday.'

She crouched down to take Louis' hand.

'He was safely in bed by dinner time,' said Will, 'but up bright and early this morning, with his usual regularity. I sometimes think I'm too old for this game. Do you have children, Apolline?'

She shook her head.

'No, I don't, which is probably why I enjoy them so much. Can I take him out this afternoon? I promised Maddie I'd take her little girl to the park in the village, I could take Louis too, give you a break.'

'Yes please, that would be amazing!'

'Good, I will meet you here after lunch. I am going out this morning to visit a Camembert factory. I have always wondered about the cheese-making process and now I will find out. It's important to learn new things, don't you agree? I'll see you later, goodbye.'

'Isn't she just stunning?' said Simon with a sigh of pure longing. He moved to the window so he could enjoy the sight of the Grecian goddess climbing into her van. 'And what a fantastic guest. Her first day and she's already volunteering for childcare duties.'

'You seem to have established quite a rapport,' said Will, giving him a stern look. 'Don't make a fool of yourself, the last thing we need is a repetition of the Nicola drama, with you playing the lovesick suitor.'

Simon was indignant.

'That's a bit rich, Will! We're still allowed to admire women here in France, if you remember. Apolline told us that herself! Free of the puritans, this side of the Channel.'

Will grinned at him, then moved towards the carafe of Calvados standing temptingly on a side table. 'Not too early, is it?'

He poured two glasses and handed one to Simon, then pulled a handful of toy cars out of his pocket for Louis to play with on the floor.

'It's never too early in France,' said Simon. 'We've both seen farmers in cafés knocking it back at breakfast time.'

'They have the excuse that they've just completed a morning's ploughing.'

'Well, so have you, in a way. Ploughing the lonely furrow of looking after your son while his mother flits around taking pretty photos. Cheers!'

Louis smiled up at them, waving his car in the air.

'Cheers, cheers, cheers,' he repeated.

'Cheers to you, darling boy,' said Simon, kissing his head. He pulled out his packet of cigarettes and headed to the fireplace.

'You don't mind, do you, as Fizz isn't here? You don't have to pretend to disapprove.'

'Go ahead, destroy your lungs,' said Will, as Simon lit up. 'Do you remember when we bought this Calvados?'

'One of our great early adventures.'

It was when Dom was still alive, the three of them had followed the handwritten sign down a muddy farm track, until they arrived at a barn where they were offered generous samples of the home-distilled apple brandy. They had responded by placing a generous order, which they were still working their way through some years later.

'Gruesome to think this Calvados has outlived poor old Dom,' said Simon. 'You never know what's round the corner, which is why you have to milk it while you can.'

'Exactly, I'll drink to that.'

'I'm impressed by Apolline going off to visit the cheese factory. We've been living here for five years and it's never occurred to us, though it's only just up the road.'

'Admit it, you'd be impressed by anything Apolline did,' said Will, 'But in our defence, we were up to our neck in building works, then so relieved it was over, we just wanted to sit back and enjoy the peace. Plus, you never bother visiting places on your doorstep. It's like people who live in Paris who've never been up the Eiffel Tower.'

He set his empty glass down next to the Calvados.

'I'll leave it there for later, save on the washing up.'

'Speaking of which, I wonder how Dougie and Mary are getting on in their pied-à-terre,' said Simon. 'They'll have to draw up a rota. We're all going to want to take turns. The missing piece in our dream existence. Life on our glorious chateau estate, punctuated by trips to the city bolt-hole.'

In a wild flight of fancy, he suddenly imagined himself and Apolline installed in the Left Bank love nest. He banished the thought at once and threw his cigarette butt into the fireplace, destroying the evidence.

'Not sure it will be an option for me and Fizz, especially when the new baby arrives,' said Will.

Louis looked up from the window, where he had been examining a fly buzzing fruitlessly in an attempt to escape through the glass.

'Daddy, let's go on the swings.'

He ran towards Will and wrapped his arms around his father's legs.

'Off you go, Daddy,' said Simon, 'and just remember, it could be worse. I believe out in the real world there are these hellish new inventions called Soft Play Centres where parents have to cower indoors and watch their kids sprawl over brightly coloured foam balls. Luckily for you there aren't any near here. Country life, simple pleasures, back to nature, enjoy!'

In the vegetable garden, Maddie and Nicola were harvesting pumpkins, ready for the weekend market. They lay scattered on the ground like giant orange hailstones fallen from heaven.

'This is an unexpected pleasure, having you help me out this afternoon,' said Nicola.

'All thanks to Nanny McPhee, otherwise known as sweet Apolline,' said Maddie, throwing a particularly large pumpkin into her wheelbarrow. 'I feel like a shot-putter, this one is massive. It was kind of her to take Lily off for the afternoon, leaving me free to lend a hand to my old mother.'

'She's such an asset already, isn't she? I'm glad she's booked in for a couple of weeks, fancy paying to stay somewhere and then offering free childcare? Do you think she's too good to be true?'

'Fizz has gone with them, I should add,' said Maddie. 'She thought I was completely irresponsible to hand over my kid to a total stranger, there was no way she'd let prince Louis go it alone, so they're out as a cosy foursome. She has a point, I suppose, but

I've become so relaxed about leaving Lily with all her chateau aunties and uncles that Apolline just seems like another helper to add to the collection.'

'It's not too much, is it, living here with us all?' asked Nicola. 'I was delighted when you and John decided to move here permanently, but I did wonder if you might come to regret it. I mean it's all very well spending a few months on maternity leave, but quite another thing to up sticks completely to join a commune of old people . . . Let's wheel this load up to join the others.'

They pushed their twin wheelbarrows towards the edge of the field to add to the large heap of squash piling up ready for collection. There was nothing like a shared task to facilitate conversation, Nicola noticed.

'Don't worry, Mum, no regrets,' said Maddie. 'Anyway, we can always move on if we want, it's not a life sentence – I guess it is for you, buying in with the others, but we're more semi-detached in the cider press. We love it, though, and I want you on hand when the new baby comes.'

'So exciting! I couldn't imagine this happening when we first bought the chateau. It never occurred to me that you'd come and join us.'

'Nor me. But there's been a lot of water under the bridge since then. First, Dad dying, then you inflicting a brand-new fake daddy on me.'

She grinned at Nicola as she emptied her barrow of pumpkins.

'It was you who encouraged me!' said Nicola. 'I'm glad you approve of Jean-Louis, you know the feeling's mutual.'

'I adore him, he's far too good for you.'

'Haha.'

'Also, he comes as the perfect package, with fake grandma for Lily. His mother is so sweet with her.'

'Hmm, I can't say it's easy, living next door to Anne. It was bad enough having one mother-in-law, but then to acquire a second one who's more or less the same age as yourself is a little complicated.'

'She's not your mother-in-law as you and Jean-Louis aren't married. And you can understand her feeling miffed at being deprived of grandchildren. He's her only son and then he goes and chooses a really old partner . . .'

'Cheeky! I'll race you back.'

Nicola set off with her wheelbarrow at a cracking pace, leaving Maddie trailing behind her.

'All right, you win,' said Maddie, catching her breath, 'but only because I'm pregnant and carrying extra weight. I accept you're amazingly fit and a worthy consort for the delicious Jean-Louis. And you only live next to his mother half the time, it's a great arrangement! Makes me feel like a complete square, with my full-time husband and nuclear family. Still, at least we have our weird chateau family to make us interesting.

'Oh look at this, what a charming scene, straight out of happy families!'

Beth came up to join them, carrying a basket of apples and a trug full of quail eggs. She set them down heavily and wiped her brow.

'Mother and daughter running through the pumpkin field, giggling with delight. I'm suddenly feeling a bit sick.'

'Ah, don't be like that, Beth,' said Maddie, putting an arm round her. 'Is it because you're missing Eva? Why not get her to move over as well? Plenty of outbuildings to choose from – she and James could take their pick.'

'That's not going to happen. Eva and I get on just fine, probably because we have a bit of distance. It was the intention, when we bought this place, to finally be free of our needy adult offspring. Now look at us!'

When they first came up with the idea of buying a communal home, Nicola used to joke that selling the family house was the only way to evict their children. Fat chance of an empty nest, with Maddie and her brother comfortably installed, post-university, in their childhood home. Beth and Simon's daughter had at least managed to move round the corner to a flat provided by her parents, but Beth complained she was still required to change light bulbs and offer daily counselling on her daughter's emotional and professional crises.

Maddie pulled a sad face.

'We've ruined it for you, I'm sorry.'

'Of course you haven't, I love having you all here,' said Beth. 'Saves us turning into a retirement village. Can you imagine those places, peopled entirely by geriatrics?'

'That's not going to happen, especially now with the *chambres d'hôte*,' said Maddie. 'The place is bursting with life. Mum and I were just saying what a great decision that was – especially with our new star guest.'

'Speak of the devil,' said Nicola. 'It looks like that's the end of the afternoon play shift.'

'Mummy!!!!'

Lily was racing towards them, arms going like windmills until she reached her destination and flattened herself against her mother. Apolline followed, a symphony in pink and purple today, Beth noted.

'Did you have a lovely time?' asked Maddie.

Lily nodded.

'Yes, we had a wonderful afternoon,' said Apolline. 'We iden- tified ten types of trees, then we went on the swings, where Lily saw a friend from school, then she wanted to come home as she says the swings are better here. Fizz was telling me all about her role as an influencer, it is incredible how she has built her pro- file. I am full of admiration for her va-va-voom, she has a lot of what you call 'get up and go'. I love that English expression! She has gone home now with Louis, but I think she will trust me next time to be in sole charge, though to be honest I enjoyed her company. I forgot how slowly the time passes when you are alone with children!'

'It can be really boring, I agree,' laughed Maddie. 'I'm incred- ibly grateful, thank you.'

Apolline was looking in Beth's trug.

'Are those quail eggs? *J'adore!* Nothing better with *l'apéritif* than a quail egg dipped in celery salt.'

'That's just as well, because that's exactly what you're getting this evening,' said Beth.

'Do you have all different sizes of chicken, Beth? Please, I want to see the hen houses. I think I know where they are, can you show me now? Then I must gather some of these magnificent pumpkins. I want to make lanterns for Halloween next week.'

She took Beth's arm and steered her in the direction of the chicken run.

'Also, I want to learn all about your business. Simon was telling me about your work for a production company. You are clearly such a clever, creative couple, you must tell me everything.'

'That's very flattering,' said Beth, 'but possibly not true, though I'm happy to talk you through my latest project, if you really want to hear about it.'

Maddie and Nicola watched them leave.

'*Elle est dynamique!* Dynamic woman!' said Maddie.

'*Epanouie!* Flourishing!' replied Nicola.

'*Bien dans sa peau!* Comfortable in her skin!'

It was a joke between them that they liked to share epithets for fulfilled women, as heard on French advertisements.

'She really is determined to be best friends with us all, I wonder what her story is,' said Nicola. 'No doubt all will be revealed.'

CHAPTER SIX

As Halloween approached, the warm weather retreated, strong winds stripped the leaves off the trees and rain came down in sheets. Nicola struggled to put up her umbrella against the breeze for the short walk from her car to the butcher's shop.

'*Allez, ma grande,*' said the butcher as she stood dripping on his shop floor. 'What can I get you?' His unfailing good humour was reassuring, reminding her how much she loved shopping for food in this land of culinary pleasures. He was seventy-eight years old, he'd told her once, clearly his enthusiasm for his job had kept him looking young.

'Some better weather would be good,' she said.

'It's coming, I have organised it for you,' he said with complete conviction. 'You will see, it is a myth that we have a lot of rain in Normandy.'

With the summer they'd enjoyed, the sunshine lingering into an *été indien*, it was easy to forget that this was one of the rainiest parts of France.

'And besides, with no rain, there is no rainbow,' said the butcher. 'How can we produce delicious beef or Camembert without green grass?'

He beamed at her through his spectacles. Nicola was always struck by how many French people wore glasses compared to the UK. Did they have worse eyesight or were they just more assiduous about tackling all aspects of their health? Judging from the long lines invariably queuing for the pharmacist, she suspected the latter.

She peered through the glass to inspect what he had on offer, running through possible menus in her head, then settled on a boeuf bourguignon. In her battered cookbook *Secrets of the Great French Restaurants*, it said this was the dish that men liked more than any other, which was the kind of sweeping generalisation you could get away with last century when the book was published.

The butcher pulled up a strip of marbled red meat and vigorously chopped it into large chunks.

'You'll want a bone with that,' he declared, disappearing into the back of the shop before returning with a large, unspecified piece of animal which he threw into the bundle.

Nicola thanked him and dashed through the rain to the *primeurs* next door. Along the length of the counter, trays of squash, ten types of potatoes, figs, grapes, endives, tomatoes of all hues and sizes were laid out with immense artistry. She passed over the *cèpes* with regret – it was such a short season, you should really eat them at every opportunity – and asked the shopkeeper instead to serve her the small button mushrooms – *champignons de Paris*, named after the city where they were first grown in the ideal conditions of the catacombs. Those on sale here were grown locally in a cave just round the corner. They'd visited it once and learned how a mushroom doubles in size every day and can be harvested after a week. She then moved down to the cheese counter, selecting a dark orange Livarot tied with a straw belt, a fresh goat's cheese rolled in ash and a sheep's cheese wrapped in a chestnut leaf.

Driving back to the chateau, Nicola was pleased to see the rain had cleared up and by the time she was home the sun was dancing on the roof tiles. Four seasons in one day – they'd often seen it, the most remarkable example was a hail storm one July, when tennis-ball sized stones of ice had dented car roofs and shattered windscreens.

She carried her shopping through the side door into the *arrière-cuisine*, then into the kitchen. Apolline was seated at the table, flanked by Simon and Will, each of them engaged in carving a pumpkin. Fizz was filming them on her phone.

'Hey, Nicola,' she said, 'come and look at this hive of creativity!'

'Occupational therapy, very good,' said Nicola, walking behind them to inspect the results. Simon had cut out large letters to spell an obscenity. He said his pumpkin was destined for the doorstep to frighten off any trick-or-treaters, though an advantage of the chateau's remote location was that you were very unlikely to be troubled by random callers. Will had opted to carve a straightforward face with cross-shaped eyes and a rictus grin.

'It's so easy to cut these pumpkins!' he said. 'When I was a kid, my mum gave us each a turnip and we had to gouge out the solid flesh inside. Almost impossible and we always ended up stabbing our hands.'

'A turnip, what the hell?' said Fizz, putting down her phone. 'Sometimes I just can't believe the age gap between us.'

'Ah, you're young enough to have grown up with Halloween pumpkins filling our supermarkets,' said Simon, 'the regrettable American tidal wave that washed over us all, even reaching France, despite their best efforts to resist foreign influence. As if it wasn't enough that the Yanks forced us into Christmas turkeys, we were quite happy with a goose before they led us astray.'

'Nicola, take a look at Apolline's,' said Fizz, 'it's amazing. I've just posted it.'

Nicola bent down to take a look at Apolline's pumpkin. She had cut out the front section to reveal the interior which had been transformed into a library, the walls lined with tiny books, shuttered windows with blue curtains, tables and chairs arranged in a familiar pattern. There was even a facsimile of the chandelier hanging from the ceiling.

'That's our library, how incredibly clever of you,' said Nicola. 'Look at the detail!'

'Thank you,' said Apolline. 'I admit I made a head start yesterday with the carving, and am just now completing the decorations. I wanted to create a tribute to the chateau, to show you how very much at home I feel here.'

Nicola then noticed her box of accessories – fabrics and paints, threads and wires. It was amazing what she must have kept stashed in those two carrier bags she arrived with.

'We're very happy to have you,' she said. 'You're obviously quite an artist.'

'You are all artists here, I sense that,' said Apolline. 'It is not a practical, sensible decision to take on the project to renovate a chateau, so therefore you must all be artists.'

'In our spirits, maybe,' said Nicola, 'but we don't all have the talent!'

'What's that about talent, are you talking about me again?'

Leo breezed into the kitchen, wearing a pair of tight trousers in the palest shade of eau de Nil that were cropped six inches above his ankles.

'What do you make of this trouser, is it too much, do you think?'

They all turned to inspect him as he held a model pose.

'Well . . . I don't like to criticise,' said Nicola, 'but aren't they a bit *short*? It looks like you've had a growth spurt in the school holidays.'

'I disagree, they are fabulous!' said Fizz. 'That's exactly what we're seeing this season.'

'One of the great things about getting older is not having to care about what's new this season,' said Simon. 'Find a style that suits you and stick with it. Leave the chopping and changing to the young, poor things enslaved to the fickle winds of fashion.'

Leo looked at him in horror.

'Simon, that's an appalling attitude! You know my belief that fashion is the fight against death. If you say you can't be bothered, it's like saying you're ready to die. What a terrible example to set!'

'That's your view and you're entitled to it. I'm not saying I can't be bothered, I mean I know what I like and I stick to it. You can hardly say I lack imagination in my choice of clothes, can you. Have you seen my latest?'

He flashed open his jacket to expose a shirt featuring a design of swirling planets and stars in bold colours.

As Apolline leaned forward to inspect his shirt, Simon held his breath, longing for her approval.

'It's original, I like it,' she said, leaning back to admire him from a distance, running a hand through her fabulous auburn hair. Gleaming chestnut tresses, thought Simon, there was something in her that brought out the poetry in him.

'And what about me?' asked Leo. 'Aren't I original?'

'Yes, Leo, you are a great original,' said Apolline, 'and what's more you are able to follow fashion, because you have kept your boyish figure. So the cigarette trousers we see worn by models on the catwalk can also be worn by you, which is quite an achievement at your age. Of course if Simon were to attempt wearing them, it would look ridiculous.'

Simon was instantly deflated.

'Well, I wouldn't say ridiculous,' he said, in a hurt voice. 'I'd say more that they are simply not to my taste.'

'Yes, that's what I mean,' said Apolline soothingly, patting Simon's knee in a gesture that sent an electric current through him. 'Now, I think we are all finished with pumpkins, we should prepare the table for Halloween dinner tonight. Leo, maybe I can help you with the decoration?'

Leo was examining Apolline's library pumpkin.

'I am lost for words,' he said. 'We must construct our table as a tribute to this work of art. Let's get started on it right away. I have a marvellous array of ghostly and witch-like accessories to set the mood.'

He lifted the pumpkin with great reverence and took Apolline's hand to lead her into the dining room.

'You will let me know if I can help you with the dinner?' she said to Nicola as she left the kitchen. 'I know how much work it entails, so please use me as you see fit.'

Nicola couldn't help noticing the way Simon was looking at Apolline as she made her offer. She remembered that yearning expression only too well. She did hope there wasn't trouble ahead.

Simon was enlisted as Nicola's assistant chef that afternoon. He wrapped himself in a large apron to protect his statement shirt, then set about the painful task of skinning the shallots that she'd brought in from the garden.

'You're a cruel woman, giving me this job. Look at me now, crying my eyes out.'

He wiped the tears away to make his point.

'Never mind, you'll soon be done. Your reward will be opening those bottles of Côtes du Rhone to pour over the meat.'

'Boeuf bourguignon, do you know, that's exactly what I fancy. Good old-fashioned French food, nothing fancy, no foreign spices. Traditional values, none of your vegetarian nonsense.'

'You are sounding more and more right wing. Make sure that nice young couple don't overhear you, they may think you really mean it.'

'Well, I do mean it. I fancy eating a hearty beef stew. And so do you, obviously, as you chose the menu. You were secretly fantasising about a right-wing dinner when you went into that butcher's shop and ingratiated yourself by buying red meat in line with his Le Pen views.'

'You don't know the butcher voted Le Pen! And how can food be political, you really are talking nonsense.'

'Then you've done apple tart for pudding! Pure Donald Trump. I rest my case.'

'You are absurd. Now pass those onions.'

Nicola poured some oil into a big pan and started frying up chunky bacon lardons. Simon pushed the shallots off his chopping board into the pan and Nicola added the mushrooms. Simon sat down to open the bottles of wine.

'"While greasy Joan doth keel the pot",' said Simon. 'What a fine sight that is, you stirring up the jumbo-sized pan.'

'What time is Beth back?'

Beth had been in London for a few days of meetings about her latest project.

'Around six, she's getting the same train from Paris as Dougie and Mary. Apolline's offered to pick them up, which is decent of her.'

'Is there anything that woman won't do for us?'

Nicola glanced at him to check his reaction, but his face was neutral.

'She likes to be helpful, keep herself busy, I think.'

He poured himself a glass from the bottle he'd just opened, took a sip and nodded his approval.

'Pretty decent, almost too good to go in the pot.'

'Have you done any digging about her home life? In view of your close connection. You've been spending quite a bit of time together.'

Simon waved his hand vaguely.

'Not that much time,' he said, with a fake nonchalance that Nicola saw right through. 'She's been showing interest in my book. I'm glad someone is.'

'That's not fair, we've all been very supportive of you and your oeuvre, but I had the impression you'd rather ground to a halt.'

'Certainly not! You have to understand that a writer is working all the time, even when he's not writing. It's all going on up here.'

He tapped his skull.

'So, in between your literary chats, have you gleaned anything about her?'

'There's a husband, but she's not very forthcoming about him. She's taking some time out to reset, she says. And she's going to visit her family in Toulouse at some point. I think actually she's planning to extend her stay here. She asked me yesterday what I thought about her booking in for a few more weeks. I said absolutely, good plan.'

'I see.'

She gave him an enquiring look, which put him on the defensive.

'What do you see?'

'Nothing. Unless there's something you're hiding from me. Can you pass me that big casserole.'

'Sure.'

Simon was relieved the conversation had moved back to practical matters. The kitchen shelves were loaded with industrial-sized stock pots and crocks, heavy iron pans that had been in the chateau for decades. He fetched one down for Nicola and she transferred the contents of the pan, then started frying the meat in the remaining oil.

'It's just as well Madame de Courcy included all these massive pots in the sale, we need them when we're cooking for twenty,' she said. 'Not that she ever touched them herself, she left that to her servants. She thinks we're really eccentric, you know, doing our own cooking.'

'Hardly eccentric, just irredeemably middle class. Not like her with her centuries of good breeding.'

'At least we've got a cleaner now. I love how she folds the end of the toilet roll into a V shape.'

The notice Leo put up in the boulangerie had brought them a stern Romanian woman whose efficiency left them giddy with gratitude. Maria came every morning and was greeted by the chatelains with warmth and respect, though she never stopped to exchange pleasantries. She did, however, show Nicola photos of the house she had built in her home village, where she employed her own cleaner, and where her daughter was recently married at an event for nine hundred guests. Nicola was taken by the traditional Romanian dress worn by the women, embroidered skirts sticking out at a ninety-degree angle as they danced sedately in heavy costumes in the blazing heat.

'She's marvellous, even if she doesn't wear the frilly apron that Leo had in mind. I think she's happy to be working for Brits, we're kinder to our domestic staff than the French are,' said Simon. 'Apolline said the same. When she came to be an au pair in London, she couldn't believe how friendly her employers were, welcoming her as a family member. All she had to do was look after the children, whereas in France, they'd have you scrubbing floors and generally treat you like a cut-price servant.'

'Ah yes, how we revel in our superiority,' said Nicola. 'How nice to be British, so decent and thoughtful compared to the French. Remember that my partner is French, so I can't entirely swallow that. Also, Jean-Louis says that we are hypocrites, so desperate to be liked that we're always making flattering remarks that we don't really mean.'

'That's true! When I told Madame de Courcy that her new house is bijou and charming, I actually meant it was a characterless box that I would hate to live in.'

'I think it's OK if you lie to be kind, though, don't you?'

'You mean like if I told you that you look amazing and surely can't be more than thirty-five years old?'

'Haha.'

'Actually, you'll always look nineteen to me. Your age when we first met. Frozen in time.'

'And here we still are, decades later, friends for life and living the dream. How lucky are we? Let's not do anything to rock the boat. I think you know what I mean, don't you?'

'This boat is unsinkable,' said Simon, 'just like the *Titanic*.'

'Unfortunate analogy.'

'Don't worry, Nicola, everything is fine and dandy. The chateau community is solid as a rock.'

'Good, let's keep it that way.'

'Well, that was slightly underwhelming,' said Fizz. 'I don't think it will go down as the most memorable Halloween ever.'

She and Will were returning to the chateau with Maddie and John and the children, after a short bout of trick-or-treating round the village. Fizz and Maddie were dressed as elegant witches, Will as old Father Time, while John had really entered into the spirit, slapping on blue face paint, blue hair dye, and some ghoulish yellow contact lenses which gave pleasingly monstrous results. Louis and Lily were a pair of small skeletons. As Fizz said, they were a little young to fully understand what was going on, but it was good for the memory bank, to show them joining in the activity. Maddie was annoyed by Fizz's obsession with recording their every move. If it didn't feature on the Madame Bovary vlog, then as far as Fizz was concerned, it hadn't happened. Too often Maddie found herself putting on a fake smile, unable to relax in the moment because she had to present a public face of enjoyment. They validated their lives through the artifice of the lens, just so Fizz could continue to receive freebies from companies keen to reach her followers.

'At least it was short,' said Will. Only three houses had opened their doors, the rest of them wisely stayed cowering indoors.'

'*Des bonbons ou des farces!*' said Lily, unfolding her hand to reveal a sticky mass of sweets.

'Luckily you didn't have to put a horrible curse on them, darling, or throw eggs at their houses,' said Maddie.

'Anyway, the best part of the evening's still to come,' said John. 'I wouldn't have bothered with this blue makeup for the sake of knocking on a few doors, this is just the preamble! Once we've put the kids to bed, we can properly enjoy dinner and ghostly tales, all ready for La Toussaint tomorrow. Considerate of the French to make All Saints Day a bank holiday, the perfect way to recover from Halloween excesses. Too bad Maddie and I work for UK companies, it'll be business as usual for us.'

They arrived at the chateau gates and crunched their way over the gravel to the front door where Simon's pumpkin with its obscene message was glowing in the dark, alongside Will's more respectable effort.

'It's a good job the kids can't read yet,' said Maddie. 'Another year and I suppose we'll have to veto that sort of thing. What a bore, respectable family life. See you both at dinner.'

They parted ways – Fizz and Will took Louis back to their barn while Maddie and John headed off to the cider press with Lily.

'I'm just going to check for eggs,' said Maddie. 'I forgot to do it earlier, I'll catch you in a bit.'

She detoured towards the hen house, thinking about their trick-or-treat outing. Next year, they'd be joined by her new baby – and Fizz's. The two witches would be pushing prams around the village. No doubt Fizz would have her newborn whipped into a strict routine in no time. As she approached the chicken run, Maddie noticed one of the birds had escaped and was standing still against the fence, making no attempt to move. She moved closer to take a look and see if she could coax it back to the pen. Then froze to the spot. The chicken's head had been ripped off, leaving the gory stem of its neck exposed, still puls-ing. She recoiled in horror, then braced herself to check on the others, shining her phone torch into the pen. Corpses of chickens everywhere, eviscerated, one looked like it had swallowed a tomato, or maybe that was part of its innards. Four survivors were cowering in the shelter. The quails had not been touched, their wire fence was unbroached. The fox had favoured the larger, meatier birds.

She walked back to the cider press. Lily was already in the bath, so she called John through to the living room to reveal her gruesome discovery.

'True Halloween horror,' he said, taking her into his arms and staring at her through his yellow contact lenses. 'We've had foxes before but never with such appropriate timing. Sorry you had to be the one to find it. I'll go and repair the pen quickly so the survivors are safe, but let's leave the clear-up until morning.'

By the time he returned, Lily was in bed and Maddie was stretched out on the sofa, recovering from her unwanted Halloween surprise.

'All secure,' said John. 'I was well dressed for the task, it would have frightened the fox off for good if he'd seen me.'

'So horrible,' sighed Maddie, 'it's almost enough to turn me vegetarian. I mean, what's the difference between us and that fox when you think about it.'

'The difference is we don't kill chickens for fun. Only to convert them into delicious food, which is far more civilised. Chicken soup for the soul, honey garlic chicken thighs, roast chicken flavour crisps. You wouldn't be without them.'

'But just think that all the time we were pretending to be scary, walking round the village in our frightening outfits, a real-life predator was ripping those poor birds to pieces. We think nature's all rosy and lovey-dovey, but it's an absolute bitch.'

'That's true. It's a wicked world, but it's the only one we have. Shall we go across for dinner?'

Leo's bedroom was located at the top of the east wing turret. He had fallen in love with it at first sight, marvelling at the 360-degree views through the Rapunzel-style windows. He knew he would always want this room, even when the roof was leaking and he couldn't sleep for the noise of rain dripping into a bucket.

Now, it was warm and dry and he was sitting at his dressing table, examining his receding gums in the mirror and thinking he finally understood the meaning of the expression 'long in the tooth'. It wasn't that your teeth were growing longer, it was just that you could see more of them, because the gums were disappearing.

At least he still had all his own hair. There was comfort in that. And comfort, too, in finding himself living in this magnificent chateau, embraced by the warm, self-chosen family who had been his bedrock since David had left him. That was before the great chateau adventure, in a previous life when he was living with someone he thought would be his forever partner.

He stood up and admired his outfit in the full-length mirror. He'd opted for a nun's costume – the black and white wimple effect was pleasingly severe, with echoes of Chanel, offset by an oversized silver cross pendant.

There was a knock at his door. He opened it to find Apolline, dressed in a green satin leotard, garlanded with fresh ivy leaves. Her normally auburn hair had been dyed bright red, and twirled into two horns before cascading down her over her shoulders.

'Poison Ivy,' Leo shrieked in delight. 'What a superb effort!'

'And you are an elegant Sister Josephine! I thought you would not mind if I took some ivy from the chateau walls to lend authenticity?'

'Not at all, it's perfect. Do you want to come in?'

'Thank you. I have been meaning to visit your room, it is the most romantic in the castle.'

She took a brief tour round the room then lay down on his four-poster bed. Leo hoped the red hair dye wouldn't stain his bedspread.

'Simon was telling me about your dating adventures,' said Apolline. 'If you would like me to advise you when you are looking at potential dates, I would be more than happy. Sometimes things get lost in translation, and I could help with the nuances. Assuming it's Frenchmen you are meeting up with?'

Goodness, thought Leo, she's also a relationship counsellor on top of everything else.

'Mostly French, yes,' he said, 'though in Paris it's more international. To be honest, I've slightly lost heart recently, I'm not sure how interested I am now in finding The One.'

'You still miss David?'

She was well briefed, she even knew his name.

'No, that's over. I realised that the moment he tried to get back in touch with me. I'd been grieving him for months, and when he finally reappeared – messaged me out of the blue – I remembered how awful he was. I think it's more that I'm settled here happily at the chateau. I can't quite see how a partner would fit in.'

'You'll know when you meet the right one. Shall we go down for dinner?'

Leo followed her down to the crystal ballroom where Simon was serving up cocktails to the assembled party. The timid young couple who were staying in the Madame de Pompadour suite were dressed as ghosts, their solemn faces peeping out of old sheets which Beth had given them, as they'd arrived without costumes.

Simon stopped mid-conversation at the sight of Apolline in her green leotard, but quickly recovered himself.

'There you are,' he said. 'Can I offer you a Dead Man's Drool? It's a little bit of seasonal fun before we move on to the classic French menu.'

He handed them each a glass of blood-red liquid.

'Cherry rum, apricot brandy, grenadine and juice. Poor old Maddie couldn't bear to look at it, too close to home after her death rampage experience.'

Maddie then had to recount her discovery of the devastated scene after the fox attack. The timid young couple looked horrified.

Nicola thought she'd better change the subject.

'Congratulations on your outfits, everyone. I'd like to single out Beth for originality. Here she comes now, dressed as a worm! Truly ingenious.'

Beth made her entrance, encased in a flesh-coloured foam tube marked with worm-like rings which left only her face exposed. She glanced over at Poison Ivy and instantly regretted her outfit choice. As a woman of character, she had always despised those who used fancy dress as an opportunity to make themselves look sexy. She had once gone to a James Bond party disguised as the villainous henchman Oddjob, while all the other women were dolled up as Bond Girls. Yet now, she would give anything to be wearing something less unflattering. A giant worm, what was she thinking?

'Very clever,' said Apolline, clapping her hands prettily.

'That's my wife,' said Simon, looking at Beth in disbelief. 'Always one to make a statement.'

'So, we're just waiting for Jean-Louis and Madame de Courcy now,' said Nicola.

'Speak of the devil! Literally!' said Leo.

Jean-Louis swept in, looking dashing in a demonic cloak and horns, followed by Madame de Courcy as an immaculate witch, holding a broomstick as if it was an elegant handbag. She beamed at everyone, admiring their outfits, happy to be included once again at a *fête* in her former home. Then she saw Apolline and her eyes widened in disbelief.

'*Apolline, c'est vous! C'est vraiment vous?*'

'You two know each other?' asked Nicola.

'No, we have never met!' said Madame de Courcy. 'But of course I recognised her at once! Apolline Fleurie, one of our great actresses, what an honour to have you here in my chateau!'

Beth suppressed her usual irritation at the old lady's use of the possessive pronoun. *Not your chateau, actually.* But this was intriguing.

'What's all this, Apolline?' said Nicola. 'Have you been hiding your light under a bushel?'

Apolline looked embarrassed.

'It was a long time ago,' she said. 'Madame de Courcy has a very long memory. It has been many years since I made a film.'

'But such films!' said Madame de Courcy, making her way across the room to stand next to her screen idol. She then reeled off a list of titles that nobody had heard of.

'I don't think they made it outside France,' Will whispered to Fizz. 'You know how the French government sponsors their film industry, so they make loads of films which remain locked in the local market.'

Fizz nodded, slightly relieved. She wouldn't want to have *too* big a star in their midst, that was her role. In a modest way, naturally.

Apolline was graciously thanking Madame de Courcy.

'It's very kind of you to say those things. I enjoyed it immensely, but then my life took a different turn. I married an Englishman, that's another story ... And these days my passion is my art. I haven't shared this yet with my charming hosts, but my creativity is now directed through my work as a painter and potter.'

'I'm not surprised, having seen your brilliant pumpkin design,' said Nicola. 'You must take a look at it when we go through, Madame de Courcy, it's the centrepiece on the dining table.'

'In fact, I meant to ask you, I might as well do it now as everyone is here,' said Apolline. 'Would you agree to extend my reservation until the end of the year? And if so, would it be possible for me to use one of the attic rooms to set up my potter's wheel? I would like to have it shipped over if you don't mind?'

Dougie was delighted by this request, the winter bookings weren't exactly flooding in.

'I'm sure I speak for us all – as chief booking clerk, if you like – when I say that you would be more than welcome.'

There was a general nodding of approval around the room.

'Well that's settled then,' said Dougie happily. 'The only outstanding question is, should I book you in as Apolline Granger or Apolline Fleurie?'

'Oh, Granger will do perfectly. Apolline Fleurie belongs only on the screen.'

Of course she's an actress, thought Simon. He knew she had that special something, could sense it the moment she stepped out of her campervan. That luminous beauty, the porcelain skin, the way she owned a room whenever she entered. And now she was staying on, just as they had discussed. What incredible good fortune. He smiled at her in pure delight, and she smiled back.

From the spyhole of her hideous worm outfit, Beth watched them grinning at each other like a couple of idiots. Here we go again, she thought. What was it Hillary Clinton said about her husband? A hard dog to keep on the porch. That sounded right. They could be heading for a long winter.

Part Two

Winter

CHAPTER 7

As winter began to bite, Chateau Lafarge glowed with warm conviviality. No risk of loneliness here, there was always someone to play cards with by the fire, or team up with in the kitchen, or take a soul-cleansing walk with through the frozen woods.

It is no accident that Christmas falls in the bleak heart of midwinter, the Christian festival latching on to pagan tradition. This year the chateau-dwellers planned a bumper gathering of extended family to drive away the gloom. Will had invited his adult sons Jack and Alex over from the States. They would finally meet their young half-brother, which wasn't without potential for stress.

'Supposing they don't like Louis,' said Fizz, holding a plank position on the mat she'd rolled out on the floor of the barn sitting room. 'They may resent him, like the ugly sisters with Cinderella.'

'They're bound to like him,' said Will, watching her from the comfort of the sofa, 'he's their baby brother.'

'He's also the child of the woman their father left their mother for.'

'That's old news. They're grown adults now, completely over it. Anyway, Marjorie's seeing someone, apparently. Jack set her up on a dating app and she's hooked up with a retired banker with plenty of cash. Blissfully happy, he says.'

'You never told me that!'

She twisted into a side plank and stared at him, hand on hip.

'You're never terribly interested in anything to do with Marjorie, so I didn't bother to mention it.'

Fizz frowned.

'So now she's got most of your money, thanks to your generous divorce settlement, plus a rich new boyfriend. While you're struggling to support your young family.'

Will shifted uncomfortably.

'I wouldn't say struggling exactly. I had to be generous with the divorce. I felt so bad about walking out, I wasn't going to leave her penniless.'

'What does her new boyfriend look like?'

'I've no idea.'

'I don't believe you, of course you've looked him up.'

'All right then. He looks like a retired banker. Red corduroy trousers. A respectable widower, conventional, quite old looking, sits on loads of boards as a non-exec director.'

'He sounds perfect for Marjorie. Maybe she'll feel sorry for you and give you some of your money back.'

'I don't think that's going to happen.'

He couldn't help feeling slightly envious of his ex-wife, enjoying a luxurious retirement at his expense from her career as a full-time mother. He could imagine her going on holidays to interesting locations with her fancy man, when his lucrative board appointments allowed. Jack mentioned they'd been cruising to the Galapagos on a ship that was so small it felt like a private yacht. Will had always fancied getting up close with those giant tortoises. It was the life he'd be leading if things had worked out differently.

Instead of which, here he was holed up in rural France with an odd-ball collection of friends and a young wife who was soon to present him with another child. No wonder he drank a little more than he used to. There was no point in thinking of what might have been. You make your bed and must lie in it.

Watching Fizz now, still holding her position with her lithe body perfectly aligned, he couldn't regret his choice.

'Shall we have a little lie-down?' he suggested, never one to miss an opportunity. 'Make the most of it while Apolline's looking after Louis?'

Fizz stared at him while she considered his proposition.

'All right then,' she said, abandoning her plank and sitting up on the mat. 'I've read that sex is good for you at this stage in pregnancy – it reduces blood pressure and promotes healthy sleeping and a feeling of wellbeing.'

'Oh well, in that case . . .'

It wasn't entirely the response he was hoping for, making him feel more like a wellness purveyor than a hotly desired lover. Still, he wasn't going to look a gift horse in the mouth.

While his parents were having sex in the cowshed, Louis was at the very top of the chateau, his hands covered in clay. Apolline was using one of the unrenovated attic rooms as her studio, her potter's wheel set up in front of the window, giving inspirational views over the valley. Next to it, she had placed a small table with a bowl of sticky clay which Louis was happily squeezing through his fingers.

Simon put his head round the door. There she was, her beautiful face concentrated on the clay taking shape between her hands.

'Not disturbing you, am I?'

'Come in,' said Apolline, glancing up at him. 'You can give Louis a hand while I finish this off.'

Simon watched her fingers running over a narrow-necked vase, steadying its shape until she was satisfied with the result. She switched off the wheel and went to wash her hands in the corner basin.

'How are you doing, Louis?' she asked. 'Have you finished?'

Louis nodded. He had made a crude but solid-looking pot.

'Good stuff, Louis,' said Simon, 'I like your style, it looks both naïf and modern.'

Apolline laughed.

'I don't think a little boy will understand that concept!'

'Oh, I always speak to children as if they are adults, it's how you bring them on. Anyway, his pot is marvellous, you can sell it alongside yours at the Christmas fair, can't you?'

'I'll certainly fire it, alongside mine, but I'm sure Fizz will want to keep it. Come here and wash your hands, Louis.'

He trotted over to join her. Simon admired the way she carefully wiped and dried the boy's hands. What a wonderful mother she would have made. He was suddenly overcome by the absurd fantasy of them a having a child together, living a parallel life in which they raised a family in a chateau all of their own. The acclaimed writer and the famous actress-turned-potter, she had left behind her glittering career on screen for the love of an English man of letters whose debut, *Après Moi, Le Déluge*, took the literary world by storm. A sort of latter day Arthur Miller and Marilyn Monroe.

'Anyway,' he said, 'the reason I came by was to tell you that I watched one of your films last night, the one with Gérard Depardieu.'

'Is there any French actress who has not been in a film with Gérard Depardieu? He made so many, it is absurd.'

'You were wonderful in it. I'm just fascinated as to why you gave it all up.'

'I have no regrets. Have you seen how humiliating it is for actresses seeking to prolong their careers? Everyone focusing on their appearance, commenting on their ageing process, comparing them in middle age to how they were in their dewy youth? I refused to take that path. As I told you, I wanted out, and out is what I chose.'

'You moved to England, where nobody recognised you.'

'That was a bonus.'

'Because you married an Englishman. You haven't spoken much about him.'

'Shall we go down? I told Fizz we'll meet them in the dining room, she's putting out some lunch.'

She wasn't going to tell him, that much was clear. And he wasn't going to tell her that he had actually watched her film three times, endlessly freeze-framing to take another look at her fabulous face, which was just as fabulous today. She had the kind of beauty that stays with you. He wanted to tell her she was as beautiful now as she was back then, and she would remain beautiful in his eyes for the rest of their lives.

The three of them filed down the servants' staircase and into the dining room where Fizz and Will had set out a welcoming spread of leftovers on the table. Slices of last night's rare roast beef, accompanied by a tabbouleh salad with roast aubergine and pomegranate for the vegetarians. A fire was crackling in the hearth, Louis was fascinated by the green flames coming off the pine cones.

'Just the six of us today, including Leo who's on his way,' said Will. '*Très intime n'est-ce pas, Apolline?*'

He always spoke French when he was feeling bullish, and he was in a good mood after his morning sex.

'Look what I found,' said Simon, who had detoured via the cellar. 'It has to be Bordeaux Left Bank to go with the beef. Here's a nervy St-Estèphe.'

He put two bottles on the table.

'What do you mean by "nervy"?' said Fizz. 'I don't see how you can apply that term to wine. Does it suffer from anxiety? More to the point, why are you drinking at lunchtime?'

'A day without wine is like a day without sunshine,' said Simon, 'and it would be an insult to that beef to wash it down with water. Don't you agree, Leo?'

Leo was heading towards them, looking very flustered, waving a copy of the local newspaper.

'Terrible news! Look at this double page spread; we have rivals! A couple of British queens have bought a chateau not far from us and they're doing it up! He's a noted interior designer; he works for royalty! And private clients who are so grand, they can't be named. I can't bear it.'

He flung the paper onto the table so they could gather round and read it. The story sounded remarkably familiar. A falling-down chateau with too many rooms to count, the roof repaired in the nick of time, the irresistible lure of a grand parade of interconnecting reception rooms. The photograph showed two handsome middle-aged men standing in front of their imposing moated castle.

'They've even got a moat! And look at the pair of them, much younger than us! Apart from that, we're exactly the same. They've stolen our thunder. We are no longer special.'

He sat down dramatically and put his head in his hands.

'Nice-looking boys, it's true,' said Simon, peering at the photo. 'Look on the bright side, they could be friends for us. I don't see why you're so upset, we weren't the first Brits to buy up an old chateau and we won't be the last.'

'But round here we are unique! Everyone knows us as the eccentric English group who formed an unlikely commune and saved the chateau from extinction. And at its heart, if I'm not being immodest, was me. The token single gentleman, a talented designer who has brought new life to a historical monument. And now I'm up against London's leading creator and his glamorous partner, who are set to take Normandy by storm.'

'Creativity fosters creativity,' said Apolline, putting her arm round Leo's shoulder. 'You should be glad that others have been inspired by this beautiful landscape and patrimony to do what you have done. It can only be a compliment.'

'Here, this will cheer you up,' said Simon, handing him a glass of wine. 'I never realised you were so competitive. But look what you've achieved in the design of this place, it's amazing and only getting better with the new guest rooms you're working on.'

Leo took a sip of wine and felt a little brighter.

'I suppose you're right.'

After a comforting lunch, they moved fireside to discuss the progress of the *chambres d'hôte*, while Leo rearranged the pyracantha sprays displayed on the mantelpiece.

'I'm so glad I've got you lot to bolster me up,' he said. 'Imagine if I lived alone, I'd be wracked by self-doubt and loneliness. What a blessing to have our community. It's a therapy centre as well as everything else. Those two up at the rival chateau won't have that, they'll be rattling around just the two of them. I feel sorry for them to be honest.'

'Hashtag feeling blessed,' said Simon. 'God, I hate that expression. But you're right that we have a fantastic set-up here at Chateau Lafarge and you, Leo, are the jewel in our crown. Unsurpassable.'

'Smile, Leo!' said Fizz, whipping out her phone.

Leo posed graciously, one arm outstretched to tweak the twig display, while Louis played at his ankles, poking sticks through the fireguard.

'This post will be captioned "Preparing for Christmas at the chateau",' she said, '"'tis the season to be merry – time to count our blessings".'

'I'll drink to that,' said Will, emptying his glass of Calvados.

'So many blessings, it's hard to know where to start,' said Simon. 'I'll kick off with the joy of being in a safe space where it's all right to use old-fashioned pronouns. He or she, his or hers, not a they in sight. "Simon is looking forward to spending their Christmas at the chateau". Sounds ridiculous, doesn't it! But you can't have that attitude if you're living in polite society across the Channel. Thank God for our sanctuary here.'

'You're sounding more and more right wing, if I may say so,' said Will. 'I hope you're not turning into an old duffer. Personally, I have no problem with people choosing their pronouns and sexuality.'

'Well said, Will,' said Fizz. It was sometimes hard to believe her husband was the same age as Simon, his views were so much more enlightened.

'Nor do I,' said Simon, 'but I can't bear people laying down the law and telling me what I can and cannot say. I'm a libertarian.'

'How about you, Apolline,' said Will, 'where do you stand on the great gender debate?'

Apolline took her a sip of her tea.

'I agree that gender is fluid, we all have personal experience of that . . . But I don't like how it has become a source of conflict and intolerance.'

'Exactly, the perfect response,' said Simon, beaming at her. She always said the right thing, he'd noticed.

'Let's get back to the business in hand – the expansion of Operation Paying Guest,' said Will. 'We all agree the soft launch has been a great success – cheers to you, Apolline – and we can look forward to four more rooms opening in the spring. My paintbrushes are ready, Leo, I await only your colour choices.'

'*Le Soft launch*, don't you love the way the French pinch all our expressions?' said Simon. '*Le marketing, le brainstorming, le manager.* All to do with money and business, of course, which is all the French think we're good for.'

'Don't forget *le lifting* for a facelift, and *re-looking* and *brushing*,' said Apolline, 'plenty of Anglicisms in the world of beauty.'

'They have no choice because they have such a tiny vocabulary,' said Simon. 'They've used up all their words, so they have to borrow ours.'

Apolline frowned.

'That is not true! The French language is the richest in the world, built up over centuries!'

'I'm not denying that but look at the figures. English has half a million words – that's five times more than French. No wonder you have to come crawling to us! I sometimes think I'd find it easier to write my book if it was in French – less choice when it comes to selecting the words.'

'Quality, not quantity,' said Apolline, 'you have said yourself that French is the most beautiful language.'

'Especially when spoken by you.'

He blew her a kiss and Will rolled his eyes.

'That's enough of your gallantry, Simon. In any language, our bed and breakfast business is set for expansion next year, so we need a realistic timetable for preparing the new rooms. The plumbing's all in, it's just the decoration. I'm aiming for two rooms completed this side of Christmas, and two more in January, provided we can get a sensible rota going. Does that sound feasible, Leo?'

'Oh the pressure!' said Leo, raising a hand to his forehead. 'I thought we moved to France to get away from that . . . But it's fine, I already have my ideas for a Rococo theme for the Jean-Honoré Fragonard and Antoine Watteau suites. Remember we sourced that wonderful curvy furniture at the *salon des antiquaires*. And you're right, we need to get ahead of those two arrivistes who've just bought the other chateau.'

'In terms of our Christmas family guests, I suggest we put my sons in the undecorated rooms, they won't mind,' said Will, 'then, Simon, your Eva and her boyfriend can have the newly painted Fragonard and John's parents can have Watteau – nothing like a deadline to get things going.'

'Are there any plans for wallpaper in the design schemes?' asked Simon. 'You know hanging paper is my forte, I can't paint a ceiling but give me a bucket of paste and a wide brush . . .'

'Yes, I bought a bargain batch on eBay,' said Leo. 'Glowing pink and gold, like Carrie Johnson had in Downing Street, but at a fraction of the price as they were end of line. I love how you men have embraced your practical strengths. Just think how Will used to be huge in corporate law, and Simon ran an advertising empire, and now you're pottering around as odd-job men.'

'Much more satisfying,' said Will in a definite voice, 'and much less stressful.'

He needed to remind himself that his glory days as a lawyer had come at a heavy price. It was too easy to look back wistfully at his past achievements and wonder what had become of him.

Fizz was doing a jigsaw with Louis on the floor. She glanced across at Will – it was nearly time for him to take on his child-care shift. From top lawyer to odd-job man, he seemed quite content with it, but she had to admit she rather missed the charge that came off him when he was so very gainfully employed. It wasn't just the money; it was the power. The respectful way people spoke to him. The expensive suits. The acknowledgement that he was so successful, he could afford to leave his original wife and treat himself to a new model, aka yours truly. Then he got fired, and here they were, which had worked out better than she feared. She had become a less materialistic person since having a child. If Will was fine with it, so was she. She just wished he didn't drink so much.

At the kitchen table in the cider press barn, Maddie was showing Lily how to make paper chains. The simple process of licking the gummed ends of the strips and looping them together took her back to her own childhood when she would hand them to her father on the ladder for him to pin them round the walls of their London home. She found comfort in these Christmas memories, repeating the rituals with her own daughter. He never met his granddaughter. He would have been so proud of her sitting here now, brow furrowed in concentration as she stuck the paper pieces together.

John came in through the front door, bringing a swirl of cold night air.

'Paper chains, great work, Lily! Now put your coats on, you two, I'm going to show you something really exciting.'

Lily's face lit up. She was so reliably cheerful that Maddie feared it could only go downhill as she got older, but it was always lovely to behold. She helped Lily into her coat and slipped hers over her shoulders, following John out into the frosty night. He led them a few paces from the front door.

'Now, turn round!'

Lily screamed in delight. On their roof, a huge, illuminated Santa Claus was climbing up a ladder with his bag of presents, one leg already poised over the chimney.

'*Père Noel*,' said Lily, clapping her hands.

'I thought we could get away with it here,' said John. 'It wouldn't be allowed on the chateau, obviously, but I don't see why we shouldn't have one, given that every other house in the village has gone for it.'

He and Maddie had often commented on the number of flashing Santa Claus figures you saw locally, leaping out at you as you drove through the dark countryside. It seemed at odds with the generally conservative approach which tended not to favour ostentation.

'I deliberately placed him on the side of the barn that you can't see from the chateau – so it's for our eyes only. Our Secret Santa.'

Maddie hugged him.

'I'm loving our Santa, well done, John. Now let's go in for a cup of tea, I'm freezing out here.'

They were all three engaged round the table with the paper chains when there was a knock on the door.

'Not disturbing you, am I?' said Nicola, putting her head round the door.

'My favourite mother-in-law!' said John. 'You could never disturb us.'

'Ah, that's nice, you're also my favourite son-in-law. I just came back from the farm and saw an unusual glow behind your barn, so thought I'd better check it out. Only to discover Father Christmas on your roof!'

'*Père Noel*, Grandma,' Lily corrected her, wagging her finger in the French way she had recently adopted.

'Isn't he great?' said Nicola. 'Come in, Mum, have a cup of tea.'

She pulled out a chair for her and went to fetch the kettle.

'Paper chains, that takes me back,' said Nicola. 'I remember making those with you and Gus.'

'And Dad – he was in charge of hanging them up. It's one of my favourite memories. He used to string them up over the marble fireplace, then in lines radiating out from the ceiling light.'

'Oh yes, and we always had the Christmas tree in the corner with the Robbie Williams doll on top that you insisted on putting up every year.'

'Robbie Williams was there the first time I met you and Dom,' said John. 'I was a bit nervous about meeting Maddie's parents, then I saw him tied to the tree and covered with tinsel and I realised everything would be all right.'

'And so it was,' said Nicola. 'And here we all are now. Without Dom, of course.'

Christmas was always an emotional time for her. Fond memories of their family life were clouded by shadows of grief and betrayal, though these grew fainter with every passing year.

'I like to remember Dad as he was then,' said Maddie. 'When we were little and he could do no wrong. Before he became a love rat.'

Nicola wished she could have spared her children the clouding of their father's reputation.

It was only after his death that she had come across hidden letters revealing a love affair he'd had while the children were teenagers. The painful discovery had brought a new dimension to her grieving. After some deliberation, she had shared the information with Maddie and Gus, but she wasn't sure now that it had been the right thing to do.

'He was a great father,' she said gently, 'and a good husband, overall.'

'Not exactly my idea of a good husband! John, I don't want you getting any funny ideas.'

'What's a love rat?' asked Lily.

'Time for your bath, Lily!'

John swept her up, glad for an excuse to leave the room. He wasn't very comfortable discussing his late father-in-law's misdemeanours, it made him feel guilty on behalf of his sex, which was ridiculous as there was nothing to reproach him with. He had always got on well with Dom. It was a tragedy him having that accident. He should have lived to a ripe old age and burned the incriminating letters before anyone got to read them. It would have saved a lot of aggravation.

'I'll read you a story when you're in bed,' said Nicola. 'We can have that lovely one about Father Christmas.'

'Bye, bye!'

Lily waved to them on her way out, then wrapped her arms around her father's neck.

'He's so good with her,' said Nicola. 'I'm glad it all worked out well in the end.'

John and Maddie had broken up before she knew she was pregnant, and there had been a lot of turbulence and uncertainty, before the ultimately happy outcome.

'Yes, he's a brilliant father, which is just as well with another one on the way. Mind you, so was Dad. You don't know how it will work out further down the line.'

'Try not to judge your father,' said Nicola. 'I sometimes wish I'd never told you about the affair.'

'That would have been really dishonest, encouraging me to keep him on a pedestal for the rest of my life.'

'Nobody's perfect.'

'Not even Jean-Louis?'

'He's pretty perfect, it's true. But then we don't have the stresses in our lives that many couples do.'

'Like children?'

'Children, and all the other pressures you young people have ahead of you. The great thing about being my age is every year is a bonus. I can live in the present and take each day as it comes.'

'Jean-Louis isn't your age!'

'No, but he is good at living in the moment. Plus, we have our separate living arrangements, which keeps it light.'

'The lightness of my sexagenarian mother. Carefree boomers living their best lives.'

'That was the idea behind this whole chateau project, that we could have fun for the rest of our days, and not sink into dreary retirement. We didn't want to become those couples who start to look like each other, his and hers matching fleeces, interchangeable short-back-and-sides grey haircuts, flicking through cruise brochures.'

'You're certainly not that. Anyway, Dad died before there was any risk of becoming half of a dreary couple . . .'

'Admittedly, it didn't quite go according to plan. Anyway, let's not be morbid, it's Christmas! Are you looking forward to seeing your brother? I know I am.'

'I am,' said Maddie. 'I'm giving him a Christmas stocking, as well as Lily. He'll say I'm infantilising him, but he'll love it really. We'll be quite a party of younger people, giving you oldies a run for your money – Eva and James, as well as Will's American boys, I really can't wait to meet them and see how they interact with Fizz! Never a dull moment here at the chateau, is there? John's parents are excited, too, especially now his mum knows she's actually going to meet the famous Apolline Fleurie.'

'She's heard of her?'

'Turns out she's a massive French film buff, knows all her movies.'

'We'll sit them next to each other. Well away from Beth.'

'Beth doesn't like her? I thought they got on well. Apolline is always chatting to her, asking about her work, I've often seen them together.'

'Beth likes her well enough. Just not as much as Simon seems to.'

'Oh.'

'You know what Simon's like. Prone to crushes.'

'Like the one he had on you?'

'That was just him being silly. I think this could be more serious.'

CHAPTER 8

Beth was woken by the unfamiliar rumble of a dustcart. She listened to the distant clattering of bins, the faint shouts of busy morning people, then opened her eyes to familiarise herself with her surroundings. Her back felt stiff, then she remembered. She was in Paris. Reaching down beneath the blanket, she felt the rough tapestry of the chaise longue. As her eyes acclimatised to the semi-darkness, she could see a sleeping figure curled up on the floor. He'd beaten her to it, taking the comfortable blow-up mattress, while she was relegated to the back-breaking couch, which was frankly not on for someone of her age.

'Thank goodness you're awake at last,' said Leo, 'I can hear you twitching. I've been waiting to get up for ages but didn't want to disturb you.'

'Yes, I'm officially awake. You can get up now and bring me a coffee. Payback for helping yourself to the only comfortable option for an overnight guest in the Paris pied-à-terre.'

'Terribly selfish of Dougie and Mary not to have bought a bigger place, then we wouldn't be going through this torture.'

Leo threw off the covers and pulled on a silk dressing gown, embroidered with dragons.

'Do you like this? I bought it at Fanny Miami yesterday. Fabulous vintage shop at Porte de Clignancourt.'

'I'll like it more when it's presenting me with a cup of coffee.'

'That won't take long. One advantage of this teeny-weeny flat – it's only two strides to get anywhere. Like being in a doll's house compared to the chateau. I'm already in the kitchen! Espresso or café au lait, madame?'

'Un crème,' said Beth. 'We don't say café au lait in Paris, as you know.'

'Sorry, that was gauche of me.'

Beth pushed herself up from the chaise, stretching her legs, and moved towards the window. She opened the shutters to look out onto the street. Two men in green boiler suits were hosing down the gutters, cleaning up after the dustcart. They looked more like university professors than bin men. Beth had noticed before how intellectual French workers always appeared, possibly because they all wore glasses. Even at this early hour, there was life on the streets, people coming out of the boulangerie with their baguettes, walking at a purposeful pace as they set about their business. A big contrast to the empty stillness of the view from the chateau.

'Paris s'éveille?' asked Leo, as he placed two cups of coffee on the table. 'Don't you love that song? It's six a.m., Paris awakes.'

He launched into song, offering a full-throated rendition of the Jacques Dutronc number.

Mary appeared grumpily in her dressing gown in the doorway of the bedroom.

'What is this, the dawn chorus? And how come there's two of you? When we went to bed, it was only Leo.'

'Sorry, Mary,' said Beth. 'My flight from London was delayed and I missed the last train home. I tried texting but you didn't see it. Luckily Leo picked up, so he was able to let me in.'

'Where did you sleep?'

'On the chaise longue. It was agony, don't worry, I won't do it again.'

'Why didn't you get a hotel?'

'Too mean. I blame our co-habitation project. I'm still in the student mindset because that's how old we were when we all met. I forgot it's no longer feasible to crash on a friend's floor, not even on the chaise longue.'

'You could have slept on the blow-up mattress if my date hadn't been such a disappointment,' said Leo. 'I was sure I'd be going home with him when I saw his photo, he looked incredibly hot. I couldn't believe it when I saw him in the flesh.'

'Was this Arnaud?' asked Beth. Leo had shown her his profile last week. He had been messaging Arnaud for days and had high hopes that he would be The One.

'Yes. Honestly, I could have wept when I saw him sitting there at the bar, little legs dangling. Double chin, pudding face, it's criminal how the camera lies. I could have overlooked all that, but he had a really annoying laugh, like a dog yapping'.

'Go for an *éboueur* next time. Don't you love that word, much better than dustman. I was watching them just now, nice and fit from hopping on and off the lorry.'

'I might just do that. I'm through with internet dating, it's so dishonest. It was better in the old days when all you could do was stroll through the park and see who caught your eye. Hyde Park late at night just isn't what it used to be, and neither are the Tuileries Gardens, I'm told, whereas they used to be such fertile hunting grounds. Much more rewarding than swiping through Grindr. How I long for the pre-internet age when you went out there to see for yourself, as opposed to hunching over your phone, peering at photographs.'

'It's a bit early in the day for this conversation,' said Mary, walking through to the kitchen. 'I'm taking tea back to bed for me and Dougie, and we'll see you in half an hour.'

'We'll get out of your hair,' said Beth. 'Let's go out for a gorgeous stroll through Paris, Leo, and leave poor Mary and Dougie to enjoy the peace.'

'That sounds like a good idea,' said Mary. 'This flat is perfect for two people, beyond that it starts to feel very crowded.'

'*Au revoir, mes amis,*' Dougie called out from the bedroom, relieved to hear their guests were leaving.

Beth and Leo dressed quickly and said their goodbyes. The silence was gratifying when the door closed behind them. Mary handed Dougie his cup of tea and they took up their respective books to indulge in the quiet reading hour they always enjoyed before getting up.

On the pavement of Rue Bonaparte, Beth and Leo debated which direction they should take, whether to head for the Luxembourg Gardens or the river. They settled on the river and soon found themselves on the Pont des Arts, the pedestrian bridge linking the left bank with the Louvre and the Tuileries Gardens. Looking right downstream there was the gothic Notre-Dame Cathedral, looking left they could see the Eiffel Tower. In the crisp morning air, the view reminded them of why Paris was so infinitely desirable.

'Did you know Kenneth Clark described this spot as the very centre of civilisation?' said Leo. 'You can see what he means, you can practically inhale the culture here, think about the artists and scholars who've hurried across this bridge on their way to study the treasures of the Louvre. Henry James, Renoir, Ruskin, they all adored it.'

'Not to mention the famous love padlocks,' said Beth. 'They had to remove them because the weight was threatening to bring down the bridge, and now it's banned.'

'That's a shame, we could have added our own. Leo and Beth forever, etched on to a pink padlock. We could have attached it and thrown the key into the Seine. Wildly romantic. And utterly inappropriate for an odd couple like us. A lonely old gay and his happily married lady friend.'

Beth paused and rested her elbows on the railings, watching the Bateau Mouche pass under the bridge, the passengers huddled on the top deck despite the cold, taking in the sights.

'Happily married is pushing it,' she said. 'Long married, maybe.'

Leo looked taken aback.

'Really? I always assumed you and Simon to be solid as a rock. The very foundations of our chateau community. I know he can be infuriating, but he's so endearing. Absolute life and soul. What's the problem?'

'You haven't noticed, then?'

'Noticed what?'

'Surely it can't have passed you by, a sensitive and observant person like you?'

'Try me.'

'Have you not noticed his embarrassing infatuation with our perfect French house guest? Who turns out not to be some randomer but is actually a really famous actress. Thereby doubling her appeal in Simon's eyes. He always has been shallow.'

'Shallow is a cruel thing to say about a person. People have pinned that on me in the past, because I like things to look beautiful. I've been accused of being entirely obsessed with appearances, but it's not true. And surface beauty often reflects inner beauty, don't you find?'

'Whatever.'

'Sorry, I was digressing, let us resume. You believe that shallow Simon has a crush on Apolline. Well, so do I, she is delightful. So do we all, I reckon. She's such a caring person, always helping out even though she's a paying guest. And very artistic – she gave me one of her self-thrown vases after I admired it. I have it on my bedroom mantelpiece and every time I look at it, I think of her and her fabulous outfits. That green velvet offsetting the auburn hair, she would definitely have won me over if she'd been sitting on my casting couch.'

'Thanks for reminding me how attractive she is.'

'But my point is, we are all seduced by her attractiveness. Simon's no different from any of us in that respect.'

'Except that you're gay and the rest of us are either straight women or men who only have eyes for their partners. Apart from Simon.'

'Trust me, it's nothing, he's just being his usual charming self and he's thrilled to have someone new to be gallant with. Now, I have a great suggestion for breakfast. Café Marly, all the fashion people go there, they have a heated terraced overlooking the glass pyramid of the Louvre. My treat, to make up for your horrible night on the chaise longue.'

Leo and Beth returned to the flat after breakfast to collect their suitcases and say a swift farewell to their hosts, before heading off to catch the train home from Gare St Lazare.

'Isn't it lovely and quiet, now they've gone?' said Dougie.

He was seated in his favourite armchair, reading yet another book about a public-school educated spy who had abandoned his comfortable English home to lead a bleak life behind the Iron Curtain. Incredible to think that someone would prefer life in a grey Moscow apartment to what could be enjoyed in his native land.

'I'm with you,' said Mary. 'I love them dearly, but I've come to see the flat as our sanctuary, which is all too often invaded. It's like having adult children who have never quite left home, not that we'd know what that feels like.'

'Shall we put a limit on it? We haven't enjoyed a single trip here when it's just been us two, there's always one or another of them who's found a reason why they must come up to Paris. Let's say, only one or two visitors per month. Or is that a bit mean?'

'It's not really in the spirit of our communal life. We told them this pied-à-terre was for everyone to use, so it won't go down well if we turn around and say we'd rather you didn't come. The trick is to make sure they come when we're not here. There's the answer. Please use the flat, but only in our absence. That inflatable mattress was a mistake, and I never want to wake up again to find someone sleeping on the floor *and* the chaise longue. Anyway, it's just us now, let's close the shutters and get cosy.'

She enjoyed the ritual in the flat of moving from window to window, closing themselves in against the dark mid-winter night. The draughty corridors of the chateau seemed far away from the warmth of the Paris flat, where the temperature was always exactly as you wanted. It never felt lonely – they were surrounded by people here in the heart of the city – but you had your privacy. This is how it could have been if she and Dougie hadn't joined in on the great chateau adventure. Just the two of them, in a conventional nuclear couple retirement.

She settled down in the chair facing her husband.

'Dougie, can I ask you something?'

'Go ahead.'

'Do you ever imagine how it would be if we left the chateau? I mean if we pulled out of the whole thing. Made this flat our full-time home?'

Dougie put his book down in astonishment.

'Where on earth has this come from?'

'I'm not saying I want to. I'm just wondering if you ever think about it?'

'Never! I'm completely committed to the chateau. I'm so proud of how we pulled it off, to make that magnificent place into a comfortable home where we live in a community of people we love – it's an incredible achievement. And the icing on the cake is having this flat for our little escapades. Would I want to reduce that rich life down to these two rooms? Absolutely not.'

'Good, that's what I needed to hear. I just sometimes think you'd be happier with a simpler arrangement. Just you and me, nobody else to think about.'

'That would leave us as an inward-looking ageing couple – I'm being realistic here. No family, friends scattered far and wide. No thank you! That's not to say I don't enjoy it when it's just the two of us, but how marvellous to have that combined with our jolly communal life. Don't you find that after a couple of days on our own, you're ready to rejoin the throng? I know I am.'

'Yes,' said Mary, 'I really am. Thank you for reminding me. But, first of all, let's have a final day of Paris pleasures. I suggest we walk up to the Musée de Cluny to look again at the Lady and the Unicorn tapestries. My great good fortune, as a medievalist, is to find myself living in close proximity to the finest artworks of the Middle Ages. Then we can stop off for an *apero* at café Flore, before picking up some sushi to bring home for dinner here.'

'Sushi? That's not very French.'

'Exactly, we're about to enter days of meat fest in Normandy, so I want to have something we can't get at the chateau. All the luxuries of Paris rolled into one day. Culture, exotic foods and people-watching at a famous café.'

'Sounds perfect. Let me just finish my chapter. What a glorious life we lead.'

On the train home, Beth and Leo were amusing themselves by speculating about the other passengers. In a rash move, they had splashed out on first class seats and found themselves in a carriage surrounded by the affluent-looking middle-aged.

'Such a relief to be travelling amongst the bourgeoisie,' said Leo, in a stage whisper. 'Look at him with his silver fox hair curling onto his collar. You know there's a term for that, one of my dates taught it to me – "*cheveux de riches*", rich men's hair, it even has its own Instagram account.'

'Keep your voice down,' said Beth, 'I'm sure he heard you.'

'It's fine, we're speaking English. *Cheveux de riches* isn't just any old hair, you know. To qualify it must be luxuriant silver grey, whooshed back and confidently nestling in the nape of the neck. Preferably with a brightly coloured sweater tied around the shoulders, but he's fine with that green Loden wool coat. Absolute classic, especially with the twirly scarf he's added, French men really do know how to dress, it's one of the things

I adore about living here. Though snappy dressers are more visible in Paris, we see precious few of them in deepest darkest Normandy.'

'Looking even darker in this season,' said Beth, peering out of the window over the landscape of fields, punctuated by the occasional disused watermill and more recent industrial developments of factories and warehouses. Dusk was already falling; it was disheartening how short the days were. You didn't notice it so much in the city, with all its distractions.

'I'm already missing the bright lights, aren't you?' she said.

'No, I've had my fill. I need to check up on Will's progress painting the new rooms. Not long until they all pile in for Christmas, I'm getting a little seasonal thrill. Deck the halls with boughs of holly – it's one of my first tasks when I get back, plundering our estate for branches with bright red berries to add warmth to all our salons, then we'll dig out all the fairy lights.'

'You're in a good mood, you seem to have got over your disappointing date?'

'Dead-to-me Arnaud? Certainly. I have all I need at the chateau for the most fabulous Christmas, especially with all those young men arriving, with whom I shall engage in a little harmless flirtation. They know I'm no threat, just a sad old queen finding happiness in a few snatched moments of connection.'

'You are absolutely not a sad old queen. You're everyone's favourite housemate and the young visitors love you too. Even Eva's dour-faced James brightens up a little under your influence.'

'Ah yes, he's a challenge, that one. It's working with money that does it to you, I think. It's far too abstract, shifting zillions of pounds that you never see between different accounts. It's bound to turn you grey.'

'I was hoping she'd find someone else, but it looks like he's here to stay, so I'd better get used to him if he's destined to be my son-in-law.'

'A game of charades might bring him out,' said Leo. 'Give him a creative challenge after Christmas lunch and you might discover he has a scintillating personality beneath that surly facade.'

'Trust me, I would have glimpsed it by now. I've been trying to find it for years. Every time Eva brings him to stay I'm hoping this will be the time I discover how wonderful he is.'

'At least he earns lots of money.'

'There is that. Though I do wish we'd gone for the arranged marriage system we used to talk about. That way I could have married Eva off to Nicola's lovely Gus, and we'd be one big happy family.'

'It would be your fault if it went wrong, though. At least if they choose their own partners, they're digging their own graves. Though I do agree about Gus, everyone's dream son-in-law.'

Leo was fond of all his friends' children, but he kept a special place in his heart for Nicola's son Gus. His light-hearted enjoyment of life, the way he lit up a room whenever he entered, his visits were always a treat.

'We also have the thrill of Will's sons arriving,' said Beth. 'Last time I saw them they were children, neat hair and short trousers, house-trained by Marjorie, so that will be interesting.'

'I expect they'll be with tinged with American glamour. Silicon Valley chic. Our chateau will be the throbbing international heart of Normandy.'

'Oh look, it's our station, that was quick.'

The train drew to a standstill and they stood up and pulled their luggage from the overhead racks.

The man in the Loden coat with rich man's hair smiled at Leo.

'Thank you for your kind words about my appearance,' he said, in perfect English. 'It is a compliment indeed to be admired by a gentleman as impeccably dressed as you.'

He turned to Beth.

'And I hope your daughter manages to persuade you of her boyfriend's worth. There is no doubt more to him than meets the eye, and I don't think a game of charades will be the best way to reveal it. And trust me, she is better off choosing her own partner than relying on her mother's choice. Happy Christmas to you both.'

'You too,' said Leo, pushing Beth down the corridor to make a quick escape.

'That was mortifying,' said Beth, as they stepped onto the platform. 'It's a terrible mistake when you live abroad, to think you can talk about people because they won't understand you speaking in English, then of course they do.'

'It could have been worse; he was quite flattered. I bet he's going to look up that *cheveux de riches* site right now, he might even find himself featured there. Now, who did you say was coming to meet us?'

'Simon, allegedly. I texted him earlier and he said he'd be here.'

'I told you so, he is your devoted husband. I don't know what you're so worried about.'

They pulled their suitcases out into the station car park and looked around for him. Gradually the crowds subsided and the car park emptied, then there was the tooting of a horn and a vintage orange campervan screeched to a halt in front of them.

'I'm sorry I'm late,' said Apolline, climbing out of the driver's seat to open the door for them. 'Simon was so busy hanging wallpaper that he forgot the time, then he couldn't let his brush dry out, so here I am.'

Was she helping him hang the paper, Beth wondered. That used to be her role.

Apolline picked up their cases and threw them into the back of the van.

'Sorry, it's a bit of a mess in there, but I think you can squeeze in between those boxes. I'm loading up my pottery, ready for the Christmas market.'

'Thanks for coming to get us,' said Leo. 'Your hair looks great, by the way. I'm intrigued by how you've worked that purple scarf into your messy bun. It's a very modern, shaggy look, suits you to a tee.'

They climbed into the van.

'How was your trip, Beth?'

Apolline locked eyes with Beth in the rear-view mirror. Beth took in her flawless, makeup-free skin, her chiselled cheek-bones. A natural beauty, damn her, and now she was graciously showing interest in those she'd selflessly pitched up to fetch in her bohemian van.

'Good, thanks,' said Beth. 'Productive, tiring, the usual. Then a sleepless night on the chaise longue at Dougie and Mary's. Let's just say I'll be happy to sleep in my own bed tonight.'

Unpacking in her chateau bedroom, Beth appreciated anew the generous space of it, the luxurious dimensions of the antique ward-robe, the dramatic overmantel mirror that had been reflecting her image over the last few years. Not too much damage, all things considered, she thought, though the light was low now as she pushed up her hair and pulled a winsome expression over one shoulder.

'Hello, are you admiring yourself?'

Simon burst in, dressed in his decorating clothes, and looked her up and down.

'Admiring myself would be pushing it. I'm assessing, I think you'd call it.'

Simon nodded.

'Sorry I couldn't meet you, I was on a roll with the wallpaper, steaming ahead. You should go and check it out. Leo's very pleased.'

'Was Apolline helping you? She seemed to know all about the wetness of your brush.'

Simon looked surprised.

'Yes, she was as a matter of fact. Do you have a problem with that?'

'Of course not.'

'Good trip?'

'Yes thanks. Hope you didn't miss me too much?'

She gave him a searching look, but he turned his back to change out of his glue-spattered overalls.

'Some Christmas cards arrived for us,' he said. 'They're on the dressing table.'

Beth picked them up, recognising most of the handwriting. Cousins, old friends, the same people they'd been exchanging cards with for years. Old habits die hard. She stretched out on the bed to enjoy the ritual of reading them.

'Amazing, really, that people still bother, especially now you have to pay so much to send a card abroad. Still, it's nice to get them. Oh God, here we go.'

She opened one from an old university friend. Beth had never really liked Cordelia but kept up the card exchange because of the entertainment value of her annual round-robin bulletins.

She snorted with pleasure and read it out to Simon.

'"You may recall that fifteen years ago, Celestine was suffering from dry eye syndrome. Unfortunately, it returned this year, but she is now responding well to the use of moist heat eye masks." I mean, hold the front page!'

'Is Celestine her older daughter?'

'Yes. The younger one ran away because she couldn't stand her parents. I quite see her point.'

She opened another envelope, from a former colleague who'd moved to Somerset to open a tearoom and yoga centre. The card featured a photo of Anna holding a baby on her lap, surrounded by her smiling adult offspring and their partners.

'God, that woman's annoying, look at what smug Anna's stuck on the front of her card!'

She held it up to show Simon, who strolled over to take a closer look.

'A charming picture of yet another friend who has been blessed with a grandchild,' he said.

'Who do they think they are, the royal family? Why send an unsolicited photo of yourself to people who haven't asked for it? It's like U2 bombarding everyone's iTunes with their album.'

'Don't be bitter, there's more to life than being a granny. Your time will come. Or maybe it won't, but that doesn't mean you should begrudge other people their happiness. A nicer person would be thrilled for Anna.'

'I've never pretended to be a nice person. You must admit it's narcissistic. "Look at me with my perfect family." Well, good for you, Mrs Boasty, I'm delighted for you.'

She reached down into Simon's bedside cabinet for the bottle of Pineau de Charentes he kept there, and poured it into two sherry glasses that were stored alongside it.

'In fact, let's raise a toast to smug Anna and her blooming family.'

'Not for me, thanks.'

Beth looked up in surprise.

'You're saying no to a drink? That must be a first.'

Simon patted his stomach.

'I'm taking care of myself. Trying to be a bit reasonable before it all gets out of hand over Christmas.'

Beth then noticed he had changed into a Lycra shirt and shorts, worn over a pair of tights, to rather comical effect.

'What on earth are you wearing?'

'I'm going for a run.'

He said it casually, as if it were the most natural thing in the world.

'But you hate running. In fact, you hate all forms of exercise, you say it's just a distraction for people with humdrum minds, to stop them thinking about the pointlessness of their lives.'

'Did I really say that? It's rather clever. But I'm over my existential phase.'

He pushed one leg out sideways, raising his arms to stretch in the opposite direction.

Beth looked at his skinny legs, which appeared skinnier than ever in the shiny grey tights, compared to the substantial bulk of his stomach. His tailor once told Simon that his shape was what they referred to in the trade as a 'Humpty Dumpty'. Rude, but accurate, Simon said at the time, and they'd had a laugh about it. He wasn't laughing now.

'What's come over you, all of a sudden?' said Beth, sipping her drink, 'you've always been the last of the heroic overindulgers.'

Simon bent forward to touch his toes.

'I'm guess I'm just making the most of the time I have left. You've only got to do the maths to realise we can't afford to squander it.'

He picked up a Fitbit from the dressing table, slapped it on his wrist and headed for the door.

CHAPTER 9

On Christmas Eve, Nicola was up bright and early, a knot of excitement in her stomach as she jumped into her car to head for the shops. It was a perfect winter morning. She knew better than to hope for a white Christmas – they usually saw in the season with grey rain at the chateau – but today the temperature had dropped, skies were blue, and frost was sprinkled like fairy dust over the chateau gardens as she drove through the gates.

Gus was arriving this afternoon, the back-seat passenger once again in James's swanky car. He'd amused them all last summer describing the journey. In theory James shared the driving with Eva but he became so clenched up with tension when she took the wheel that she'd refused to continue and they'd had a stand-up row at the services while Gus the pacifier tried to smooth things over. Nicola was very much thinking of Gus when she'd planned this year's Christmas menus, about what would give him pleasure. It brought back memories of Dom, too. Their last ever Christmas as a family had been celebrated in the London house, how casually they'd gone about it, little dreaming they'd never spend another one together.

She pushed those unhelpful memories aside as she parked alongside the boulangerie then joined the queue on the pavement, breathing in the smell of freshly baked bread while she inspected the cakes in the window and made her selection. Two *bûches de noel* should be enough after everything else. She'd take the classic chocolate log, realistic with its brown ganache like wood bark, also the white one, decorated with berries and shiny foil lettering urging revellers to enjoy *bonnes fêtes*. The mood in the queue was unusually jovial as they stood in line, wrapped up snugly in scarves and gloves. She'd noticed before how the level of animation rose at this time of year, though not to the over-the-top limits you found in Britain. You couldn't imagine French people snoring in their paper hats after falling asleep on the train home from their office Christmas party. Moderation in all things was the French way. Excellent food and wine, naturally, but in respectable quantities.

Nicola carefully stored the cakes in her basket, balancing the fragile cardboard boxes beside the stack of baguettes, croissants, two large rye loaves and a blowsy brioche, which always made her think of Marie-Antoinette, who did *not* say 'let them eat cake' when the peasants ran out of bread, but rather *qu'ils mangent de la brioche*, which is not cake but a slightly sweet, buttery bread. In fact, these words were never spoken by Marie-Antoinette, Rousseau's words were attributed to another, unnamed *grande princesse*, but it was a shame to let that ruin the story.

Wishing *au revoir* and *bonne journée* to the other customers, she left the shop and walked down the road to the ancient butcher to collect the pre-ordered capons – not something you could buy easily in Britain, where the process of castrating chickens to fatten them up was considered inhumane. But in France, food traditions were sacred, the old ways were the best. As usual, the butcher issued strict instructions about how to cook the birds, the same advice he'd been issuing for fifty years.

Why invent new ways of presenting dishes, when the quality of ingredients spoke for itself, and needed only the classical treatment they'd rejoiced in for centuries?

At the supermarket, Nicola loaded her trolley with oysters and *foie gras* and chose the best of the seasonal cheeses – Vacherin, Pont L'Eveque, Beaufort – plus a box of La Vache qui rit for Gus – the bland creamy portions always reminded him of his childhood holidays in France. She hurried to the car, tightening her coat against the cold, and texted him a picture of the Laughing Cow cheese.

Just for you. Much else besides. Safe journey x

He responded with a photo of a drum of cheese footballs, placed beside him on the back seat of the car.

The winning snack at home or away. Wouldn't be Christmas without them.

Back at the chateau, Nicola parked up by the side entrance, looking forward to a coffee and croissant after unloading the shopping. Beth came out to greet her, grim-faced.

'What's up?' said Nicola. 'You don't look very filled with Christmas cheer.'

'What's the worst thing that could happen, on the coldest day of the year, when we're about to receive a chateau-load of guests?'

'Tell me.'

'The boiler's on the blink. Will and Dougie are looking at it, with very glum expressions.'

'Ah. Can't we call an engineer?'

'On Christmas Eve? Yes, we can. Miraculously he's coming out this afternoon.'

'That's all right then, he can sort it out. Here, take these oysters. I was agonising about whether to choose *claires* and *spéciales*. I went for the *claires* in the end – more light and Christmassy, I thought. And I bought rye bread to go with them. Classic. Unchanged. The Same Forever. Served simply with lemon and shallot vinegar. Can you imagine if we dared to adulterate them or actually *cook* them?'

'You're such a Pollyanna, how come you're always so cheerful?' said Beth, picking up the shopping bags. 'What makes you think the boiler will be mended this afternoon? Why can't you imagine that we're about to spend a miserable Christmas shivering in our coats?'

Nicola noticed a shambling figure trotting slowly towards them.

'Oh look,' she said, 'here comes Usain Bolt.'

Simon wheezed to a halt beside them. He had added a headband to the Lycra outfit, his hair was hanging dankly down beneath it. Even in this cold weather, his face was red and sweaty.

'Don't have a heart attack,' said Beth, 'that would be a real own goal.'

Simon slumped to a halt beside the car and pulled a packet of cigarettes out of the pocket of his shorts.

'It's my reward,' he explained, lighting up and inhaling deeply, 'you have to be kind to yourself. Rome wasn't built in a day.'

'And other clichés,' said Beth.

'Did you know about the boiler?' asked Nicola.

'I thought Will was on it? He was fixing it when I went out.'

'It's a case for the professionals, they're coming this afternoon.'

The three of them went into the kitchen and Nicola put the coffee on. She lit the range and opened the oven door to take the chill off the room, then went through the grand salon and into the crystal ballroom. Mary was sitting by the roaring fire, wrapped in a blanket and calmly working on a large jigsaw of a night sky. Three-quarters of the pieces were dark navy, so it was challenging.

'It's a good job we have an unlimited supply of logs from our grounds,' she said. 'Come and sit here. As long as you're only a couple of metres from the fire, you wouldn't know there was a problem with the heating.'

Nicola stood in front of the flames and stretched out her hands to warm them. She thought of all the previous occupants of the chateau who would have done the same down the centuries, burning wood from the estate, the only source of heat.

'Terrible timing,' she said, 'let's just hope it's resolved this afternoon.'

Outside in the frost-covered grounds, the children were screaming in delight as they crunched over the crisp grass in their wellington boots. They ran down to the lake, which had frozen over, and began smashing at the icy edges with sticks, under the watchful gaze of their mothers, intent on preventing a death-wish scramble over the shiny surface.

'It's outrageously beautiful,' said Fizz, 'looks just like a Christmas card with that sparkling frost.'

She stepped back to take a photo of Louis and Lily, then handed her phone to Maddie.

'Would you mind? I'd like one of me and Louis in profile, with the chateau in the background.'

She led her son a few steps away from Lily. She didn't mind the little girl appearing occasionally on the fringes, but it was important to remember who the star of this vlog was. The clue was in its title. Madame Bovary. In other words, Fizz. She should always be centre stage, and by extension, so should Louis, her dauphin son. She'd made the decision to exclude Will from all the photographs, and not just because he was now really starting to look his age. It was more a question of maintaining the mystique. Don't let the daylight in upon the magic of monarchy, the saying went. In other words, she should keep her followers guessing about the dauphin's father. Maybe when she announced her new pregnancy, she would come clean, and include a shadowy image of him in the background.

She crouched down, drawing Louis in front of her, and raised an arm to point towards the chateau, glistening in the sunlight.

Maddie took a few shots, then handed back the phone so Fizz could check the results. She was pretty good at this now, she knew what Fizz liked. You had to capture her jawline at a particular angle, offset today by the collar of a luxurious fake fur coat. Nothing below the waist, now she was beginning to show. She should put in a bill for her photography services, or at least receive a portion of the free products Fizz kept hoarded in the spare room of their barn.

Fizz nodded her satisfaction.

'Great, thanks, the perfect shot for Christmas Eve at the chateau. Are you excited about seeing your brother?'

'Yes I am, so is Lily, she's made a sweet card for Uncle Gus. How about you, I'm guessing your feelings are a little more complicated about finally meeting Will's boys?'

'I'm actually looking forward to it. We've done a few Zoom calls recently so that's broken the ice. And I think they've finally forgiven me for marrying their dad. It's about time, they're practically middle-aged. I mean, how long can you bear a grudge for, really?'

'Grudges are forever, if you want them to be. I'm going up to the chateau now, to help get ready for this evening, will you come too?'

'Yes, let's go.'

The children were reluctant to abandon the frozen lake, so Maddie told them they could hang on to their sticks, and they set off running up the slope, bashing the grass on their way.

'What is it with kids and sticks?' said Fizz. 'You give them all these educational toys and all they really want is a bit of old wood.'

'And we have plenty of that.'

'I told Will I'd make the beds up for his sons,' said Fizz. 'Wicked stepmother comes good.'

'And I'm making up the Watteau suite for John's parents, like a good daughter-in-law. It's the same word in French, did you know that? *Belle-mère* means stepmother *and* mother-in-law. "Beautiful mother", it could sound ironic in both cases.'

'Which brings us back to Simon's theory about how small the French vocabulary is.'

'I told John's parents they were staying in the newly decorated Watteau suite, and Rosemary misunderstood and thought I said "the what-ho! suite", as in P. G. Wodehouse. It would suit them, though, they're very old school English.'

'What time are they arriving?'

'About the same as the others, I think, teatime. They're big on tea, in the tradition of those Brits who can't go for more than a couple of hours without putting on the kettle. Thank goodness you don't get that in France.'

They pushed open the front door of the chateau and were greeted by Will.

'I'm just going upstairs to make up the beds, can you take Louis?' said Fizz. She stopped and looked at him. 'Why are you wearing a coat?'

Will's face was solemn.

'You probably can't feel it as you've just come in from the cold, but we have no heating.'

'No heating!'

Fizz had a sudden flashback to their first months in the chateau. The huge, draughty rooms, one functioning lavatory shared by nine people, wondering if she'd made a terrible mistake moving to this old ruin with a bunch of people old enough to be her parents. They slept in a huge shabby room on the first floor then – she remembered Nicola showing her the basic basin in the corner and laughing when she asked where her bathroom was.

Thank goodness they'd moved into the barn. Unless . . .

'Is it just the chateau boiler? What about ours?'

She tightened her grip on the banister handrail, but soon relaxed it.

'Ours is fine,' said Will. 'And the chateau boiler should be sorted this afternoon when the engineer appears. I'll take Louis back now to play in our nice warm barn!'

There was an advantage, after all, to their demotion to the humble outbuilding.

'Thank goodness for that,' said Fizz, climbing the stairs. 'I'll be over to join you as soon as I've made the beds, I'm not hanging around here to freeze to death.'

Maddie took Lily into the salon where they found all the chatelains sitting in a tight ring around the fireplace, as if at a prayer meeting. Nicola and Beth were chopping vegetables on trays balanced on their knees. Leo was swathed in a lilac pashmina, wearing gloves as he wrote out place settings on silver pieces of card. Simon, still wearing his running gear under a puffer jacket, threw an extra log on the fire, while Will was assessing the quality of the woodpile, ensuring that only the extremely dry pieces made the cut. The last thing they wanted was a room full of smoke, on top of everything else.

'Close the door, darling, keep the heat in!' said Nicola, looking up from a pile of sprout leaves.

'Granny!'

Lily ran over to Nicola and wrapped her arms around her legs.

'We're keeping warm in here, for the time being,' said Nicola, 'just until someone arrives to mend the boiler. It won't be long.'

The engineer stared regretfully at the boiler. He'd run several checks but had failed to identify the problem. Then his face brightened.

'*Ça y est*, I have it! It is the connector! This one small part, he is perished.'

He pointed it out to Dougie, who inspected the plastic joining piece and nodded knowledgeably, though it made no sense to him.

'Well done, that is good news,' he said. 'Do you carry a spare one in your van?'

The engineer wagged his finger in that infuriating French way. Back and forth it wiggled. Absolutely not was the message. *Don't do this to me*, thought Dougie.

'*Non!*'

'So, you need to pick one up from your office?'

'Ah no, it is more complicated than that. Our office is not a warehouse!'

'But you can get hold of one?'

'As I said, *c'est compliqué.*'

'Complicated? I don't like the sound of that.'

'Of course it is possible, everything is possible. But this is a German boiler, and the supplier for this boiler is close to the German border, in Alsace-Lorraine. I can order the part *en urgence* today but of course tomorrow is a holiday, then it is the weekend . . . I must be frank with you, the piece will arrive in time for New Year's Eve celebrations, but for the next few days, you will have to make do with the fires in your magnificent chimneys, of which I'm sure you have many!'

Dougie saw him out, then went to break the news to the others. He opened the door to the salon and was greeted by a row of expectant faces turned towards him.

'Don't shoot the messenger,' he said.

'That doesn't sound good,' said Simon. 'Tell us, Dougie, we can take it.'

Dougie explained the situation, and everyone fell silent. Leo covered his face with his hands, then removed them to ask a question. 'Does this also mean no hot water?'

'No hot water, unless we heat it on the stove or in the kettle,' said Dougie.

'Imagine how many saucepans I'd have to carry upstairs to achieve even the shallowest bath!'

'We could use medieval methods,' said Beth. 'Hang a big pot over the open fire, then pour it into a copper tub by the hearth. Take it in turns to have a dip.'

'Oh God, can you imagine,' said Leo. 'I'm going to go full French. No washing, just slap on loads of makeup and perfume.'

'It sounds like you are being rude about the French again,' said Apolline as she entered the room. She was wearing a floor-length sheepskin coat and a fur hat like the one Margaret Thatcher, and later Liz Truss, wore on their trips to Moscow.

Leo forgot his discomfort for a moment.

'What an outfit, Apolline! I am stunned by the extent of your wardrobe. What else have you got hidden away in that campervan?'

'I have a few essentials, for all eventualities,' said Apolline, adjusting her hat as she noticed Simon giving her an adoring look.

'Anyway, I'm never rude about the French,' said Leo. 'I'm a firm believer in minimising washing, the French have it right as usual. No point in flushing away the body's natural sera.'

'And yet I fear the French have now gone the Anglo-Saxon way,' said Apolline. 'They wash excessively and use deodorants just like you English, with no respect for the natural odours of the body.'

Simon thought how much he would love to experience her natural odours.

'Never mind all this silly talk about French versus British hygiene, we need a plan!' said Nicola. 'We have seven guests already on their way. It's too late to cancel, which would have been the obvious solution.'

She slumped back in her chair. Just that morning, she had been in such high spirits, preparing for a wonderful Christmas. And now it stretched ahead of her like an icy wasteland. What were they to do?

*

Half an hour later, Jean-Louis pulled up outside the chateau and opened his van to reveal a stash of electric heaters that were seized upon by the grateful chatelains.

'Jean-Louis, you are my absolute hero,' said Beth, picking up an industrial-looking piece of machinery and grimacing under its weight. 'Are you sure this is a heater? It looks like a giant meat grinder.'

'It is amazing what I have hidden away in my outbuildings,' said Jean-Louis. 'I'm afraid they are old and dusty, but they do the job. I bought them years ago when we were rearing cattle and I needed to keep the new-born calves warm, but now they will do the same for my English friends!'

The heaters were soon distributed through the chateau, with mutterings from Dougie about the disastrous electricity bill that was bound to follow. One per bedroom for the residents, but there weren't enough for the visiting family members.

'I suggest we regroup along family lines,' said Nicola, as she threw another log on the fire in the salon. 'Gus can stay with Maddie in the cider press barn, and Will's boys can move in with them – a chance for them to get to know their new brother.'

'That won't go down well with Fizz,' said Beth, 'she's sure to think it's too close for comfort. We'll have to let them know the news, there's been no sight of them since this morning when they went racing back to their cosy love nest.'

'What about your Eva and James?' said Nicola.

'I've already texted her,' said Beth. 'As I predicted, they've booked a room at the Hotel de France down the road. They're such high maintenance, I think that's the best solution.'

'Which just leaves John's parents. We can't let them sleep in a freezing cold room.'

Once again, Jean-Louis came to the rescue. He was carrying a fresh supply of firewood into the room and overheard the conversation.

'Maddie's in-laws? Of course, they must stay at the farm with us,' he said. 'My mother will be delighted to be with people her age. So, there we have it, everything is settled.'

He put his arms round Nicola.

'Now you can go ahead and prepare the Christmas dinner you have been planning. Just tell me how I can help out in the kitchen.'

'I told you, he is *perfect*!' said Beth, smiling at the sight of them embracing like teenagers. 'Nicola, you are one very lucky woman.'

Simon insisted on carrying Apolline's radiator up to the Louis XIV suite.

'You forget you're supposed to be a paying guest,' he said, panting with the effort of heaving the dead weight of cast iron up two flights of stairs, 'which means you're not expected to install your own heating.'

He dropped the radiator on the bedroom floor with a sigh of relief. Apolline closed the door behind them and stretched out on the gilded bed.

'You are very kind, and it's true it would have been a struggle for me.'

She removed her fur hat, so her hair fell down over her shoulders.

Simon was embarrassed by the sudden intimacy. He plugged in the radiator then went to look for a cloth in the bathroom.

'It's a bit dusty, I'll wipe it down for you.'

He found what he needed, trying not to look at her silk underwear draped over the bidet.

'You look like you've stepped right out of *Dr Zhivago* in that get-up,' he said, touching the radiator to make sure the warmth was coming through.

'Thank you, I am a big fan of fur. I think there is no problem if they are vintage, it's not like I am having the animals killed to meet my needs. That would be different.'

Simon stood up, the radiator was fine, his work here was done.

'You're very adamant, aren't you?' he said, as he took the cloth back to the bathroom. 'I like that about you, you always have an opinion.'

'Of course. And there is something else I have an opinion about. The book you are writing. I read the pages you gave me, and I think they are very, very good. They bring to mind a New Wave film. With their lucidity, their passion, you write with the sensibility of a French *auteur cinéaste*. When reading, I could see it as a film by Truffaut.'

'You like my book!'

He'd sent her the early chapters the other day, after their decorating session. He'd assumed she was merely expressing polite interest when she asked to see his work, but not only had she read it, she found that it was very, very good. Could she be any more perfect?

'Oh Apolline, do you really think so?'

The London car was the first to arrive, bang on schedule as you'd expect with James in charge. He stepped out of the driving seat, stretched his limbs, and to Beth's surprise, gave her a friendly wave when she came out to greet them. He's probably relieved they're staying in a hotel, she thought, less exposure to the in-laws and their absurd extended household. She couldn't blame him for that. Eva emerged in a fluffy coat the colour of mink, her nod to the fur that was no longer socially acceptable, which was a crying shame in these arctic conditions.

'Hey, Mum, thank goodness we're here. I was sure we were going to go skidding across the icy roads, even though James has put winter tyres on the car.'

'Winter tyres, how very organised!' said Beth, hugging Eva and breathing in her perfume, which smelled of faraway city sophistication.

'Essential when you're driving up to the ski slopes,' said James. He didn't add, 'as any fool knows', but he might as well have done. Beth tried not to be annoyed.

'Oh yes, I'd forgotten about that, you're going on after Christmas.'

'There she is, my own flesh and blood!'

Simon came out with his arms outstretched, beaming at the sight of his daughter, a chip off the old block with her dark good looks.

'Dad, are you wearing trainers? And shorts, beneath that massive coat! What's happened to you?'

'Please also note the running cap, the latest addition to my sporting wardrobe. It's supposed to make you more aerodynamic, along with shaving off your body hair. What do you think?'

He struck an athletic pose and Eva burst out laughing.

'I can't believe it! How long have I been telling you to take more exercise? I lecture my patients about it all the time. Half of them wouldn't need to see me if they weren't so fat, though I can't say to them, obviously.'

'Your father has decided to take himself in hand,' said Beth.

'You don't look too delighted about it, Mum,' said Eva. 'Aren't you happy for him?'

'It's early days.'

Nicola came outside, still holding a kitchen knife, wearing an apron over her quilted coat.

Where's my boy?' she said.

'Here I am!'

Gus climbed out of the back seat and hugged his mother. She was glad to see he still had the rock star long hair and hadn't gone for that shaved up the sides look favoured by many bearded young men these days.

'Look what I've brought, it's my new toy. Thought I could entertain us over Christmas.'

He reached back into the car to bring out an accordion which had been travelling on the seat beside him.

'A squeeze box, how thrilling!' said Nicola. Gus was a joyful music maker. He loved playing his guitar and took no offence at being dubbed a 'pub pianist' by more accomplished musicians, for what could be better than delighting people by belting out crowd-pleasers on the keyboard?

'I've named it the Gift of Music,' he said, stringing it round his neck, 'a portable piano. You won't believe how often my friends beg me to bring the Gift of Music when I go over for dinner.'

'The perfect way to warm us up,' said Nicola. 'You can do an Irish jig for us to dance to, though it's not as cold as it was a few hours ago. Come in and see for yourself.'

James and Eva drove away to check into their hotel and Gus followed Nicola into the imposing entrance hall of the chateau.

'I always forget how fantastic this place is,' he said, looking up the sweeping staircase, dominated by the chandelier, 'but you're right, it's pretty cold!'

'Come into the salon, you'll see what a difference the fire makes.'

She opened the door and watched Gus's face light up at the sight of the blazing fire.

Leo was standing by the fire and opened his arms to embrace his favourite child of the chateau.

'Gus, my darling boy, come and kiss your poor old uncle. How marvellous that you're here to lighten our darkness!'

'You don't need lightening up, Leo, you're a shining beacon. Look at you in your sparkling trousers.'

He kissed Leo on both cheeks.

'Thank you for noticing,' said Leo. 'They have a lurex thread running through the woollen cloth, so they're warm as well as decorative. I've changed early for Christmas Eve dinner to avoid chilly trips to my bedroom. And they team so well with my silver-grey pashmina, don't you think?'

He flung one corner of the scarf over his shoulder to make the point.

'It's actually really cosy in here,' said Gus, 'I might even dare to take off my coat. I love the holly and mistletoe decorations. I bet you did them too?'

'You know me, self-proclaimed Head of Style. I just need to put the finishing touches to the dining table. Why don't you come and help me?'

'I'll leave you to it, I'm going to check out my accommodation at my sister's place. For once, the humble cider barn is better than the chateau. It's warm as toast apparently. Don't be too jealous.'

For the second time that day, Fizz was making up beds for the stepsons she had yet to meet, this time in their barn house. Alex would sleep on the sofa bed in the living room, while Jack was to take the room they'd allocated for the baby, currently used as a storeroom for the boxes of booty that she'd acquired thanks to the power of her vlog. Will had loaded up the car with heated hair rollers, miracle skin products, dozens of pairs of trainers, forty handbags and an exercise bike, and moved them to an old barn by the orchard. The room looked bare now, with just a single bed and a bleak bedside table.

She heard the front door open.

'Will, is that you? This wasn't how it was supposed to be! The whole point of having that huge chateau is so we can accommodate guests at a civilised distance. And now we're all going to be packed together like sardines, in a student house-share arrangement with only one bathroom.'

Will took off his coat and shoes and walked through the sitting room where Louis was engrossed in lining up his toy cars on the floor. He patted his son's silky head and wandered in to inspect the newly emptied bedroom. It occurred to him that it was feasible that Fizz could have shared a student house with Jack and Alex, since they were of a similar age. He would have been the odd one out. The father, dutifully loading up the car with his teenage child's belongings, rather like he'd done just now. Sometimes it felt lonely, being an older husband.

'It will be fine, we couldn't let them sleep over there in the cold, they're from California. And it will be a chance for us to bond at a more intimate level.'

He stared at the single bed and thought about the last time he'd spent a night under the same roof as Jack and Alex. Probably when he was still living with Marjorie. After the divorce they tended to meet in neutral territory. Pub lunches, trips to the cinema, football matches, the usual venues for ex-husbands trying to keep in with their adult sons.

He was less confident than he sounded about how this would pan out. He hadn't seen Jack and Alex since pre-pandemic days, if you didn't count Zoom, which he didn't. Peering up the nostrils of fish-like images of people – sorry, 'loved ones,' as we were re-educated into naming our friends and family – casting around for small talk, it was even worse than talking on the phone.

'You're making intimate sound like a good thing,' said Fizz. 'I'm not sure that's true in this case. Remember, I've never met your sons and for them I'm the scarlet woman who wrecked their parents' marriage.'

'Hey, Dad.'

She spun round to see a younger version of Will standing in the doorway. He looked taller than she'd expected, on the computer screen she'd only ever seen his head and shoulders.

'Jack, my boy, is it really you?' said Will. 'And there's Alex too! We weren't expecting you for ages, how did you get here?'

He moved forward to embrace them in an awkward three-way man-hug. Fizz stood back, hoping that Jack hadn't overheard their recent conversation.

'We took a cab from the station. The driver knew exactly where to find the chateau. What a place! I mean I've seen pictures, but the reality's something else. At risk of sounding like an American, it's so old!'

Jack spoke with a cool mid-Atlantic drawl which Fizz found rather attractive.

'It looked a lot older when we first moved in, you should have seen it then,' said Will. 'Untouched for centuries, it wasn't for the faint-hearted. Sorry you took a taxi. I was expecting you to call, I would have come to meet you.'

'It's fine,' said Jack.

He turned to Fizz with a smile.

'Good to meet you in the flesh at last. The scarlet woman!'

'I'm so sorry,' she said, flustered. 'I didn't realise you were there.'

'Sorry to creep up on you like that. We met up with our brother on the way in. Cute kid.'

On cue, Louis came trotting into the room, clutching a toy fire engine, and wrapped his arms round Fizz's leg. She picked him up, grateful for the distraction.

'Say hello to Jack and Alex.'

Louis buried his head in her chest, overcome by shyness.

'I'm so glad you could both make it at last,' said Fizz. 'I'm sorry we can't offer you a grand room in the chateau. Well, we could, but you'd probably to freeze to death, so we thought you'd be better off with us here in the warm.'

'Nice and intimate, as you were just discussing with Dad!' said Jack. He clearly wasn't going to let it drop.

'It's great to be here,' said Alex.

He sounds like he means it, thought Fizz, and he has a lovely smile. She knew he was the easier of the two. Classic second child. From all accounts he didn't seem to bear quite the grudge against her that Jack did. It was always hardest for the older child, she knew that. She wondered whether that would be the case for Louis, forced to break new ground, while his younger sibling glided along in his wake.

'You must be exhausted, with the jet lag.'

'No, we're good,' said Alex. 'We've just spent a couple of nights in Paris so we're in the right time zone.'

'Americans in Paris, in the time-honoured tradition,' said Will. 'What did you do there?'

'Usual stuff. Eiffel Tower, the Louvre. Then Jack made me go to the Crazy Horse, which was kind of embarrassing.'

'Ah, what happens in Paris, stays in Paris,' said Will. 'How is Lydia, by the way?'

'It's Livia actually.'

'Sorry, Livia.'

'Don't be sorry, you've never met, why should you remember her name? Anyway, she's fine. Gone to spend the holidays with her parents in Ohio.'

'Have you met them?'

'Yes, they came to visit us in San Francisco for Thanksgiving, the same time as Mum and Roger.'

'You met Roger! That's the man she found on the internet, right? The retired banker?'

'Yes, I've met Roger. Seems like a nice guy. And most couples today meet on the internet so it's not exactly newsworthy.'

'Quite the family gathering, then,' said Will.

All playing happy families without me, he thought. No doubt banker Roger had forked out for that little expedition. Ingratiating himself with the future in-laws, ready to usurp the father of the groom, if ever it came to that.

'How about you, Jack?' he asked. 'Is there anyone special on the scene?'

'Come on, Will, less of the Spanish inquisition,' said Fizz, 'the poor boys have only just arrived and you're bombarding them with questions. Let's go and have a cup of tea and let them settle in.'

'We can do better than that,' said Will, 'I have a bottle of vintage champagne chilling, I've kept it for this special occasion – my first Christmas with my three sons.'

'Isn't it a little early in the day to start drinking?' said Alex.

'It's never too early at Chateau Lafarge.'

CHAPTER 10

Darkness fell, candles were lit and the fireplaces in every reception room roared with flames so that when the time came for Christmas Eve aperitifs, the chateau was a warm blaze of sociability.

Nicola was already slightly drunk on champagne but accepted another glass when Leo came over with the bottle. She grabbed his sleeve so he could bend down to listen to her. There was such a hum of conversation, she had to raise her voice to be heard.

'We're making memories,' she said. 'When I look out over this room and see everyone enjoying themselves, I know this will be a moment I will keep in my mind forever. This is why we bought the chateau, Leo, this is what it is for. Just take a look.'

Leo stood beside her, their backs to the chimney, and looked out over the room full of people laughing and drinking.

'Our loved ones! When you think I could have been a lonely old queen on my own, and yet here I am at the glowing heart of our chateau family. Those young people are getting on like a house on fire, look at them. Even James is looking slightly relaxed, and that doesn't happen very often.'

Nicola watched them laughing over something Gus was saying. As ever he was the centre of attention, the life and soul of the party. She felt a stab of warm maternal pride.

'I'm so pleased that Maddie and John have some young company for a change,' she said.' I do worry about them sometimes, locked away here with us oldies. Will's sons are delightful, aren't they? And have you noticed Jack flirting with Apolline. I think he's quite taken with her.'

'As we all are. She's old enough to be his mother, though. Not that that counts for anything in that family, look at his father. Which is probably what he's thinking. Let's go and join them.'

As they approached the group, Nicola noticed Simon hovering nearby looking at Apolline, who was leaning into Jack, enjoying his anecdotes about his time in Paris. She recognised the expression on Simon's face, it was the same one he wore during their first months in the chateau, when Nicola had been the object of his embarrassing infatuation. She did hope he'd snap out of it soon; it was the only cloud on her rosy horizon.

'Hey, Nicola,' said Jack, 'I've just been hearing from Apolline that you are all fabulous hosts. I can't argue with that, but on the other hand I'd be pretty happy if I advertised for a paying guest and someone like Apolline turned up, though I guess you had to kiss a few frogs along the way.'

Apolline smiled prettily and Simon's face darkened.

'She's perfect, of course,' said Nicola, 'but all of our guests have been lovely, even if we do allow ourselves to have a favourite.'

'No favouritism here,' said Simon, advancing with a bottle, 'we're a chateau democracy, if that's not a contradiction in terms. Anyone for a top-up?'

Jack held out his glass.

'When in Rome. Or even in Normandy. I can't get over the quality of food and drink in this country. The guy in our hotel was telling us you can be fined three hundred thousand euros and put in prison if you're a registered artisan baker and use frozen dough instead of fermenting it yourself. Sounds pretty harsh to me but I guess that's why the bread tastes so good.'

'It's reason enough to move to France,' said Nicola. 'No matter how small your village, you can always buy a delicious baguette.'

Jack turned his attention back to Apolline.

'That's enough about me and my adventures, let's talk about you. How long are you planning to stay here at the chateau?'

Apolline looked down at her glass.

'I'm not entirely sure, but I will be moving soon to Toulouse for a while. It's my hometown.'

'How soon? '

'Maybe in a couple of weeks.'

Simon was topping up her glass and looked up, aghast.

'Two weeks! When were you going to tell us?'

At the other side of the room, Madame de Courcy was entertaining John's parents with tales of her reign at the chateau. It was unthinkable to imagine a Christmas at Chateau Lafarge without her. The new chatelains had invited her on a whim during their first year of ownership, and now she showed up every year as a matter of course. At six-thirty on the dot, she would arrive on Christmas Eve, bearing her usual gift of a poinsettia which Leo couldn't bear as it ruined his decor. If the friends ever felt oppressed by the unavoidability of her attendance, they consoled themselves with the knowledge that surely she couldn't live forever. And the advantage of having a very old person in the room is the way it makes everyone else feel young and sprightly by comparison.

This evening, she was advocating the old-fashioned virtue of not being a wimp about the cold.

'You wouldn't believe the fuss they were making earlier about the boiler not working. I told them I lived here my entire life without the absurd luxury of central heating. It is merely a question of ensuring the fires are properly maintained. And of course, having the discipline to endure a certain discomfort, wouldn't you agree, Madame?'

She directed her question at Jean-Louis's mother, translating into French for her benefit. She prided herself on her command of English, and it was gratifying to have a new audience in the form of this distinguished older English couple, but it was important to be inclusive of the farmer's mother, whose family had been associated with this terrain almost as long as the de Courcys.

Anne nodded her agreement; you didn't need to tell her anything about battling the elements after spending her life on the farm where she was born. Her father had failed to produce a male heir, so Anne was allowed to install her husband, and then her son. It was all very feudal.

'I find thermal underwear is key,' said John's mother Geraldine. 'I packed my vests and long johns which are standing me in good stead – though of course we are very comfortable staying with Anne . . .'

She rested her hand on Anne's arm. It was so kind of her to put them up.

'Long johns, is that how you call *les caleçons longs*?' asked Madame de Courcy. 'You Anglo-Saxons, I love how you give nicknames to everything!'

'Named after a nineteenth-century boxer, I believe,' said John's father, draining his glass and looking around for a refill.

Geraldine put her hand over his glass.

'Pace yourself, Geoffrey, we haven't even sat down yet.'

Jack came over to introduce himself.

'Hi, we haven't met, I'm Will's son. I live in California so obviously I'm blown away by the drinking levels in the chateau. I'm amazed they've all lasted this long, the amount they put away.'

'Not me, I'm on the Champony,' said Maddie, coming up to join her in-laws with a glass of fizzy apple juice in her hand. 'Though to be honest I can't wait to deliver this baby so I can return to the full pleasures of the French table. They regard a glass or two of wine as part of the meal, not as an evil source of alcohol units. I like that attitude.'

'You're looking very well, Maddie,' said Geraldine.

'Oh sacred vessel that is woman!' said Geoffrey, who had succeeded in intercepting a passing bottle of champagne in spite of his wife's best efforts.

'Don't make me sound like a stately old ship, Geoffrey! It's bad enough galumphing around wearing a tent, you don't need to rub it in.'

'Don't worry, my dear, you'll be back in your jeans in no time. You were last time!'

'I'll ignore that remark because I know you mean well,' said Maddie, 'but you can't say things like that anymore.'

'Things like what? I'm just being gallant, what's wrong with that?'

'Never mind.'

She gave him a kiss and he turned back to talk to Madame de Courcy.

'The un-woke chateau,' said Jack to Maddie. 'Deep in the French countryside lies a castle where anything goes and you can say what you like, no matter how fattist.'

'And the rest,' said Maddie with a laugh.

'He's right though, you do look great.'

'Thanks.'

'It's quite a weird life here for you and John isn't it? Don't you miss the city? I mean it's a spectacular place, but you're pretty much locked in with a bunch of retirees.'

He was looking at her with genuine curiosity. What on earth could have persuaded her?

'We love it,' she said. 'When we stayed here for my last maternity leave, I literally couldn't bear the thought of leaving. So here we are.'

'That sounds pretty definite.'

'We visit London often for work. We stay with John's parents.'

'To get your top-up of sexist compliments.'

'He's a sweetheart.'

'I can totally get my dad living here, at his age, but it's odd for Fizz, too. She's almost as young as me.'

'She's making a good stab of it with her vlog. Loads of followers, and loads of freebies – lucky we have so many outbuildings to store them all.'

'Yeah, that Madame Bovary, I don't really get it.'

'You're not exactly the target market.'

'I guess not. Oh look, your mother-in-law's gone to talk to Apolline. What a beauty she is, that French woman.'

'Geraldine was desperate to meet her, she's seen all her films.'

'Apolline's an actress? I'm not surprised with that face.'

'Ex-actress. Now an artist and potter.'

'And about to go off to Toulouse, I hear.'

'Oh really? First I've heard.'

'She told me earlier.'

'Well, Beth will be pleased.'

'She doesn't like her?'

'She doesn't like the fact that Simon so obviously likes her.'

'Aah. I saw him giving me thunderous looks when I was talking to her. It's all going down at the chateau, clearly. Thank you for filling me in on the gossip!'

'I wish I hadn't said anything, now. Please forget it, and don't say anything to Will.'

'My lips are sealed and I'll be out of here soon. I'm a ship that passes in the night. A bit like you, sacred vessel.'

Their conversation was interrupted by Leo climbing on to a chair and clapping his hands to attract everyone's attention.

'Ladies and gentlemen, *messieurs-dames,* I have the *énorme plaisir* of announcing that dinner is served. Please take your seats according to the plan displayed on the board by the door ... oh James, I've only just noticed your sweater, how very original!'

Everyone turned to look at Eva's boyfriend, who was usually a conventional dresser in city suits or smart casuals. Tonight, he was wearing a red and green jumper featuring a large snowman standing on his head, with its carrot nose sticking out at the bottom. He looked embarrassed as everyone applauded.

'Bravo, James,' said Jean-Louis from the other side of the room, 'that is the best *pull moche de Noël* I have seen this year.

'I was just trying to be light-hearted. I thought it would appeal to your parents,' James whispered to Eva as they filed into the dining room. 'They always seem to find me so boring, so I thought I'd mix it up, and now I've become an object of ridicule.'

'Of course you're not,' said Eva soothingly. 'You know how Leo always likes to comment on what people are wearing, don't take it personally. And at least your jumper matches the table decor.'

The dining table was decorated with holly branches and red velvet deer that Leo had sourced at a flea market. He had also managed to find some illegal crackers with satisfyingly dangerous indoor fireworks. The French guests, who were as unfamiliar with the concept of Christmas crackers as they were with the British oddity that is pantomime, were particularly pleased by the fizzing and spitting of Wiggly Snakes and Smokey Joes. Truly, said Madame de Courcy, the *rosbifs* were masters of fun, they knew exactly how to make *les fêtes* go with a swing, although she was relieved they had opted to end with the *buches de noël* rather than the Christmas pudding they had inflicted on her on a previous occasion, like a deadly heavy stone from which her digestion had still not recovered.

It was late into the evening, many courses down, before Nicola declared it was finally time for Secret Santa. It had been her idea to replace the random gift policy of previous years, whereby some chatelains gave presents of breathtaking extravagance, while others thought a 'token' was quite sufficient, notably Dougie who set a new low when he ordered a multipack of disposable rain ponchos, price per person less than one euro. Maddie was put in charge of generating the list via an app and each guest tonight on their way in had placed their anonymous gift, wrapped and labelled, beneath the Christmas tree.

James was elected postman by virtue of his character sweater. He distributed the presents around the table while Gus played 'The Twelve Days of Christmas' on the accordion, accompanied by raucous singing – FIVE GOLD RINGS! – and spirited impersonations of lords a-leaping, maids a-milking and geese a-laying. Finally, every parcel was allocated and the guests could begin the ritual of ripping open the paper of the mystery gift before them. One at a time, so the entire table could enjoy the fun.

'You see what a great system this is,' said Nicola, waving a pair of lacy black knickers in the air, 'not only do we have the thrill of a present, we can also try to guess who chose it for us.'

'Wasn't me, honestly,' said Simon.

Maddie unwrapped a tiny babygro for her unborn baby, Mary received a first edition of a Doris Lessing novel, Will had a bottle of Puligny Montrachet, while Jean-Louis was delighted with a vintage toy tractor.

'It's a Massey Ferguson, best of British!' Will shouted from his end of the table.

'Will, it's supposed to be a surprise who it's from!' said Fizz.

'Oops. Anyway, rarely available on eBay. Enjoy it, Jean-Louis.'

Simon's parcel was small and book shaped. He tore off the paper to find a striking black cover with the author's name Murakami and a pen nib in white standing out from a red circle, along with the title, *What I Talk About When I Talk About Running*.

'Oh God, please don't encourage him, whoever that was,' said Beth, glancing over her shoulder.

Simon was transfixed. He opened the book and started reading.

'It is entirely me,' he said, 'the philosophical diversions, the drive to exercise, the writer's imperative . . . Whoever chose this book for me knows me better than myself. Listen to this: "I run, therefore I am . . ." "Most runners run not because they want to live longer, but because they want to live life to the fullest." That's me, in a nutshell!'

Eventually the table broke up and the guests drifted off, James and Eva walking down to their hotel, while the gallant Jean-Louis drove his mother and John's parents home to the farm, dropping off Madame de Courcy on the way.

Will and Fizz accompanied Jack and Alex back to their barn, Fizz urging them to keep the noise down as they approached. The baby alarm had not disrupted the evening but she didn't want Louis to be woken by the sound of them crashing in through the door. She had never been a drinker but her enforced abstention during pregnancy made her painfully aware of the excesses of others, especially Will. Alex mentioned his concerns to her as they walked across the frosty lawn. He said his father was drinking noticeably more than he remembered, though he realised that Christmas was hardly typical. They were interrupted by a shout and the sound of breaking glass – Will had tripped on a flagstone and dropped his precious bottle of Secret Santa wine. Laughing, Alex pulled him to his feet.

'My Puligny Montrachet, I'll never get to taste it!'

'Don't worry, Dad, I'll buy you another bottle. And yes, full disclosure, it was from me!'

Walking in the other direction from the chateau, Gus was serenading Maddie and John on his accordion as they headed back to the cider barn. 'Green grow the rushes-o!' he sang at full pelt, with John adding an impressive bass line. Maddie opened the door and rejoiced in the warm snugness of their home. Gus and John stumbled in after her and Gus picked up the empty Christmas stocking he had left on the kitchen table.

'I'm hanging this on the end of my bed, Maddie, and if I wake up in the morning to find it's not stuffed full of presents, I'm going to scream my head off.'

'You really are retarded, I should never have come up with the idea, I'm not your mummy.'

'Too late, you've started the tradition now, so every year from now on you'll be filling three stockings – mine, Lily's and mystery baby's. Do you know what it is yet, by the way? Am I getting another niece or a nephew?'

'You'll just have to wait and see, like the rest of us.'

*

Simon broke away from the clear-up party in the kitchen to intercept Apolline on her way up to bed. He challenged her on the staircase as she was turning into her wing.

'It was you who chose that book for me, wasn't it?'

She put her finger to her lips.

'I cannot possibly say, it is a secret, no?'

She was swaying a little, and he put his hand on her arm to steady her.

'But I know it was you,' he persisted, 'because nobody understands me the way you do.'

'All right, I admit that I was your secret Santa!'

She giggled; the wine had gone straight to her head.

'I first intended to buy you *un jogging*, because I knew you would enjoy the way we French have stolen the English word since our own vocabulary is so paltry.'

'Ah, we're back on the vocab tease, are we?'

He put his other hand on her shoulder, trying to concentrate on their *jeu de mots*, when all he really wanted to do was kiss her.

'You may have stolen our English word, but it is absurd to refer to a pair of tracksuit bottoms as *un jogging*. Jogging merely means the act of running.'

'*Touché*. Very well, I admit that I did give you the Murakami book.'

'Thank you. I love it.'

Their faces were close now. He waited for a sign from her. Then she spoke more softly, in French.

'I knew you would enjoy it, because you are my hamster.'

'Excuse me?'

She repeated the words.

'Your *hamster?*' he said. 'What on earth do you mean by that?'

'*Tu es mon âme soeur*. My sister soul. My soulmate.'

'Soulmates, exactly. That's how I feel. You read my book, you know me, Apolline, like nobody does. We're made for each other. Tell me you're not leaving. I can't bear the thought of you leaving. Stay here, I beg you. Forget about Toulouse.'

She took a step back.

'I must go, surely you see that? I cannot stay here on the fringes of your life.'

'I will have no life if you go away. Please stay.'

Beyond the fire-fuelled warmth of the reception rooms, the staircase and landings were bitterly cold. Beth opened her bedroom door and appreciated the warm air pumping out of the inelegant but effective heater. As she slipped into bed, there was another treat in store. Simon had unearthed an electric blanket from the back of the wardrobe which he had fitted earlier under the bedsheet.

'Oh yes!' said Beth, stretching her feet through the luxurious warmth and reaching across to Simon who was already in bed with his back to her. 'You know the way to a girl's heart.'

'I ordered it weeks ago, forgot all about it until today,' he murmured. 'I deliberately kept it quiet, didn't want Dougie bitching about the electricity cost.'

He didn't mention that he had in fact ordered two electric blankets. The other one he had secretly installed on the twirly gilded bed of the Louis XIV suite, where he now imagined Apolline delighting in the miracle of her warm sheets. Like a courtly knight, he would win her favour by performing such duties. He would prove his worthiness to be her soulmate.

'Delicious dinner, I'm completely stuffed,' said Beth. 'It was great having all those visitors, everyone behaves better. What about James and his jokes sweater?'

'He's a dork.'

'If we were being charitable, we could say at least he was making an effort.'

'We're not charitable.'

'There is that.'

Although in reality Beth was feeling pretty charitable right now. While they were clearing up after dinner, Nicola had given her the happy news that Apolline would soon be leaving the chateau. It was the best Christmas present she could have asked for, certainly better than the four threadbare linen napkins she had received as her Secret Santa from Madame de Courcy, all chance of anonymity blown as they were embroidered with her initials.

'Did you hear that Apolline's off to Toulouse?'

She asked the question casually, the darkness meant she couldn't read Simon's expression but she felt him tense up.

'Mmm.'

'I assume it was her who gave you that silly book?'

'No idea. It's not silly by the way.'

'She's certainly had a good long stint with us. Night night.'

Simon listened to her breathing grow heavier as she sank into sleep. A good long stint, was that how they were to treat the miraculous arrival of Apolline into their lives? He couldn't bear the thought of her leaving, and now he knew she felt the same, she must change her mind. She was his soulmate, she told him so. He held that thought as he, too, drifted off to sleep in the warm cocoon of the electrically heated bed.

CHAPTER 11

If Christmas is a family event, New Year's Eve is when the net should be cast wider, to welcome new blood in the form of friends and neighbours. So said John and Maddie. Energised by the presence of people their own age for a change, they had decided to organise a spontaneous party in the chateau. The theme was techno rave and a DJ friend of Gus's was coming from London to host the event. A flurry of messages last night had established a surprising number of attendees, considering they were only giving three days' notice. 'I'm amazed they don't have other plans,' said Dougie, who announced that he and Mary would disappear to Paris for the occasion, rather to everyone's relief. Will and Simon were flattered at the thought of being down with the kids, while Nicola and Beth were just relieved that someone else was doing the organising.

Leo appointed himself senior statesman at today's planning meeting which was taking place around the dining table. James and Eva had made their excuses as they were out visiting the D-Day landing beaches, so Maddie and John were joined by Gus, Fizz, Jack and Alex.

'May I say how excited I am about this event,' said Leo, after they had run through the first items on the agenda. 'It's New and Young, vital qualities for our ongoing life at the chateau. I have one question concerning "techno rave". Can someone please explain to me what on earth it is?'

Gus turned up the volume on his laptop and played him a hardcore example of electronic dance music.

Leo nodded his head in time to the beat.

'That really is quite something. I can't resist dancing to that!'

He stood up and moved wildly on the spot, arms and legs jerking, to the great amusement of his spectators. Fizz clicked away at her phone. Here was something she could certainly use.

'You're owning it, Leo!' said Gus.

'The oldest swinger in town, that's me.'

'One more smile for the camera,' said Fizz.

Leo obliged, then offered up a deep curtsey and sat down, exhausted by his efforts.

'The next thing we need to do is clear the crystal ballroom,' said John. 'Luckily we have so many rooms in the enfilade that the furniture can simply be stored in the grand and petit salons.'

'Do be careful when you're moving it around,' said Leo, 'I don't want anything scratched.'

'What's great about the venue is we don't need to worry about the noise,' said Gus. 'It was very thoughtful of you to buy this huge chateau in the middle of nowhere where we don't have to notify the neighbours.'

'Naturally our priority when home-hunting was to find somewhere to host a techno rave party without consequences,' said Leo, rolling his eyes. 'Right, let's get on to the most important subject – my outfit. Now you've given me a flavour of the music, I'm beginning to envisage what I might wear. How about a see-through black vest and legging combo, edged with a rainbow colour trim with "LOVE" printed on it, accessorised with a few chains and rings plus a pair of vintage Converse Allstars?'

'That's perfect, Leo,' said Fizz.

'I wonder what those rival gays will wear,' said Leo

'You've lost me there,' said Jack. 'Who are the rival gays?'

'You mean you've been here for days, and Leo still hasn't told you about his nemesis?' said Fizz.

'It was a crushing blow, but I've risen above it, ' said Leo. 'Two English gays bought a chateau nearby, rather like ours but with the added bonus of a moat. That was bad enough, but to cap it all, Oscar turned out to be a hugely successful interior designer whose clients include royalty. In other words, an enhanced version of me. It almost brought me down, but then I thought, no. Befriend your enemies. So, I went over to introduce myself. Their chateau is less imposing than I feared, and Oscar and Jeremy are older than they looked in their photographs, so it's all fine. They're coming to the party!'

'The good and the great of Normandy,' said John, 'and we have a carload of friends coming over from London, it's going to be such fun.'

Nicola came in, pushing a tea trolley.

'Sandwiches for the working lunch committee,' she said, putting out plates of half-baguettes. 'French style, old-school, *jambon*-Emmenthal.'

'You wouldn't want to be a vegetarian in this country,' said Alex, helping himself to a sandwich and biting through the satisfying layers of cheese and ham.

'I'm vegetarian and I get by,' said Fizz. 'I assume that's for me, Nicola, with the hummus?'

Nicola nodded.

'You're all right making them at home,' she said, 'but there's only ever one veggie sandwich option at the boulangerie and that's *thon-crudités,* tinned tuna with bits of lettuce. It always looks really unappetising. How's the planning going, all set?'

'Pretty much,' said Maddie, 'I'm excited – our last wild night before we become dreary parents of two and all fun disappears.'

'You know that won't happen, darling.'

'Is Apolline still all right with Lily?'

'Yes, she's taken her out for a walk with Louis. We're so going to miss her when she goes, and it leaves us with another guest room to fill.'

She turned to Jack and Alex.

'How have you two found it, sleeping in the chateau?'

Since the boiler had been repaired, they had moved out of Will and Fizz's barn and into the guest wing.

'Amazing,' said Jack. 'I mean, Dad's cottage is nice and cosy, but you could pretty much be anywhere. Whereas upstairs, just walking down the corridor feels incredibly grand, and the views from the big window over the lake are to die for. Dad said he's going to get on with decorating them after we've gone.'

'I haven't seen the new rooms yet,' said Maddie, 'let's go and check them out.'

'I shall lead the tour of inspection,' said Leo. 'Eat up, then follow me.'

They finished the sandwiches then followed Leo through the crystal ballroom, the interconnecting salons, and up the grand staircase. It was a beautiful winter's day and the light came dancing in through the tall windows.

In the manner of a tour guide, Leo pointed out the rooms.

'Here is Antoine Watteau. Your parents were destined for this room, John, but they like it so much at the farm they decided to stay on there instead once we had the heating back. And next door is Jean-Honoré Fragonard, where Eva and James are sleeping. They've gone out for the day, I believe, so let me show you that, too.

'Who are Watteau and Fragonard?' asked Jack. 'I've never heard of them.'

'After all that money your father threw at your education, I'm amazed,' said Leo. 'They were pioneering painters of the Rococo movement. Take a look at this.'

He flung open the door to reveal a room bathed in the rosy glow of sunlight reflecting off elaborate pink and gold wallpaper. Above the bed hung a reproduction of Fragonard's *The Birth of Venus*, with pink-faced cherubs on billowing clouds. A curvy lacquered wood sideboard, images of birds, acanthus and sea-shells on the curtains, everything combined to set a playful, luxurious mood.

'Wow, I thought my room was pretty impressive, but it has nothing on this,' said Alex.

'It will soon be transformed, it's my next project,' said Leo. 'Ideally I'd have fresco ceiling paintings, but that is a little too challenging for your father. I'm going for a similar mood to this for yours and Jack's rooms, so we'll have an entire Rococo wing. The François Boucher room and Madame Le Brun, it's time we had another room named after a woman.'

He opened the next door, bare but for a bed and Alex's suit-case in the corner.

'Here you see the bare canvas. Next time you come, you will enjoy the finished item.'

He stared round the room and couldn't wait to get started. It was the most thrilling sensation for him, to feel the potential of an empty space and imagine how it would soon take shape.

By early evening on New Year's Eve, the scene of the party was set. The crystal ballroom, stripped of all furniture, looked vast beneath the strobe lighting, flashing out green and purple, moving across the room together with laser beams piercing through a ghostly haze. The atmosphere was of heightened, energetic excitement.

'The chateau as we've never seen it,' said Beth, as she and Nicola watched the lighting engineer at work. He had arrived that afternoon in the van with the DJ and was putting the final touches to his installation.

'I hope that hazer machine doesn't leave a stain on the floor. Mary will go nuts.'

'Good job they're not here, it really wouldn't be their thing.'

'Makes a change from string quartets around the piano.'

'And finally we're hosting an event to which we don't have to invite Madame de Courcy,' said Beth. 'I'm really looking forward to it! Let's go and have something to eat in the kitchen. I know they've organised some snacks for later, but I can't wait that long.'

They closed the door to the crystal ballroom and walked back to the kitchen where they found Leo staring into the fridge, wondering what to eat. He was wearing a diaphanous black jumpsuit with a lurid trim repeatedly featuring the word 'love', large silver rings on his fingers and a pair of white ankle-length trainers.

'Great minds think alike,' said Beth. 'This reminds me of the scene in *Gone With the Wind* where the girls are made to eat before the party so they look dainty later on, just picking at their food in front of the boys.'

'What do you think of my frockage?'

He gave them a twirl.

'Quite a departure from your usual look,' said Nicola. 'What do you think of ours?'

Leo studied their outfits. Both were wearing grungy black tracksuit bottoms. Nicola had topped hers with a fluorescent pink top, while Beth had a baggy black T-shirt bearing the slogan 'Nice People Dancing to Good Techno Music'. They both wore matching neon glow necklaces.

'They're . . . different,' he said. 'It's important to remain open to change at our age.'

They found a tub of pork rillettes in the fridge and sat down to eat them with the remains of the lunch salad.

'Remind me what time everyone's coming,' said Beth.

'I think they said nine o'clock,' said Nicola. 'That way people should have already had supper so there won't be great food expectations. And three hours is more than enough to throw yourself around on the dance floor, I would have thought.'

As they were clearing away their dishes, they heard a noise outside. Two carloads of Gus and Maddie's friends had arrived and were making their way into the chateau, cheerfully chatting to each other and carrying sleeping bags and rucksacks. Leo spied on them through the window.

'I do hope it's not going to be one of those disasters you read about where someone has posted an event on social media and thousands of people descend on it. Can you imagine, our precious chateau being trashed by the mob.'

Nicola joined him at the window.

'No, it's fine, personal invitation only – I recognise that girl, she's an old school friend of Maddie's. I'm relieved that people are turning up, it would be too tragic if it ended up with just us oldies throwing our dance moves.'

'I could do a solo,' said Leo, 'a jerky electronic version of the Dying Swan.'

He demonstrated by lifting his arms over his head, standing on tiptoe and impersonating a ballerina receiving electric shocks.

An hour later, the dining room was full of young people loading up on shots from an alarming number of vodka and gin bottles lined up on the table. The host chatelains moved amongst them, graciously welcoming them to their home.

'You make us look like teetotallers, the way you're knocking back those shots,' said Simon to a pretty girl wearing a bodysuit with reflective piping. 'We like our wine here, as you'd expect, but tend to take it easy on spirits.'

'Speak for yourself, Simon,' said Will, raising a glass, 'I'm making a point of entering the spirit of New Year's Eve. It only comes once a year and at our age who knows how many more we have left?'

'Quite a few more, I hope, Dad,' said Jack who had strolled across to join them, 'but I like the attitude of you all here at the chateau. It's like, eat drink and be merry, for tomorrow we die. You can't argue with that.'

'Are you talking about death?' said Maddie. 'That's no way to get this party going.'

She hugged the girl in the bodysuit.

'This is Siena, we were best friends at school. Siena meet Simon and Will, who are my housemates, and Jack who is just visiting.'

'Housemates, that's hilarious,' said Siena, 'in a place this size you need to talk about chateau mates.'

'It's a strange life for Maddie and John, don't you agree?' said Jack. 'I totally get it if you're retired and you want to just go off-piste for the rest of your life. But I was saying to Maddie the other day, don't you miss engaging with the real world?'

'Define "real",' said Maddie. 'I know you have us down as a bunch of hippies, but we're just sunny nihilists, we focus on everyday pleasures.'

'Happy in your bubble, I guess. Well I'll drink to that. Oh look, here are some more people arriving.'

Leo was welcoming Oscar and Jeremy, the couple who had had the temerity to buy up the neighbouring chateau. It was their first visit to Chateau Lafarge and they were looking around in a suitably impressed manner, to Leo's gratification. Oscar was dressed in non-committal black but Jeremy was sporting a daring pair of tight psychedelic flares, which made him look rather like one of the stationery products he designed and sold online to a discerning clientele.

Fizz was thrilled by Jeremy, snapping away at him with a little too much enthusiasm as far as Leo was concerned.

'This will be an absolute first for my vlog,' she said, 'in all my years as Mademoiselle, then Madame Bovary, we've never held an event like this. Jeremy, can you just stand there by the door to the crystal ballroom and look back at me over your shoulder . . . that's fantastic.'

She looked at her phone, satisfied with the results.

'Madame Bovary, I must look you up,' said Oscar. 'I heard someone mention you the other day, it seems you're quite a big noise in our corner of Normandy.'

Fizz was delighted to find herself socialising with someone as distinguished as this famous designer. It could only be good for her to foster the friendship. She locked him into a corner and engaged him in a conversation from which he found it difficult to escape.

The music ramped up and the crowd moved onto the dance floor in the crystal ballroom. It was, they all agreed, a massive success, the senior members moving seamlessly with the younger ones, any self-consciousness banished by the light effects that made even the stiffest dancer appear to be the epitome of cool.

As midnight approached, the DJ paused the music and entered the countdown, after which the revellers fell indiscriminately on each other's necks, blearily wishing everyone a happy new year. Simon was looking around the room, searching for Apolline. He'd been watching her dancing with Jack and she had been ignoring him all evening. She must have slipped out. He left the crowded room and set out to find her.

She was sitting in a dark corner of the petit salon, studying her phone.

'There you are,' said Simon, 'I wondered where you'd gone.'

She looked up at him.

'I'm not comfortable with those big outpourings at midnight, it is alien to my introvert soul.'

'I know what you mean. It makes me want to run for the hills.'

She laughed.

'You! You're the biggest extrovert I know! What is that English expression, "life and soul of the party", that is you, no?'

'That's what everybody else sees, but it's not true, I'm a sensitive introvert, just like you! Come outside with me, I'll show you what I'm really like.'

He pulled her by the hand and they slipped out onto the terrace, then beyond, away from the party lights and the people, until they were leaning up against an oak tree, safely out of sight.

'No one can find us here,' said Simon, wrapping his arms around her against the cold.

'Are you warm enough, are you all right with this?'

She nodded. Finally, they kissed, and Simon saw his future stretching in front of him.

'My *âme soeur*, my hamster,' he murmured.

'Yes, I'm yours. I'm not going to pretend any more. But you understand now why I must go away. I cannot stay here when I am in love with you, it's not possible.'

'And I cannot stay here without you. We will leave together, it's the only way.'

You're taking a *sabbatical*! A sabbatical from what, exactly?? Last time I looked, you didn't have a job, or did I miss something?'

Beth's face was a picture of fury. It was the morning after the party, they were sitting up in bed, and Simon's calm explanation of his plan was not going well.

'It's just for a month or two, to allow me to really kick-start my book.'

'Kick-start? You've been at it for months, years even, and now you're telling me that you haven't even started it? Are you a Jack Nicholson-style lunatic bashing away at your typewriter "all work and no play makes Jack a dull boy", all the while planning your killing spree?'

'I've done a few chapters. Apolline thinks they're amazing, by the way.'

'Oh, does she indeed? You didn't think to show them to me?'

She waited for his explanation.

'You can be very scornful, Beth. I worried your criticism might dry me up entirely.'

'Whereas Apolline's approval has opened the floodgates of your creativity!'

Simon said nothing. Beth then knew the truth, it landed like a dead weight in her stomach. It was exactly as she suspected. She felt like crying, but what was the point, she mustn't appear weak.

'I'm not an idiot,' she said. 'I've seen you following Apolline around with your doe eyes, hanging on her every word. It's pathetic, but it's what you do. You have crushes on people. It doesn't mean you should walk out on your wife on the pretext of going on a bloody *sabbatical*!'

'It's not a crush.'

'Oh, don't tell me you're in love with her?'

'Yes, as a matter fact I am. We are. We love each other. I'm sorry if that sounds harsh, that's why I wanted to present this as . . . a sabbatical.'

'Sabbatical, my arse! If you're leaving me for her, at least have the guts to admit it.'

Simon put his head in his hands.

'Oh Beth, please don't make this any harder than it needs to be!'

'Ha! Make yourself the victim, why don't you? Have you really thought this through? You may believe you and Apolline have some kind of special relationship, but I think you're kidding yourself! She'll get sick of you, or you'll get sick of her, then you're going to regret everything you've lost. Me, in other words.'

'I'll take that risk.'

He sounded so cold. Forty years together, and now this. She locked up her hurt, and vented instead on the practical repercussions.

'What about all the work here at the chateau, what makes you think you can just wriggle out of your responsibilities? It's supposed to be a joint venture, or had you forgotten?'

'We all have our side hustles. You're always going off to London, I never complained about that.'

'Excuse me, you can't compare me earning a good whack by going off *on my own* for meetings about TV projects with you fannying around Toulouse with a French actress!'

'So, she's a "French actress", now, is she? Don't sound so bitter.'

'I *am* bitter! No doubt you'll be reading out passages from that stupid Murakami book to each other. Maybe she'll take up running too, so you can go together along the banks of the Garonne and she can admire how aerodynamic you are, now you've shaved off your body hair like a gay porn star.'

She leaped out of bed and pulled on her dressing gown, then walked to the window to look out over the grounds. Yesterday's sunshine and frost had given way to a dull greyness.

'I've made my mind up, Beth. I'm doing this,' said Simon.

She turned to look at him.

'Well in that case, there's nothing more to say. You have clearly decided you need a sabbatical from me. In which case, good riddance.'

She waited until he had left the room, then climbed back into bed and burst into tears. Simon was a nightmare, of course, but he was her nightmare, and she never thought he'd leave her. They were partners for life. This couldn't be happening.

Part Three

Spring

CHAPTER 12

Simon's departure cast a shadow over Chateau Lafarge. Everyone agreed he had treated Beth appallingly, but she refused to play the victim. There was nothing worse, she said, than people coming up to her, eyes soft with sympathy, asking how she was feeling. Life went on.

Spring was announced by banks of daffodils brightening the lawns in shades of cream and yellow, some with vibrant orange centres. They were planted in clusters around the fruit trees in the orchard and swathes of them lined the driveway to welcome visitors under the bright sunshine. Their arrival coincided with the return in force of the paying guests. Great for the bank balance, hard work for the hosts, including Beth and Nicola, who were grumbling in the kitchen.

'I know we should be grateful when they book in for dinner, but it's quite a faff, isn't it?' said Beth, frowning over the pile of potatoes they were peeling. 'Don't you just dream of handing them the keys to their own Airbnb apartment at the far end of the chateau and letting them get on with it? Rather than having to rustle up something delicious and then make polite conversation while we serve it?'

'Ouch!'

Nicola rubbed the end of her finger which she had just nicked with the kitchen knife. Her left hand was battle-scarred with cooking injuries. She had tried using cut-proof gloves, but they made her hands sweat.

'I agree,' she said, 'self-catering is far less effort for a chatelain. Maybe we should have bought a chateau attached to a caravan park, that's a nice little earner.'

'But then we'd have to stare at the caravans.'

'We could screen them off with a row of conifers. Keep them out of sight, the way nobles used to build secret tunnels, so they didn't have to look at the servants.'

'Never mind caravans, we should knock up some glamping tents, there's money for old rope,' said Beth, who was always looking out for new income streams. 'Just because the tent is big and purple. Hello! It's still camping, don't kid yourselves it's a luxury hotel.'

'Or get the guests to build their own accommodation, like Chris up the road. Did you hear about his new venture? He's selling residential mud-house building courses. Visitors pay to stay for a week on his land where they sleep in huts, then learn how to build them from wattle and daub. Paying for the privilege of working as medieval labourers! They use ditches as toilets.'

'Clever old Chris, he's very enterprising for a hippy draft dodger.'

There was no evidence that American Chris had escaped to France to avoid conscription during the Vietnam War, but they enjoyed the story. The favourite entertainment of expats in rural France involved speculating about other expats, it went with the territory. Chris was one of the most colourful, an antiques dealer who lived in a massive watermill attached to a disused cheese factory on the outskirts of the village, where he constantly dreamt up new schemes for making money.

'Still, we are where we are,' said Nicola. 'Seven for dinner tonight, I think. At least only half the rooms are booked, imagine how we'll feel when it's a full house.'

'Yes, today we've got a family of boffins spending the school holidays inspecting the DD landing sites. Then there's Julian and Anthony from Gloucestershire, with their dogs. I kind of wish we'd said no pets, don't you? It's bad enough being jovial with human guests, never mind having to feign interest in their animals.'

'Accepting pets does broaden our market, loads of *chambres d'hôtes* won't take them.'

'Sensible people,' said Beth.

She sliced the last potato and dropped it into the pan of water. They were cooking *tartiflette* tonight, a delicious gooey bake of Reblochon cheese with bacon and cream. It was a mountain recipe from the Haute-Savoie, not local at all, but they'd become rather bored with cooking Norman dishes so most of their dinners now were based on recipes from other parts of France. To mix it up, they had tried occasionally to offer Italian or Asian cuisine but that didn't go down well with the guests who, understandably, wanted the full French experience.

'This is when I really miss Simon, when the new guests arrive,' said Beth. 'He's so great at doing the meet and greet. An arsehole at all other times, obviously, but he makes it feel like fun when the guests arrive, rather than a chore.'

'That's true,' said Nicola, glancing up to assess her friend's mood. 'Have you heard from him recently?'

'We're not communicating. I think it's best. Even after that screaming row when he left, we still kept in touch for the first few weeks. Then, nothing. Which I assume means he's still loved-up with dream girl.'

'Poor Beth.'

'Poor Beth nothing! She could be doing me a favour. Maybe I'm better off without him.'

'Are you?'

'I'm not sure. I'm managing perfectly well without him. I'm really enjoying working away, without him guilt-tripping me about leaving him on his own, though the whole point of chateau life is that you're never on your own, so that makes no sense. I'm also glad to be spared updates on his fitness schedule and the non-progress of his book. Speaking of books, shall we go through for the reading hour?'

It was a ritual they had established, to break up domestic duties and remind them that this new life was all about enjoying every moment. Once dinner prep was completed, they would hang up their aprons and go through to the petit salon, where they would sit in grand armchairs to read their books in companionable silence. Servants transformed into ladies of leisure. That afternoon, Nicola was reading a novel set in Morocco – she liked to be transported to a different climate – while Beth was lost in the brutal details of a violent thriller.

The Gloucestershire gentlemen were the first to arrive, in a Land Rover fitted with a cage for their two dogs who leaped out of the back the moment the boot was opened and went sniffing around the grounds to familiarise themselves with the new premises.

Dougie was sent out to receive them. Beth had taken one look at their tweeds and decided they were just his cup of tea. Dougie was delighted, they were exactly the sort of visitor he had hoped for when they first decided to take in paying guests. They showed such an intelligent interest in the history of the chateau, listening to his in-depth account of the various stages of its building, enraptured by his mini lecture on the nature of architectural turrets. As he explained to them, leading the way up the spiral staircase to Leo's room, turrets were originally built projecting from chateau walls to provide a defensive position, but then became decorative, offering panoramic views such as this.

'It's what we're missing at home, a turret with a view!' said Anthony with a sigh.

Dougie had forgotten quite how spectacular Leo's room was, and as he looked out over the sunlit fields and forests in three directions, he had a niggling regret that he should have held out for this room for Mary and himself. But Leo had been so insistent, and on a prosaic note, their room on a lower floor involved fewer stairs, which was something to think about as they grew older, especially with his knees. You needed to be practical about these things. He brushed aside the thought, it was something that had been badgering him recently – what would happen when they could no longer manage the stairs? They would have to install a Stannah Stairlift of baronial proportions, it would probably take half an hour to convey a user from ground to top floor and would hardly be in keeping with the chateau aesthetic.

'Let me show you to your room,' he said, focusing on the here and now, which was the only way to live. 'You're in the Antoine Watteau suite – your namesake, Anthony, designed in the Rococo style by our resident designer Leo. You can get a sense of his talent from his own room, but you'll find the Watteau even more striking.'

The men and their dogs followed Dougie through the laby-
rinthine corridors until they arrived at their suite.

'It's heaven!' said Julian, sitting down on the pink counterpane.
The terriers jumped up beside him, which Dougie tried to ignore.
Their policy was to welcome only well-behaved pets – unlike this
annoying pair – but he was prepared to let it go in this case as he
liked their owners.

'I'm having that classic Brit reaction when entering a chateau,' said Julian. 'I'm thinking, why don't we trade in our small
house in England for something like this? Because it's about the
same price, right?'

'Depends where your small house is,' said Dougie, 'but yes, it
can appear astonishingly cheap to buy a ruinously large chateau.
And then to be faced with a chateau-sized bill for the renovations.'

'That's true, maybe we'll stay as we are!'

'We're fortunate because we bought in as a group venture,'
said Dougie, 'so all the costs are shared. And every day we count
our blessings for living here. Or should I say we acknowledge
our privilege, isn't that the modern turn of phrase?'

'Oh, very good, glad to see you're still up to speed on correct
English even if you do live abroad! Tell me one thing, though,
why is it always the Brits who buy up the chateaux? Don't the
French want them?'

'No. Crumbling chateaux are a liability. If you're French
and there's one in your family, you only want to visit it once
a year and hope someone else will pay for the new roof. You
certainly don't want to buy one, that's only for British dreamers
who enjoy DIY, or rich foreigners from other countries who can
throw money at it. Then there's the French tax man – the last
thing a French person wants is to attract his attention by buying
a *monument historique*.'

Dougie left them to settle in, after confirming dinner at eight, then went outside to enjoy the spring sunshine in a productive way, wandering down to the vegetable garden where he picked up a stool and a trowel from the shed and sat down to weed the beds of leeks. He found the act of weeding therapeutic, the careful removal of seedlings from where they shouldn't be, but at the same time it was a futile exercise because nature abhors a vacuum and another seed would soon find its way into that bare earth to take the place of those removed. His musings on the joys and pointlessness of gardening were interrupted by Louis, who came running up to him and stuck his small hands into the soil beside him. Fizz and Will followed behind, Fizz capturing the moment, as usual, on her phone.

'What's the caption for this one?' asked Dougie. '"Old man shares gardening knowledge with next generation"?'

'I don't think you quite get social media, Dougie, but that's the general idea. What a glorious day, isn't it? We're just taking a stroll to admire the daffodils.'

Daffodils were on the dining table that evening, displayed in a row of unpretentious jam jars for the enjoyment of the dinner guests – a slightly awkward combination of the Gloucestershire gentlemen with their dogs, and an earnest family of four, the goal-driven parents determined that the children should acquire a detailed knowledge of the Normandy landings during their Easter holidays. The father had engaged Dougie to lead them on a tour of the principal sites the following day and there was much talk of Juno, Utah and Omaha beaches as Dougie set the *tartiflette* on the table and they finalised the details. He apologised to Anthony and Julian for excluding them from the conversation and said they were more than welcome to join the tour if it was of interest.

'No thank you,' said Anthony, 'we're committed to a tour of the chateaux and gardens of the region. We're intent on pleasure rather than revisiting the horrors of the past but thank you for thinking of us.'

Their dogs were sniffing under the table, pressing their muzzles into the groins of the other guests, which didn't bother the children, though the parents were radiating disapproval. Dougie had asked them if they were all right with the dogs being present for dinner and they had agreed, without knowing what they were letting themselves in for.

When the guests had finished dinner, Dougie cleared the table with Beth and Nicola, then the three of them sat down for a leisurely staff supper. It was always the favourite part of an evening, when the guests were safely dispatched, and the on-duty friends could relax and enjoy themselves. Mary and Leo were in Paris, while the barn-dwellers, as they had come to be known, were at home in their nuclear households.

'Do you think we should offer separate tables for dinner?' said Dougie, loading up their plates with *tartiflette*. 'It can feel a bit forced sometimes, don't you think? Disparate people stuck at a table together, feeling obliged to make conversation.'

'Certainly not,' said Beth, 'that would mean even more work for us, having to put up different tables all over the place. It's clear on our website: dinner available on request, served at the communal table. It's not our fault if sometimes they don't like each other.'

'Ever the charmer,' said Nicola with a smile. 'No wonder we scored that one-star review last week.'

'Don't remind me about those awful people!'

Their reviews were generally favourable, but Beth had got on the wrong side of a couple recently when they had dared to suggest that her *blanquette de veau* was a little under-seasoned.

'You're far too sensitive to criticism,' said Nicola, 'the first rule of hospitality is that the customer is always right.'

'But the whole point of *blanquette de veau* is that it's a subtle dish. If they want someone who's going to blow their brains out with a cheap smattering of strong spices, they should go elsewhere.'

'Which is pretty much what you told them, unfortunately.'

'Well, they deserved it. Anyway, there's too much grade inflation in those online reviews, where everyone expects five stars. It makes us stand out a little, to have the attitude you might expect from a temperamental top chef.'

'"We would have given Chateau Lafarge five stars, had it not been for a bizarre outburst from one of the hosts who reacted badly to our suggestion about how a recipe could be improved upon."'

Nicola laughed as she repeated it word for word, imprinted as it was on her memory.

'All right, give it a rest,' said Beth. 'I wouldn't have minded if it had come from someone who knew what she was talking about, but this was the women who the previous day had asked for tomato ketchup to go with her lamb navarin. Ignorant to the core.'

'Remind me never to comment on your cooking,' said Dougie, 'you are completely terrifying.'

'And massively judgemental,' said Nicola. 'Plenty of chefs endorse tomato ketchup.'

Beth slammed down her knife and fork in a fit of temper.

'I suppose you think that's why my husband's left me!'

There was an awkward silence.

'Oof, that's a bit of a leap,' said Nicola eventually. 'I thought you appeared to be handling it a bit too well.'

'I am handling it well. Then suddenly it hits me – how come he gets to run off with a French actress while I'm stuck here as a kitchen maid, dishing up dinners to an unappreciative audience?'

'Because you were born to serve?' said Nicola, with a straight face.

Beth gave her a playful slap.

'OK, I asked for that. Moan over.'

'The guests were appreciative tonight, to be fair,' said Dougie, feeling out of his depth with all this relationship talk. 'Anthony said it was the best *tartiflette* he'd ever tasted, and the chocolate tart went down well with the children.'

They were interrupted by a knock on the door. Anthony came into the room and they could tell from his expression that he was the bearer of bad news.

'Sorry to disturb you,' he said, 'but we don't appear to have any running water in our bathroom. I'm not sure whether it's only us, or a general problem . . .'

'Oh dear, I'm so sorry about that,' said Dougie, 'let me just check.'

He went into the kitchen and ran the cold tap, which gushed forth then reduced to a trickle before drying out to nothing.

'Something's up, I'll ring Will now. He's our resident plumbing expert, I'm sure he can deal with it. Please accept our apologies, Anthony, I'll keep you updated.'

Anthony nodded his thanks and left the room, while Dougie spoke to Will on the phone.

'At least the other guests will be safely in bed by now,' said Nicola. 'She said they were heading for an early night.'

'Let's hope Will can sort it out, whatever it is,' said Beth. 'I've just thought of another reason why you should stay living in the city rather than buy a gigantic money pit out in the sticks – not that I'm compiling a list, by the way. Emergency plumbers, twenty-four-seven, respond within an hour, you can only dream of that in rural France.'

Nicola's phone rang.

'Who's that calling you at this outrageous hour?' asked Beth.

'Oh really!' said Nicola talking into the phone, her eyes widening. 'Yes of course. I'll be right there, give me five minutes.'

'That was John,' she said. 'Maddie's waters have broken, I'm going over to be with Lily while he takes her into hospital.'

'Honestly, Mum, I thought I'd died and gone to heaven when the nun came in to take the baby.'

Maddie was sitting up in bed, looking extremely well, in a graciously appointed private room in a Catholic maternity clinic. Since John had become an employee of the French office of his company, he was a member of a private health insurance scheme which came with astonishing benefits. It was a far cry from Maddie's experience after Lily's birth, surrounded by the noise and chaos of an NHS ward.

Nicola hugged her daughter, giddy with relief that all was well, that her daughter had come through the trauma of giving birth. As a doctor, she knew only too well how often things went wrong, though it was rarely discussed. She felt now the same sense of wonder as when Lily was born, witnessing the miraculous launch of a new life. Her daughter, now her grandchild, the generations rolling on, the old must give way to the young.

She found herself unable to speak for a moment, then focused her attention on a vase of fresh flowers on the bedside table.

'You wouldn't be allowed those in a British hospital,' she said, 'they're considered a health risk these days.'

'I'm not sure you'd even call this a hospital,' said Maddie, touched by the sight of her mother's heightened emotional state. 'It's more like a boutique hotel and health spa, run by nuns in their darling wimples.'

Bang on cue, a nun entered the room, dressed in a long white gown, looking like an angel from a school nativity play. She handed Maddie a tiny bundle – wrapped in swaddling clothes, thought Nicola, continuing the biblical theme – then smiled at Nicola before retreating as discreetly as she had arrived.

'That's Sister Beatrice,' said Maddie, cuddling her baby. 'She's one of the *petites soeurs*. That's what they are called, it's so cute, having all these little sisters, most of them quite old to be honest, running around after you.'

'And they don't mind that you're not Catholic? Let me see my gorgeous grandson!'

She gently took him from her daughter's arms and examined his minute wrinkled fingers, the spiral of his fair hair, the strength of his body folded into foetal position. She remembered the last time she had performed this rite, on the ward of St Thomas' Hospital in London, after Lily was born. She had cried then, as she was crying now. For the usual grandmotherly reasons, but also because, for the second time, she was thinking how this baby would never know his grandfather, and how much Dom would have adored it all.

'The birth was a breeze, I hear,' she said, focusing on the practical details.

'I know what you're thinking, Mum,' said Maddie, who also had tears in her eyes. 'Dad's first grandson.'

Nicola nodded; they were in perfect understanding.

'And yes, the birth was a doddle!' said Maddie. 'All that Anglo-Saxon nonsense about working through the pain with gas and air – completely out the window. Remember when the doctor here asked me if I wanted an epidural, I said I didn't have one last time, but thought I'd give it a go this time round. He told me I'd find it very comfortable, and he wasn't lying.'

She took the baby back from Nicola and put him to her breast where he latched on and suckled happily. Nicola noticed her wincing slightly and brought a tube of Kamillosan ointment out of her handbag. She unscrewed the cap and the smell of chamomile took her back to the birth of her first grandchild, and beyond that, to the early months of her own babies, when this nipple cream was her biggest ally in her determination to carry on breastfeeding.

'I brought this for you, thought it might be useful.'

'Thanks, Mum. They're not as evangelical about breastfeeding here. Remember when Lily was born and it was all about how you must not under any circumstances give her a bottle, otherwise your milk will dry up? Whereas Sister Benedict whisked him away last night, telling me I needed a good sleep – '*Vous avez la petite tête blanche,*'– then reappeared in the morning, like a heavenly white vision of angel with child. He latched on good as gold, no apparent ill effects from the demon bottle.'

'I like that, putting the mother first,' said Nicola.

'I also have the French speciality of *réeducation périnéale* to look forward to.'

'Oh yes, retraining your perineum! What is that exactly?'

'As far as I can work out, they stick an electric device up your "birth passage" to shock the muscles back into working order. I'd really rather not think about it.'

'I couldn't imagine that going down well with my British patients, back in the day.'

It was years since Nicola had stopped working as a GP. It seemed a lifetime ago that she was sitting in her consulting room, hearing all her patients' stories, hoping to improve their lives, praying she wouldn't mess up and miss a vital diagnosis. The chatelains agreed it was a definite plus to have a doctor in their midst, though Beth thought Nicola should go on a refresher course. No disrespect, but things had moved on since she was practising.

'You look such a natural with him,' said Nicola. 'I can't wait to have you both back at the chateau.'

'I'm here for a few more days, getting our money's worth from that health insurance. I'll be quite institutionalised by then, waiting for my lunch tray at midday. John's bringing Lily along later, she can't wait to meet her little brother.'

'Be warned, she will appear massive,' said Nicola. 'I remember when Dom brought you up to the hospital after Gus was born, I couldn't believe this great galumphing child who I used to think of as being so small.'

There was a knock at the door and they both looked up, expecting another appearance from Sister Beatrice. Instead, it was Beth, wearing a big smile, bearing a bottle of Bollinger and a vase crammed full of daffodils.

'Maddie, you star, look at you, you look fantastic!'

She placed the vase on the table – 'I brought it from the chateau, didn't want to go hunting through the clinic for a suitable receptacle' – then reached into her handbag and pulled out three flute glasses.

'They're only plastic, but it's proper champagne. Bolly for the *bébé*. What will you call him? Alain? Emmanuel? Gérard? Let me take a look and decide for you.'

Maddie held the child up for inspection.

'Sacha, definitely,' said Beth, 'he looks like a Sacha to me. Also, it's a suitably trans name, so all bases covered. He's perfect, by the way, well done.'

She poured three glasses, encouraging Maddie to enjoy her first drink for months.

'It will pass directly through you to Sacha, so he can join our celebration. And though it pains me to say so, it's two–nil to you, Nicola. Two beautiful, bouncing grandchildren for you, but where oh where are *mine*?'

'It's not a competition!' Nicola protested.

'So, I'm the goal scorer, am I?' said Maddie. 'You two make me laugh with your competitiveness, anyone would think you once had the same boyfriend!'

'Ooh, sore subject,' said Nicola.

'Sorry, my brain is fuddled with hormones, I didn't mean to mention Simon.'

'It's fine,' said Beth, 'no subject is off the table in our great big happy family. But today's all about you, Maddie. That, and the joyful news that the water supply is once more restored to the chateau, so we don't have to go grovelling to the guests explaining why they can't brush their teeth or flush their loos.'

'I'll drink to that,' said Nicola. 'Here's to a beautiful new life in the chateau, and a functioning plumbing system.'

CHAPTER 13

At a riverside café in Toulouse, Simon slipped off his jacket and rolled up his shirtsleeves to soak up the afternoon sun while he enjoyed his post-lunch cigarette. He could abandon the vitamin D tablets now that winter was over. His sponge bag was bulging with food supplements since he'd decided to take his health seriously, and it had become a bit of a bore to be honest. He poured the last dregs of rosé from the carafe into his empty glass. It was the obvious wine choice in this weather, when at lunchtime you could kid yourself it was high summer as you looked through your sunglasses over the wide expanses of the Garonne. It was only later in the day that the chill came down and reminded you it would be months before the warmth really set in.

He stared at his laptop, open in front of him as it was most days, usually at this café where he often chose to have lunch because of the sweeping river views in both directions. It was also a good vantage point for viewing the small red sculpture of a boy in a donkey hat perched under one of the arches of Pont Neuf. He was supposed to symbolise the city's outcasts, and in his more self-pitying moments, Simon liked to imagine he identified with the little fellow, for were they not both rootless souls, alone in the pink city?

Not exactly alone, he was living with Apolline, in the apartment she had rented on a charming pedestrianised street in the old town. His study was a box room with barely room to swing a cat. It was a far cry from his stately quarters back at the chateau. But if he'd been looking for an artist's garret, he couldn't have asked for better. Up a rickety staircase to an attic space with sloping ceilings and a view over the rooftops which changed colour exactly as was promised: pink at dawn, red at midday and mauve at twilight. It really was the perfect spot for him to carry on with his great work, as was his stated intent. The only thing was, he hadn't.

The memory of the journey down from Normandy would stay with him forever. On a cold January morning, he had climbed into the passenger seat of Apolline's orange campervan. Leaving at dawn, they made the ten-hour journey through narrow country lanes, along broad motorways, and eventually into an underground car park deep beneath the medieval heart of Toulouse. He never dreamed when he first caught sight of that Volkswagen van and its flame-haired owner that this fantasy of freedom and escape could become a reality. A beautiful woman like that falling for a fat old bloke like him – what were the chances? Whenever they stopped for petrol at a service station or for lunch at a village café, he wanted to shout out to everyone there, *Look at me, the luckiest man in the world, on my way to an amazing new life with this incredible woman.*

He believed it would be forever. How could it not be, when he had found his soulmate, his *âme soeur*? True, he and Apolline had not discussed the future, she was a free spirit who lived one day at a time, but it was clear to him how it would evolve, and during the course of that journey south, he saw the rest of his life mapped out ahead of him. The great writer and his actress-turned-artist muse, nurturing their talent and their love in the cultural heart of south-west France. If they made a film about them, he could be played by Gérard Depardieu. Apolline could play herself, naturally, or Isabelle Huppert could step in. Though come to think of it, those actors were both rather old now, maybe Timothée Chalamet and Audrey Tautou would be more appropriate.

Simon finished his lunch, called for the bill, then packed away his laptop and set off on a leisurely stroll along the embankment. He'd decided to visit the modern art museum this afternoon, so he crossed the bridge and walked to the scruffy side of town where a former slaughterhouse had been converted into an imaginative space with plenty of room to display exhibitions of rather obscure artists and photographers. Simon favoured pho-tographs over paintings – at least you could tell what you were looking at, and didn't have to wonder what was in an artist's head when he splashed a couple of lines of colour across a large canvas. He needed to rest after his walk, so he sat down on a yellow metal lounger that was bolted to the ground in the yard in front of the museum, one of a number of isolated chairs ran-domly dotted around in a pattern that baffled Simon. He really didn't understand modern art at all, but no doubt somebody thought this unsociable seating plan was a good idea.

Apolline was home when he returned to the apartment. She had been out visiting her family and was stretched out on the sofa, drinking a tisane, her auburn hair casually spread out over the cushions.

'Hi, how was your day?'

Her tone was light, politely interested.

'Great, thanks. Lunch at the café down on the *quai*, then I went to see that exhibition at Les Abattoirs that you recommended.'

Apolline had already seen it, she had been with her sister. Simon hadn't met any of her family yet as she said it was too soon and didn't want them to jump to conclusions.

'What did you think?'

'I think I should have seen it with you, you might have helped me understand the artist's strengths.'

'Ah, my poor British philistine,' she teased.

'Philistine, phlegmatic, any other national characteristics beginning with "ph" that you'd like to attribute to me?'

'Photogenic?'

'Thank you, I'll take that.'

He put the kettle on to make himself a tisane. He would rather have something stronger but he was trying to be more sensible. Having some distance from the chateau made him realise how decadent their life there was. Endless aperitifs, wine with every dinner; it was around now when the first warm spring weather came in that they would have their first picnic of the year, spreading blankets on the lawn, carrying out trays of amuse-bouches and bottles of Crémant de Bourgogne, to welcome in summer with a kir royale.

'Are you going for a run later?' Apolline asked.

'Of course! You know my routine.'

Like an old married couple, he thought. He would set out soon, puffing his way along one of the routes he'd worked out, through the royal gardens and the Jardin des Plantes, round the *vieux quartier*, along the Quai Daurade. He often spotted more of James Colomina's red boy statues on his runs. At least there was an artist he understood, you knew exactly what you were looking for, and they popped up all over the place, illegally installed – he was like the local Banksy. The hope was that with all this self-improvement – the fitness and the culture – he would win over Apolline, she would commit to the relationship he knew they were destined for, if only they could ramp it up again. The truth was, that since those first crazy couple of weeks, their sex life had rather petered out.

'I picked up a red snapper for our supper,' said Apolline. 'I'll prepare it for your return.'

He opted for a shorter run today, the *bougnettes* meatballs he'd had for lunch were still sitting heavily in his stomach, so he simply jogged up to the magnificent place du Capitole to drink a pastis at one of the many café terraces that were perfect for people watching. He observed a young couple flirting over balloon-shaped glasses of a bright orange drink, and two men of his own age, enjoying a beer together, before going home to their wives, he imagined, though he had no idea of their lives. He'd never felt more alone. Throughout his life, he'd always been at the heart of things, surrounded by people who knew who he was. Nobody here had a clue.

Back at the apartment, he sucked a breath-cleansing mint then took his usual shower and changed into one of his more flamboyant shirts, featuring multicoloured butterflies, before setting two places at the small table beneath the eaves. Apolline had her back to him as she fried the fish, her hair held up with a large tortoise-shell clip, exposing her delicate neck. Simon longed to release it so her hair would tumble down her back.

He poured them each a glass of Badoit sparkling water, and she set the fish on the table, alongside a rocket salad and a tray of oven chips. Like most French cooks, she favoured short cuts.

It was only the silly Brits who thought you should prepare everything from scratch. Simon couldn't recall them ever having frozen chips at the chateau.

'Any news from the chateau?' asked Apolline, as if reading his mind. 'They will be missing you, I think.'

She looked up to check his response. They discussed the chateau often, in passing, but she never asked if he was missing it, if he regretted his decision to leave with her.

'The daffodils were out, was the last I heard,' he said vaguely.

He and Beth had been texting until recently, bland exchanges about practical matters, both of them rowing back from the stand-up argument they had when he announced he was leaving. But he had stopped communicating a couple of weeks ago. He needed a clean break if he was to have any chance with Apolline. Enough of this halfway house, he needed to give this love affair his all.

Apolline took a sip of water and speared a chip with her fork.

'Daffodils, they were the *fleur fétiche* of your poet Wordsworth, I think?'

'That's right, and I love how you say it by the way, much better than 'fetish flower' which sounds a bit pervy in English.'

'"A host of golden daffodils",' she said. 'I remember it from school. We recited it in English lessons, I knew all the words once upon a time.'

'Not my favourite poet, all that goody-goody nature talk,' said Simon. 'I prefer Philip Larkin; he said deprivation was to him what daffodils were to Wordsworth.'

'That sounds rather sad. Are you putting any deprivation in your book? You could rename it *Après Moi Le Déluge – et La Déprivation*. How's it going, you haven't shown me anything since we came to Toulouse?'

'Don't hold your breath.'

'But you are making progress? Your work is important to you, I know that. It is also why I fell in love with you. When I read your words, I could see the beautiful man behind the more . . . comical façade.'

'Comical! Thanks very much.'

Had she not noticed his efforts at self-improvement? The running, the weight loss, the bloody mineral water? It was all for nothing if all she saw was a comical old bloke.

'You know what I mean. You like to be flamboyant, to play the fool, it is part of your charm. But I want to see more of the inner Simon, more of my *âme soeur*. The poet who chose to leave his life behind to follow his destiny, to become my lover.'

At last. There was a glimpse of the passion he feared they might have lost. Simon pushed his plate aside and leaned earnestly across the table.

'He's still here, Apolline. Believe me, I'm still me.'

Simon was in celebratory mood. Maybe it was the red snapper, or maybe it was Apolline's appeal to his inner poet, but something had put the fizz back in their relationship and they'd just spent the most amazing night together.

He came back into the bedroom, his silk dressing gown loosely tied, bearing a morning tea tray.

'Here we are, a tisane for my muse.'

He presented her with a cup of her favourite infusion and admired the way she sat up and drank it, wearing an apricot-coloured negligee. He was endlessly impressed by her trousseau of lingerie: an aubergine baby doll, a lavender satin corset, a rose-pink lace slip. Unlike Beth's functional, shapeless nightdresses.

British women could learn a trick or two from their French counterparts in that department.

Apolline gave him an approving smile.

'We are back to how we were, *mon amour*, that is good news.'

Hooray, he had passed her test! He did wonder if it was his feelings of inadequacy which had caused things to go awry. He had a constant nagging worry that he wasn't good enough, that he was 'punching', to use that horrible expression. What was a goddess like her doing with a regular bloke like him? It could play terrible tricks on a man's performance when you started to have those thoughts. None of that was in evidence last night, he was proud to say!

He snuggled up beside her.

'Look out the window, it's a beautiful morning! Shall we go somewhere together? Shall we feed animals in the park then sing to each other later. "It's such a perfect day, I'm glad I spent it with you." Shall we?'

'You're sweet,' she said. 'But I'm seeing my brother, he's back from Paris for a few days so I'm having lunch with him and our mother.'

'Ah, your mysterious family. I pound the streets alone while you have assignations with all your siblings and cousins, and school friends ... It's the million-dollar question. When am I going to meet them? Are you really so ashamed of me?'

'I am not ashamed of anything I do and that includes you.'

'Phew.'

'But it is too soon for me to introduce you to my family. I need to be sure we are going to last the course. They are still coming to terms with what happened with my husband, and you are an Englishman, like he was. I don't want them to think I'm making the same mistake again.'

'That's intriguing. I'm glad you've mentioned your husband, because you've never actually talked about him. All I know is that when you booked to come to the chateau, you said you were looking to escape your circumstances. I reread the email many times after you arrived, because I didn't like to ask and you never seemed inclined to discuss exactly what it was you were escaping from.'

'I can tell you now,' she said, 'because since I have been with you, I realise that it wasn't my fault. It sounds silly, I know, but I thought there must be something in me that made him . . .'

She paused and rested her head on his chest, preferring not to meet his eye.

'Made him what?'

'It's all right, I will tell you, face to face.'

She sat up and turned to him.

'He left me for somebody else.'

'He's mad, then. Why would anyone leave you, just look at yourself.'

She squeezed his hand.

'*Merci, cheri*. But the person he left me for was much younger. Only twenty-four.'

'Oh, that old cliché! Midlife-crisis man ditches gorgeous wife for younger model,' said Simon, before realising he could be referring to himself. Although he was surely too old to be in a midlife crisis. Possibly not, he'd read the other day that middle age had been pushed back, that sixty was the new forty. In which case, he was at the prime age for committing acts of midlife madness.

He focused his attention back on Apolline and her treacherous husband.

'Where did he meet her, was it online? Or was it old school, in the office, or in a bar?'

'Him.'

'Sorry?'

'He left me for a man. He's gay, you see, but I didn't realise.'

'Oh.'

'I know. How could I not have known? Imagine how stupid I felt.'

She put her hand over her eyes, as it to shield herself from the memory.

'All the clichés that we French believe about Englishmen. You know we joke about you, with your single-sex boarding schools, and your all-male gentlemen's clubs. Your fondness for dressing up in black tie to attend soirées where only men are present. My husband fell into all those categories, and sure enough, he turned out to be gay. And his idiot French wife didn't have a clue.'

'You poor thing, what a shock for you, but how were you to know? After all, there are plenty of Englishmen who went to boarding school and wear black tie who aren't gay.'

'But I didn't marry one of those. I fell for a gay man, dazzled by his charm and good looks. He had beautiful manners and I was very young when we met, I have that in my defence. I was a *jeune fille au pair* and he was a friend of the family where I worked. They invited him to dinner and then he asked if he could show me around London. He took me to restaurants, and many time to the theatre, which I adored, of course.'

'Musicals, I suppose?'

'Yes, lots of musicals, how did you know?'

'Just a hunch. It's one of our clichés about gay men. That they love musicals.'

'Ah. So maybe if I had been English, that would have been a warning sign. How do you call it – my gaydar would have picked it up.'

'Maybe. Though I love musicals and I'm het to the core.'

'Het to the core, I love that!'

She smiled at him. 'I can't tell you what a relief it is to talk to you about this. You're the first person I've told, apart from my family.'

'I'm a good listener, as well as a legendary sexual athlete. At your service.'

She laughed.

'You're funny. So was he, I think that is what attracts me to British men.'

'Our famous sense of humour. Benny Hill. John Cleese. Austin Powers. It's how we lure women into bed.'

'And I was happy to be lured by him. The sex was fine to begin with, but in retrospect I now see that things were not as they should be after a while. I was away a lot when I started working in films, and we lost the habit of intimacy, you might say. But it was nevertheless a big shock to me when he told me he was leaving me for Riccardo.'

'Italian?'

'Yes. He clearly prefers foreigners.'

'It must have been very difficult for you.'

'And for him, if I'm honest. I can see that now.'

'That's very forgiving.'

'At least I didn't realise we were living a lie for all those years. Whereas he must have been painfully aware.'

'And that was when you decided to come away to France. To my great good fortune.'

'Yes, I wanted to see my family and explain to them in person. It's not the kind of detail you can casually throw into a phone call. But I wanted to spend some time in neutral territory first, which is why I booked to stay in Chateau Lafarge.'

'I'm so glad you did. Serendipity.'

Strolling down to the café later that morning, Simon processed the information Apolline had shared with him. He felt keenly for her, the betrayal she must have felt. He admired her subsequent acceptance, and the sympathy she felt for her husband. She had behaved impeccably, as she always did. It was flattering to think that after her trauma, it was he, Simon, who had restored her sexual confidence, though of course it was important not to make this all about him. But come on! Simon the notorious woman-pleaser, he couldn't help it if it put a spring in his step as he nodded to the waiter and sat down at his usual table.

He ordered a carafe of rosé and pulled up his WIP on the laptop. WIP was shorthand for work in progress, he'd learned that at a creative writing course he'd once attended in Wales. A lot of very earnest women, and him, though on that occasion he'd managed not to fall in love with any of them. There was a gloomy sense of everyone arriving with their WIPs, then leaving a week later with them barely changed, apart from a few tweaks. They had to read their work out to each other, which was mortifying, a bit like group therapy, not that he'd had any experience of that. Most of the WIPs were appalling. He wasn't being immodest when he said that his stood head and shoulders above the others. The bar was pretty low.

That first WIP of his had been finished during lockdown. He'd been grateful to have a project to focus on during that strange, static time, when they thanked their lucky stars every day for the giant chateau household that gave them the space and company most people could only dream of. How awful it was for many, trapped in small flats, alone or with people they didn't much like. To his surprise and disappointment, Simon's first novel did not find a publisher and he was too proud to go down the self-publishing route. Instead, he turned his attention to his new work. Forget the artifice of fiction, with its silly plots and character development, he was moving on to deeper matters: philosophy, the meaning of life, introspection on a grand scale were at the heart of *Après moi, Le Déluge*, a non-fiction work of deadly importance. It would prove to Apolline that he was a serious introvert, not the flibbertigibbet extrovert he sometimes appeared.

He scrolled down to read yesterday's paragraphs and was pleased with his progress. Sometimes he surprised himself with his own brilliance. The waiter arrived with the wine, poured some into a glass and set the carafe down on the table. Simon took a sip, then lit a cigarette and sat back in his chair to think about the launch party he would organise when *Après Moi* was published. He knew he'd have to organise it himself, the days of publishers paying for them were long past. Parties don't sell books, as a friend in the business had mournfully informed him. Maybe he could host it here, on the *quai*, he'd seen several private parties taking place on this café terrace, cordoned off with silken ropes. Then there was the guest list, which was a little trickier. It was a bit of a trek to drive down from the chateau, always assuming that things were OK with Beth by then. He was trying not to think about that right now, better to focus on the here and now, take each day at a time, that was Apolline's view.

But it was unthinkable that Beth and his friends wouldn't be there for his launch party. Who on earth was he going to invite, if not them? Eva and James, of course. Or maybe by then he would have made lots of new local friends, but as things stood now, he spent every evening alone with Apolline, in a strange new couple bubble from which they were yet to emerge.

His thoughts were interrupted by his phone ringing, an event so rare that it took him by surprise. Nobody called these days, why would you when you could text? It was Nicola. He stared at her name on the screen. It took him straight back to the chateau, the chaotic community, the hustle and bustle of shared dinners and laughter and arguments.

He cleared his throat to take the call.

'Hey, Nicola, there's a lovely surprise.'

He hoped it wasn't disastrous news, for that was the only time people made actual person-to-person calls, wasn't it? She sounded upbeat, so that was unlikely.

'How are you, Simon? We're all wondering how you're getting on.'

'I'm very well, thank you. I could put you on video chat and show you the mighty Garonne, by whose banks I am currently sitting. But it might make you jealous, especially as I'm sitting here in my shirtsleeves with the sun beating down.'

'Slightly jealous, it's true, but it's warming up here, too.'

'I saw on the website you've updated it with the spring daffodils. Looks very enticing, should bring the bookings flooding in.'

'Already happening! Anyway, I'm ringing with joyful news. We have a brand new chatelain. Maddie's given birth to a little boy, all fine and dandy.'

'A second dauphin! That will put Fizz's nose out of joint! Great news, Nicola, do give my love to the proud parents.'

'Will do.'

'You'll have to source a christening font, hold a humanist baptism in the crystal ballroom, ring in the changes for the new regime.'

'Gorgeous idea! You could officiate, I can just see you as a secular celebrant. Any chance of you coming home, dare I ask? We miss your smiling face and general bonhomie. There's a Simon-shaped hole at the heart of our chateau life.'

'That's very touching.'

There was a pause.

'But you're not answering my question?'

'Not right now. Good news on my book, though, it's progressing well.'

'How about the running?'

'That too. You should see me, I've bought a new mauve running kit. As I zip along, I blend in with the pink stone of Toulouse. The colours here are amazing. Did you know the wealth came from a blue pastel plant that provided luxury dye for the good and the great of Europe during the Renaissance? The merchants made a fortune which they spent building these incredible mansions. You should come down and see for yourself.'

'Too busy, I'm afraid. The chateau doesn't run itself, not to mention the market garden.'

'You're so industrious, you put me to shame.'

'Well, that's partly why I'm calling. There's a feeling here that it's about time your sabbatical ended. We need all hands on deck. Beth was saying the other day how brilliant you are at welcoming the guests, it's your special talent.'

'Right . . .'

'How's Apolline, by the way?'

'Yeah, she's good, thanks. She's got her potter's wheel up and running . . .'

'Say hi from us. Beth tells me you've gone a bit quiet on her recently. She said you were in touch, but she hasn't heard from you for a couple of weeks.'

'As long as that? I guess I've been busy.'

He waited for a response, but Nicola said nothing.

'Is she OK?'

'She's busy, too. Both at the chateau and on her work projects.'

'I see.'

He was suddenly hit by an overwhelming desire to see Beth. Beth who thought he was brilliant at welcoming the guests, Beth who was busy at work and in the chateau, where she would be sleeping in their bed. He missed that room with the ludicrous shepherdesses on the wallpaper. He missed Beth.

'Simon? Are you still there?'

'Sorry. Yes, still here.'

'So you'll let us know, then? When we can expect you home?'

'Yes, I'll let you know.'

They followed up with a few pleasantries, then the call ended. The waiter arrived with a pan of mussels and a bowl of chips, which he set down on the table, warning Simon to be careful as the pan was very hot. Simon thoughtfully dipped a chip into the thin, parsley-strewn wine sauce and put it in his mouth. As he worked his way through his lunch, he thought back to the last occasion he had enjoyed *moules frites*, on a trip to the

Normandy coast last year, just before they opened the chateau to guests. The high summer crowds had disappeared, but the heat lingered on. They took a long table at their favourite restaurant, looking out over the sea. After lunch they sprawled on the beach until they'd taken so much sun that they all had to go for a swim, even though Dougie hadn't thought to bring his swimming trunks, so went in wearing his Y-fronts, to everyone's delight and Beth screamed with laughter at the sight of him in his droopy drawers.

It was pure nostalgia, Simon knew, to cling on to these memories. Yesterday was over, it was tomorrow that counted. He ordered a coffee and a Cognac digestif and reopened his laptop.

CHAPTER 14

'Simon sends his congratulations,' said Nicola to Maddie, who was feeding little Sacha in a nineteenth-century nursing chair which Leo had found at a local auction. She complained it made her feel like a fainting Victorian maiden, the angle of it meant you had to lie in a semi-swooning position, but it looked authentically at home in the crystal ballroom. Beside her stood a rocking wooden cradle which they had discovered hidden away in one of the many attic rooms of the chateau. Leo was pleased with these additions to the room's furnishings, it meant that Maddie could keep the nasty modern baby equipment out of sight, in the cider barn.

'That's nice,' said Maddie, 'did he say when he might be coming back?'

'How about never, there's an idea,' said Beth, pushing a tea trolley into the room, cups and saucers rattling alongside a rich chocolate cake she had made with a view to nourishing the nursing mother.

'You don't mean that,' said Nicola, 'otherwise you wouldn't have kept in touch with him.'

'He's left me, Nicola! More fool me to carry on texting. Anyway, as I told you, he stopped returning my messages a while back. Too busy shagging Apolline. Sorry, Maddie, close your ears.'

'It's all right, now I'm a fully fledged adult, I'm allowed to join in this type of conversation,' said Maddie. 'That cake looks amazing.'

'Nigella's chocolate Guinness cake, packed with iron, see how it even looks like a pint of the black stuff with its frothy cream topping. It's the sweet equivalent of a bottle of stout, which is what they used to give to breastfeeding women.'

She cut a generous slice and placed it on the table next to Maddie.

'Delish, thanks for that, Beth,' said Maddie, helping herself to a mouthful with one hand whilst holding the baby with the other. 'They say it takes a village to raise a child, but actually it takes a chateau – you've all been marvellous.'

Nicola frowned; she found it hard to fathom Beth's feelings about Simon.

'It's probably just a fling,' she said. 'He's bound to come crawling back. The question is, will you find it in your heart to forgive him?'

'My flinty old heart? I don't think so. Did he say anything about the home-wrecking Frenchwoman?'

'Only when I asked. He said she'd set up her potter's wheel.'

'Is that a euphemism?'

'Put it this way, he didn't say he *wasn't* coming back,' said Nicola.

'And as I just said, maybe it's better if he stays away. I'm fine as I am. Did I tell you I'm going to Paris this evening? I've got a work meeting, then I'm meeting Leo for dinner. He's going to introduce me to Luc, his new love interest. Will you manage without me?'

'That's fine. None of the guests are booked in for dinner, so I'm going over to the farm tonight. Dougie and Mary will handle breakfast, you've done more than your fair share recently.

Make sure you report back on Leo's new beau, he sounds very keen on him.'

'I hope it doesn't end in tears. Still, nothing ventured. Luc works in luxury, apparently. Which means he works in the luxury business, it doesn't mean he literally works in the lap of luxury, you know, bathing in asses' milk with servants pouring non-stop champagne. *Il travail dans le luxe*, which he claims is actually very hard work, according to Leo.'

'Intriguing, we'll expect a full debrief.'

Maddie stood up, holding the baby against her shoulder, rubbing his back until he burped.

'I'm going back to the barn, thanks for lunch, you two.'

She walked through the salons into the entrance hall and opened the heavy oak door. The heft of it always charmed her, the thought of it swinging on those hinges for centuries, allowing other women to step outside with their new babies. She could imagine a procession of them, wearing floor-length gowns and conical headdresses with trailing veils, epitomising the elegance of bygone chatelaines. A far cry from her own slouchy tracksuit bottoms. She was still in the comfortable post-birth haze where the days roll into one, rather like an extended Christmas holiday.

Strolling through the grounds, admiring the creamy white narcissi that grew in clumps beneath the fruit trees, she recalled her previous maternity leave, when she and John had arrived from London with baby Lily, aged two months. They slept in the chateau then, while they worked on renovating the cider press, which turned into such an appealing home that they decided to stay forever. Sometimes she had to pinch herself, it seemed too good to be true. Living in this rural paradise instead of the grimy, noisy compromise of a London suburb.

John saw her through the window and opened the barn door. Lily pelted out from behind him and flung her arms around her mother.

'I told my *maîtresse* that my baby brother was called Sacha, she said it's a pretty name.'

'That's sweet, how was school?'

'I'm going to Marie-Louise's party, look!'

She thrust an invitation into Maddie's face.

'We have to go *déguisé*.'

'Fancy dress, wow! Good job Daddy's on paternity leave, he can help you plan your outfit.'

'Four weeks pat leave, can't argue with that,' said John. 'Thank God for the socialist paradise that is France.'

'And for the support of our chateau mates. There's a lot to be said for moving into a retirement community. I just had a lovely lunch with Mum and Beth. They said any time we want to go out, they're very happy to babysit. All of them have said that, actually. When you think what we could be paying a nanny.'

'Just a shame there's nowhere to go,' said John with a laugh. 'We're hardly going to take in a show and a couple of cocktail bars. At a pinch, we could go for a quiet dinner down the road in the Hotel de France.'

They went inside where the domestic chaos contrasted with the stately grandeur of the chateau – brightly coloured plastic toys strewn all over the floor, crayons and paper on the table, small clothes hanging on racks, shoes and boots jumbled up beside the front door. Maddie handed Sacha to John and stretched out on the sofa, patting the seat beside her. Lily jumped up next to her, holding a book. Maddie read her the story, about a scary monster who turns out to have a heart of gold. As she turned the pages, admittedly with the feeling of stifled boredom that always accompanied reading aloud to a child, she thought again how happy she was with the way her life was panning out.

In the bar of Hotel Costes, Beth was on her second mojito, served up by one of the impossibly glamorous waitresses who were obviously models. You could tell by their off-hand manner, which let you know it was a bit of a nuisance you being there. Beth had stood around for several minutes when she arrived, waiting to be noticed while two of them finished their conversation. Now safely ensconced in a dark corner of the opulent room, she could relax and enjoy the spectacle of thin, good-looking Parisians admiring themselves in the mirrors lining the walls.

She was waiting for a contact in the TV world who had asked to meet her, but he was running late. As people mostly were in Paris, she had noticed. She ran a hand over her hair, checking out the sharp new cut. The salon had been recommended and she was pleased with the result, which complemented her severe black clothes. You couldn't go wrong with black, especially in Paris, and especially when you were slightly larger than your average Parisienne. She always used to be a snappy dresser, but it was noticeable how much of a country bumpkin she'd become since moving to the chateau, happily slouching around in baggy old gardening trousers like something out of a Molly Keane novel.

'Beth, *désolé pour le retard,* sorry I'm late.'

A well-presented man of around her age slithered into the seat opposite. She was relieved to be joined by someone who didn't look thirty-five like the rest of the clientele. That was her first impression. Her second impression was that she had seen this man before, but she couldn't place him.

'I am Olivier,' he said. '*Enchanté* to meet you. How was your journey? I know you spend most of your time at Chateau Lafarge, which is what I want to talk to you about. I am familiar with your home because I am from that part of Normandy; I used to visit the chateau when I was a child. More recently I have been following the vlog of your rather alluring fellow chatelaine, Madame Bovary.'

He was straight to the point, Beth thought, and he certainly seemed to know all about them.

'Her real name is Fizz Hodgkins,' she said, 'and her vlog used to be called Mademoiselle Bovary, but she recently changed it to Madame Bovary. An odd way for a woman to change her name – keep it the same but go from Miss to Mrs – but I guess we all have different methods of asserting our feminist credentials.'

'If indeed that is what is what she intended. I thought rather it was a humorous acknowledgment that she has transitioned from a determinedly child-free person to a mother, as happened to Flaubert's heroine.'

'That's true, sorry for my rather po-faced assessment of the name change.'

He smiled at her and she noticed that he really was rather good-looking.

'What fascinates me about your arrangement is the communal aspect of your life in the chateau. We know all about Brits buying our best chateaus *en couple*, those programmes are two a penny, when we see the husband and wife weeping over insanitary conditions and the six figure quotes to repair the roof . . . They are simple-minded, these people, if they think they can afford to restore those palaces on a modest income or from the proceeds of selling their small apartment. We French know it is *hors de prix*, we don't give it a thought, we are far too sensible! So thank goodness for you British. Without you, our *patrimoine* would be crumbling into the ground!'

He beamed at her, inviting her to join in pitying the British fools whilst simultaneously thanking them.

'I'm not sure if that's a compliment or an insult?' said Beth.

'I am not referring to you! No, that is my point. You are not just a boring British couple with a pipe dream, you are a fascinating community of friends, who have established a different way of life. I see it through Madame Bovary's posts. You are mostly – forgive me – quite old, but in your midst you also have young people, new life coming through. I see there is another baby coming soon to join *le petit dauphin*.'

'We already have another one! Born a couple of weeks ago, to my friend's daughter. She and her husband moved over to join us during her first maternity leave, so we have three children now, and one on the way.'

'Perfect! I had no knowledge of that.'

'I think Fizz – sorry, Madame Bovary – is keeping her powder dry. She wants the big splash when her own baby is born. She's already annoyed that Maddie has beaten her to it!'

'That is exactly the kind of rivalry I am looking for. The tensions and joys, the highs and lows of creating a new community within the noble walls of an ancient chateau. *Les Nouveaux Châtelains*, that is my working title. *A New Life in the Chateau* in English. You must agree it has the makings of an excellent TV show, with legs to carry it forward through the coming years, as the children grow up and the original buyers grow old. It is TV gold, in my opinion.'

Beth's mind was spinning as she absorbed the idea. Potentially it could be horribly intrusive, so they would have to control the cameras. The disparate storylines, the paying guests, a walk-on role for Madame de Courcy, Leo camping it up in his glamorous outfits. Professionally, she felt excited. Personally, she believed that provided they maintained full editorial control, it could be an absolute hoot. And lucrative.

It was slowly dawning on her where she had met this man before.

'When you say you are from that part of Normandy, do you still visit the area?' she asked.

'Yes! I grew up in a village a few kilometres away. When I say grew up, of course I went to school in Paris, but my family home is a *gentilhommière* not far from your chateau. I am a frequent visitor.'

'So you sometimes take the train down, to visit your *manoir*?'

'Yes, quite often. I prefer not to drive, the queues leaving Paris are horrendous.'

It was him! She knew it now.

'I think we've met before,' she said.

This was none other than Monsieur *Cheveux de Riches* – she saw the same silver hair curling onto his collar. He was the one who'd eavesdropped on her conversation with Leo all the way down from Paris, then embarrassed them by challenging them in perfect English.

She watched the dawning recognition on his face, as he, too, remembered the shared journey.

'Of course! I thought you looked familiar; I remember thinking there's an attractive British woman with attitude! It's all coming back to me. You were with that very elegant man, who was kind enough to admire my own appearance. He said I had rich man's hair – I immediately looked up the Instagram account when you left the train.'

'I'm sorry, we were both mortified. I'm afraid it's an occupational hazard when you live abroad, you think you can get away with talking about people in English, forgetting that they probably understand every word.'

'It could have been much worse, at least you weren't rude about me.'

'Slightly rude, I think. My father used to tell me, don't make personal remarks, which is exactly what we were doing.'

'I presume your companion on that train was one of your fellow chatelains? I didn't think he was your husband.'

'No, not my husband. That was Leo. It's fair to say he's the darling of the chateau, we all adore him.'

'He's very photogenic. As are you.'

He gave her a smile that made her blush. Then she was annoyed at herself for blushing.

The waitress who had served Beth earlier sidled up to their table. She was wearing a skimpy black dress and had a small, sequinned handbag strapped across her chest. The idea was that the staff looked like sexy customers, rather than paid employees.

'*Je vous écoute*,' she said, without interest. I'm listening, just in case you want to annoy me by ordering something.

'At last, I thought I might die of thirst,' said Olivier. He asked what Beth was drinking, then ordered the same.

'Mojitos, we can embrace our inner Hemingway,' he said, when the waitress had gone. 'Have you been to Cuba?'

Beth was already two cocktails ahead of him, so was more than ready to discuss the joys of Havana with this very agreeable companion, who turned out to have stayed in the same hotel as her, the Nacional, at exactly the same time, a few decades before.

'Most of our best memories are from around thirty years ago, don't you find?' he said. 'It's a function of our age.'

They launched into a warm exchange of recollections, with that particular bond that comes from shared experience, for they might have bumped into each other in the hotel corridor, or unknowingly sat next to each other at breakfast. They recalled going for dinners in private houses in Cuba – there were few restaurants back then – where you risked tripping over hens running wild in ramshackle gardens, before sitting down to the inevitable menu of chicken or fish with rice and black beans which appeared without fail on every table.

'You can imagine, for a French person with our passion for gastronomy, it was a challenging diet,' said Olivier.

'Even for us Brits, the food was disappointing. We're not so far behind you these days. But what a city, with those colourful falling-down Spanish houses and people dancing in the street and vintage pink cars driving so slowly. It was like being on a film set, didn't you think?'

'You're right, I remember looking out over the boulevard towards the ocean and having the same sensation. And imagining I was a 1930s American film star, escaping Prohibition by visiting Havana for a weekend of gambling and drinking, with cigars rolled on a maiden's thigh.'

'I don't suppose they do that anymore. Cigars on thighs I mean.'

'Another pleasure denied. Whatever happened to fun?'

'That was our brief, when we bought the chateau. We wanted to have fun in retirement. We didn't want our lives to sink into a boring decline.'

'And did you succeed? Do you mind if I vape? It's all this talk of cigars. One thing I like about this place is they are very tolerant, they have to be, in order to attract the fashion crowd, who stay thin by smoking instead of eating.'

He pulled his e-cig out of his pocket.

'Not so tolerant of customers who don't pass their beauty test,' said Beth.

'True.'

'Coming back to your question . . .Yes, we did have fun. We *are* having fun. It was a risky thing to do but moving to the chateau was a good decision.'

'Especially now you're going to be stars of the small screen. Tell me what you think of my idea.'

The waitress arrived with their mojitos, removing Beth's empty glass with a disapproving look.

'I think it's a great idea,' said Beth, who had been mulling it over during their conversation. 'I'd need to sell it to the others, but I think they'd be up for it. The money would be handy, there's a ceiling on what we can earn from paying guests and it's so exhausting having to be nice to them all the time. I'm slightly bothered about the loss of privacy, but the beauty of having all that space means that anyone who doesn't want to take part at any point need not do so. They can hide themselves away, the cameras don't have to be everywhere.'

'Exactly. Now I need to hear more detail about your household. I know all about the chateau, I've seen it before, but talk me through the dynamics of the people who call it home.'

Beth gave him a potted history of how the friends had decided to buy a big house together, originally in England, until they realised how much more they could afford in France. The fantasy googling of dreamy chateaux all over the country, the focusing in on Chateau Lafarge, their rapture when they saw it in real life for the first time.

'So, you were four couples and only Leo was single?'

'That's right. Then there was the terrible accident. God, that was awful.'

She took a sip of her drink. These mojitos were pretty strong, in that deadly way of cocktails which taste like fruit juice, then creep up and surprise you.

'Nicola and Dominic,' she continued. 'It was all down to them, really. They were the instigators of the whole project – it was Nicola who came up with the idea. That first year was so chaotic, with all the renovation and adapting to group living. We'd just pretty much settled into it, then we had this gorgeous summer party to celebrate, loads of people came up from the village, it was just how we imagined it should be, living the dream . . . It was that same evening. Dom cycled off to buy some more bread, and never came back.'

She fell silent as she thought back to that terrible night. It was hard not to see it as the defining moment of their history at the chateau. They tried not to think that way, but it eclipsed everything else.

Olivier reached across the table to squeeze her hand.

'I remember reading about that and thinking how awful for you all,' he said. 'It was in the local paper.'

'Front page news. You know how the only stories they have in that paper are about traffic deaths.'

'That would be front page material in any paper with a heart. But you're right about the local paper, which reflects life in the countryside. There is no news there, apart from traffic deaths and *foires à tout* – boot fairs, I think you call them. People live there in order to escape the news, it's the whole point of a rural existence.'

'It was a terrible time; we all did a lot of soul-searching. You know, maybe this wasn't meant to be, we should sell up and go back to our old lives. Though that wasn't possible for Nicola, of course. But then she didn't want to leave, and we realised this was the whole point of the exercise – we were there for each other, it's a massive mutual support system. As well as being fun. Which is what we will focus on for the TV show, obviously. We must hope for no more deaths.'

'I like that idea, it's a strong thread – the community pulling together in terrible times. What about the other couples within the group? Your husband, for instance, where is he this evening? Does he mind that his wife is being entertained by an admirer at a fashionable Paris hotel while he is chopping wood or whatever he does at the chateau?'

'An admirer?'

'Yes, why not?'

'But this is a business meeting.'

'And this is France, we are allowed to admire people even at business meetings.'

He gave her a look. Which she enjoyed. To hell with it, she might as well tell him.

'If you must know, he's not at the chateau. He's in Toulouse with a glamorous French actress. She was one of our paying guests, and he ran off with her.'

'What a fool! If I had a wife like you, I would not be looking elsewhere. I would be keeping you close to me.'

Was he hitting on her? Or was this simply French gallantry?

'And do you have a wife?'

He drew on his vape, and as he exhaled, she noticed the sensuous curve of his lips.

'We're not talking about me, it's all about you, remember. I was wondering why any man would turn his back on a woman like you.'

She watched him devour her with his eyes, a frank, invasive stare as he assessed her. He was sexy, there was no getting away from it.

'Simon – that's my husband – tried to tell me it was just a "sabbatical".'

'Ha, a much-abused term. He's not a professor, is he?'

'No, but he's supposed to be writing a book.'

'Pfft!'

Olivier took another drag, then exhaled his disapproval.

'It beats me why everyone thinks they must have a book inside them. Such a lonely, fruitless task. You can unzip me from here to here . . .'

He drew an imaginary line from his throat, past his chest – she saw it was tautly muscled beneath his close-fitting shirt – and down into his lap.

'. . . and I can assure you, you will find no trace of a book.'

He leaned forward to smile at her, then her words came out before she could stop them.

'I'd like to unzip *you*.'

He raised his eyebrows. 'Interesting. Now, should we order another mojito?'

'Yes, I'm feeling reckless.'

Beth woke up with a fuzzy head and what the French brilliantly describe as a *gueule de bois*, a mouth of wood. This was unusual for her as she prided herself on never suffering from a hangover, no matter how much wine she drank at the chateau. She wasn't at the chateau, though, and – as she gradually recalled – she hadn't been drinking wine, but cocktails. With a man. Oh God.

She slowly opened her eyes and noticed a Christian Liaigre lamp on the bedside table. She knew it was Christian Liaigre because Leo had recently shown her a picture of one in a magazine. It was made of heavy bronze, in the shape of a figure of eight, with an expensive cream shade which blended with the pale, neutral decor of the room. It was a far cry from the colourful huntsmen and maidens featured in the *toile de jouy* wallpaper of her chateau bedroom.

She turned over and was relieved to find she was alone in the bed. She wouldn't say she regretted last night, but she needed space to get her head around it. Then she saw a note tucked under the lamp.

Sorry, early meeting. *Fais comme chez toi* with coffee, etc.
À bientôt, O x

Was that still the form, these days, after a one-night stand, to leave a note? Rather than send a text? Beth wouldn't know, the last time she had a one-night stand, mobile phones hadn't been invented. Slowly, she sat up, then swung her legs round, down to the ground, feeling her way onto the unfamiliar terrain. She padded across the wooden floor, in search of her handbag and clothes which were piled up neatly on a chair. Olivier must have picked them up from the floor on his way out. Should she be offended or grateful that he hadn't woken her? Maybe she had been snoring with her mouth open and he hoped never to see her again. But on the other hand, he did leave the note, so it can't have been that bad.

She gathered up her clothes and went into the bathroom – a gleaming monument to minimalism with a huge walk-in shower and twin basins, though only one toothbrush, she noticed. She stood beneath the raindance showerhead, as she believed it was called, the name suggesting you should raise your arms in a primeval gesture as though bathing in a jungle downpour. She stepped out and wrapped herself in a luxurious towel which bore the embroidered initials 'OdB'. He had a *particule*, she recalled, the all-important '*de*' before your surname which denotes your noble ancestry.

Sitting on the bed, she dried herself slowly and replayed the details of last night. The extra mojitos, the giggling climb into a taxi for the short ride here, the impassioned embrace against the front door before they'd even reached the bedroom, the whispered consent, the no-holds barred sex. She couldn't quite believe it. The joy of it. The whole thing was an amazing, unexpected delight.

Once dressed, she thought about using the single toothbrush, but decided that was an intimacy too far, despite everything that had taken place last night. Her own toothbrush was sitting chastely in the sponge bag she'd left at Mary's flat, where she'd intended to spend the night, before the evening had taken a different turn and she had texted to announce that she had run into a friend who lived in Paris, so wouldn't be requiring the blow-up mattress on Rue Bonaparte. As if. That would take some explaining, but she'd think of something. Or maybe she didn't need to. Mary wasn't her mother, for goodness' sake, and surely when you reached this age, you didn't have to pretend anymore. There had to be some compensations.

She picked up her phone and wandered into the kitchen, opening the cupboards to see what was on offer. This is what it must feel like to be a burglar, prowling through an empty apartment, praying that nobody will come in and disturb you. She would be mortified if the door opened, and she had to explain her presence. She fixed herself a bowl of muesli and slotted a capsule into the coffee machine, then sat down to read her messages.

Leo had texted a reply to hers, when she had cancelled their dinner, claiming her business meeting had run on. Which it had.

Gutted you won't meet my new beau. I'll keep him for next time x

Then another one, sent later last night.

Mary says you ran into an old friend and you spent the night together???!!!

She rinsed her bowl and cup, then walked through to the living room, where two pairs of exceptionally high French windows looked directly on to the gardens of Palais Royal. It had been too dark last night to appreciate the astonishing view – the formal gardens lined up in a long, enclosed courtyard, just a stone's throw from the Louvre. It was built for Cardinal Richelieu, Olivier told her, and he then passed it on to Louis XIII, in the casual way that royalty and high church figures interacted.

She couldn't resist taking a photo and sending it to Leo. He replied instantly.

> Your friend lives in Palais Royal!! Who is it? We must invite them to the chateau, that is exactly the RIGHT SORT of Parisian friend for us. X

CHAPTER 15

Ten days later, Beth was back in full rustication at the chateau. Her Paris adventure seemed from another world as she joined Nicola in the kitchen, preparing the Easter feast. She and Olivier had been messaging about the TV project, but neither of them had alluded to the night they spent together. Nevertheless, she felt a surge of excitement at the knowledge that today she would meet him again. He was staying at his family home nearby, so she'd invited him to join them for lunch. Ostensibly, to meet the chateau residents, the cast of the programme they planned to launch together. In reality, she simply longed to see him again.

There were no believers living at Chateau Lafarge, but Easter Sunday was a big day of celebration. Any excuse for a feast, after all, and the arrival of spring, with its promise of sunny days ahead, was the perfect opportunity to serve up giant platters of lamb. It was always lamb, a convention they'd established in their first year. They did worry about becoming too conservative, but livened up the menu with different side dishes to show they were not stuck in a rut. This year the theme was Middle Eastern, the *gigots* studded with spices, accompanied by a watercress salad with jewel-like pomegranate seeds.

Before lunch, there was an important ritual to prepare: the annual Easter egg hunt. They pretended it was for Louis and

Lily, but in fact Leo had started the tradition before either child was born. It was so tempting, he said, with all that space, and he'd bought up bags full of shiny foil-wrapped eggs which he'd hidden around the garden, just like he was doing today. John was helping him, grateful for an excuse to avoid childcare duties. He adored his kids, but it was pretty relentless, and he was happy to escape with a basket of chocolate treats which he and Leo had scattered through the vegetable plot, the flower borders and now the orchard.

'I've held a few back for us,' said Leo, patting his pocket, 'it's not fair that we should miss out just because we're doing the hard work.'

He reached up to place a couple of eggs on the branch of an apple tree.

'That's a bit high up, don't you think?' said John. 'Anyone who's shorter than you and me would be challenged to find those.'

'People should be challenged, it will encourage them to raise their sights! There are plenty lying around at ground level for those who prefer low-hanging fruit.'

'You sound like you've been reading a business book, whipping yourself up for greater achievement.'

'I have never read a business book, nor will I ever. I can't bear their empty language.'

'How do you know it's empty if you've never read one?'

'I've dipped in, that's enough. Luckily there's no need for business books in the creative world I inhabit. A world where shiny chocolate eggs grow on trees. Now, let's go back up to the chateau and hide the rest of them on the terrace. I'm thinking of those who can't be bothered to tour the entire demesne for the sake of a bit of chocolate.'

Beth came out to find them as they were disposing of the last of the eggs beneath the lavender and rose bushes which grew in large pots the length of the terrace.

'This is exactly the sort of scene that Olivier was imagining,' she said, handing them each a Kir Royale from the tray she was carrying, 'three generations of chateau-dwellers living the dream as they celebrate another annual high point – the great Easter egg hunt.' She had decided it was warm enough for drinks on the terrace and was setting out bowls of nuts alongside the champagne buckets.

'Ah yes, the amazing TV producer who is going to make us all rich and famous,' said Leo, sipping his drink. 'What do you think of the idea, John?'

'I'm all for being rich and famous,' said John, 'but I'm also quite happy living as we do. I like the plan, provided Maddie and I can remain on the sidelines, which we would do, I guess, as we're not living in the actual chateau.'

'It's true, you can opt in and out as you like,' said Beth. 'Nobody has to be filmed if they don't want to be, but Lily and Sacha will be lovely additions, even if their father is camera shy. What a thing it is to be a child with no inhibitions.'

'Can you imagine *not* wanting to be filmed?' said Leo. 'I actually can't wait.'

'It's still early stages, the next step is getting Olivier over to meet us all.'

Beth clinked glasses with them both, then spilt the beans.

'In fact, full disclosure, I've invited him to lunch today. He happens to be staying with his family nearby, so I thought it was the perfect opportunity for him to get to know us in a relaxed setting.'

It was safety in numbers, too, as far as she was concerned. The thought of meeting one-on-one after their last encounter was intimidating. Far better to do it publicly, in the comfortable setting of a chateau family lunch.

'Ooh, I must get changed at once,' said Leo. 'I can't let him see me in these gardening slacks – first impressions are so important.'

'Too late,' said Beth, 'here he comes.'

She watched Olivier walking towards them, cutting an elegant figure in a dark grey jacket and a white scarf. Sex on legs, she loved his loose, confident stride. He was escorted by Nicola, who was pointing out the orchard and the vegetable garden, explaining what they had planted, describing the brassicas they would be taking to market next week. Everybody was arriving now to enjoy the midday sun, little Louis holding his parents' hands, though Fizz had her sights set on Olivier.

Beth admired the way Fizz made a beeline for her target, sweeping up a glass of Crémant on her way. She was in full-on flirt mode, determined to impress.

'Olivier, please take this, so I can have vicarious pleasure from watching you drink it.'

'Ah, Madame Bovary, *merci*!' he said, glancing down at her flowing dress. 'I recognised you at once. Not long now, I imagine, before you will once again be able to indulge in an aperitif.'

Beth was amused to eavesdrop on their conversation. Now Fizz was pretending to be surprised that he knew who she was.

'Am I really that famous? My reputation clearly precedes me! I'm counting the days, to be honest, although I am a moderate drinker. It's just the fact of knowing you're not allowed something that makes you want to have it, don't you find?'

She gave him her most winning smile.

'We are all excited about the TV project,' she continued. 'Beth told us of your plans, I'm thrilled you're a fan of my vlog, which is why I think you'll agree I'm the perfect person to. . . .'

'Yes indeed . . .and there is Beth herself, I must speak with her, please excuse me.'

He dismissed Fizz with a courteous nod, and turned to Beth and Leo.

'Hello again,' he said, and Beth couldn't stop herself blushing as he kissed her on both cheeks. She was glad Leo was there to defuse the moment.

'You remember Leo,' she said, 'though of course you've never been introduced.'

'*Enchanté de vous voir*,' said Leo, bending his knees into a little curtsey. 'What a coincidence that we already met on the train. Beth told me all about it.'

'And how is my hair today, do you find?' Olivier asked with a smile.

'Oh, it's still unbelievably rich. And it's offset perfectly against your charcoal jacket. Silver meets dark grey, couldn't be better.'

'High praise indeed from someone as stylish as yourself.'

'I had no idea you were joining us, Beth just sprung it on me. I told her I would have dressed with more care had I known. As it is, I'm straight from the garden – we've been hiding Easter eggs. I hope you'll be rising to the challenge?'

'I adore a *chasse aux oeufs*. Will that be before or after lunch?'

'After, we'll need the exercise to work off the *gigot cuit a la persane*. Does that sound right? Persian-style lamb?'

'Perfectly expressed,' said Olivier, turning to watch the assembling throng on the terrace. 'I see we are quite a crowd; do you have any of your paying guests joining us for lunch?'

Leo shook his head.

'That would be a step too far. It's like they say about marriage – for better, for worse, but never for lunch. Dinner for the guests is by arrangement, but lunch is family time. We have a full house at the moment – all six rooms are taken, so breakfast and dinner give us more than enough exposure. Now, if you'll excuse me, I can see Nicola beckoning me over, I suspect she needs a hand in the kitchen.'

He walked off, leaving Beth and Olivier standing together in an awkward silence, looking at their shoes. Olivier spoke first.

'So, Beth, how have you been? This is a very different setting from our last meeting in Paris. And for the first time, I see you in daylight.'

She looked up.

'Not too frightening a sight, I hope?'

He smiled. Devastatingly handsome, thought Beth.

'Not at all,' he said. 'If anything, you look even more ravishing in the natural light, away from the artifice of the hotel Costes and the mood lighting of my apartment.'

'Listen, about the other night—'

Olivier raised his hand.

'I know, it's fine. There is nothing to discuss.'

'Oh. I see.'

It meant nothing to him, then.

'What is it you have written on your cushions? I have seen it in many British homes. Ah yes, I remember – "Keep Calm and Carry On".'

'Those awful cushions with a picture of the crown?'

'Yes!'

'So, I remind you of our royal family?'

'No! I mean . . . we don't need to make a drama of it. If you don't want to. Of course, I would love us to carry on . . .'

Her heart leaped. He *did* want her.

'But I know your circumstances are a little more complicated than mine . . .'

'I don't think we discussed your circumstances.'

'I thought you may have gathered that I am a respectable divorcé?'

'It's true I only spotted one toothbrush in your bathroom . . .'

'Ah, but there you were jumping to conclusions. Suppose that apartment was my *garçonnière*, the bachelor apartment where I entertain my mistresses, while my wife languishes in the countryside.'

He was teasing her, she realised.

'You keep a wife in your Norman residence? But no, I think you would have mentioned it.'

'Yes, I would have mentioned it. You see, not all French men are faithless seducers. Though naturally I would love to take you off to bed right now, to do those unspeakable things again.'

His smile made her feel weak. Then Dougie and Mary came over to introduce themselves, and the conversation took a different turn.

'Thank goodness we didn't offer the guests dinner tonight,' said Nicola, 'that would have been a step too far.'

She was sitting in the petit salon with Leo and Beth. The nights were still chilly enough to merit an open fire, which flickered before them as they discussed the day's events and looked forward to the week ahead. The other chatelains had drifted off to bed, but the three of them were too cosy to move, curled up in their armchairs, drawn to the confessional warmth of the fire.

'I put a mini bowl of Easter eggs in each of their rooms,' said Leo, reaching forward with a poker to stir the embers. 'It's those little touches that make the difference when it comes to the reviews.'

'There was plenty of chocolate left over. I'm completely stuffed,' said Beth. 'Though I wouldn't mind a few negative reviews now. I can't help thinking we've become victims of our own success. Slaves in our own chateau. To be honest, I preferred it when we only had two guest rooms.'

'Says the touchiest of us all!' said Nicola. 'You go mental when anyone makes a critical remark on Tripadvisor.'

'Our new maid Sylvie starts tomorrow, that will make a big difference,' said Leo.

'You shouldn't use that word,' said Beth, 'it makes us sound like Downton Abbey.'

'Maid is a respectful term in my book.'

'It's demeaning and outdated. And gendered. You don't get male maids.'

'Well, she's starting tomorrow anyway, our *femme de ménage*. Maria has met her and given the thumbs up and I'm glad she's French. Madame de Courcy remembers Sylvie's grandmother working at the chateau, so we have ancestral continuity.'

'Thank God for that.'

'That's enough servant talk,' said Nicola. 'Don't you think today was our best Easter lunch ever?'

'Definitely,' said Leo. 'Everyone was on their best behaviour because of Olivier. He's quite a dish, isn't he? A bit of a flirt, too. Do we know anything about his private life?'

'Divorced, I believe,' said Beth, looking at her fingernails.

'A bit of chemistry between the two of you, I'd say,' said Nicola.

'Hmm. We'll work well together I think.'

'He told me he thought about approaching our rivals at the other chateau!' said Leo. 'Thank goodness he didn't, I would have been beside myself at the thought of Oscar and Jeremy being on telly instead of us. Luckily, he knew from Fizz's vlog that we were a multigenerational group, so much more interesting than a nuclear couple of gays. Plus, you have me to play that diversity card.'

'Our exotic bird,' said Nicola. 'When are we going to meet Luc, by the way? You're keeping him very much to yourself.'

'I'll invite him to stay at the chateau when the time is right, but for now it's a Paris-based relationship. I'd introduce you if only you'd leave the garden behind and come to town. Beth missed her chance the other week. Luc was all set to meet the family, then she claimed she couldn't make dinner as her meeting had overrun.'

He turned to Beth.

'You were with Olivier, I suppose. You could have brought him along, he's a nice piece of eye candy.'

'Oh yes, I remember now,' said Nicola. 'Mary said you ran into an old friend and spent the night at her apartment. I meant to ask you about that, was it someone from uni?'

'She's obviously done all right for herself, whoever it was,' said Leo. 'She lives in the Palais Royal, no less, Beth sent me an appetising photo of the view over the gardens.'

'The Palais Royal? That's a coincidence,' said Nicola. 'I was talking to Olivier today about Paris and he said that's where he lives. I wonder if he knows her?'

Beth shifted in her chair. Her silence spoke volumes. Then Leo shrieked in delight.

'No! You dark horse, I can't believe it! Come on, tell us all. How, when, what? All the details, please.'

'What do you mean?' asked Nicola. 'Have I missed something?'

'Keep up, Nicola!' said Leo. 'Palais Royal, massive coincidence? I don't think so. Beth spent the night with none other than that smooth-talking silver fox, Olivier.'

'Beth, is it true?' asked Nicola.

Beth nodded.

'It's true. But it's fine, honestly. I'm telling you because . . . well because I have no choice actually, you kind of backed me into a corner.'

'As long as Olivier didn't back you into a corner?'

'Oh no, nothing like that! Totally consensual.'

'Consenting adults over the age of sixty,' said Leo, 'who'd have thought it? I'm in awe.'

'I can't quite believe it myself,' said Beth. 'But don't worry, it's not going to interfere with the TV project in any way.'

'Never mind the project,' said Nicola, frowning. 'I'm only interested in you. In your mental wellbeing.'

Beth laughed.

'You think I'm not right in the head because I slept with Olivier?'

'It sounds very sane to me,' said Leo. 'There I was feeling sorry for you because Simon's gone AWOL, and you're having a marvellous adventure of your own. Hats off, I say.'

'How often? Was it a one-off?' asked Nicola.

'Only that once. So far. I would say it was down to the mojitos and reminiscing about Cuba, but that might make me sound irresponsible. I was thinking, maybe I shouldn't tell you, but then I thought, why not? I'm a free agent after all since Simon's deserted me. If you can't be frank at our age, when can you?'

'Exactly. I'm not judging you, not at all. I'm just amazed.'

Jean-Louis was almost asleep when Nicola slipped into her bed beside him.

'At last,' he said. 'I thought you were giving me the cold shoulder, that you prefer to sit by the fire with your English friends, rather than share your bed with your French lover.'

'Never! Well, I do like sitting by the fire, it's true. But guess what? You're not the only French lover round here.'

'Really? You have someone else?'

'Not me. Beth.'

Jean-Louis flipped around to face her.

'That is news, indeed! But should you be telling me? It's not very discreet.'

'She says it's no secret. Says she's too old for all that. And they are both free agents.'

'I'm not sure Simon would agree.'

'He's not in a position to disagree.'

'True. So, tell me, who is her beau? '

'Olivier. He was at lunch.'

'The TV person? *Oh là là!*'

'I can't believe you really say that. *Oh là là.* It sounds like you've stepped out of a comedy sketch.'

'He's a charming man. I hope she knows what she's doing.'

'I think she does, she's very cool about the whole thing. I'm not, though.'

'Why not? She is a grown woman.'

'I know it's ridiculous, but it's as if I've just found out my parents were cheating on each other. First Simon and now Beth. Why can't they just be happy together. I'm worried it's threatening the stability of our chateau family.'

He drew his arms around her.

'It's their business. It will all work out, believe me. What is important is that you and I are happy together. We had a wonderful Easter Day, and we have many years ahead of us.'

'It was a wonderful day, wasn't it?'

'My mother loved it too. When she sat at the table next to your adorable grandchildren, she said she felt privileged to be part of this community. That she was blessed to see the chateau come to life again, even if it is full of British people. That she couldn't think of a better way to celebrate our Lord's resurrection. I know you will excuse the religious reference.'

Nicola was glad she'd invited Anne. The advantage of a large gathering was that tensions were lost in the crowd. Far better than sitting in a quiet threesome, which they sometimes did down at the farmhouse, when Nicola would invite her quasi mother-in-law to dinner. On one occasion, Nicola had cooked a *côte de boeuf* which wasn't entirely to Anne's satisfaction, leading to the cooking lesson. She had invited Nicola into her kitchen the following week to show her how it should be done.

'I'm pleased your mother was there to remind us of the religious significance, we're such a godless lot. Normally Madame de Courcy plays that role, but she had to stay at home with a cold.'

'The ex-chatelaine and the tenant farmer's widow. Your real French neighbours, always around to remind you of the chateau's place at the heart of our village,' said Jean-Louis. 'Here, I have something for you.'

He reached down to fetch a box which he'd stored under the bed, then presented her with a dark chocolate bell, tied with a red and gold ribbon.

'You must know the story of the *Cloches de Pâques*? On the Thursday before Easter, the church bells fall silent in mourning. They sprout wings and dress up in fine ribbons, then fly to the Vatican to be blessed by the Pope. On Easter Sunday, they fly home to their steeples, dropping off chocolate eggs and animals on the way. Then they ring out in celebration, someone will shout out, '*Les cloches sont passés,*' that is when the children know it is time for the egg hunt! I explained this at lunch, but alas, you were at the other end of the table. So, here is your bell. Happy Easter, *chérie*.'

'Ah, thank you, I love it. You Catholics and your fanciful stories.'

'But we must have stories! They make our lives much richer, don't you agree?'

'I do. A world with no stories is no world at all.'

'And my favourite story is the love story which began when you arrived at Chateau Lafarge and stole my heart.'

He was so romantic, she thought, as she sank into his arms. She was possibly the luckiest woman alive.

A few doors down the corridor, Beth was lying in bed, reading a text from Olivier.

> Thank you for a wonderful afternoon. I adore your chateau community. And I adore you.

She paused before replying. How much did he adore her? Did he adore her more or less than he adored her chateau community? And how could he adore either, based on such fleeting encounters? Then she remembered how easily the French used the word 'adore', bandying it around on any occasion. She had heard them adore a coffee eclair, a pair of shoes, a flower arrangement. It was nothing personal.

She tapped out her response.

> They liked you too.
> *Tant mieux.* Just as well.

Should she let him know that their affair – if indeed you could count it as such – was now out in the open? True, she had only told Nicola and Leo, but she hadn't sworn them to secrecy.

> In fact, I've told them about us.
> Really??!!
> I thought, why not. You don't mind?
> *Au contraire*. But I had the impression you wanted discretion? For me, there is no reason to be discreet.

She might as well put her cards on the table. Recklessly, she tapped out a message.

> I want to carry on seeing you.
> ☺ ☺ ☺. Oh, but maybe you mean only for the project?
> Not just the project.
> I want you now. *J'ai envie de toi.*
> I'm in bed.
> *Précisement*. See you in ten minutes x.
> You're mad! *Tu es fou!*
> *Fou de toi.* Meet me by the front door, I'd better not ring the bell.

Beth leaped out of bed and pulled on her dressing gown. She picked her dirty clothes up off the floor and stuffed them into the laundry basket. She didn't want to put him off. Then she opened the bedroom door and stood silently in the corridor, making sure there was no sound of life. Everyone was asleep, she was safe. She tiptoed down the vast staircase. If anyone saw her, she was going to make a cup of tea.

Standing in the darkness by the window, she saw the head-lights approach. She opened the huge oak front door as quietly as she could, then took her lover by the hand and led him up the unlit stairs, praying that nobody would choose that moment to leave their room.

She closed the bedroom door behind them, and they laughed like children. Such behaviour! Then he took her in his arms and they stopped laughing.

CHAPTER 16

Easter Monday saw a mass evacuation of the guest rooms; Sylvie's arrival was well timed to assist Leo with the breakfast service. He was delighted by her trim black dress and the upticks of her eyeliner. She was, in his opinion, the quintessential chic French maid.

'We're one step closer to a fully staffed home,' he said, coming into the scullery with a tray of dirty plates for Mary to stack neatly in the dishwasher. 'Sylvie is delightful with the guests. I can see we'll get great mileage out of her telling them about her family connection with the chateau. As long as they speak French, of course, her English isn't up to much.'

When the last guests had driven away, Sylvie joined Maria to strip the beds and make up the rooms for the next arrivals. Mary shooed Beth and Nicola out of the kitchen. They had done more than their fair share putting on yesterday's lunch and she wanted them to relax and let her do what she did best and restore the kitchen to gleaming cleanliness.

Nicola set a pot of coffee on a tray and suggested to Beth that they take it outside: the sun was warm and the terrace the perfect place from which to admire the frothy blossom on the plum trees. These early flowerers were the warm-up act, followed by pear, then apple blossom at the end of April through early May, when trees burst into life throughout the cider orchards of Calvados. The women sat in silence for a while, each wondering how to broach the subject that was on both their minds.

'I was up early this morning,' said Nicola eventually, 'and happened to notice a Tesla driving off as I was waiting for the kettle to boil. As you know, I'm not big on cars, but I recognised this one because Olivier was talking me through its merits at lunch yesterday.'

'Ah. It's a very smooth drive, apparently.'

They both started laughing.

'You're a dark horse, smuggling in your lover!' said Nicola. 'I've got to hand it to you.'

'It was a spur of the moment thing, we were texting, then suddenly, there he was! I hope no one else noticed.'

Nicola's expression grew serious.

'I have to say this to you. I do hope you're taking precautions.'

Beth rolled her eyes.

'Thanks, Mum, but I've got news for you. At my vast age, I am beyond the risk of unwanted pregnancy. It's one of the few advantages.'

'I'm not talking about pregnancy. I mean STDs. They are massively on the increase amongst the elderly, you know, I was reading about it the other day.'

'Oh God, what a horrible thought. And who are you calling elderly?'

'We are all elderly. Or borderline elderly.'

'So elderly that we were brought up with the fear of VD rather than STDs. Which do you think sounds worse, venereal disease or sexually transmitted diseases?'

'Whatever it's called, you don't want it.'

'Obviously.'

'So?'

'This is completely mortifying.'

'Think of me as your GP, not as your friend.'

'Well, Doctor, the answer is no. We did not take precautions, as you put it. And can we please stop this conversation here, it's making me feel very uncomfortable. I'm happy to talk about other old lady matters such as beard hairs and sneezing incontinence, but I draw the line at sharing details of my sex life. I wouldn't ask you about your intimate relations with Jean-Louis.'

'Fair enough. I just felt it was my doctorly duty to share that health advice.'

Nicola poured them each a cup of coffee.

'So come on then, talk to me. What is this thing with Olivier?'

Beth took a sip of her coffee.

'I don't know what it is, but it feels fantastic! Possibly the most fun I've ever had. Entirely reckless and thrilling. Does that shock you?'

'It's not about me being shocked!'

'I'm just living in the moment, isn't that we're supposed to be doing at our age? That's what Simon's done!'

'Simon will come back, we all know that. And then what will you do about Olivier?'

'I'll just see what happens. Olivier knows the situation. He thinks I'm having a revenge affair to get back at Simon.'

'Hmm. Well, I guess it's your business, that's what Jean-Louis said.'

'You told Jean-Louis!'

'Yes! You said it wasn't a secret and I took you at your word.'

'That's true, I suppose.'

'Anyway, he said it was your business, and had nothing to do with us, but I disagree. It's a family matter.'

'Since when did you become so judgemental! I didn't have a go at you when you fell into Jean-Louis' arms with what might be considered indecent haste after poor old Dom died! In fact, I encouraged you. Oh no, sorry, Nicola. That was low of me . . .'

Nicola shook her head.

'No, you're right, maybe it was too soon. But my romance was a long time brewing. It wasn't a drunken one-night stand to get back at my husband.'

'Ouch.'

'Sorry.'

'Two-night stand, actually, and counting. Many more to come, I hope. I'm having the time of my life, it's just so wild! Can't you understand that?'

She turned to Nicola, wanting her friend's support on this exciting new chapter. But Nicola shook her head.

'The whole thing's going to implode when Simon comes back. There will be a horrible atmosphere in the chateau, all recorded on camera under the supervision of your lover! Can't you see how this will affect us all?'

Beth slammed down her coffee cup.

'If I can just stop you there! Firstly, remember that Simon left *me* and probably has no intention of returning to the chateau. Secondly, how do you know it will all end in tears, are you a soothsayer? And thirdly, since when is it up to you what I get up to in my private life? It's all right for you, in your cosy arrangement with your cute French boyfriend and your perfect grandchildren, but maybe I've got a bit more fire in my belly! Maybe I want to look beyond the chateau walls to see what else is out there! I'm not quite ready to crumble into group retirement with an ageing bunch of losers.'

She stopped to draw breath, then qualified her last remark.

'Not that I think we are losers, by the way. We are an adventurous group of friends committed to seizing the day and making the most of our autumn years. Or winter years. Our later years, anyway. In my case, I've had something unexpected and rather marvellous come my way, and I'm not about to walk away from it because you're worried it might upset our goody-goody family life at the chateau.'

Nicola stared at her in admiration.

'Wow, that's an impassioned plea for the rights of the autumn-aged. I'm in awe. "Rage, rage against the dying of the light." Our very own Dylan Thomas right here in the chateau. I take it all back. You must do your thing, and we'll just see what happens. Friends?'

She reached across to take Beth's hand.

'And congratulations on being a legend.'

'So ends the awkward sex chat,' said Beth with a laugh, 'which is just as well since here comes your daughter. The last thing she'd want to hear is her mum talking STDs with her mate.'

Nicola looked round to see Maddie hurrying up the terrace steps towards them, baby Sacha balanced on her hip.

'Will's taken Fizz to hospital,' she said, 'the baby's coming.'

Will sat beside the hospital bed, cradling his new-born son. He'd pulled the curtains around them for some privacy. They were on a public maternity ward with three other families – there were no nuns or fancy treatment for Fizz, who was staring at her child in a state of shock.

'I was convinced it was a girl,' she said. 'I felt it in my bones, and I could tell from the scans.'

'None so blind as those who will not see,' said Will with a smile. 'He's gorgeous, I couldn't be happier.'

'I know. He scored ten out of ten on the Apgar test, did you see? It's just . . . I can't get my head around it, I've been talking to her for nine months, and now it turns out she's a he. I should have asked the doctor, I told her I didn't want to know the sex because I thought I already did. How could I be so stupid?'

Her eyes filled with tears and Will leaned in to hug her, sandwiching the baby between them.

'He's perfect, we are so lucky, you know that's true.'

'It's your fourth son,' said Fizz, 'you should be even more disappointed than me. Don't tell me you weren't looking forward to finally having a daughter?'

'Well, yes, but mainly because that's what you wanted, what you thought we were getting.'

He should have paid more attention during the scans, in retrospect, but it was difficult to make anything out on those grey screens which showed nothing noticeably human. Instead, he'd just nodded along each time and relied on Fizz to interpret the results.

'I can't believe I got it so wrong,' said Fizz, smacking her hand on the bedcovers. 'I have all those baby girl clothes at home which I'm meant to be promoting. I'll have to send them back, I'm going to look like an idiot. Lunatic woman fails to understand her baby scans and thinks she can tell the sex of her child by second sight. It's not very credible, is it?'

Will gently passed over her infant son.

'Don't think about things that don't matter,' he said.

Fizz took the baby and lowered her face to brush her lips against his wax-covered head. She ran her fingers over his silky brown hair and breathed in the smell of him. It was musky and sweet, but also like fresh bread. There were no words for that smell, she thought.

Suddenly her face lit up.

'I have it!' she said. 'I don't know why it didn't occur to me right away. I'll dress him in girl's clothes, it's bang on trend! Well, gender fluid clothes are on trend, but I can go further and actively put him in girly dresses. It's how baby boys were always dressed in Victorian days, you've seen the photos. Long hair and dresses until at least the age of three! It's a perfect look, it will go down a storm on the vlog. A tiny Harry Styles for the chateau, and just in time for the TV show.'

She was always full of surprises, Will thought, as he watched her becoming energised by her new idea, channelling her disappointment at the unexpected into an opportunity, though you couldn't possibly think of that beautiful little boy as anything other than a total gift. He'd been present for the births of all his children, but this time he had felt it particularly keenly. An emotional rush, that this small child was his legacy. It didn't matter at all what happened to him, it was this baby who was the future. He would literally give his life for him.

He leaned forward to stroke the child's head.

Fizz looked at him in disbelief.

'Will, are you *crying*?'

He briskly wiped away a tear.

'What if I am? I'm allowed to feel things, aren't I? I'm looking at my son here, and you. And thinking, how did I get to be so lucky?'

*

In Toulouse, Simon and Apolline were strolling through the Victor Hugo covered market. Apolline's floaty orange dress was accessorised by the carrot fronds, dill and parsley leaves emerging from her elegant wicker basket. Simon was pulling a shopping trolley laden with provisions for the week ahead.

'You wouldn't see this in the UK, you know,' he said. 'British men don't use baskets on wheels, full stop. They are considered the preserve of frail old ladies, who favour the four-wheeled models, which can double as a walking frame.'

Apolline frowned.

'But that is a silly attitude, the *caddie* is such a practical device, perfect for shopping in the market, unless you want to exhaust yourself by carrying heavy bags. *Vraiment*, you English could learn a great deal from us.'

'You're right as usual,' said Simon, 'though I do think we're more creative when it comes to choosing place names. Why, for instance, is this called the Victor Hugo market? He wasn't from Toulouse, was he?'

'No, but I happen to know there are more than two and half thousand streets throughout France which are named after him.'

'That's the thing about you French, you know who your heroes are, and you stick with them. Let's hope Victor Hugo is never cancelled, think of the massive work involved in renaming all those addresses.'

He paused by a butcher's stall, inspecting the trussed birds laid out in ascending order of size, legs neatly tucked beneath them.

'Shall we have quail one night, what do you think?'

Apolline nodded and the butcher gave her an admiring glance.

'It's her, isn't it, Apolline Fleurie?' he whispered to Simon as he wrapped up the birds. 'My wife adores her films. You are a lucky man!'

Simon smiled his acknowledgement that, yes, he was the fortunate consort of this French screen legend, then took the small parcel from the butcher and placed it in his trolley. It weighed so little – he was still adjusting to living in a two-person household. At the chateau, they would have bought fifty quails, at least, for their mass catering operation. He thought about their own quails in the grounds there, housed in a cute wooden hut which Will had constructed, and how unthinkable it was to even suggest slaughtering them for the table. They were pets with a purpose, as Beth referred to them, whenever she returned, glee-fully, with a trug full of their freshly laid eggs.

'I used to love the quail eggs you served at the chateau, with the aperitif,' said Apolline, as if reading his mind.

'I know.'

'Let's buy some, we can have them for lunch,' she said. 'Look, he has them for sale.'

The butcher handed her a box of the tiny eggs, pleased to have interacted with this famous actress. He would tell his wife all about it later, how she was accompanied by a rather stout man with a foreign accent. He had heard she was married to an Englishman, this must be him.

Back at the apartment, Apolline boiled the eggs and served them up on a bed of lettuce, along with some sliced radishes. Saturday was the one day in the week that they had lunch together; on Sundays she usually visited her family, which didn't involve Simon. There was plenty of time, she said, for him to meet them, it was still early days.

Simon took a bite of the egg, seasoned with celery salt, the way they did at the chateau, but it didn't taste the same. When he ate them there, it was in the crystal ballroom or the dining room, full of his friends, laughing together. Or on the terrace, looking out over the gardens and orchards that had been nurtured by generations of chatelains before them. Here, in this bijou apartment, his view was restricted to the – admittedly very alluring – sight of Apolline, daintily nibbling on her sensibly light lunch.

His phone buzzed, and he guiltily pulled it out of his pocket. They weren't supposed to have their phones on at mealtimes, but Apolline nodded her assent.

It was a message from Nicola, announcing the birth of Will and Fizz's baby son. They had a group WhatsApp for the chatelains, but Simon had signed out shortly after arriving in Toulouse because reading the messages made him feel like a ghost, as if he'd died, and was revisiting the people and places he'd left behind. Sometimes he imagined sneaking back to the chateau, then pulling a sheet over his head to jump out from behind a pillar, offering a surprise haunting.

'Any news?' asked Apolline.

'Nicola, letting me know that Fizz has had a baby boy. She seems to have adopted the role of town crier for Chateau Lafarge. Every time she contacts me, it's to announce the birth of a child. I can just imagine her ringing her bell and pinning a note to the chateau gates.'

'Fizz wanted a girl, I think. But he is healthy? That is all that matters.'

'Apparently so. And she's planning to dress him in girls' clothes to make up for it. They're having a celebration dinner tomorrow, to welcome him home. Fizz left hospital this afternoon.'

'That is good news for them. And they always find a reason to celebrate in that chateau, don't they? When I think back to my time there, it was non-stop parties, I couldn't believe it when I arrived from my quiet life in Henley-on-Thames.'

Non-stop parties. Those were the days, thought Simon, with an almost physical ache.

'That was the idea, when we clubbed together to buy a massive house,' he said. 'To make the most of our autumn years. You must admit it's a good plan?'

'For the gregarious, of course. And I think you miss it?'

She looked at him quizzically across the table.

'They're about to become even more gregarious, with the TV series,' said Simon. 'Filming starts next month, according to Nicola.'

'That must be tempting for you, in view of how you like to play to the camera.'

He shook his head, trying to convince himself.

'No, that's the old Simon. The new Simon is here, this is what I am now. Living with you in this bohemian loft, dedicated to writing my book. That is my focus.'

'Are you sure? I'd hate to think I was keeping you from where you'd rather be?'

Her tone was playful, not at all possessive. Could it be, he thought, that she was finding their relationship less all-consuming than he liked to believe it was.

'Apolline, I'm here because I want to be! And I thought you wanted me here, but correct me if I'm wrong.'

'I love you being here,' she said, 'but we are grown-up people. If ever you felt you wanted to return to the chateau, I would understand. Especially with the opportunity to be part of the TV programme. I have had my time in front of the camera, it holds no appeal for me. But for you, I think it is a different matter. And I might enjoy watching the results.'

There was no doubt about it, she was definitely giving him the Get Out of Jail Free card, should he wish to take it.

He immediately banished the thought. Get out of jail, indeed. When he was living this wonderful life with a beautiful woman way out of his league. Who might be showing signs of indifference? No! She was just being her usual considerate self.

'Thank you for lunch,' he said. 'If you'll excuse me, I'm going to work this afternoon. I haven't made quite the progress I'd hoped for this week.'

'Fine by me, I'm going shopping with an old school friend. It's been so long since I've bought any new clothes.'

Simon kissed the top of her head and went into the spare bedroom, wedging himself into the armchair which shared the small space with the potter's wheel. Apolline didn't like him working in their bedroom, so when she was at home and not working with clay, this was where he sat, his laptop perched on his knees as there was no room for a desk. He thought about the enfilade of massive reception rooms at the chateau, each salon leading into the next, a fantasy of space and luxury.

He opened his laptop and corrected a couple of words in his last paragraph. Fiddling while Rome burns, he thought, when you considered the enormity of the task ahead. Still, one day at a time. His phone rang – thank goodness, a reprieve – and it was his daughter Eva. She often rang him on a Saturday, he'd noticed, probably while James was watching sport. She had been remarkably non-judgemental about his change in circumstances, he had been pleasantly surprised.

'Hello, darling, how lovely to hear from you.'

'Hey, Dad, how are you? Listen, never mind the small talk, have you spoken to Mum recently?'

'No, not recently. I thought it was better to leave things for the time being.'

'I'm worried about her. I think she's gone a bit weird.'

'How do you mean?'

'Well, she keeps going on and on about this TV programme they're going to make at the chateau. Terrible idea, by the way, I think you'll come to regret it. Not you, obvs, as you're not there.'

'I heard about it. Sounds quite exciting to me, but I hear your reservations.'

'And she doesn't stop talking about this producer whose idea it was. He's got a house nearby, she says, but it sounds like he's round there all the time.'

'That's normal, surely, if he's putting the show together?'

'It's more than that, I think she's got an embarrassing crush on him. It's bad enough you running off with another woman, I don't want Mum behaving badly as well. It really is quite cringe. I think you need to get back there and see what's going on.'

Back to the chateau, thought Simon, *what a very enticing prospect.*

'I will go back at some point, but I'm sure you're making a fuss about nothing.'

'I just don't want her making a fool of herself. I'm like, please don't become the most embarrassing mum ever. He's French, too, and we know what they are like.'

'That's a very prejudiced remark, we love the French. We live amongst them.'

'Of course *you* do. One in particular, the willowy Apolline. Is she there, by the way?'

'No, she's gone out clothes shopping.'

'Don't tell me. Emerald green robes and ribbons for her auburn tresses, rocking that pre-Raphaelite look.'

'Now, now.'

'The thing is, if you were at the chateau, you could keep an eye on Mum.'

'She's not likely to think that's my role.'

'I know it's not your role, I'm not asking you to control her or anything. But think of me! How mortifying it would be if it goes out on telly, and there she is, mooning after this Olivier . . .'

'He's not going to appear in it, is he?'

'She says yes! He's going to appear as the visiting neighbour, you know, like Mr Knightley riding over on his horse from the nearby manor house. It's going to look like he's sweeping Mum off her feet, it could be ghastly!'

'Mum's far too sensible for anything like that.'

It was true that the idea of Beth being swept off her feet was absurd. For a start, she wasn't exactly bimbo material. A handsome woman of a certain age, for sure, but not a candidate for becoming a Frenchman's mistress! Plus, it just wasn't in her nature to have her head turned. It was her caustic, no-nonsense attitude that he loved about her. And which would always prevent her from doing anything stupid.

Eva was in full flow now, putting the pressure on.

'And anyway, quite apart from that, I think you should be in the show. I know I said it's a terrible idea, but if it's happening, you need to be there. You have charisma, just like me, and you need to share it. When it does go out, I want to be able to tell my friends that my dad's on the telly.'

'Well, when you put it like that. I promise I'll give it some thought.'

Their conversation ended and he picked up his laptop to return to work. The open document had vanished from the screen, so he clicked on the icon to get it back. Then frowned.

The version he was looking at was just two paragraphs long, from when he started writing *Après Moi*. Months ago. Years ago. He must have opened the wrong file. He went in to search later versions. There were three others saved, none of them longer than a couple of pages. That couldn't be right. Then he remembered, you didn't need to save files to your computer anymore, it was all stored in the cloud. He clicked on the fluffy cloud icon – he loved the imagery, all your important thoughts clustered and stored in heaven. Then searched in vain. There were documents going back years, parking permits from when they lived in London, screenshots of theatre tickets, the manuscript of his unpublished novel - that was a waste of time. But of his latest work, to which he had devoted all his waking hours over the last months – apart from those spent wooing Apolline – there was no sign. He took a deep breath. It couldn't be true, he was a technological dunce, he knew that. He'd go through everything calmly now; it was bound to be there somewhere.

CHAPTER 17

Fizz gave a lot of thought to finding a gender-neutral name for her baby and presented Will with a shortlist of three: Clay, Grey or Wren. Will settled on Wren, he liked the thought of his son flying free, the sky was his limit, unlike the terminally earth-bound Clay or depressingly monochrome Grey.

In the best chateau tradition, Wren was welcomed home with a sumptuous multi-course dinner. It was just as well they had no guest bookings, serving breakfast the morning after would have been a stretch for the bleary-eyed hosts.

Olivier slept over for the first time since their late-night tryst on Easter Sunday. Beth saw no reason to keep their affair under wraps after her conversation with Nicola, though she did feel a little uneasy about him publicly settling into the bed she so recently shared with Simon. The clandestine fling, when he'd left before breakfast, was one thing, but this was quite another. It was all a bit too respectable. As if she'd shoehorned in a new, fake husband. She didn't feel that way on their Paris trips – that was Olivier's territory, and she didn't give Simon a second thought when she was lying in bed in the Palais Royal.

Before braving the breakfast table, she decided to take Olivier for a reviving walk around the lake, sizing up the views of the chateau. It looked particularly impressive from this distance, the stone terrace running the full width between the turret towers, with the lake in the foreground reflecting the sun.

'That's definitely our opening shot,' said Olivier. 'We can start every episode with that, have the viewers swooning with chateau envy, before zooming in on the detail. Look, there's your bedroom window – I can tell because I left it open.'

Beth felt a twinge of remorse. That was her and Simon's bedroom – what was she thinking, inviting someone else into their private space? But, no regrets, she was still reeling from their latest night of passion. It was true what they said about French lovers, if hers was anything to go by.

She focused her attention on the task in hand.

'The wisteria will be out next month,' she said. 'It's the best time of year for the south facade.'

The wisteria was her favourite, with its chunky, gnarled branches spreading possessively across the wall, soon to be festooned with heavy clumps of mauve blossom. It was over a hundred years old – Madame de Courcy had shown them a photograph from the 1920s when the plant was already well established, forming the backdrop to a group portrait with the family sitting in line on the stone bench, unsmiling in their starched shirts.

'Ah yes, the *glycine*. We have one at my house, too, you must come and admire it. It's about time you saw my other home, so far you have only seen my Paris apartment. The country house is in a very different style, and I can introduce you to my mother!'

Beth didn't care for this talk, as if they were a courting couple getting to know each other's home lives. She wanted hot sex, not domesticity. She brought the conversation back to the wisteria.

'It's the timing of the blossom that's so appealing, the way it announces that summer is on the way. By the time you get to August, everyone is sick of flowers, don't you think?'

'August is a terrible month for the garden, I agree. It is best spent on a beach with a bottle of chilled rosé. Shall we go together? I will collect you in my car and take you up to the Côte de Nacre, with a cool box containing an elegant seafood picnic, which we will enjoy as we gaze out over the ocean.'

That was more like it. Excitement and outings, never mind meeting his mother.

'I'd love that,' she said, pulling him in for a kiss.

He moved her behind a tree.

'I think here we are safely out of sight.'

'You weren't so out of sight this morning when we ran into Dougie on our way down the stairs. He didn't know where to look, poor man.'

Olivier squeezed her waist and slipped his hand inside her trousers.

'I'm sure Dougie took it in his stride. I like him, for me he is the quintessential English gentleman. A little bit awkward, easily embarrassed, but very knowledgeable. We can use him a lot, I think, to present the history of the chateau.'

He pressed against her and stopped talking about Dougie.

'Last night was one we will always remember; I hope you agree.'

They were steamily getting down to a repeat performance when they were rudely interrupted. Fizz had been following them across the lawn, then turned behind the tree to find them snogging like teenagers.

'Ooh, sorry, that's really embarrassing!'

'No, no,' said Beth, quickly separating herself from Olivier. 'We're the ones who should be sorry. Not appropriate.'

Fizz couldn't help smiling.

'There was me, thinking how you looked like a couple of characters from a Jane Austen novel, strolling round the lake, then I walk in on you in flagrante delicto.'

'Jane Austen, yes,' said Beth, smoothing down her hair. 'Which characters, Darcy and Elizabeth?'

'More like Elizabeth's parents, I'd say. Mr and Mrs Bennet.'

'Cruel, but accurate.'

'So, I just wanted to run something past you,' said Fizz. 'It's an idea Simon had off the top of his head, he mentioned to Nicola when she rang to tell him about Maddie's baby. He suggested we might stage a humanist baptism. It's actually called a naming ceremony, but I prefer to say baptism, and I don't see why we shouldn't have a font. Maddie wasn't interested, but I've been wondering about it for Wren and I thought it would make a great scene for the show. Grand setting in the crystal ballroom, loads of godless godparents in our fake extended family, and I could launch Wren in a beautiful christening gown, anticipating all the dresses that they will wear in the subsequent episodes.'

'Did you just say "they"?' Beth asked.

'Yes. Wren's pronoun is they/their.'

'He's four days old.'

'Oh Beth, you sound so old fashioned! I'm deputising for them, keeping an open mind, then when they get older, they can make their own decision. But this would tie in perfectly with my vlog, where I'll be making a big gender-neutral statement by dressing Wren in female clothes.'

'That sounds very modern,' said Olivier. 'I think it would make a great feature for the programme, so let's talk about it at the meeting this afternoon.'

'Fab, see you then. I'd better get back to my baby!'

They watched her hurry off as quickly as she had arrived.

'We have a very dynamic team here,' said Olivier, putting his arm around Beth's waist.

'Yes, especially Fizz. She really has the bit between the teeth, all that post-birth energy. I hope she doesn't come crashing down.'

'And we have a few hours before our planning meeting. I feel I need a lie-down after all this walking and it looks like it's going to rain. Shall we go back upstairs and continue our unfinished business?'

The crystal ballroom was transformed into a conference centre for the first planning meeting that afternoon. Will had brought down some stacking office chairs that he'd found abandoned in an attic room, covered with dust. Even now, they were still uncovering forgotten items of furniture. There were so many rooms at the chateau that nothing was ever thrown away, as there had always been somewhere to store things no longer required. Will brushed down the chairs and laid them out in rows, then brought in a tray of water glasses. It reminded him of his office days, though normally he wouldn't be doing this lowly work, he would be the one who came in to lead the presentation.

Olivier had erected a screen to display the PowerPoint slides from his laptop, setting out the content and time frames for the filming.

'This is all very professional,' said Mary, settling into a front row seat. 'Do you remember last century when we used to have carousels for colour slides, you had to load them upside down?'

'Oh Mary, you're showing your age there!' said Dougie. He was looking forward to this afternoon, embracing his role as chateau historian. It was exactly the challenge he needed at this point, and he felt rejuvenated by the project and wanted to hear more about it. His only doubt concerned the relationship between Beth and Olivier, so rudely revealed to him this morning when he caught them emerging from her bedroom. He hadn't known where to put himself, it just seemed so inappropriate, and where did that leave Simon when he returned from his sabbatical?

Fizz and Maddie sat side by side, their babies in their laps. John had taken Lily and Louis outside, so they didn't create a distraction. To Nicola's surprise, Jean-Louis had turned up, wearing his signature blue boiler suit. She teased him that he'd be buried wearing it. He said he couldn't think of a finer outfit, and he'd be hopping back onto his tractor after this so there was no point changing. Looking round the room, she was pleased to see how enthusiastic everyone was about making the series. The only person missing was Leo, as he was due back from Paris this morning, but his train had been cancelled.

'I suppose we are all "stakeholders",' said Beth, sitting down next to Nicola. 'One of the pleasures of my long career has been watching the evolution of bullshitty business terminology.'

'You've always had a good ear for that nonsense,' Nicola replied. 'Let's see how we score on bullshit bingo once your lover boy starts speaking. Three points for a "red flag", "synergy" or "think outside the box". Oh look, we're on.'

Olivier rose to his feet.

'Thank you for coming this afternoon to hear about the series we'll be making together about your wonderful life in this spectacular setting. I know that you British are keen on cricketing metaphors, so let me assure you that our programme is going to knock all the other chateau shows for six. They will be on the back foot, clean-bowled by the brilliance and human interest of *Les Nouveaux Châtelains*, or to use its English name, *A New Life in the Chateau.*'

Will smiled at Olivier's use of cricketing terms, knowing how the sport was a mystery to the French. He and Dominic had planned to create a cricket pitch in one of the fields when they bought the chateau. They talked about assembling a local team and inviting other clubs of expats to join them for matches. Dom's death put an end to that project, but maybe it could be revived. Give it a few years and the kids could join the team; he would train them up. He'd be quite old by then, but age was nothing but a number.

Olivier's presentation was met with enthusiastic applause, and excitement at the news that the camera crew would be arriving in two weeks. They would be accommodated in a couple of the attic rooms and would install a provisional kitchen so they could be self-contained. It was important to keep the boundaries.

Nicola was passing round glasses of water, together with some madeleines which she'd baked earlier, when the door burst open, and Leo made a theatrical entrance.

'I'm here! So sorry I'm late, what have I missed? This is Luc, by the way, I know you've all been dying to meet him.'

A tall young man followed him into the room and waved shyly at the group. He was wearing an artfully ripped pair of baggy jeans, a chunky cream cardigan and platform-heeled trainers with colourful stripes.

Everyone took a good look and Nicola came forward to greet him.

'Luc, at last! Welcome to the chateau, you see we have just been briefed on the programme we are about to make here, did you hear about it?'

'Yes, Leo say to me. Please, my English is very bad, I am ashamed.'

He flapped his hand in front of his face, impatient at his inability to master the language.

'Oh, you'll soon pick it up,' said Nicola. 'We pride ourselves on being bilingual, but in reality we are a very British bubble, and you'll be fully immersed. Have a madeleine.'

Luc picked a cake off the proffered tray.

'Very Proustian, *très proustien*,' he said. 'Do you mind if we speak in French? Leo tells me you are a wonderful cook, I am amazed at how you English *emigrés* have seized the French way of life. I don't know any French person who cooks madeleines, yet here you are in your chateau, serving up the iconic gateau which is supposed to transport me back to my childhood. As I often say to Leo, you are more French than the French!'

'I think it's because we chose it,' said Nicola. 'If you're actually French, it doesn't have the novelty appeal. For us Brits, it is our romantic ideal. Now, let me introduce you to everyone . . .'

Fizz was already at her shoulder, wasting no time in rushing up to kiss Luc on the cheek.

'Hi Luc, I'm Fizz, and I'm *thrilled* to meet you! I'm sure Leo has told you all about me and my vlog.'

She handed him her baby and while he anxiously held the child against his chest, she talked to him about herself in her signature, animated style.

Beth slipped into the seat next to Maddie.

'Me, me, me, here we go again,' she said, nodding towards Fizz who was in full performance mode.

Maddie giggled.

'She's marvellous, really, so much energy,' she replied. 'I can safely say she'll be featuring more prominently than me in this programme. My instinct is to hide away with my kids in our cottage.'

'What do you think of Luc? Pretty easy on the eye, wouldn't you say?'

'Not bad at all. Lucky Luc, to have won Leo's heart.'

'He's very young, I wasn't expecting that. I hope Leo's not having a midlife crisis.'

'Midlife? You're all a bit beyond that age, if you don't me saying.'

'I know, we're in denial.'

'Speaking of midlife crises, any word from Simon? I kept thinking of him during the presentation, how brilliant he would be in front of the camera.'

'You're as bad as your mother, treating my husband as though he's some kind of gift from God! He's left me, and I really don't care. You may have noticed that I have other fish to fry.'

'*Un autre poisson*, indeed.'

Beth glanced across at her.

'You don't approve?'

'I neither approve nor disapprove, it's nothing to do with me!'

'What's more, he's taking me to Paris tomorrow for fun and games. While you sit there like the sainted mother you are, baby on your lap, passing judgement on a flighty old woman.'

Maddie laughed and passed Sacha over.

'Here, take him for a bit, I'm going to say hello to lovely Luc.'

It was a big crowd for dinner that night, with six of the *chambres d'hôte* guests booked in for *lapin aux pruneaux*, braised to perfection in local unfiltered cider, followed by a roasted rhubarb clafoutis. Luc was assessed and approved by the chatelains, he was fulsome in praising the food and cleared the table with remarkable speed and grace before heading off with Leo for his first sighting of the turret bedroom.

After the others had drifted off to bed, Beth and Nicola retreated to the grand salon to relax and chew over the day's events.

'It seems strange, Leo having a partner,' said Nicola. 'He's been single for so long, ever since David walked out on him.'

'We would never have invited Leo on the chateau venture if he'd still been with David,' said Beth. 'I couldn't stand him. Snobbish with no justification, I don't know what Leo saw in him. Luc is much nicer, as well as decades younger.'

She took a sip of her tea.

'I'm loving this linden infusion, did I tell you I discovered a tree we'd never noticed, on the other side of the lake? Beautiful yellow blossom. Olivier told me it's *tilleul* in French, he picked handfuls of it this morning.'

'Very gallant, I see he shares your passion for foraging.'

'Foraging and harvesting, we could almost be self-sufficient now at the chateau, we just need to start breeding fish in the pond. Carp are good, according to Olivier, we could serve them up for an Eastern European Christmas lunch.'

'Olivier knows, clearly. You talk so much about him, is he not staying over tonight?'

'No, he went back to his house. Breakfast with his mother in the morning. He wants me to meet her, I said absolutely not.'

'Too soon. I can tell you from experience that a French quasi mother-in-law isn't all plain sailing.'

'But he's taking me to Paris tomorrow, I hope that's OK? We're going to the Rodin museum, then a *super petit resto* he's mad about.'

'Lucky you, of course it's OK.'

'I'll do breakfast duty before I go. Don't you sometimes feel like a school dinner lady? The endless round of mass catering.'

'Yes, but we love it really. Remember what we *didn't* want for our retirement. Two grey heads nodding over a quiet dinner table. Or TV meals on a tray as we sit in front of yet another crime series.'

'Sounds quite tempting. Anyway, I'm off to bed.'

As Beth stood up, her phone started ringing.

'Who's that, calling at this outrageous hour?' asked Nicola.

'It's Simon. I'd better answer. My inclination is to blank him, but it could be about Eva.'

Nicola pretended not to be listening as Beth wandered into the next room to take the call.

'Hello stranger, I'm assuming this isn't a trouser call?'

There followed a long silence from Beth as she paced the room, her phone clamped to her ear. Then she spoke.

'Are you drunk? And by the way, what if it's not what I want? You seemed to think it was fine to bunk off to Toulouse with another woman, and now you're bored with her, you want to come crawling back? . . . All right, so it's not that you're bored, that makes me feel a lot better, carry on digging that hole, why don't you?'

Nicola thought about going to bed, then decided she'd better wait to hear the full debrief. Beth eventually ended the call and came back to flop into the chair beside Nicola.

'He's coming back. Oh Nicola, what am I going to do?'

'What did he say?'

'He's had an existential crisis. Triggered by losing the book he was writing. It evaporated into the ether, apparently. You know Simon and computers.'

'Not his strong suit.'

'He says he's come to terms with it, says Hemingway lost all his manuscripts once, when his wife packed them up in a suit-case and left them on a train.'

'That must have been a challenging moment in the marriage.'

'Simon sees it as a sign. Like Hemingway, he will rise above the loss, and achieve greatness.'

'He certainly has grandiose ambitions.'

'But to do that, he must return to the chateau. And to me, as an afterthought.'

'What about Apolline?'

'He says she's fine with it. Clearly not quite the grand passion after all. He was also talking about the TV project. Obviously fancies himself in a starring role.'

'As we've all said, he would be excellent.'

'And he was asking about Olivier. According to Eva, I wouldn't stop going on about this handsome Frenchman and she fears I'm making a fool of myself, by having a silly crush on him.'

'Crush! It's gone a bit further than that!'

'I know!'

Beth took her head in her hands.

'Why couldn't he just stay put? I don't want him back! It's my time now and Simon's gone and ruined it, I'm furious with him.'

Nicola reached across and patted her hand.

'I won't say I warned you, that wouldn't be helpful.'

Simon plugged his phone in to charge and slipped into bed beside Apolline without turning on the light, so as not to wake her. But as he put his head on the pillow, she turned to face him.

'Did you tell her?'

'Sorry, I thought you were asleep. Yes, I told her.'

'It's fine, you don't need to creep around in the dark because you think I'll be upset. You are doing what you want to do. I always said that must be the basis of our relationship. Just as I will do whatever I want to do.'

'I rather hoped you'd beg me not to leave.'

'I don't want you to stay against your will. You can visit me whenever you like. We are free, remember. What did Beth say when you told her you were going back?'

'She wasn't exactly over the moon.'

'Perhaps she was enjoying having her own space? You two have been together for so long, it must have been refreshing for her.'

'I hadn't thought of that.'

'Let's sleep now and talk about it tomorrow.'

Simon listened to her breathing turn slow and steady. Never a snore, she was far too dainty for that. Unlike Beth. He could imagine her now, stomping up the chateau stairs, still cross with him after their conversation. She'd be climbing into their bed, wearing one of her scruffy old nightdresses, so unlike Apolline's immaculate lingerie. He would see her soon, would take the train via Paris. Maybe she wouldn't meet him at the station but one of the others would. He would drive between the imposing gateposts, push open the heavy oak door and once again become the life and soul of Chateau Lafarge. He had missed it so much. He couldn't wait to go home.

'You're all right, it's not too windy with the roof down?'

Olivier glanced across at Beth, who was happily ensconced in the passenger seat of his Tesla.

She shook her head.

'I'm enjoying the fresh air. Do you know, I've never been to Paris by car, I always get the train.'

'The car's more private.'

He stretched out his hand to squeeze her leg.

'My first car was a Citroën 2CV, a *deux chevaux*. You know it was designed so you could drive across a freshly ploughed field with a basket of eggs on your lap without them breaking, it was such a soft ride. I adored my *Dedeuche* I'd drive round Paris, you could park anywhere then, not like now.'

They slowed down to pass through the *péage*, and Beth noticed a man in the adjacent queue was looking at their car approvingly, then checking out its passengers.

'You prefer this one, I expect.'

She wasn't that interested in cars, but it seemed rude not to show appreciation.

'It is beautifully silent, as you can see, the joy of electric. Let's listen to my Paris playlist.'

Beth let the sounds of Paris wash over her: Charles Trenet, Ella Fitzgerald, Josephine Baker, Edith Piaf. She imagined herself in a tiny garret, gazing out over the rooftops, regretting nothing.

'Oh look, the Eiffel Tower, how corny!'

As they approached the Pont St Cloud, there was a clear view of the iconic structure dominating the city, no other building came near its height. Twenty minutes later, Beth had a closer view as they drove along the embankment, before parking up on the Boulevard des Invalides, close to Napoleon's tomb.

'We'll save him for another occasion,' said Olivier. 'Today I want to show you something more elegant, Hôtel Biron, where Rodin worked right up until his death.'

They entered a classically proportioned mansion, the perfect foil for the sculptor's sensuous statues: a giant pair of hands, hefty-limbed figures embracing, and suffering, and thinking.

'We could do with a couple of these at the chateau,' said Beth, as they wandered through the gardens. 'I love how the sculptures seem so embedded in the flower beds, much better than looking at them behind a rope indoors.'

'It's my favourite museum in Paris,' said Olivier. 'I knew you'd like it; you have an intense feeling for the physical. Now, let's cross back to the right bank, we can work from the apartment until dinner.'

Back at the Palais Royal, Olivier worked on his laptop while Beth rested in the bedroom, remembering her first time here, the giddy excitement of that night when he brought her home in the taxi, through the coded entrance doors, kissing her in the tiny lift, leading her into an unknown apartment. The spontaneity of it. Suddenly she became the mistress of an elegant Frenchman, desired once again after her husband's betrayal. It was straight out of a bodice-ripper.

It wasn't quite so spontaneous now. Olivier put his head round the door and tapped his watch. Almost time for dinner, they could walk as it was a pleasant evening.

They crossed the Rue de Rivoli and strolled through the formal grid of Tuileries Gardens, past the imposing glass pyramid and the stern quads of the Louvre palace. Olivier then ushered Beth into their destination, guiding her through the welcoming curtains of the restaurant, beyond the gleaming, weathered curves of the marble-topped bar, to a table in a dining room with a 1940s feel that was both spacious and cosy. The atmosphere was warm and animated, every table was taken, buzzing with conversation.

'You can't beat the ambience of a Paris restaurant,' said Olivier. 'I rarely eat out in the country because it feels too hushed, don't you agree?'

'True, in our local we often find that we're the only table, or there's a handful of other people, staring at us if we're being too noisy.'

She remembered one occasion in Le Petit Moulin du Village, ten of them seated round three tables pushed together to accommodate everyone, while a silent couple glowered at them from the corner. It was for Mary's birthday, and it did get fairly boisterous, but then Simon went over to the other table, talking them over with his customary charm, and the next thing you knew, they'd pulled up their chairs to join in the birthday cake celebrations. It was a high point of their first year in the chateau. She still recalled the feeling of joyful inclusion, the undoubted rightness of their decision to make their brave move to the chateau.

She picked up the menu from their table for two. On the next table, a tense-looking couple with angular faces were considering their choices. Dressed in black and grey, unsmiling , their eyes darted critically across the card, then Beth heard them order fish and steamed greens. You didn't stay that thin by ordering soufflés.

'I'm starting with the asparagus with gribiche sauce,' said Olivier. 'I also recommend the goat's cheese and anchovy wrapped in courgettes.'

After dinner they strolled back again through the Tuileries, and up to the apartment, where Olivier proved himself, as always, an attentive and accomplished lover.

'There's something I've got to tell you,' Beth said afterwards, as he was returning, naked, to the bedroom, carrying two glasses of water. 'Simon's coming back to the chateau. He rang me last night to tell me.'

Olivier handed her a glass then crossed to his side of the bed.

'Is he now?' he said, slipping in beside her. 'And how do you feel about that?'

'I feel quite a lot of things. Mostly, I feel annoyed.'

'In that case, you must ask yourself what you must do to feel less annoyed. We are having a wonderful time, I think you agree. We mustn't let the return of your husband put an end to that.'

Part Four

Summer

CHAPTER 18

Simon's return to the chateau coincided with the arrival of a glorious heatwave. The sun shone steadily every day, highlighting the beauty of the chateau and gardens which responded by putting out blooms of roses and delphiniums, campanula and alchemilla. The hot weather prompted a flurry of last-minute bookings for the guest rooms and for the glamping tents which Fizz had set up in the grounds. Beth had come up with the idea of the glamping offer, but Fizz was the one with the energy to bring it to fruition, assisted by Maddie and John, erecting a swathe of luxurious satin dwellings in the field beyond the orchard. Which was the advantage, Beth said, of having younger people on board.

She was stretched out on a lounger now, soaking up the rays, getting ready to see Simon for the first time in months.

Leo brought her out a glass of home-made lemonade.

'You're looking sexy in that leopard-print sundress, all set to welcome home our Prodigal Son? It's the theme for my dinner, you know, I'm cooking a Fatted Calf.'

'Or veal, as we call it.'

'Remind me what time his train gets in?'

Beth sighed as she looked at her watch.

'An hour and a half. I could really do without this, Leo. I finally get over him leaving me, I'm having a fabulous time with my hot French lover, then back he comes to rain on my parade!'

'Oh, Simon could never rain on anyone's parade, he's such an enhancer! I'm thrilled at the thought of having him back. Are you sure you don't want to collect him yourself?'

'No thank you. I'll leave the emotional platform scene to you.'

'Right, in that case, I'll go and get changed. I can't be greeting him in my pinny.'

Beth sipped the lemonade, a perfect blend of sugar and acid, then checked her phone. There was a message from Olivier, suggesting she join him in Paris next week. He wanted to take her to a new restaurant on the Left Bank with a pretty little terrace, perfect for a hot summer night. *Yes please.* She sent her reply then closed her eyes, enjoying the sensation of the sun on her face. She didn't believe in cowering in the shade to protect your skin, who knew how many more summers she had ahead, there was no point in taking a pale body, unblessed by the sun, to the fastness of the grave.

She must have dropped off, because it was a couple of hours later when she was woken by a familiar voice.

'Wakey-wakey.'

She opened her eyes to find Simon standing over her. He'd lost some weight, she could see it in his face, which was tanned and handsome. He was wearing an apple-green linen suit that she didn't recognise and the battered panama hat he'd bought decades ago on their first trip to the Caribbean, when they'd stayed on a plantation in Bequia, drinking rum punch on the veranda, then walking hand in hand through a mango grove to the hot white beach. It had been one of their happiest holidays.

'Oh, it's you,' she said.

'Yes, it's me.'

He gazed down at her, suntanned and foxy on the lounger. She was always the first to get the reclining chairs out at the first hint of warmth, and she'd be there, soaking it up on the terrace.

'You look great,' he said. 'You changed your hair?'

She dismissively ran her hand through it.

'Months ago, it needs cutting again. Next time I'm in Paris.'

'Ooh la-la, so it's a Paris hairdresser these days.'

'You're blocking my sun, can you stand aside please.'

Simon sat down on the chair beside her.

'Seriously, Beth, you look really good. It feels great to be home.'

'Did you miss me?'

She shot him a challenging look.

'When you were there, on your "sabbatical", did you miss me at all? I'm guessing not, to start with, when you were all loved up with Apolline.'

'Ah. Listen, I know there's an awful lot of explaining to do . . .'

'Explain away! How long in, I wonder, before you gave me a thought? At what point did you come to realise that actually, you're a bit of a prick?'

'Ouf.'

He scratched his head.

'I admit it. You got there first but yes, I am a bit of a prick. I behaved badly. I'm sorry, but I couldn't help it. I don't know what else to say. Except that I'm here now. I love you and I want us to make it up. There. I've said it, and I haven't even unpacked yet.'

'Where are you going to sleep?'

"Oh. Well, I suppose I was hoping . . .'

'You didn't really think you'd be slipping back into our bed, as though nothing's happened?'

'No, of course not.'

That was exactly what he'd been thinking.

'Rome wasn't built in a day, I get it,' he said. 'I'll earn my spurs. You'll see, Beth, I'm going to make it up to you.'

Simon was plunged straight back into duties the following morning. With the influx of guests, breakfasts had become a massive operation, the chatelains had sourced vintage bistro tables and chairs from local *brocantes* and set them up on the terrace, where croissants and coffee were served up beneath lilac umbrellas which toned beautifully with the lavender bushes.

'The conditions are perfect for eating outside,' said Nicola to Simon, as they ferried trays between the tables. 'The guests love to see the bees and butterflies fluttering round the lavender, but we're not yet troubled by wasps, they'll come to curse us in August.'

Simon mopped his brow with a handkerchief plucked from the breast pocket of his linen shirt. He'd chosen his outfit with care, to convey the air of a bohemian chateau owner graciously opening his home to members of the public.

'I'd forgotten what hard work it is. I was planning a run after this, but I'm going to lie down under a tree instead. Won't you come with me? I want to talk to you about Beth.'

They left Maria and Sylvie to clear the last tables and walked down the steps, setting off across the lawn towards the lake.

'The grass is so green still,' said Simon, 'early summer is when it's best, not yet scorched yellow by weeks of relentless sun. I missed it, you know. Toulouse has some beautiful parks, but it's very much a city on a river, you don't get this sense of living in a bucolic paradise, in the middle of nowhere.'

They sat down on a bench which Will had crafted from a fallen tree, slicing off the curved bark to make a seat, and carving out a lion's head at each end to form fanciful armrests.

'Good old Will, honing his carpentry skills,' said Simon, stroking the lion's head. 'The great thing about this chateau adventure is having the opportunity to find new things to be good at, digging into your creativity.'

'Speaking of which, any news of your missing manuscript?'

'An inappropriate word these days, "manuscript". Meaning written by hand, whereas we all now use computers.'

'Thanks for the Latin lesson.'

'But no, I have to accept that my great work is gone forever. The odd thing is, I really don't mind. Which suggests it wasn't as great as I liked to think.'

He held his hands up in a disarming show of self-knowledge.

'I'm sure it was very good,' said Nicola, loyally, 'but now you can write something even better.'

Simon waved his hand dismissively. Nicola remembered what a serial enthusiast he was, always ready to move on to the next project.

'Plenty of time for that, I'm just enjoying being back at the chateau. It's lovely to be home with my friends and I'm pumped for this TV show. The only fly in the ointment is Beth! Do you think she'll ever forgive me?'

'You did abandon her; you can understand she might not be best pleased.'

'I came back, though – she knew I would. We've had similar . . . episodes . . . in the past but I always come to my senses in the end, she's used to it.'

'Are you counting me as one of your "episodes"?'

She was referring to the embarrassing infatuation he developed for her when they first moved to the chateau, which had created some tension.

'Oh no, there was nothing in that, just me being silly!'

'Ah. So easily dismissed.'

She hung her head in mock despair. Simon looked concerned, at which point she took pity on him and punched him on the arm.

'I'm only teasing. We're just mates, you know that.'

'That's a relief, mate. May I just add that you are an exceptionally attractive mate. I find you far more physically appealing than Will, for instance, even though he too is my mate.'

'There you go, at it again.'

'However, I accept that I did lose my head over Apolline, but look at me now – voting with my feet – which are firmly replanted on the fertile terrain of Chateau Lafarge.'

He stuck his feet in the air and hitched up his trouser legs to show off an elegant pair of navy suede loafers.

'Do you like them? Apolline bought them for me. I think she was trying to sharpen up my look. She also bought me that pale green suit, my arrival outfit yesterday in case you didn't notice?'

'Very stylish. Was she sad to see you go?'

'Weirdly, it was absolutely fine. I think we both felt our thing had run its course. Relief on both sides that neither of us had a broken heart. It's funny how it can go like that. Madly in love one moment, ho-hum the next.'

'Especially you. Most of us are steadier than that.'

'How are things with you and the delicious Jean-Louis? You looked pretty loved-up at dinner last night.'

'Wonderful, thank you.'

'It must be true what they say about French lovers.'

'Well, you should know. I've no complaints about mine.'

'Which brings me back to Beth. It was something Eva said to me. I've yet to meet this Olivier person, but according to Eva, Beth was being weird about him on the phone. Kept mentioning his name, that sort of thing. You don't think there's anything in that, do you?'

Nicola shifted on the bench; she knew this would happen. Beth had dropped her in it, forcing her to play piggy in the middle. It really wasn't fair.

'Why don't you ask her?' she replied. 'I have nothing to report, I am not my brother's keeper.'

'Quoting from the Bible, that sounds ominous!'

He turned to face her.

'I expected you to laugh and say what a ridiculous idea. But you're not saying that, are you?'

'Oh look, here comes Madame de Courcy.'

Nicola had never been more pleased to see the old lady, who was wearing a floral chiffon dress and a straw hat, accessorised by a pleated fan which she flipped open as she approached them.

'I thought it was you, Simon, you've been away for so long I had almost forgotten the shape of your silhouette, but then I thought, no, that is him, my favourite Englishman, just a little thinner than I remember!'

Simon gallantly rose to his feet and kissed her hand.

'And what a pleasure to be reunited with my favourite French aristocrat. You're looking remarkably well, Madame de Courcy. Come sit with us.'

Their flirtatious exchanges continued as she settled comfortably between them, patting Simon's knee and fanning her face. Playing Scarlett O'Hara to Simon's Rhett Butler, thought Nicola, it was a well-rehearsed ritual.

'I came to find you because I just happened to be walking past your gates and I noticed two vans arriving. They were carrying equipment round the back of the chateau, which seemed irregular to me. You cannot be too careful, I hear it is a method employed by burglars, to appear as if they are delivery men.'

'That's kind of you, but it's nothing to worry about,' said Nicola, while thinking to herself that this woman was the biggest snoop ever. 'It will be the camera crew arriving, we start filming this week and they're getting everything set up.'

'Camera crew? Are you hosting a wedding you haven't told me about?'

'No. Have you not heard about our latest enterprise? I suppose not, it all happened so quickly . . .'

Simon jumped to his feet.

'I would have told you right away, Madame de Courcy, you know I can't keep anything from you, but I'm only just back in action myself. I'm happy to announce that your ancestral home Chateau Lafarge is to become the subject of multi-part television series, featuring me and all the other inhabitants, who are destined to become stars of the small screen.'

He took a bow, and Madame de Courcy frowned.

'I don't like the sound of that at all, it is considered very vulgar amongst the French ruling classes to show off our homes. I made peace with the idea that you were taking paying guests to help cover the bills incurred in running the chateau, that is a practical measure and I respect your British *pragmatisme*. But to turn my home into a circus, prying into every corner with a long lens, that I cannot allow.'

She flapped her fan vigorously, transforming it from a flirtation aid into an instrument of protest.

'I'm sorry we didn't tell you sooner,' said Nicola gently, 'but it's our home now, and we can do as we choose. I had reservations as well, but we have made the decision and we are seeing it as an exciting opportunity. I think you will reach the same conclusion when you see the results. You may even be persuaded to take part.'

'Never. Now, if you will excuse me, I must attend to my affairs.'

She nodded a cool goodbye and set off across the lawn.

'She'll come round,' said Simon. 'I bet you once she's seen the first episode, she'll be begging to perform *Tout Va Très Bien Madame la Marquise* to camera.'

'The thick stone walls of a chateau, you can't beat them for staying cool,' said Beth, stretching out on a chaise longue in the grand salon. They remarked on this whenever there was a heatwave. It was as if the chateau had been constructed for the sole purpose of insulating its occupants against extreme weather. The south-facing curtains were drawn to keep out the sun, enhancing the impression of living under natural air conditioning.

Dougie and Leo were languishing in armchairs, while Olivier stood, seigneur-like, by the fireplace, his arm resting on the mantelpiece. They had just completed their first meeting with the TV crew, and Olivier was pleased with the way it had gone.

'So, we're all set for the opening sequence, I'm glad everyone's on track. Beth, it's important that you remain the key contact, in terms of making sure all the residents know the schedule.'

'Yes, boss.'

Beth gave a mock salute.

'You're very much subaltern to his captain,' said Leo. 'I wish you'd both wear uniforms.'

'I won't be here every day, ' said Olivier, 'but my producer Denise will be keeping me up to date. She is a capable woman, you will like her very much.'

'I'm already thinking about my outfits,' said Leo. 'What I really need is a Winnebago trailer where I can lie down between takes and flick through my wardrobe. I can't be climbing the stairs to my turret room every time I want to change.'

'Leo, we are not making a movie and you are not a movie star, although I admit you look like one,' said Olivier with a smile. 'This is a fly-on-the-wall documentary about the realities of communal living in a grand chateau. We are looking for, to quote that wonderful English expression, "warts and all".'

'"Warts and all"!' came a voice from the far side of the room. 'That doesn't sound very aspirational!'

They all turned to look at Simon who had come in from the garden. He approached Olivier and offered him his hand.

'And you must be Olivier, looking very much at home in front of our fireplace. Delighted to meet you at last, I've heard so much about you. I think we want less of the warts, though, and more of the celebration of our wonderful life here, don't you agree?'

Olivier shook his hand. So, this was Beth's husband, he looked like a proper English eccentric with that gaudy-coloured handkerchief stuffed into his shirt pocket.

'Warts are just part of life,' he said, 'the lows only serve to emphasise the highs. Good to meet you too, I understand you have been away on a "sabbatical"?'

The way he asked the question was definitely a challenge. Simon withdrew his hand. Had Beth told him about Apolline? What exactly was the extent of their relationship? He didn't care for this man, with his annoyingly fit physique and superior air of authority.

'Yes, you know that other English expression, "a change is as good as a rest"? I'm back now, refreshed, and ready to go. I couldn't pass up the chance to star in a programme about our beloved Chateau Lafarge.'

'I would say "feature in" rather than "star". As I just explained to Leo, this is strictly a documentary.'

'I was only joking. I thought you French loved our crazy British sense of humour?'

Leo jumped to his feet.

'Right, I'm going to love you and leave you. I've promised to give Luc a tour of the local hotspots, obviously that won't take long in our one-horse town.'

Dougie followed him out, leaving Beth alone with Simon and Olivier in an awkward threesome where suddenly they found nothing to say to each other.

'I must leave, too,' said Olivier, breaking the silence. 'I promised my mother I would take her to lunch.'

'I'll see you out,' said Beth, relieved that he was going.

'Beth tells me you have a house nearby,' said Simon. 'That's convenient.'

'Yes, my connection with the region gave me the idea in the first place. I knew all about the mad English people who bought the big chateau, it was the talk of my village. Then I followed your housemate's Mademoiselle Bovary vlog, which made me see the potential.'

'And so handy for you to call in, I hear you've been a frequent visitor?'

Simon's tone was neutral, but the question made Olivier uncomfortable.

'Everyone has been very welcoming,' he said carefully. 'You have a special set-up here; it is unusual to find oneself so embraced by a community. I'll see you again soon, it's good to meet you at last.'

Beth accompanied him out while Simon took her place on the chaise longue. He stretched out and tapped his fingers on the upholstery, waiting for her return.

'Not bad looking, for a silver fox,' he said when she came back in.

'Glad you think so.'

'I quite fancy him myself. *Très* French, that blend of neat and sexy. Bit full of himself, though.'

'Hmm.'

Beth picked up her phone and slumped into an armchair.

'It's baking hot out there,' she said.

'Don't change the subject. I was talking about the allure of Olivier, the discreet charm of our neighbouring bourgeois.'

'He's doing a great job of putting the programme together.'

'Eva thought there was more to it than that. She said you sounded obsessed with him.'

'Did she now!'

Beth threw down her phone.

'That girl's got a cheek! She was asking me what I was up to, so I told her all about the TV thing, and then she goes sneaking to you! What did she say?'

'She wasn't sneaking, she was worried about you.'

'Worried about me? She should worry about herself, it's about time she had a baby, that would give her something to think about, instead of making up stories about me.'

'Oof, that's a bit off topic! She wasn't making up stories, why would you say that? And what would those stories be? Fanciful tales of a middle-aged woman taking a liking to a dishy Frenchman?'

'Right, because that would be so embarrassing, wouldn't it? A silly old woman getting giggly over a man, because there couldn't be anything in it, could there? Nobody's going to fancy her at her age!'

She glared at him. Looking quite magnificent, he had to admit.

'Oh my God, it's true. You're shagging him, aren't you? Damn. What have I done? It's all my fault.'

He put his head in his hands, overcome by this revelation. He'd honestly thought it would be fine; he'd apologised and was all set to return to his normal life at the chateau. But now Beth, his Beth, had fallen for somebody else. And it was all his fault.

Beth was surprised to find she actually felt sorry for him.

'Well, that's a first,' she said. 'You putting the blame on yourself!'

'It's true, though. You fell into his arms because I left you.'

'And as a weak and vulnerable single woman, you think I was easy prey?'

'I guess that's how it happened.'

'Or maybe I fell passionately in love with him, like you did with Apolline?'

He looked up and frowned.

'Now you're being silly. That's not the sort of thing you do.'

'Who are you to judge what "sort of thing" I do? Maybe you don't know me at all. I admit, it probably wouldn't have happened if you hadn't fucked off with another woman, but who knows? Maybe it would?'

'I wouldn't have allowed it!'

'You wouldn't have known! I met him in Paris, the first time.'

She got up from the armchair and went to perch beside him on the chaise longue.

'It's quite a relief to tell you all this, by the way. I've been stressing about it ever since you announced you were coming home.'

He studied her face, and for the first time he realised what he'd done to her, the effect of him blithely abandoning her for another woman.

'In Paris! Where did he take you?'

'Hotel Costes. It was a business meeting, to discuss the TV programme.'

'And then he took you back to see his etchings?'

'Yes. Charmingly hung in the Palais Royal.'

'Spare me the details.'

'You asked!'

'I don't want to know!'

His mind was racing. There he'd been, grovelling to Beth, and all the time she was having her own affair, making a cuckold out of him! And now he had to face that wretched Frenchman every day while filming that programme he'd been so excited about. How on earth did it come to this.

Fizz was lying on the bed, blindly feeding Wren who was suckling at her breast while the cooling gel masks worked their magic on the new mother's eyes. She absolutely must look her best for the first day of filming. Unlike her housemates, she already had an online presence, she didn't want to disappoint her followers by appearing saggy or less than perfect. This heat was a worry, there was nothing worse than a shiny face in close-up under high definition.

'Will, are you there?'

He wandered through from the sitting room, wearing only a pair of cotton shorts, it was too stuffy in the barn to put on anything else.

He touched her arm.

'Here I am.'

'Can you put Wren down. I just need another ten minutes with this eye mask, then I'm going to do a hair treatment.'

She handed him the baby. Wren was wearing a floaty yellow dress over his nappy. His wardrobe consisted entirely of girl's clothes, and while Will respected Fizz's decision, he was a little nervous about his son's infantile cross-dressing being recorded for posterity. Supposing Wren grew up to resent it? Children could be so cruel – he could picture the scene at school, the poor boy being taunted in the class when someone produced an image from *Les Nouveaux Châtelains*. Everyone seemed to think the show would be a smash hit – it was one thing to invade your own privacy, but what about the privacy of the children too young to give consent? He had sympathy with those parents who had a strict policy on keeping their offspring offline.

'Then can you take a look at the bathroom in Fuchsia tent? The woman – Jemima, I think – told me this morning they were having issues with the hot water. We don't want to have a grumpy customer ruining the vibe.'

'Yes ma'am,' said Will. He didn't mind being the odd job man, he had proved to be the most practical of the chatelains, with the result that he was the first port of call when something went wrong. There was a certain pride in that, but he sometimes needed to remind himself that once upon a time, in the pre-chateau age, he was the biggest earner of them all.

'And can you make sure those nappies are in the wash? I want the best ones to hand for tomorrow, casually showing how eco-aware we are with our stylish reusables.'

'Consider it done, domestic god that I am.'

'Great, I really need to focus on myself for the rest of the day, get my head round coordinating my vlog posts with the filming. I need to mention the show, but I don't want it to be the only thing I'm talking about.'

Will obediently took Wren off to his cot, setting him down gently and stroking his head until he went to sleep. Louis was playing with Lily at the cider barn, so now would be a good time to take care of the problem bathroom. The glamping site was a great initiative and a good money-spinner, but more plumbing meant more maintenance, so more work for the resident handyman.

He set off across the lawn to the chateau to pick up his toolkit, working up quite a thirst on the journey with the sun beating down on his bare back. The chateau was cool, thanks to the high ceilings. He wandered through the crystal ballroom, marvelling at the quiet grandeur, so different from the barn where he was surrounded by the noise and equipment that came with young children. He carried on through to the grand salon, thinking he might just help himself to a little refreshment from the drinks cabinet. There, he found that Simon had beaten him to it and was pouring himself a glass of Calvados.

'Great minds think alike,' said Simon, waving the decanter at him. 'I heard the footsteps and I said to myself, what are the chances that's my old friend and drinking partner Will, looking for a late morning pick-me-up!'

Will gave him a complicit smile. He was glad to have Simon back, he'd missed him.

'I'm actually here to pick up a toolbox, but decided I deserved a bit of time out before I get down to the grubby business of waste pipe maintenance.'

Simon passed him a tumbler.

'You're a marvel, Will, this place would fall apart without you. Behind the glamorous facade of our fairy-tale castle, there is our unsung hero, fixing all the breaks and ensuring the show goes on.'

'A safe pair of hands, that's me,' said Will, taking the glass and sitting down on the chaise longue. 'And yet I used to be so much more.'

'You still are so much more! Father of four, husband of an internet-renowned hottie, you've got it all. Not like me, I'm the one who really needs a drink.'

He slumped down beside Will.

'You presumably know what's been going on between Beth and that poncy Frenchman?'

'Ah.'

'Is that "ah", as in "ah yes, I was going to tell you about that"? Since we are friends.'

'Listen, Simon, I don't know much about it, it's not my business, to be honest. Did Beth tell you?'

'Let's just say I challenged her about it, then she confessed.'

'Well, that's a relief, at least it's all out in the open. I was wondering what was going to happen.'

'We still don't know what's going to happen. I could challenge him to a duel, we have the right setting for it. Throw down my gauntlet, then pistols at dawn.'

Will took a swig of his brandy.

'I wouldn't do anything if I were you. It's bound to fizzle out. If you ask me, it was an act of revenge. After you went off with Apolline.'

'Hmm.'

'Is that 'hmm', as in you admit that it could be your fault?'

'That was my first reaction: it's my fault. But when I thought about it, I realised there's no room for blame in affairs of the heart. I had no choice, it wasn't my fault I fell in love with Apolline. You should understand that. You left Marjorie because you fell in love with Fizz, you couldn't say it was your *fault*.'

'The divorce judge thought otherwise, which is why I'm not as rich as I used to be.'

'Anyway, the point is, I came home. I sacrificed my life with Apolline to come back to Beth, only to find she's making a fool of me! But you think it will be all right, do you? Just a moment of madness on her part?'

He looked at Will, hoping for reassurance.

'Yes, exactly so,' said Will, with a nod. 'No doubt it will all work out. I'm not even sure how often she was seeing him, none of us knew anything about it until Dougie bumped into him coming down the stairs one morning.'

Simon sat up straight.

'What did you say?'

'Yes, poor old Dougie, covered with confusion, you know how old fashioned he can be.'

'He was coming down *our* stairs? Do you mean to tell me that Frenchman was staying overnight in *my* bedroom?'

'That would be a reasonable assumption. I thought you knew, didn't Beth tell you?'

'What a cheek! Beth didn't say anything about that. I assumed she was meeting him elsewhere. Not literally taking my place in the Napoleonic bed! Putting his pyjamas under *my* pillow, what was she thinking? I need a refill, will you join me?'

He went to pick up the decanter and poured them both a generous top-up.

'I need to do something to take my mind off that horrible image. Let me come with you and sort out the pipework. I'll be your plumber's mate and hold the spanner. Calm my nerves before I have to face that smooth-talking Casanova tomorrow.'

CHAPTER 19

The first day of filming dawned with a radiant blue sky, the sun shining unchallenged to showcase the chateau and its grounds in the best possible light.

'I'll give you a hundred euros for every cloud you can see in that sky,' said Beth. 'Honestly, if you had even the vaguest idea that you might want to buy a chateau, wouldn't this view just swing it for you?'

They were self-consciously assembled on the terrace, watching the drone circling above them. Any minute now, it would zoom in on them, and when the director gave them the word, they were to wave up at the camera, inviting the viewers into their fairy-tale home. It was just the original eight chateau-buyers for this shot, there would be plenty of time later to feature the others, the director explained, but she wanted to start with the core group. Efficient, bilingual, and wearing a strong pair of statement spectacles, Denise knew exactly what she was about.

'Denise, darling, I'm slightly desperate for breakfast, will it be much longer?' said Leo. 'It's a terrible strain putting my best profile forward.'

Denise held up her hand.

'Here it comes, look happy and wave NOW!'

They all put on fixed smiles and waved obediently at the drone. Then they were dismissed and allowed to go in for breakfast. There was a half-hour window before the guests would arrive for service.

Leo loaded a tray with a plate of croissants and a pot of coffee.

'I'm taking this up for me and Luc, I hope that drone won't come spying on us through the turret window. See you later.'

Fizz picked up a couple of fruit smoothies from the row of glasses she had prepared earlier, the strawberry colour matched the shade of her long dress. It was important to wear strong colours on camera, particularly from a distance, so as not to fade into the background.

'Drink up, Will,' she said, handing him a glass, 'we'd better get back to relieve John and Maddie. It was good of them to watch the kids. It's handy that the second-tier chatelains weren't required this morning. Denise said it was just for the opening shot, though. Much less structured from now on, they will just be creeping up on us randomly with those cameras, you'll never know when they are going to appear!'

'Yes, it's rather concerning,' said Dougie, pouring himself a coffee and sitting down at the table. 'I'm very happy to talk to camera about the history of the chateau, but not so keen on the idea of my daily routine being recorded.'

'Don't worry, Dougie,' said Simon, 'that would be far too dull to make the final cut.'

'How brutal of you,' said Dougie. 'Mary, aren't you going to defend my honour?'

'We know he's only joking,' said Mary, spreading butter thickly on a slice of baguette. 'If you're looking for seriously boring, how about a shot of me poring over my jigsaw, that will have the viewers enthralled.'

'They'll love you, Mary,' said Simon. 'I hope your cleaning skills will be on display, there could be a whole spin-off series there – *How to Freshen your Chateau.*'

'I gather you're serving breakfast, Simon,' said Dougie. 'It looks like your first customers are in, all ready to experience your famous oleaginous charm.'

Simon went over to greet them, it was the couple from the Fuchsia tent, elegantly dressed in shades of cream. Simon put a solicitous arm around Jemima's shoulder. He hoped the plumbing was behaving itself following his intervention? He soon had them both eating out of the palm of his hand as he escorted them out to a table on the terrace.

'They're a bit precious, those two,' Beth whispered to Nicola. 'You'd think if you're going for the glamping option, you might be on the bohemian side, but she's a right fusspot. Complained to me yesterday that she'd found a stain on the mattress – I mean, honestly, who looks? And said the tent lets in too much light so she woke up earlier than she would have liked. I felt like saying, well it is a tent!'

'We have a spare room in the chateau tonight, someone cancelled the Antoine Watteau suite, shall I offer them a free upgrade?' said Nicola.

'And reward their bad behaviour? Certainly not! Have you noticed it's always the younger guests who make a fuss. The old ones are far less trouble, not as spoilt, I suppose.'

'Survivor generation, as opposed to victim generation. But you're forgetting the customer is always right, I'm not sure you're cut out for a career in hospitality. Luckily your husband's got them wrapped round his little finger, look at him.'

Through the French windows they could see Simon in action, the young couple breaking into smiles as they listened to whatever tall story he was telling them.

'You must admit he's an asset,' said Nicola.

'He's all upset with me, keeps giving me wounded looks.'

'Because of Olivier?'

'Yes, he was hoping there was nothing in it. I was unable to reassure him to the contrary.'

'Oh.'

'Then Will let slip that Olivier had slept over in our room. That went down badly.'

'Which you can understand.'

'I admit I had misgivings about that myself.'

'Speak of the devil,' said Nicola, 'here comes lover boy.'

Olivier was striding towards them, looking sexy in white linen trousers and a figure-hugging navy shirt.

'*Salut, les filles.* I hear the opening sequence is looking good. I thought I'd just pop in and see how you were all doing.'

'All the better for being addressed as a *fille*,' said Nicola, 'but I'm on breakfast duty, and I can see we're filling up, so I'll leave you to it.'

Olivier sat down on the chair she had vacated next to Beth. He took a croissant from the basket on the table and bit into it, brushing the crumbs off his white linen lap.

'I haven't seen your face for a few hours, *ça me manque*, I miss it.'

She turned to him.

'You're seeing it now. Not looking at its best in the cruel morning light. Luckily the drone camera was at a distance.'

'It looks good to me. I was wondering when we would see each other again. In private, I mean. I have tickets for us for the Bastille next week, but I can't wait that long.'

He put his hand, unseen, on her thigh and she felt her usual electric reaction.

Simon passed by their table, carrying a tray of herbal infusions, looking daggers at his rival.

'Good morning, Olivier! Can I get you anything, or is my wife taking care of you?'

'*Merci*, Simon, I have everything I need. Like most French people, I am not a big eater of breakfast. A black coffee and a cigarette is how we like to keep slim, although I no longer smoke.'

'As long as you haven't turned your back on all of life's pleasures. I gather that's not the case.'

He swept off and Olivier raised his eyebrows at Beth.

'I am sensing a little tension there.'

'I'm afraid so. He found out about us.'

Olivier looked concerned.

'You told him. Was that wise?'

'I didn't exactly tell him. But he knows, and it's all rather difficult.'

'Ah, you British! I fear you lack our elegance when it comes to affairs of the heart. Discretion is all important.'

'I know, we're no good at subterfuge.'

'Come to my house this afternoon, where there is no need for subterfuge. Three o' clock?'

She nodded.

'I'm just going to have a word with Denise, I'll see you later.'

She watched him weave his way out between the tables, giving Simon a friendly pat on the shoulder.

Simon recoiled, then spun round to Beth. He pulled a face of revulsion, and she couldn't help laughing.

*

Leo pushed open the door to his turret bedroom with a flourish and placed the breakfast tray on the dressing table. Luc was still asleep, so Leo took his coffee cup and sat on the end of the bed, waiting for him to wake up, admiring the contours of his face and the tousled dark blond hair spread across the pillow. Eventually Luc opened his eyes, then sat up, slightly disturbed to find Leo staring at him.

'How long have you been sitting there?'

'Five minutes. Enjoying the peace. And your beautiful face. I've even brought you breakfast.'

He brought the tray over and laid it out on the bedcovers. Luc's face lit up at the sight of the pain au chocolat. Leo knew it was his favourite.

'I am a lucky person, to have met you, Leo.'

'And you are the first person I have ever invited into this bedroom. Can you imagine what a monk-like existence I have endured for the last five years?'

'I think you have many offers,' said Luc, 'as you are a handsome English gentleman.'

'Thank you,' said Leo, trying to ignore the crumbs that were falling wide of the tray. He knew he must be less fussy about such things, now he was in a relationship. 'I kissed a few frogs, as we say, but it was worth the wait, to find you.'

'So I am the *grenouille* who become a prince. And now I am in your *magnifique* chateau. *J'adore!* Where are the cameras today? I must be filmed before I return to Paris! Let's swim in the *lac*, I have a *maillot de bain* in a delicious colour of *pistache*. It looks very beautiful under this *ciel bleu*, they will want to film me!'

'I don't think it works like that,' said Leo, 'we are briefed to carry on as normal and to ignore the cameras.'

'Let us just go then, and hope they find us!'

He leaped out of bed and pulled a pair of tiny swimming trunks from his rucksack. He slipped them on quickly and Leo noticed that they barely preserved his modesty.

'*Qu'est-ce que tu penses?*' Luc asked, striking a pose the same way that Leo did when he wanted to show off his wardrobe. Maybe that was what first attracted them to each other.

'I adore summer,' he continued, 'you only need one small item of clothing, and you have an entire outfit.'

He took a towel and draped it, toga style, over his shoulders.

'Come on, *on y va. Il faut qu'on se bronze*, let us start our summer tan.'

What a thing to be young, thought Leo, remembering the days when he would lie in the sun at every opportunity, without a thought for how it might impact his skin. Nobody cared about cellular damage in those days, it was the here and now that counted, acquiring a honey glow to enhance your youthful beauty.

He picked up a tube of factor 50, just for his face. He had no intention of stripping off or swimming in that chilly lake. His pleasure would come from resting on the bank, watching Luc entering the water. He would be like Gustav von Aschenbach in *Death in Venice*, only without the dyed hair – no need of that yet, thank you – as he sat observing the beautiful boy.

Luc slipped his feet into a pair of metallic blue fisherman sandals – 'They're from Prada, Leo, do you like them?' – and took Leo by the hand. They must *en profiter*, he said, take advantage of this blissful weather. Leo followed him down the spiral stairs, through the gracious reception rooms and out on to the terrace, smiling at the guests who had turned their heads to take a look at the scantily clad young man who had just walked by to liven up their breakfast.

They crossed the lawn and spread the towels on the grass beside a tree at the water's edge. Leo sat in the shade and watched Luc plunge into the water, screaming at the chill of it. He swam a few strokes, then emerged, like a Greek god, to sprawl luxuriously beside Leo, exposing his miraculous body, glistening in the sunlight. *I am truly, miraculously happy*, thought Leo. His reverie was soon interrupted by the sight of Simon, running towards them in an orange Lycra outfit that did little to flatter his florid complexion and sturdy physique.

'Hello, boys!' said Simon, grinding to a halt beside them. 'That water looks tempting, I'm going to follow Luc's example.'

'*Ah oui,*' said Luc, 'it is very energising. *La natation sauvage.*'

'Oh yes, "wild swimming". Or "swimming", as we used to call it. God knows why we needed to add the "wild".'

He pulled off his figure-hugging top. Leo was relieved he stopped short of removing his skin-tight shorts.

'My favourite mutton,' said Leo, 'you're punishing yourself this morning, breakfast service *and* a jog, let's hope you don't keel over.'

'It's not a *jog*, Leo,' said Simon, 'nobody's been jogging since the 1990s! I'm *training*, that's what everyone calls it now.'

'Training for what? The eternal peace of the grave?'

'All right, let's call it running. And now a cold dip.'

He went crashing into the water. Leo was struck by his ungainly, splashy style of swimming, in contrast to Luc's elegant breaststroke. After a few minutes, Simon staggered out to stand on the bank, shaking his head like a dog to get the droplets out of his hair.

'Well hello, Ursula Andress,' said Leo, 'all you need is a white bikini and you'd be a dead spit for the girl in *Doctor No*.'

'I'll take that as a compliment. Mind if I sit between you? I didn't bring a towel, wasn't planning a swim.'

He plonked himself down between them.

'May I say, it warms the cockles of this old man's heart, to see how loved up you two are. You know, Luc, we've been waiting a long time for you. It's about time Leo found the happiness he deserves, he's been our token singleton for too long.'

Luc propped himself up on his elbows. He had just noticed the camera crew coming their way. He tossed his head and ran his fingers through his hair in preparation, but instead of continuing towards the lake, the crew diverted in the direction of the vegetable gardens.

Simon watched Luc's disappointment with amusement.

'Don't worry, Luc, they'll be back! I expect they're going to film the animals, that's quite a petting zoo that the girls managed to assemble. Who knew you could rustle up a pen load of livestock at such short notice.'

At three o'clock, as agreed, Beth drew up outside Olivier's substantial manor house. A classic eighteenth-century facade, set squarely at the end of a formal line of trees, it couldn't have looked more French.

He walked across the gravel to greet her, carrying two glasses of champagne.

'At last you get to see my *gentilhommière*!'

His gentleman's abode, though the charm of the word was lost in translation. Beth noticed how the box shrubs in front of the house were all cut to an identical height, spaced out in pots at regular intervals. Controlled precision, *à la française*.

'This could be my Mr Darcy moment,' said Olivier, 'remember how Elizabeth Bennett finally falls in love with him when she visits his magnificent country estate. Though I admit my humble cottage has nothing on your chateau.'

He leaned down to kiss her as she opened the car door.

'It's hardly a cottage,' said Beth.

She took the glass of champagne and followed him into the house. Generous floor-to-ceiling windows, a light-filled room with the usual spindly chairs you'd be too nervous to sit on, parked primly in uninviting groups.

'I'll take you to my boudoir, I'm aware that time is not on our side this afternoon.'

He led her up the elegant staircase. Beth appreciated the scale of this house, gracious without being intimidating, she could imagine living here in another, parallel life.

'You will see I am more maximalist in my decor, here in the country. I took a designer for the Paris apartment as I wanted stripped back minimalism. But here I have just absorbed the clutter of my ancestors, it's an organic growth, laid over the palimpsest of my forbears.'

Beth caught sight of herself in the mirror of the huge armoire, and saw a no-nonsense woman of a certain age, wearing a practical shirt dress. Whereas these rooms cried out for a Regency heroine in a flowing robe. She looked wrong.

Photographs in silver frames were cluttered up on the chest of drawers and Beth caught sight of one of a much younger Olivier standing in front of this house, with a small boy. That must be the son he rarely saw. Olivier hardly mentioned him, only to say their paths didn't often cross these days.

Olivier stretched out on the bed and patted the covers, inviting her to join him.

She kicked off her flip-flops and lay down beside him, trying to drum up her earlier excitement.

Olivier sensed her lack of engagement.

'So, your husband returns from his dalliance and you must now play the faithful wife, is this what it's about?'

Beth sighed.

'It's complicated. I'm cross with him, and I'm annoyed that's having an effect on the way I feel about you. I know it's illogical.'

'Affairs of the heart are by their very nature illogical. But he is an irrelevance to us, you don't have to decide between us.'

He traced his finger on her collarbone, feeling the slim golden chain she had put on that morning.

'I haven't seen you wear this before.'

'Simon gave it to me, years ago.'

'I see! So, you're making a point?'

He was teasing her.

'You know, Beth, serial monogamy is a very British obsession. We French know that love takes many forms and there is always room for one lover to complement another.'

'Oh, so you don't care what I do when I'm not with you?' She raised a protective hand to the necklace. 'That doesn't sound very caring to me.'

'I care about you, of course. But your husband is your business, and I have no right to ask about your relationship with him. All I care about is that I love my time with you. It's enough, don't you agree?'

He drew her close and they launched into their well-practised routine. Beth closed her eyes and allowed her body to go through the motions, while her mind wandered and wondered if this really was what she wanted.

The animals were a new addition. Jean-Louis had fenced off an area of the orchard and arranged the delivery of an appealing range of sheep, goats and pigs. Guests at the chateau were encouraged to feed the animals from scoops of food provided, and plans were in place to expand the offer to encourage visitors who weren't residents to come by – for a small fee – and enjoy the destressing sensation of stroking a baby animal or two.

The children were delighted by this development, and this afternoon, as usual, Lily and Louis were chatting happily as they mingled with the animals, watched over by Maddie who was sitting on the grass, breastfeeding baby Sacha. She was wearing a white seersucker sundress and looked the picture of health with her lustrous blonde hair pushed up into a loose bun. John came to join her. He had been weeding the vegetable plot before beginning his remote working day. It was a fulfilling rhythm he had fallen into. He sat down beside her, putting his arm around her and smiling up at the sun.

'This is the life,' he said. 'Can I risk sounding really smug as I remind us again how very fortunate we are?'

'Damn, I thought we'd be safely out of the way here,' said Maddie. 'But look, here come the crew.'

Robert, the cameraman, gave them a friendly wave, then turned his lens to focus on the children enthusiastically patting a baby goat with their chubby little hands, before moving round and capturing John and Maddie as they sat in the sunshine. Soundman Eric followed in his wake, his furry boom attached to the end of its pole. It was surprising how little that piece of equipment had changed over the years, John thought. It always looked like it belonged in the early days of film history.

'That's a lovely sequence, ' Robert said. 'Chateau-dwellers at one with nature.' He and Eric both spoke fluent English. Denise had selected them because she thought a bilingual crew would make for a relaxed atmosphere.

'Mummy!' said Louis, waving at Fizz who was hurrying towards them. Her long pink dress was accessorised with a pair of oversized sunglasses, and her hair was cascading down over her shoulders. She'd obviously been at the curling tongs, thought Maddie.

'I saw you heading this way,' Fizz said to Robert, giving him her most winning smile. 'I thought, I bet they're filming the animals, I did the same yesterday for my vlog. Where do you want me?'

She leaned against the gatepost, one leg in front of the other to give the most flattering angle.

'I think we're done here for the moment,' said Robert, 'we have some great stuff with the kids and the goats, and Maddie looking so natural there, feeding her baby.'

Fizz looked annoyed.

'I'm breast-feeding, too, you know. I could have brought Wren out if I thought that was a factor. Surely there's no harm in getting a little more footage here. Let me go in and play with the animals. Louis, darling, here comes Mummy!'

She entered the pen and embraced her son, then hoisted him on to her hip and took Lily by the hand whilst crouching to admire a cute black and white lamb.

Robert signalled to Eric, they might as well carry on filming, anything for a quiet life. Fizz beamed her approval as she saw them pick up their equipment. She was back in the spotlight where she belonged.

Maddie and John watched Fizz perform for the camera, her face expressing delight and wonder as she roamed amongst the animals with her two junior sidekicks.

'She just loves it,' Maddie whispered. 'I've never seen anyone look so animated by the sight of a snuffling pig.'

'Not shy and retiring like us,' said John. 'Oh look, here comes Luc, there's another one who's not afraid of putting himself in the limelight. He and Leo are made for each other. Can you believe that tiny swimsuit!'

Maddie watched Luc and Leo draw near, Luc's bathing slip shimmering in the sunshine.

'I thought you were coming to find us at the lake,' said Luc to Robert, ' then Simon guessed you were on your way here to the petting farm, so we thought, let's go!'

'If the mountain won't go to Mohammed, then Mohammed must come to the mountain,' said Leo. 'Though, as I'm not a massive fan of animals, I'll remain this side of the fence.'

He stood beside Maddie and John while Luc entered the pen and delighted the children by giving names to each animal and inventing stories about them as the camera crew kept it rolling.

Simon ambled up to join them, looking like a pumpkin in his fluorescent running kit.

'Mind the goats don't eat your swimming pants, Luc,' he said. 'You know they are notorious omnivores, they'll leave you naked if you're not careful.'

'That's too risky, this swimsuit is by Gucci!' Luc hurriedly slipped through the gate to join the spectators on the outside.

'I'm with Leo when it comes to animals,' said Simon. 'I've never seen the point of having pets, but I can see this petting farm will be an attraction. And in the event of a disaster, we can eat them, like during the Siege of Paris in the Franco-Prussian War when they consumed all the animals in the zoo. They were more exotic than our specimens – including a pair of elephants called Castor and Pollux.'

'You are a mine of information,' said John.

'I know, a walking encyclopaedia, as well as a sporting legend. Did you see me running round the grounds earlier?'

'I saw you,' said Maddie, 'fast as a flash of lightning.'

'Don't forget the swimming,' said Leo, 'he's a veritable triath-lete, if you also count him cycling off to buy the bread first thing.'

'That trip to the boulangerie is the favourite part of my day,' said Simon. 'Everything fresh and new, the wonderful scent of the hedgerows as I freewheel down the hill. It's a reflective time, too. I always think of poor Dom and how awful it was that he died that way.'

'Poor Dominic,' said Leo, 'that seems a lifetime away. And now Nicola has found a new love in Jean-Louis. I like to think of the chateau as a breeding ground for romance, don't you? When you think how over the centuries it has witnessed love and loss, births and deaths. And here we are, continuing that noble tradition.'

He squeezed Luc's hand.

'*Tu es tellement romantique,*' said Luc, 'but now I must return to the turret boudoir for a shower. After the wild swimming in the lake, and then the proximity to those animals, I must refresh myself, and make sure I am ready for the cameras this afternoon.'

Leo and Simon watched him as he made his way slowly back up to the chateau.

'At least your love life is falling into place,' said Simon. 'Mine is looking very dicey. I thought Beth would be pleased to have me back, but now I find she's been canoodling with that wretched Frenchman.'

'Handsome Frenchman, I think you mean,' said Leo. 'We all rather fancy him. And you must admit you haven't really got a leg to stand on, when it comes to the moral high ground.'

Simon sighed.

'You know, I was really excited to come back to the chateau. It was a wrench to leave Apolline, but I needed to follow my heart, and she completely understood, wonderful woman that she is. And then I find out that Beth is intent on ruining my life. Flaunting her relationship with Olivier in front of all my friends, not caring about my feelings. It's like I don't know who she is anymore.'

'Do you want my advice?'

'Yes!'

'You have to win her back. She's put up with you for all these years – I'm very fond of you, Simon, but you can be a nightmare, especially when it comes to your crushes. The most recent of which resulted in you walking out on her. No wonder she's furious! And no wonder she responded to the attentions of the alluring Olivier. You need to remind her why she married you, tell her how fabulous she is.'

Simon nodded.

'And one more thing. Don't wear that orange running kit. Trust me, it does nothing for you.'

Carry on as normal, was the brief from Denise, but it was hard for the chatelains to act casual when you never knew when a camera was going to appear around the corner. Nicola had spent the morning safely out of the picture, selling produce at the market with Jean-Louis, but late afternoon found her in the kitchen with Beth where they were preparing dinner for a full house. All the guests had asked to be catered for, which was unusual, they were naturally curious about the filming. Judging from their careful appearance at breakfast, some of them were clearly hoping to end up featuring on screen.

Beth was seated at the table, topping and tailing gooseberries which had failed to sell at the market. The fruit grew well here. They had planted a row of bushes in a nostalgic nod to their home country, but the French were suspicious of a berry that was defined as a *groseille à maquereau*, used only for stewing as a sauce for mackerel.

'What a chore this is,' she said, staring at the big box of fruit in front of her, 'remind me what we're serving them with?'

'Mascarpone cream, with a hint of Marsala, Italian style.'

'Perfect combination, but I think I need a little tipple to keep me going if I'm going to get through all this prep.'

'I was thinking the same,' said Nicola. 'Are you seeing Olivier today? You've gone a bit quiet on him.'

She lifted two large salmon onto a foil-lined baking sheet, their open bellies stuffed with lemon slices, dill and parsley. She washed her hands, wiped them on her apron and opened the fridge to bring out a bottle of wine.

'Not today,' said Beth, 'to be honest, I think I might be slightly over him.'

'Oh really? That does deserve a special toast!'

Nicola showed her the bottle.

'It's a Meursault Premier Cru, your quasi son-in-law James brought it at Christmas. I thought it looked too good for the general table, better suited for best friends enjoying an intimate pre-aperitif.'

She poured two glasses, while Beth inspected the label, then pulled her phone from her pocket.

'Let's have a quick Google, find out what it's worth … blimey, I'm going to find this even more delicious now I know how much it cost.'

She showed her phone to Nicola who raised her eyebrows.

'Criminal price,' she said, 'let's drink it slowly.'

They clinked glasses and solemnly took their first sips.

'I'm getting hazelnuts,' said Beth.

'Oatmeal, with a burst of honeycomb.'

'Flinty, with a lime edge.'

They laughed.

'Honestly, listen to us,' said Nicola. 'When you think of all the problems in the world, and here we are thinking of adjectives to describe obscenely expensive wine.'

'At least James can afford it. He may have his shortcomings, but he's a good earner.'

'Poor James, you are hard on him. I quite warmed to him at Christmas with his character sweater.'

'Is that my possible son-in-law you're talking about?'

Simon burst into the kitchen. His hair was dramatically swept back, and he was wearing a cream linen suit, with a rose-pink shirt to tone with the crimson handkerchief in his breast pocket.

'You look very dashing,' said Nicola.

Beth looked at him. Her expression was neutral, but she had to admit he scrubbed up well.

'I'm dressed for dinner, but I'm here to do whatever needs doing, so please, instruct me. I may also join you in a glass of that wine you were so expertly assessing.'

Nicola poured him a glass and he picked up a knife then sat down next to Beth and set about the gooseberries.

'It's good to be back in harness,' he said, 'there's such a buzz about the place now, thanks to you, Beth. Amazing initiative on your part, to get this film project underway.'

Beth looked surprised; it was the first time he had spoken to her in days.

'To be fair, it was Olivier's idea, I just went along with it.'

Simon winced slightly at the mention of his name.

'You brought in this project, it's down to you. So well done. And may I say how fetching you look in that outfit, it really suits you. Strong and classic.'

'Thanks, a linen jumpsuit is just the thing for this weather,' said Beth. 'But what's got into you? When did you ever pay me a compliment?'

'I'm allowed to admire my wife, surely. Other people do.'

Nicola exchanged glances with Beth.

'I'm going to get changed,' she said. 'I'll let you two to get on with the dinner prep if that's all right.'

'Leave it to us,' said Simon. 'We are the devoted couple that every hospitality establishment dreams of. Tried and trusted, with decades of shared domestic experience.'

There was an awkward silence between them when Nicola left the room, neither of them ready to address their real feelings. Eventually, Beth spoke, but only to continue the banter.

'I wouldn't say your domestic experience runs to decades. You barely lifted a finger when we lived in London, you didn't even know how to turn on the oven.'

Simon was relieved to stick to their light-hearted sparring. He faked indignation.

'I was too busy being a big cheese and commanding a huge salary in the cut-throat world of advertising! But those were different times. Now I am a reformed character, I have learned the joy to be found in small basic tasks, the sense of satisfaction to be gleaned from perfectly preparing a gooseberry.'

He held one up for her to inspect.

'Consider this gooseberry, in it we find an entire world. I believe it's called mindfulness.'

'Whatever.'

He moved his chair closer.

'Joking aside, Beth. I believe everything I said. We really are a devoted couple, our relationship built on decades of shared experience. I've loved every moment, and I love you. What's more, the best is yet to come, I can feel it in my bones.'

He leaned in to kiss her. For a moment she was about to give in, then pulled herself back.

'Fine words, Simon, but that wasn't the line you took six months ago! Don't think you can brush it all under the carpet with your Tiggerish optimism that everything will be all right! Let's just get on with the work, shall we?'

'Of course! I'm here to prove my worth and earn my lady's favour.'

He gave her a cheeky grin, reminding her how attractive she found him, and humbly turned his attention back to the gooseberries. Beth washed the soil off a bowlful of tiny red-skinned *grenaille* potatoes she had harvested that morning. She placed them in a pan of water, then wiped her hands on a tea towel and turned to Simon.

'I think that's it for the moment.'

'Good work, I think we've earned a breather,' he replied, picking up the half-empty bottle. 'Shall we take this outside?'

They wandered out to the terrace and sat down on the stone bench which was still radiating warmth from the day's sun.

'What a perfect summer evening,' said Simon. 'Do you remember when we planted that lavender? Tiny little plants, dwarfed by those massive pots, and now grown to fruition. They're a symbol of our life at the chateau, wouldn't you say? Bigger and better than ever, reaching its climax in a ground-breaking documentary series.'

He shared out the last of the wine and clinked glasses with her.

'Here's to the next chapter, and here's to us.'

Beth had no time to reply, as Maddie was approaching them, her baby tucked on her hip.

'Come and sit with us, Maddie,' said Simon. 'We were just discussing the glorious future of the chateau, embracing the new life within it. You look like an advertisement for fecundity with that baby, de Gaulle would have been proud of you for repeopling the nation.'

'Well hello, boomers, are you drinking already?' said Maddie with a smile. She handed Sacha to Beth and sat beside her.

'Say hello to Auntie Beth, you know she gave you your name.'

'Less of the "auntie", thank you, just "Beth" will do nicely.'

Beth bounced the baby on her knee and was rewarded with a gummy smile.

'A bit early, I agree,' she said, 'but it is an exceptional Meursault. Try a sip, unless it's one of your days off? I know you millennials are far more sensible than us.'

'I won't, thanks,' said Maddie, 'but by the time I get to your age, I'll probably do the same, the stakes will be lower by then.'

'That makes us feel better, cheers!' said Beth.

'You don't know what you're missing out on, with your self-loathing "days off",' said Simon. 'To quote Lord Bryon, wine cheers the sad, revives the old, inspires the young, makes weariness forget his toil, so why wouldn't we drink it every day?'

'He died aged thirty-six so not a great example,' said Maddie.

'Not of the booze, he died of derring-do!'

'Anyway, I'm glad to see you two are back on speakers,' said Maddie. 'I don't like strife at the chateau, that's not what it's about. We're one big happy family, remember.'

'You're so right,' said Simon, 'that is exactly why I'm committed to reminding Beth why she married me and why we will always be together, regardless of whoever else comes and goes.'

'Wow, there's a statement of intent,' said Maddie. 'Are you guys going to renew your vows? It's about time we had another wedding at the chateau.'

'Certainly not,' said Beth. 'Even if I did decide to forgive Simon, I would never do that. It's such an unappetising sight – an ageing couple trying to turn back the clock, determined to make themselves the centre of attention.'

'Ooh, sorry I asked!' said Maddie.

'Never mind *you* forgiving *me*!' said Simon. 'You seem to be forgetting that I'm the injured party here! I'm not the one canoodling with a French Casanova in front of their poor deceived husband.'

'Right, on that note, I'd better leave you to it,' said Maddie, taking back the baby. 'I'll see you both at dinner, assuming you haven't killed each other by then.'

She blew them a kiss, and they watched her walk back across the lawn, her shoulders golden from the sun, her long white dress skimming the grass.

'She's a lovely girl,' said Beth.

'And a perceptive one. She could sense the chemistry between us. It's indestructible.'

He stroked the back of her neck, then leaned back to examine the structure of her jumpsuit.

'That romper suit is a modern-day chastity belt, hard to know where I'd find my way in, if that was my intention.'

Beth laughed and tugged at the fabric round her waist.

'It's also really annoying when you go to the loo, you have to strip off every time.'

'It's been a while since I saw that.'

He put his other arm around her and pulled her to him. This time, she didn't resist.

CHAPTER 20

'Back where I belong, lord of all I survey.'

Simon stretched out luxuriously in the Napoleonic bed, his arm wrapped around Beth. It was the morning after their passionate reunion, and he was feeling very pleased with himself.

'There's a word for how I feel right now,' he said. '"Uxorious". It means "excessively devoted to one's wife".'

'You are insufferable with your Latin vocabulary,' said Beth, enjoying the warmth of his leg against hers. It was early morning and still cool in the room.

'But you're glad to have me back, admit it.'

'We are partners for life, like a couple of swans.'

'A lovely image, swimming towards our shared future.'

'And you have your uses. Especially at dinner last night. If I had never met you before, I would have been blown away by your charm and charisma. You certainly know how to light up a room, even though you are a terrible show-off. The camera loves you, too, they were filming you leading the rousing singalong of "La Marseillaise", everyone standing on their chairs.'

'Best national anthem in the world, it brings tears to my eyes every time.'

He sat bolt upright in bed, arms outstretched and launched into song.

'*Allons enfants de la patrie, Le jour de gloire est arrivé.*'

'I can't wait to see the film, it will make the perfect ending for the first episode. Olivier will be thrilled.'

Simon frowned.

'Now you've spoiled it all by mentioning his name. Reminding me that I am a cuckold.'

He stuck his fingers up over his ears to simulate the horns.

'Sorry,' said Beth, 'but remember you started it.'

'Let's get back to us. I'm glad my performance at dinner won you over. That was my intention – to be the joyful master of ceremonies, piano-thumper and all-round lifter of spirits that you've been missing so dreadfully. And now, you lucky woman, you even have me back in your bed. Our bed. Our Napoleonic bed. "I'm coming home Josephine, don't wash!"'

He pulled her closer to emphasise his point.

She laughed and pushed him away.

'I realise that's what you've been missing, our great big antique bed, never mind me!'

'True, it's been a shocker sleeping alone in that maid's room, it's the only reason I wanted you back.'

Beth shoved him with her foot so he fell out of the bed.

'No, please let me back!'

He jumped in beside her again.

'Thank goodness we've rekindled the flame, though,' he said. 'Better than ever, wouldn't you say?'

'Oh, it's like putting on a comfy old pair of slippers.'

'As opposed to a toe-pinching, brand-new French moccasin?'

'I'm not going to make comparisons. Unless you want to talk me through your experiences with Apolline, which would be ungallant. Let's just say that, after our adventures, we are – as you put it – back where we belong.'

'Quits, you could say.'

'You could, but it's not a game.'

Beth cuddled up to him again, appreciating the familiarity of his body.

'I've missed the bulk of you,' she said, running her hand over his well-upholstered stomach. 'In spite of your fitness regime, you're still quite chunky.'

He spun round defensively to face her.

'Unlike skinny Olivier, you mean? There is something insubstantial about that man, in every sense.'

'He's very trim, it's true.'

'But you are going to end it with him, I take it?'

'He doesn't think there's any need for that. He says that it's only we Anglo-Saxons who are obsessed with monogamy and there is no need for exclusivity.'

'I beg to differ! Maybe it's all right for the French to go all *Jules et Jim* with their kinky threesomes, but I'm an upstanding Englishman!'

'Spoken like a true Anglo-Saxon!'

'And why are the French so obsessed with that term? I don't think of myself as a wild-bearded Anglo-Saxon, following the horse-drawn plough or wearing a warrior helmet, so why are the French so keen on it?'

'It's a useful generic word, to include Americans and Aussies, as you know very well, but you are clearly determined to take umbrage at everything Olivier says.'

'Hmm. Well, he can say whatever he likes, as long as you agree that it's over between the two of you. I know you well enough to know that's what you want too. Like me, you're basically a straightforward person. We've both had a holiday romance, now it's back to reality. Though our reality is pretty damned romantic, you must agree. A charmed life in a turreted chateau, surrounded by people we love. It's the stuff of dreams. As well as TV gold, of course. It's a good job I'm so fit these day, the camera puts on half a stone so you can't be too careful.'

He took a deep breath to hold in his stomach, and propped himself up on his elbow.

'Promise me you'll speak to him today. Please.'

'I can promise you that – I'm meeting him for lunch today. But I can't promise what I'm going to say because I haven't decided yet.'

Olivier had set up a lunch table in the orchard, beneath the shade of an apple tree. A bread basket and a seafood platter were laid out on a chequered red and white cloth, along with a bottle of pale rosé chilling in a silver wine cooler.

'Such attention to detail,' said Beth, as she approached him. Olivier stood up to kiss her, rather formally, on both cheeks.

'I wanted us to meet away from the crowds at the chateau,' he said. 'Whenever I see you these days, we are surrounded by other people. Please, sit down, and taste this wine, it is a delightful Côtes de Provence from the vineyard which happened to belong to Brad Pitt, but which owes its finesse to the skill of the Perrin family who make it.'

'I try not to drink at lunchtime . . .'

'I agree, but this is such a delicate rosé that it really doesn't count.'

Beth sipped the wine. It was chilled and delicious, provoking a sense of wellbeing as she contemplated the crustacean feast before her and wondered where to start.

'It's perfect weather for seafood,' said Olivier. 'You remember not long ago I promised to take you for a picnic by the sea, but I realise this is not the moment, we are far too busy. So I decided to bring the picnic to you. I made the mayonnaise myself; you should try it with the *bulots*.'

'*Bulot* meaning whelk, as opposed to *boulot* meaning work, it's very confusing,' said Beth.

She picked up a thin metal prong, and drove it into the rubbery flesh of a large whelk. After some coaxing, it pinged out of its shell, a long yellow plug with a trail of glutinous liquid.

'It looks so unappetising,' she said, 'you need the mayo to help it down, along with a good spritz of lemon juice.'

She dipped it in the mayonnaise and chewed it thoughtfully.

'It's exactly like eating snails,' she said, 'pieces of gristle which are only made bearable by the garlic butter, or in the case of whelks, your excellent mayonnaise.'

'Sacred combinations, both of them,' said Olivier, 'but move on to the langoustines if you're finding the whelks heavy going. I boiled them myself this morning so they couldn't be fresher.'

He loaded some on to her plate, as Beth admired their prehistoric heads and dainty pink fronds.

'I've seen the rushes from last night,' said Olivier, cracking open a crab with the aid of a vicious-looking tool. 'It's fantastic stuff. I have to hand it to your husband, he certainly knows how to start a party.'

'Doesn't he just!' said Beth. 'I knew you'd like it, especially when he gets everyone singing your national anthem.'

'It made me so proud to be French, seeing the love it inspired in you Brits who have adopted my homeland as your own.'

He leaned across the table to take hold of her hand, an awkward gesture as she was engaged in pulling the head off a langoustine.

'I have a proposal for you,' he said, in what she recognised as the low, seductive tone he favoured when talking about sex. He put his head on one side and stared intensely into her eyes.

'Why don't you come back home with me after lunch, and we could look over the footage together? My mother is still away, we would have the place to ourselves . . .'

Beth gave a snort of laughter.

'So, you have a free house? Honestly, Olivier, we aren't teenagers!'

Olivier looked hurt.

'It was just an idea. I thought that offering you this aphrodisiacal seafood lunch would be a way back to rediscovering our intimacy. Then we could escape for the afternoon, just the two of us, back to my *gentilhommière*. Our last visit there was so rushed, and you were in a funny mood. Please, let us get back to how we were. I understand your circumstances have changed now, with Simon's return. Which means we simply need to adapt, to seek a new framework.'

Beth shook her head.

'I can't Olivier, I'm sorry, but I can't do it. I've loved our time together but, as you say, my circumstances have changed. It was one thing when my marriage was up in the air and I didn't know which way things would go. But now I've decided, I'm back with Simon and I'm too pathetically Anglo-Saxon to keep both of you on the go! The truth is, I lack the French sophistication to conduct an affair.'

Olivier looked at her, wondering whether he should make one further effort to persuade her to change her mind.

'Do you need me to be more persuasive?' he asked eventually. 'We have great chemistry, it is a shame to put an end to our pleasure. You must agree we have enjoyed each other, and for me, that enjoyment can stand quite independently of your relationship with your husband.'

'It can for you, but not for me. Sorry.'

Olivier made an equivocal gesture with his hand, rocking it from side to side, which Beth recognised as meaning that he was not of the same opinion.

'I think you should be sorry for yourself, not for me,' he said. 'It is a puritan instinct to deny oneself pleasure, to find reasons why one should not explore the possibilities of love. But I know that you are a woman who knows her own mind, so if that's your decision, I shall say no more.'

'Thank you.'

'But it you ever grow tired of Simon – and I sense that is entirely possible – you know where I am. Now, let me top up your glass and we will drink to our ongoing relationship – as co-producers of this excellent television series.'

Beth felt a sense of relief as she parted company with Olivier. It was all very civil as she helped him load the lunch things into his car, clearly there would be no ill effect on their working relationship, and she couldn't help thinking that their affair had been a rather wonderful thing. There were no disastrous consequences, it had given Simon something to think about, and she would shore up the memories forever, something to revisit in her old age. Recently she had come to regard her life in these terms. As a young woman she was unselfconscious about her actions, never had the feeling that she was making memories, she was just doing what she wanted to do. Looking back now, it seemed that her entire existence had been about creating layers of memories that she could later relive.

She walked back to the orchard, wanting to inspect the hornets' nest they'd recently discovered, and smiled to herself as she thought about the good times with Olivier. The overnight stays in his Paris flat, the secret kisses in the grounds of the chateau, the nights when he joined her in the Napoleonic bed. It was perfectly possible, she realised, to have a love affair and suffer no regrets, something she could never have imagined in her younger days. Maybe this was a side benefit of growing older. There had to be an upside.

The hornets had constructed their nest in the hollow trunk of a dead plum tree on the edge of the orchard. It looked like an exquisite, pale wood carving with smooth curves which reminded Beth of the art nouveau designs of some Paris metro stations. The hornets were bustling in and out. They were twice the size of honey bees, and luckily did not have the yellow legs and orange faces that distinguish the Asian hornet. The chatelains had spent a panicked half-hour consulting images on their phones and peering at the insects, trying to ascertain whether this was an outbreak of *frelons asiatiques* – a notifiable event they should report to the *mairie*.

Her inspection of the nest was interrupted by the sound of Simon calling her name. He was running towards her. He'd taken Leo's advice and was wearing a more restrained Lycra outfit, in a navy colour that was more flattering to his figure than the orange. He puffed to a halt beside her.

'Have you done the deed? I was watching from the sidelines on my run, it looked quite civilised. No violent scenes, and luckily no passionate clinches, so I assume we are back to business as usual?'

Beth put her hands on her hips.

'Business as usual? If I was looking for an excuse to run back into the arms of my French lover, I think you just supplied it! Where's your romantic soul, you useless Englishman?'

Simon put his arm on her shoulder.

'Let me rephrase that. I'm quietly hoping that you've given Olivier his marching orders, so we can continue uninterrupted in the red-hot revival of our love.'

He sank to his knees.

'Be mine, Beth, and only mine! For you are my one true love, and if you hadn't written it off as being so naff, I would be calling for us to renew our wedding vows.'

'That sounds so fake. But you can stand up now, and let's get on with our real lives. And yes – I can confirm that Olivier and I have agreed that we should call time on our romantic attachment.'

Simon rose stiffly to his feet.

'Thank goodness for that, I am truly relieved.'

'Now you do sound sincere. I admit that I'm also relieved. My mum told me that relief was her favourite emotion as she got older, and I see what she meant. Come here.'

She pulled him close and kissed him on the lips.

'Shall we go upstairs,' he suggested, 'and celebrate the deep, deep peace of the double bed, after the hurly-burly of the chaise longue?'

'No, we have guests arriving and I'm on check-in duty, come and help me.'

She took his arm, and they made their way across the lawn and up onto the terrace, where Leo was playing cards with Dougie and Mary beneath the shade of a parasol. Leo looked up as they approached.

'My God, are you two holding hands?!!'

Beth quickly dropped Simon's hand.

'So what if we were?' she said. 'It's not as if you're averse to public displays of affection yourself. Where is Luc by the way?'

'Gone to Paris, he'll be back in a few days. Meanwhile, Dougie and Mary are helping me cope with his loss.'

Mary laid down a spread of three kings.

'I haven't played canasta for years,' she said, 'I'd forgotten what a marvellous game it is.'

Dougie peered at his hand and considered his next move, while Leo beamed with delight at Beth and Simon.

'I'm *so* glad to see you back together. I told him, Beth, he had to win you back and it looks like he took my advice. It hasn't been the same without you, Simon. I know you've been here but not in the full sense so it's such a relief to see my mum and dad reunited.'

'We are *not* parents to an elderly man like you, don't be grotesque,' said Beth.

'You know what I mean. I'm just glad to have the chateau family back in full emotional health.'

Simon leaned down to give him a man hug.

'We're going to wait for the new arrivals,' he said, 'come and join us when you've finished your game.'

'Certainly not, we can't spare him,' said Dougie, gesturing to Simon to leave them in peace, 'we're set for an all-day marathon here. It's extraordinary how these games can draw you in. It's the great joy of our community here, isn't it, the chance to discover new enthusiasms with our friends? I never thought of myself as a card sharp, but look at me now!'

'You enjoy it, Dougie, we'll see you all later,' said Beth.

The new guests had already parked up and were approaching the front door by the time she and Simon arrived in the entrance hall.

'It's so annoying when they come early,' Simon whispered to Beth. 'I mean, which part of "check-in from 4 p.m." don't they understand? Rude beyond belief.'

He then turned seamlessly to greet the couple coming through the door with his most winning smile.

'How lovely to meet you, bright and early! You must have had good journey?'

'Eight hours, from Lyon, including a brief lunch stop,' said Ralph, who was wearing shorts, sandals with socks and a rather too tight polo-shirt. 'In this heat, I can tell you it pays to have a quality vehicle. Mind you, it's a lot more bearable here, it was over forty degrees in the south – not what you want.'

'For us, Normandy has the perfect climate,' said Beth. 'Slightly warmer than the UK but never unbearable.'

'What a place,' said Ralph's wife Maggie, looking around her in admiration. Tall and statuesque, she was wearing a floor-length linen shift dress in pale lavender which complemented her straw-coloured hair. Beth exchanged pleasantries with her about the joys of linen clothes in high summer, then said she would show them to their room.

'It's like Fawlty Towers but on a grander scale!' said Maggie, as they trundled down the corridor with their suitcases. 'You and your husband are the dead spit of John Cleese and Prunella Scales, or the dead spit of how they would look if they were indulging in lovely French food!'

Beth's smile froze.

'We're not the only owners,' she said, 'it's a sort of coopera-tive really. We bought in with a group of our closest friends. It's our home first of all, and a guest house second. So not really like Fawlty Towers at all.'

'Oh no, I was only joking!' said Maggie. 'It's a beautiful place, I'm completely in awe of you for taking it on, especially at an age when many would be thinking of winding down to retirement.'

'Age is just a number, that's our motto here,' Beth said firmly. 'The other thing I need to tell you is that we are filming a TV series about our life here, so you will see cameras around the place. Most of our guests love the idea, but I wanted to let you know.'

Ralph was delighted by this news.

'So we might actually be on telly, what a marvellous end to our holiday! I expect you'll also want to get a shot of our car, you don't see many Aston Martins like that, red with cream uphol-stery. It looks perfect parked out in front of the chateau.'

'Here's your room, the Jean-Honoré Fragonard suite,' said Beth, opening the door and watching the guests delighting over the decor. She still got a buzz from sharing the beauty of the chateau.

'Saucy picture over the bed,' said Ralph, nodding at *The Birth of Venus*. 'Don't you start getting any funny ideas, Maggie.'

'I see you're booked in for dinner, with no allergies,' said Beth, 'so we'll see you at seven thirty for an aperitif in the grand salon.'

'Is it dressy?' asked Maggie. 'I'm especially asking because of the cameras. I don't want to embarrass myself by wearing the wrong thing!'

'We don't have a dress code – which stresses out our American guests – so just wear what you like. And don't worry about the cameras, we filmed dinner last night, so we won't be repeating it tonight.'

'Oh, that's a relief,' said Maggie, although she looked disappointed.

Beth went down to complain to Simon, who was staring at the screen.

'Well, there's another stage-struck couple desperate to get themselves on camera,' she said. 'I can't believe they compared us to Basil and Sybil Fawlty, what an insult . . . Why are you frowning?'

Simon looked up at her.

'I'm just looking at this booking. In the name of Fleurie, arriving tomorrow for two weeks.'

'That's good, we like the long stayers, far less laundry involved.'

'Fleurie, doesn't that ring a bell? Clue: it's an address in Toulouse.'

'Toulouse, that dead-to-me city where you went after abandoning me for . . . Oh God, it's her, isn't it? I was thinking Granger, but Fleurie's her maiden name, her film star name . . .'

Simon took his head in his hands.

'Why would she do that? Just as I'm getting my life here back together.'

'Have you been in touch with her since you left?'

'No. We parted on good terms, but agreed it was best to cut contact.'

'Sounds like she's discovered she can't live without you.'

'I'm going to ring her, find out what she's up to.'

He went outside and Beth watched him through the window as he paced around the forecourt between the cars, the scene of their first meeting with Apolline.

Simon ended the call and came back in.

Beth tried to read his expression.

'Well? Is she intending to win back the love of her life? Will she be challenging me to pistols at dawn?'

He shook his head.

'You'll be relieved to know that she is completely over us. As in me and her. But she wants to come back to the chateau. She's bringing her ex-husband, as she needs to show him where she began her healing. You remember, when she stayed here last time, it was to get over their split . . .'

'She got over that with a vengeance, thanks to you.'

'Yes, all right, don't rub it in. They're back together again, obviously. She says she texted me last week to check I was OK with it, but I didn't see the message. She took my silence as approval, apparently.'

'Reunited with her husband, that didn't take long!'

'I knew she was seeing him again, she told me before I left Toulouse that they were back in touch. I assumed it was only as friends. It didn't take us long, either by the way, once I'd set myself the task of winning you back.'

'Congratulate yourself, why don't you.'

'No surprises there. But I am very surprised about Apolline and her husband. Let me tell you why.'

CHAPTER 21

Ralph and Maggie were the last down to breakfast the following morning, arriving at an obscenely late hour, in Leo's opinion.

'I think we should just tell them, *Sorry, loves, this isn't a hotel, you can't just pitch up whenever you feel like it.*'

He poured coffee into Beth and Nicola's cups. The three of them were seated at a table on the terrace, impatient to finish the morning service.

'Except we are a hotel, basically,' said Nicola, 'we certainly charge luxury hotel prices.'

'So, we just leave a Thermos and bread basket on the table and tell them to fend for themselves. I don't see why we should have to dance attendance because they're too lazy to get up at a respectable hour.'

'And earn ourselves a two-star review'?' said Nicola, biting into a pain au chocolat. 'We can't afford it!'

'It does beg the question, are we really cut out for a career in hospitality?' said Beth. 'I've decided I really don't like people very much. Especially when I have to deal with them, when I'd much rather be discussing the burning issue of the day with my best friends.'

'Are you saying we're not people?' said Leo.

'You're not members of the public. Let me qualify my remark, it's members of the public I don't really like. Specifically, our paying guests. I've rather had enough of them.'

Ralph and Maggie chose that moment to make their entrance onto the terrace. Leo jumped to his feet, all welcoming smiles as he ushered them to their table.

'Just look at him,' said Beth, 'he can certainly turn it on.'

'Where is everyone?' asked Ralph, looking around the empty tables.

'They've been and gone,' said Leo. 'Most people want to get out and make the most of the day, it's blue skies and sunshine again.'

'We couldn't have managed it any earlier,' said Maggie, patting her stomach in a ladylike way. 'We were still digesting the excellent dinner you served us last night, you've certainly earned a five-star review from us.'

'That's good to hear,' said Leo, 'now we are all slaves to our customer ratings.'

He served them coffee and fruit juice, then wished them a pleasant day and returned to join his friends.

'So, spill the beans,' he said, 'what is this burning issue you want to discuss? I assume it's to do with the return of Apolline? Simon mentioned last night that she's booked herself in, arriving today I believe! I think that's rather lovely, that they can continue as friends. We must all be terribly British when she arrives, and not talk about the time she seduced your husband and lured him away from the chateau.'

Beth scowled at him.

'I wish you wouldn't be so flippant about everything.'

'I am never flippant, but I try to keep things light. Do you know that quote from Aldous Huxley? "Just lightly let things happen and lightly cope with them." I live my life by that sound advice.'

'Whatever. Anyway, I am resigned to seeing her again, we are all grown-ups after all. But what I wanted to discuss with you is the fact that she's bringing her husband. They are reunited, apparently.'

'That was quick,' said Nicola, 'and surely good news, proving things are amicable with her and Simon, and she's not still carrying a torch for him.'

'Carrying a torch for Simon, what a funny idea,' said Leo. 'I adore Simon, don't get me wrong, but I was always mystified by what the lovely screen goddess Apolline saw in him. You've got to admit he was really punching!'

'Better suited to an old dowd like me, you mean?' said Beth. 'You're really not endearing yourself to me this morning, Leo.'

'Darling, you're perfect, you know I'm only teasing. If I were straight, you'd be top of my list – alongside Nicola, naturally, I could never choose between you two.'

Beth looked slightly appeased.

'Let me get to the really juicy part, if I may,' she continued. 'You remember Apolline came to stay here to get over the breakdown of her marriage? Well, it turns out her husband left her for a younger model, as they often do. But in this case, it was for a man! He left her for a twenty-four-year-old Italian called Riccardo.'

'Ooh, that *is* exciting,' said Leo. 'So what's happened to Riccardo?'

'He's moved on, apparently. And Apolline's husband has decided that he's not gay after all, and he's back with his wife!'

'How very modern,' said Leo, with an approving nod. 'We're all supposed to be on the rainbow spectrum now. Whereas I'm just a dinosaur, a boring old gay man, it's terribly last century. When I think how people like me were once considered cutting edge and slightly dangerous. Now we're as dreary as our het counterparts. I'm no more interesting than all the other men in this chateau.'

'Better dressed, to be fair,' said Nicola.

'There is that. I must cling to my outfits.'

He lovingly brushed his hand over his pale pink shirt.

'Do you like this blouse? It's vintage Dries van Noten.'

Nicola stood up.

'That is great gossip. Beth, I feel we need to discuss it further, shall we stroll down to the lake and stretch out on the grass for a well-deserved break?'

She picked up a couple of the cotton throws they kept folded up on the bench, then the three of them walked slowly down the stairs, across the lawn, to their favourite spot near the lake.

'Such memories,' said Nicola, throwing herself down on the ground. 'Do you remember how we re-enacted *Le Déjeuner sur l'herbe* for Fizz's vlog in this very spot? She made us take our clothes off while the men were in nineteenth-century top hats and tails. That was when she was still Mademoiselle Bovary, before she launched into motherhood. Oh look, speak of the devil . . .'

Fizz was approaching them, her baby strapped to her chest, little Louis running ahead, careering into the water, splashing his limbs in delight.

'Come and join us, Fizz,' said Leo, patting the towel beside him, 'we have been mulling over the latest news of Apolline. Did you know she's arriving this afternoon, with her *husband*?'

Fizz sat down beside him, releasing Wren from the sling and laying him down between them. He was wearing an exquisite primrose yellow smock which Fizz had been sent by an eye-wateringly expensive children's clothes brand. She was remaining true to her intention of dressing him like a girl.

'No, I didn't,' she said, 'we've been a bit out of the loop recently, hunkering down with the children in the barn, though Robert did come and film some charming footage of me with my children. I posted a picture of it on my vlog, as a teaser for the chateau series. There was a big response. I tell you that show is going to be *huge* when it goes out. So, back to what you were saying. Apolline is reunited with her husband?'

'The same husband, who left her for a man,' said Beth, 'but now he's changed his mind, and they're back together.'

'How very interesting! It just goes to show how gender fluid we're all becoming,' said Fizz.

'Some of us, maybe,' said Beth, 'but I can safely say I don't have a gay bone in my body.'

'As we can tell from your recent behaviour,' said Leo. 'Moving between two incredibly hot men. Well, one hot man, and darling Simon.'

'We were just discussing the phenomenon of middle-aged men who walk out of their marriages,' said Nicola. 'Humiliating for the wives, but what do you think is worse? To be abandoned for another woman, or for a man? I think a man is better, at least there's no question of competition. As opposed to being traded in for a younger, prettier model.'

Fizz looked uncomfortable.

'I hope that's not a pointed question, I know you all disapproved when Will left his wife for me.'

Nicola clapped her hand to her mouth.

'Oh sorry, Fizz, that hadn't crossed my mind! Honestly, you and Will have been together so long that I think of you as the same as us!'

'Thanks. I think.'

'Though of course you are still incredibly young and gorgeous,' Nicola added quickly.

Fizz lay flat on her back and picked up her baby, whooshing him through the air to mimic an aeroplane, while she put her thoughts together.

'What time is Apolline arriving?' she asked, sitting up and strapping Wren back into the sling. 'I must go and tell Olivier. I caught him earlier and we were discussing today's schedule. I think he'll be very interested to hear that our famous actress friend is coming back, just think of the ratings.'

That afternoon, Simon slipped into the salon and took a seat by the window, with a view of the entrance gates. Apolline had texted him that they would be arriving slightly ahead of check-in time, and she hoped that was all right. He didn't tell the others, he wanted to be the first one to see her, and he didn't want everyone looking at him and judging his reaction. He especially didn't want Beth to be there, her sharp eyes taking in his every emotion.

A few minutes later, the orange campervan moved slowly through the gates. Simon remembered the last time it was on these premises. A crisp winter morning, the sun just rising and he'd thrown his suitcase on the back seat, jumped in next to Apolline, and they'd headed south, giddy with love and excitement.

No such feelings now, as he watched the van approach, clocked Apolline wearing her signature Ray-Ban sunglasses and tried to make out the figure who had taken his place in the passenger seat.

Apolline stepped out, graceful as ever, while her husband unfolded himself more stiffly – he was older, of course, a friend of the family where she'd been employed as an au pair. Simon remembered every detail. He was a handsome man still, tall and slim, apparently with all his own hair, though that could be a careful disguise.

Simon thought then about the very first time he'd seen Apolline, emerging like a Pre-Raphaelite goddess from that van. He'd suffered *un vrai coup de foudre*, a thunderbolt, as if she'd been sent from heaven to bless him. What a difference a few months made, now he felt only slight embarrassment, as he opened the door and went out to greet them with a polite smile.

'You must be Cyril,' he said, trying to summon his usual charm, which was difficult in the circumstances.

But Cyril was completely disarming.

'Yes and you are obviously the famous Simon,' he said, shaking him warmly by the hand. 'Such a pleasure to meet you. Apolline has filled me in on the wonderful life you and your friends have created here. Gosh, it really is every Englishman's dream, isn't it? A turreted chateau in France, isn't that what we all aspire to?'

He looked around him admiringly, and Simon realised, with relief, that it was all going to be all right, a feeling that intensified when Apolline came up to kiss him on both cheeks in that casual friendship way that meant nothing.

'It's good to see you, Apolline.'

And it really was. How extraordinary that they could be standing there as if nothing had ever happened, as if they hadn't both lost their heads for a wild few weeks. He saw before him a nice-looking woman, that was all.

They looked up as Beth came out to join them.

'I thought I heard a car,' she said, smiling broadly, 'and here you are again, Apolline. It's been a while.'

Simon detected an undertone in her voice, but if Apolline was aware of it, she showed no sign as she greeted Beth with the same double kiss she'd shared with him.

'It is such a pleasure for me to be back at Chateau Lafarge. May I introduce my husband Cyril?'

'Oh yes, we've heard all about you,' said Beth, shaking his hand and exchanging glances that confirmed that while they all knew everything about his sexual history, it would never be discussed. True British reticence would prevail.

'Let me show you to your room,' said Beth, 'it's the same one where Apolline stayed last time, the Louis XIV suite.'

'It's OK, I remember the way,' said Apolline.

Of course she did, thought Beth, just as she no doubt remembered the doe-eyed Simon panting after her during those early days. She quashed her irritation. They were grown-ups, that was all in the past.

'Come and have a drink on the terrace first,' said Simon, putting a convivial hand on Cyril's shoulder. 'You can take a relaxing view of our grounds with a glass of something cold before you unpack.'

The women followed them through the front door into the salon, towards the French windows opening on to the terrace.

Apolline touched Beth's arm.

'You look so well, Beth. Simon told me that you, too, have had *une petite aventure*? Sometimes it can do a woman good, don't you agree?'

Beth stiffened; she wasn't ready for this intimate girl talk with the one who had caused such havoc in her marriage.

'Oh that's all in the past,' she said briskly. 'I didn't realise Simon had shared that with you.'

'Only yesterday, when we had a brief conversation. I hear your former *amoureux* is directing the television programme. That sounds very exciting. I'm hoping you may allow me to make a cameo appearance?'

'That is exactly what Olivier hoped you'd say! I wasn't sure as I know you're rather camera shy these days . . .'

'I can make an exception, to promote this beautiful place and the community where I began my healing. And now we have come full circle, have we not? You and Simon together again, just as Cyril and I have rediscovered each other.'

She might at least apologise, thought Beth. That clearly wasn't going to happen. If you were French, that's what you did, apparently. Enhance your life with a love affair – sorry, '*une petite aventure*' – and then get back with your original life partner. In this spirit of openness she was moved to ask Apolline about her husband being gay, and then not, all of a sudden.

'Cyril changed his mind, then?' she said.

'Oh, it's not a question of changing one's mind! It is the person one falls in love with. We are all on a spectrum of sexuality, gender is irrelevant, that is what I have learned. And now, thanks to my liaison with Simon, and Cyril's adventures elsewhere, we have reignited our passion – it is exactly as we were at the start of our marriage and I couldn't be happier. You too, I think?'

If she thought Beth was about to share the details of her sex life with Simon, she had another thing coming.

'As I said, we are all back where we belong, which is the main thing. Oh look, here comes Olivier.'

Olivier was hurrying towards them on the terrace, his face lighting up with recognition at the sight of Apolline. He took her hand and kissed it. Beth watched their very French exchange.

'*Quel plaisir*, what a pleasure. I never thought our paths would cross in this way, I am such a fan of your films, especially the one with Gérard Depardieu. And now with great serendipity, you are back at the chateau, just in time for a scene we are planning to shoot tomorrow. How would you feel about that? The great Apolline Fleurie makes a comeback, relaxing with her husband, who as an Englishman completely understands the great British fantasy of retiring to a chateau!'

'But of course, I am happy to participate.'

'*Génial!* Would you be ready for that tomorrow, or are we pushing our luck, it is perhaps too soon for you?'

'Tomorrow is fine. Now, if you will excuse me, I am going to take my husband for a walk around the lake, so we can breathe the fresh air of the Chateau Lafarge *domaine* before I introduce him to all the chatelains . . . this is such a homecoming for me.'

The heat had achieved a new intensity, bringing with it those unwelcome companions of high summer: wasps. In the orchard, they feasted noisily on the early windfall plums, while at the chateau they buzzed around the breakfast tables. It became a game amongst the guests, to trap them under a glass.

'They send out scouts, you see,' Ralph explained to his wife, as he peered at the one he had lured onto a plate with a spoonful of jam, which was now busily hitting its head against its glass prison. 'Once they've found a food source, they go back to the colony to bring their friends.'

Ralph and Maggie had made it down earlier today. They had been told about the filming schedule, and Maggie had selected a pair of bright yellow wide trousers with a lime-green cropped top.

'They said they are going to be filming a lot in the grounds today,' she said, checking her lipstick in her hand mirror. 'Simon – you know, the tubby one who checked us in – is setting up a croquet lawn and inviting all the guests to join a tournament. I said they could count us in, it's been years but I still remember the rules.'

'Not sure about that,' said Ralph, 'supposing we lose, it will be embarrassing to be caught on camera coming last!'

'So what if we do? It's taking part that matters and I've not spotted a single camera so far. It will be so disappointing if we're not featured at all. I think we should spend all day on the premises, make sure they get us.'

She glanced up and saw Apolline and Cyril strolling across the terrace to take their place at a neighbouring table.

'Ooh look, there's that French actress I was telling you about. I thought I recognised her last night, and Nicola – the pretty blonde – told me it was indeed her – Apolline Fleurie. But don't be so *obvious*!'

She frowned at Ralph as he swung round on his chair to take a good look at Apolline.

'She's still a corker,' he said. 'I've always liked a redhead.'

Nicola came up to clear their plates.

'Anything else I can get you?' she asked.

'A couple of croquet mallets please,' said Ralph, 'I gather we're signed up for it?'

'They're ready and waiting for you, starting soon.'

'You must be rushed off your feet with all this serving,' said Maggie. 'Such a lot of work, running a business like this, especially at your age, if you don't mind me saying.'

'Very true, ' said Nicola, 'we have Maria and Sylvie working full time for us now, but we still need to pitch in for breakfast service. Do you have any plans for today, apart from the croquet?'

'It's too hot to go anywhere,' said Maggie. 'We thought we'd just lounge by the lake.'

'Good plan. Just to warn you, we're doing a lot of shooting outside today, so you may find yourselves caught on camera.'

'Oh well, we'll just have to take our chances,' said Ralph, 'and as I suggested to your colleague, you might like to feature my car in the filming. It's the red Aston Martin with cream upholstery – you don't see many like it, it looks stunning parked out there in front of the chateau.'

'Yes, you've mentioned it before, 'said Nicola.

Outside, the producer Denise was eyeing up the locations with Olivier.

'So we'll have plenty going on,' he said, 'Jean-Louis on his tractor, the children of the chateau playing by the swings, a couple of the chatelains harvesting salad in the vegetable garden, the guests playing croquet on that pitch over there, some others taking a dip in the lake – I'm hoping they will self-edit on that one, we only want the swimwear-suitable in those shots. Then we will zoom in on Dougie giving his chat on the history of the chateau, and then our pièce de resistance – Apolline coming down the steps of terrace, the chateau rising up behind her, and she will talk to camera about the special place it holds in her heart.'

Beth came up to join them.

'I've done as you said, I've put those tasteful poolside towels round the lake, carefully coordinated, so we won't get any jarring notes. It's filling up already, nobody wants to leave the premises today, it's too damn hot, plus they don't want to miss out on becoming stars of the small screen. I've sent Maddie and Nicola with their ornamental trugs to be charming pastoral princesses in the walled garden.'

'Good. What about Fizz?'

'Ah yes, she's cast herself as yummy chateau mummy. She's spread a huge play blanket out over there, and she's got Louis and Lily making daisy chains, while Wren and Sacha lie on their backs, gazing up at the skies. You'll see that Wren is wearing his pink pinafore dress, she's not letting go of that gender stereotype bashing.'

'That all sound very good. I'll leave you to it, Denise, and take a walk with Beth to check on the croquet.'

'Inspired idea of yours, the croquet,' he said to Beth as they headed towards the pitch that Simon had laid out earlier. 'I had been thinking about a boules court, but that is such a cliché of French life. I prefer the croquet, it is also more aristocratic, as befits the chateau. Boules is too often seen played in public squares by fat Frenchmen wearing those sleeveless *débardeurs*. I think you call them "wife-beaters"?'

Simon looked up as they approached. He could smile at Olivier with genuine warmth, now he was no longer a love rival.

'All in hand, Olivier? We've got a full house for the croquet – wave to our director, everyone!'

Maggie and Ralph, together with the other guest players, obligingly did as they were told.

'I'm the score-keeper and general entertainer,' said Simon, 'you will see that in spite of the suffocating heat, I'm wearing my entertainer's striped blazer – Beth calls it my end-of-the-pier jacket. I thought it would strike a jaunty note.'

'That's good,' said Olivier, 'then we're going to do a more serious piece with Dougie talking to camera about the history of the chateau, then cut to Jean-Louis on his tractor, with John and Will presenting the perfect image of muscular masculinity . . . Then over to Leo and Luc cutting flowers – look at them, what a pretty pair they make amongst the Japanese anemones.'

'It's going to look like one of those films where they've hired too many extras,' said Simon, 'an unnaturally busy scene with everyone manically doing their thing.'

'Doesn't matter, I want to convey the energy of the community here, even in this heat, chatelains and guests alike making the most of it. And then, we come to the grand finale of this episode – our much-loved actress Apolline Fleurie, floating down those steps, the first time in decades that she's been seen on screen, talking about the significant role that Chateau Lafarge played at a pivotal time in her life. It's going to be great – all in the editing of course, but I think this will be our strongest episode yet. Viewers will be yearning to live at the chateau!'

'I think you're right,' said Beth, 'it's going to be fantastic, just as we dreamed it would be.'

Later in bed, Beth and Simon were unable to sleep, their minds buzzing with the day's events. The windows and curtains were wide open to welcome in the night air.

'Do you remember how we used to count those shepherdesses on the wallpaper, when we couldn't get to sleep?' said Beth. 'That *toile de jouy* was the embodiment of our rural fantasies.'

'Imagining ourselves as milkmaids and farmhands, toiling the land, the chateau in the background. I especially like the way the pattern continues on the curtains, matching paper and fabric, like matching tie and handkerchief.'

They lay in silence for a while, contemplating the green figures on the walls, reliving the many nights they'd spent in this room.

'You know what was great about today?' said Beth. 'I could really enjoy working with Olivier, and seeing him only as the executor of our excellent project, nothing more.'

'As opposed to your red-hot lover?'

He pinched her thigh.

'Ouch! Yes. And I'm sensing it's the same for you and Apolline? You're not hanging on her every word the way you used to, like a pathetic love-struck dog.'

'Touché. And no. She is nothing more to me than a delightful woman who is giving her best to the chateau – with a charming English husband, I might add. What a lovely man he is.'

'Agreed, I'm keen on Cyril.'

'But keener on me, I hope?'

'Yes, keener on you.'

'And you've come round to the opinion that British is best? When it comes to choosing a life partner, that is, as well as a bedmate?'

'I never saw Olivier as a life partner. I don't know what I saw him as, it was just exciting and different. A beacon of light after you cruelly deserted me. I don't think he saw me as his life partner either, by the way. He made that clear when you came back and he saw no reason to end the affair.'

'"Bof, ze 'usband, 'e need not put an end to our fun."'

Beth laughed.

'They are hard work to be honest, French lovers. All that glowering and moodiness. The endless drive to seduce. Admit it, you found the same with Apolline?'

'I thought we agreed to not talk about our exes – now that they *are* our exes, thank goodness.'

'Just this once, then?'

'All right. Apolline is a beautiful woman who has high standards I sometimes found it hard to live up to. Trying to please her all the time, constantly aware that she was the *grande dame* and I was the oafish British chancer who was punching above his weight. She also has a very refined range of lingerie; in fact she once told me that Cyril liked to try it on . . .'

'That was a bit of a clue.'

'Exactly. Anyway, that's all in the past, look at them now.'

'Very loved up. Just like us.'

'Anyway, you know how well dressed she always is, and that extends right the way through to the lacy bedwear. She had these amazing baby doll things where you had all kinds of silk ribbons and . . .'

'That's enough detail, thank you.'

'You asked! But the point is, I've always been less interested in the frilly fripperies than in what lies beneath.' He put his arm around her. 'It felt too try-hard, to be honest. I was longing for you and your no-nonsense bedshirts. Or wearing nothing at all, like you are now. I just wanted you.'

He pulled her towards him.

'I know,' said Beth. 'We think the same way, we like the same things. Basically, we're the same person, boringly enough. We love our life in France, we love the chateau , and most of all we love each other.'

EPILOGUE: FIFTEEN MONTHS LATER

'I never thought I'd say this, but I think I'm through with black,' Leo whispered to Beth, huddling into his black coat against the cold wind. They were standing in the graveyard of the village church, where the chatelains and other mourners were attending the burial of Madame de Courcy.

'It's terribly ageing, just look at everyone, they look like death. Dark brown and navy are much kinder on the older complexion. I'm going to throw everything away when we get back, no black above the waist, though trousers are all right and I suppose I'd better keep this coat for the next raft of funerals, though I might stipulate rainbow colours as the dress code for my own final function.'

'Shh . . . stop that depressing talk,' said Beth, 'this is supposed to be a celebration. At last, Madame de Courcy has left us alone, in the most definitive way. No more risk of her dropping round to tell us how we should be running her chateau.'

'She's gone to the great chateau in the sky, barging her way in there like she did to us on a daily basis. Ooh, here comes the bit I like – throwing handfuls of dirt into the abyss, it sends shivers down my spine every time.'

The *curé* delivered his final benediction, and the crowd of mourners slowly made their way back to the chateau where, for the last time, Madame de Courcy would be celebrated, though today, for the first time, she was not there to raise her own glass.

The fire was roaring in the crystal ballroom, where Sylvie and Marie had set out platters of petits fours to be served alongside the vintage champagne which Madame de Courcy had laid down for the occasion, in an act of unprecedented generosity.

'At last, the chateau is truly ours,' said Simon, splashing the champagne into a tray of glasses, 'and yet I know I'm going to miss her horribly next month when she doesn't turn up on Christmas Eve. Here you are, you gorgeous newlyweds.'

He handed glasses to Leo and Luc. They had formalised their relationship last month in the village *mairie*, followed by a party at the chateau, and were still bathed in what Beth called the magic of the early years, dividing their time between Lafarge and Luc's flat in Paris. She came up to them now and put her arm through Simon's.

'Three weddings and a funeral at the chateau, if you count our renewal of vows.'

'Yes, that was a volte-face,' said Leo, 'you were so against the idea, finding it "naff and attention-seeking", I think was how you put it, then the next thing you know, you're holding hands and exchanging new rings.'

'My romantic husband talked me into it' said Beth, 'and as you know, I embrace any excuse for a party.'

'It's party central here, all right,' said Cyril joining the conversation. 'I was only saying to Apolline, it's the best decision we ever made, to buy into this fantastic chateau commune.'

Following Apolline's appearance in an episode of the show, she had agreed to stay on for the filming of the entire first series. After that, she and Cyril were so embedded into chateau life that it made perfect sense for them to take up permanent residence in the Louis XIV suite. This extra cash injection plus the extraordinary success of the television series meant they could afford to scale back on the *chambres d'hôtes*, offering only premium packages for die-hard fans of the show who took part in a ballot for the chance to pay to stay at the dream chateau – and the possibility of appearing on screen.

'Series three in the bag, and on to the next!' said Beth. 'It certainly exceeded our wildest expectations.'

Olivier came up to them, looking suave in his black suit.

'Are we congratulating ourselves? It's well deserved. I knew it would be a winner, you must never underestimate the British appetite for wishing themselves into a stately home. Especially with such an endearing cast of characters.'

'A chateau full of lunatic Brits – and me, your token Frenchie,' said Apolline, giving a deep curtsey.

'Excuse me, you're not the only one, don't forget Luc and Jean-Louis, even if they are part-timers,' said Simon, 'and I'm practically French, you've heard me sing "La Marseillaise" – unrivalled passion and patriotism!'

The room thinned out, as Madame de Courcy's relatives and some people from the village drifted off, until only the residents of Chateau Lafarge were left. The champagne was still flowing, Nicola banged a spoon on the table and climbed up on a chair.

'Thank you, everybody, I'd like to make a toast – it's what we do here, let's face it, it's one of our special skills.'

'We're so special!' said Leo, clapping his hands.

'Save the applause for the end, please,' said Nicola.

'Let the woman speak,' said Beth.

'Thank you, Beth. So, this has been a momentous year for us, and I wanted to acknowledge the part you all played in the latest transformation of the chateau. Since moving here, we've passed through different phases – the renovation, the opening of the guest rooms, and finally – and most dramatically – the launching of our own TV show. It's true to say that when we first bought the place, we never imagined we'd be the subject of such scrutiny, with millions of viewers watching our every move. But now the cameras are off, I'd like to give a special mention to my particular heroes. First, the man who started it all – it was his idea, he had the energy and drive to pull it off – our favourite suave Frenchman, Olivier.'

Olivier bowed his head graciously.

'He's so hot,' Leo whispered to Beth, 'don't you sometimes regret your decision?'

'No, and be quiet.'

Nicola continued with her tributes.

'Secondly, our resident history nerd, Dougie. His fascinating insights into the lives of those who previously occupied in these magnificent premises gave proper gravitas to the show, so well done to him and his wife and fellow researcher Mary. Then I'd like to especially recognise the young ones, though they're not in the room, the children of the chateau: Louis, Wren, Lily and Sacha, their artless appearances melted the hearts of all the viewers, so thanks to their loving parents, Maddie and John, and Will and Fizz who of course gave them special prominence in her fantastic vlog, which has kept us topped up with endless freebies – all power to our in-chateau influencer!'

Fizz gave a twirl to demonstrate the full skirt of her black dirndl.

'Thank you, Nicola, I'd like to point out that I'm channelling Madame Bovary in my choice of funeral-wear, and that I actually bought it myself.'

'Then, we come to our joker card,' Nicola continued, 'the screen legend that is Apolline, who brought that undoubted *je ne sais quoi* to the show. French class on legs, she embodies the elegance and culture of our glorious chateau.'

Apolline raised her glass and leaned into Cyril.

'But finally, I'd like to point the finger at the couple who are the heart and soul of our chateau community. Beth and Simon, my absolute best friends. I speak for us all, when I say, thank goodness you made it up, you're the bedrock of our life, and don't you dare to ever fall out again. Right, now you can all clap your hands!'

She jumped down from the chair, and kissed Jean-Louis, to tumultuous applause around the room.

Simon leaped to his feet, beaming round at them all.

'Inspiring words, Nicola, I'm humbled by the warm things you say about me and Beth. You'll be delighted to know that I am already well on the way to completing my latest book . . .'

A ripple of laughter rang out.

'I know, you all think I never finish anything! But this is different, it celebrates the great new beginning that's happening not just for Beth and me, but all of us, celebrating our love and the love we have for everything here. I'm dedicating it to all the chatelaines, it's a companion piece to the show, and I'm calling it *A New Life in the Chateau*. Here's to the next ten years!'

Catch up if you missed . . .

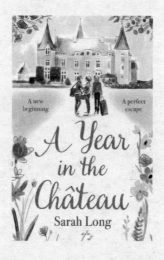

When Nicola's husband, Dominic, retires they decide not to
spend their days finding hobbies to fill the time until Countdown
is on channel 4. Instead, they fulfil their life-long fantasy of
buying a house in the French countryside and filling it with
their dearest friends. Reliving their youth and spending
their children's inheritance.

Joined by seven of their friends they club together to invest
in a château in Normandy. Group dinners, fine wine,
beautiful scenery – they're living the dream!

Available now

And don't miss the sharp, irreverent and funny novel from Sarah Long . . .

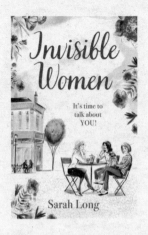

Sandra has a naughty secret.

Harriet has been ditched with her ailing mother-in-law one time too many.

Tessa is desperate for distraction after her youngest flies the nest for uni.

With the big 5-0 around the corner, isn't it about time they put themselves first?

After Tessa responds to a late night Facebook message from an old flame, she finds herself impulsively waiting at the airport for a plane from New York. Will it reunite her with The One That Got Away, or land her in a heap of trouble?

And is this the long-awaited moment Tessa and her friends grab their lives back and start living exactly as they choose?

Available now